WHITE OAK RIVER

A Story of Slavery's Secrets

Ora Smith

Ora Smith

LIGHTEN PRESS

Published by Lighten Press
www.lightenpress.com

Printed in the United States of America

This is a work of fiction.

ISBN
978-0-9980410-5-6

"Come, Thou Fount of Every Blessing" by Robert Robinson (1758) in public domain
Quote from "Little Ida's Flowers" by Hans Christian Andersen (1835)

Cover design by Lynnette Bonner of Indie Cover Design
https://www.indiecoverdesign.com
DepositPhotos #39341105 Woman; Jim Snyders photo of White Oak River

BISAC Subject Headings
FIC014000   FICTION / Historical / General
FIC014060   FICTION / Historical / Civil War Era
FIC042030   FICTION / Christian / Historical
FIC049000   FICTION / African American / General
FIC049010   FICTION / African American / Christian
FIC049020   FICTION / African American / Women
FIC049040   FICTION / African American / Historical
FIC027050   FICTION / Romance / Historical / General
FIC027360   FICTION / Romance / Historical / American
FIC027230   FICTION / Romance / Multicultural & Interracial
FIC074000   FICTION / Southern
FIC044000   FICTION / Women
ET020   CULTURAL HERITAGE / African American
TP020   TOPICAL / Black History
TP028   TOPICAL / Christian Interest

Dedication

To all who wish to join in the reconciliation between
descendants of the African enslaved
and descendants of American slaveowners.
Some of us are one and the same.

And to
my mother, siblings, children, grandchildren, nephews, nieces,
and cousins—hoping you will see the family through my eyes
and enjoy the experience.

AUTHOR'S NOTE

This story is based on true events of my ancestors. I was drawn to it as a means to discover my own identity. It is not a story of slave beatings or violence, although those horrendous experiences absolutely did happen to enslaved Africans. During my research, while poring through thousands of slave narratives, I read of violence, but I also found stories about life without those evils. While some slaves were not physically abused—and may have been cared for or even loved by their white enslavers—they still never knew freedom. Confusing and emotionally unhealthy on so many levels, the mental turmoil of the enslaved is something we may never comprehend. I did not write this side of history to soften the effects of one person owning another but instead to study the situation on an intimate level. My attempt to tell this story does not diminish in any way the atrocities that occurred because of the Transatlantic slave trade. We cannot rewrite history, and we certainly shouldn't lie about the abhorrent facts. My hope is that in sharing this story we can discuss where those who came before us went wrong and find a way to move forward. Ultimately, now it's up to each of us to decide to do better than our ancestors may have done because when individuals begin to stand up for what's right, that's when the world changes for the good.

CAROLINE GIBSON MATTOCKS

JOHN FREDERICK MATTOCKS

The painting of Caroline is modeled after a very faded daguerreotype. The drawing of John is modeled after a photograph once seen in an archive by researcher Roger Kammerer, who drew this image as a teenager.   (see more photos in back of book)

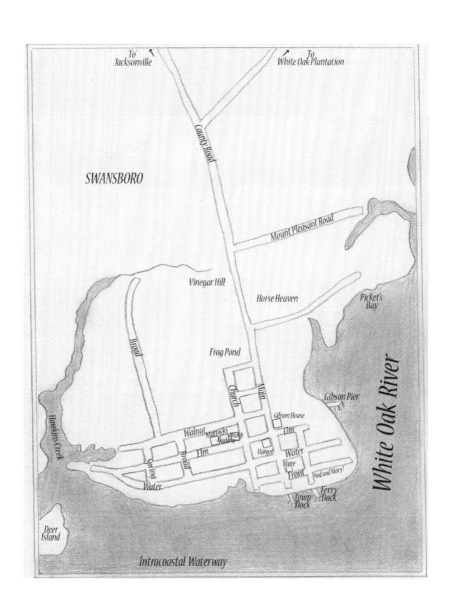

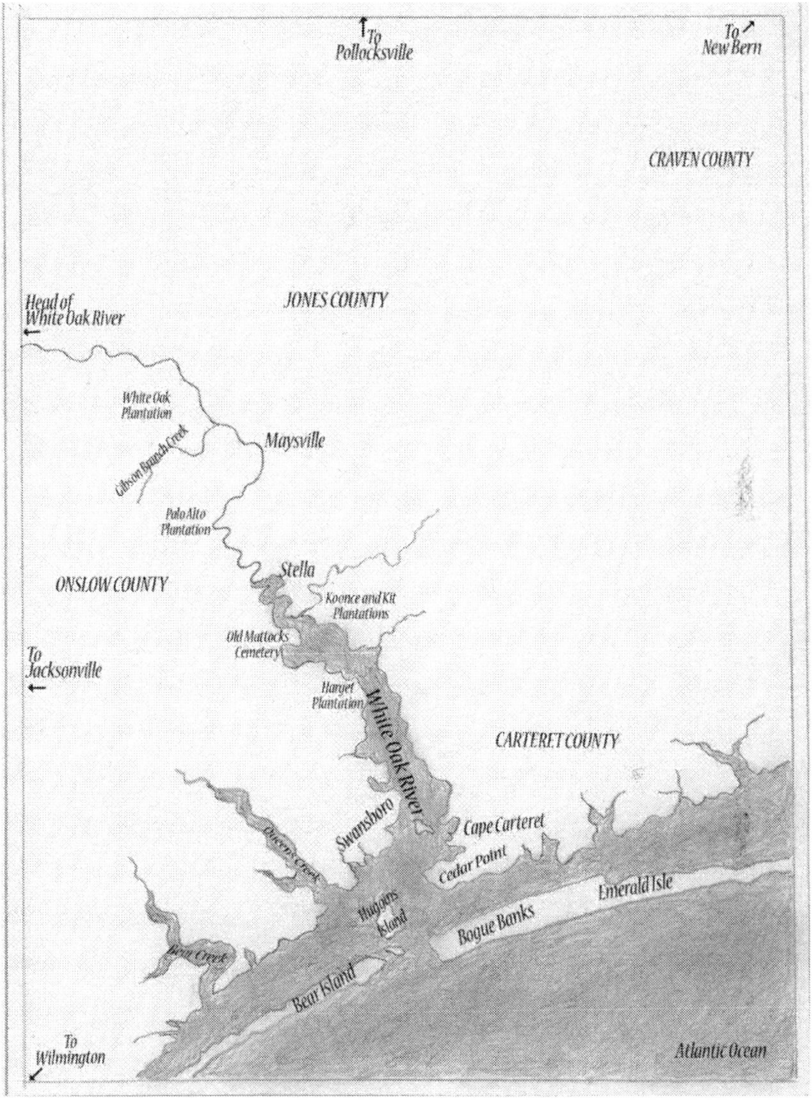
To Pollocksville
To New Bern
CRAVEN COUNTY
Head of White Oak River
JONES COUNTY
White Oak Plantation
Gibson Branch Creek
Maysville
Palo Alto Plantation
Stella
ONSLOW COUNTY
Koonce and Kit Plantations
Old Mattocks Cemetery
To Jacksonville
Harget Plantation
White Oak River
CARTERET COUNTY
Swansboro
Cape Carteret
Cedar Point
Emerald Isle
Huggins Island
Bogue Banks
Bear Island
To Wilmington
Atlantic Ocean

CONTENTS

The White Oak River runs approximately forty-five miles along the coastal plain of southeast North Carolina and empties into the Atlantic Ocean. Having served as a highway of travel and transportation for hundreds of years, it flows east through a variety of habitats including swamps, hardwood forests, and salt marsh flats and is what is known as a blackwater river.

White in name.

Black in color.

NOVEMBER 9, 1865

Seven months after the American Civil War cease fire
Koonce Plantation home, Carteret County, North Carolina

Caroline wished Mama were here to massage the pain from her back and give her words of comfort and strength as she had with Caroline's two previous childbirths. This time labor had come on three weeks early when her waters broke, and there'd been no time to fetch Mama to the plantation home so far in the country. Caroline's mother-in-law, Eliza, had brought in Chany, an old slave, to act as midwife. It seemed highly inappropriate, but so did much of what had occurred since war's end.

Chany's gnarled hands pushed against Caroline's hardening belly. "Some's ain't got it in 'em to git that babe out." She sat on the bed. Her face, the color of molasses, was heavily lined and showing a life of strife. She wore a faded yellow scarf covering most of her grizzled gray hair.

Eliza stepped to the other side of the bed. "Hush now, Chany! She's done this before and needs strength to do it again." She patted Caroline's knee, the first time she'd touched her since the labor began five hours before, then walked out of the bedchamber, her rigid back and tight brown hair-bun the last thing Caroline saw.

Why did they talk about her as if she weren't in the room? Being in labor didn't make her deaf.

The contraction grew and clutched at her abdomen, pain burning her belly and between her legs. At its peak, she could no longer suffer through with only moans. As a primal scream burst into the otherwise quiet room, she hardly recognized her own voice.

"Didn't 'spect her to caterwaul," Chany said into the air, still not directly talking to Caroline. "Let's hope this ain't gonna go much longer." Chany wiped her forehead with a sleeve then walked to a chair and sat down like she was settling in to endure something she'd rather not.

Caroline's contraction receded. She dropped onto her pillow to catch her breath, knowing another would soon follow. The experience was so unlike the births with Mama as her attendant. Chany's reactions were cold and indifferent. Perhaps because she knew only hardships and this was one more burden on her back. Not a single word of comfort or encouragement came from her mouth. Was she angry at being a midwife to a white woman?

Chany pulled a tobacco tin from her apron pocket, pushed a wad into her cheek, puffing it out to the size of a pheasant egg. Her eyes large and glazed, more yellow than white, looked about the room. The days of slaves keeping their gaze to the floor had left, replaced with equal protection under the law and black men being granted the right to vote. Caroline couldn't imagine how the new government was fixing to enact those decrees in the South.

After she endured two more fist-clenching contractions, Eliza returned carrying a pile of folded cloth and set them on the bureau. "Chany has birthed many of my slaves' . . . *former slaves'* . . . babies." Her face colored in apparent frustration at the slip. "She'll do you right."

Another contraction grabbed Caroline in its iron jaws. Instead of starting gradually and working its way up, it came at its peak to tear her in two. Tears stung her eyes. She clenched her teeth, but her shrieks won over her will and rent the air.

Eliza shook her head, looking toward the ceiling.

Caroline needed Mama.

Pain ripped and tore with a great pressure. She struggled to regain control of her body and mind, the contraction never ebbing completely.

Walking to the bureau, Chany snatched a cloth from the stack. She came to the end of the bed and wiped Caroline between the legs.

She could hardly feel it opposed to the pain.

Chany's otherwise indifferent face took on a look of puzzlement. She rubbed the back of her neck. Without making eye contact, she said, "Next pain yo' needs to bear-down as iffen it the most importan' thing ya'd ever done in yo' life."

The need to push soon overwhelmed Caroline, and she directed the last of her strength to free herself from the great pressure consuming her body. The baby slid from its confines more quickly than her others had. She took a deep breath and pushed herself up on elbows to see over her still protruding belly.

A boy! Arriving earlier than expected and much smaller than her two daughters, his head was covered with wet wisps of black, curly hair. John would be so pleased to finally have a son.

Chany pulled her finger from the baby's mouth and his high-pitched, desperate wails pierced the otherwise quiet room.

Caroline ached to have him in her arms and reached for him.

Chany ignored her and rolled the baby toward herself as she looked him over. Her milky eyes stared wide-eyed at the baby's back. "I'z neber see'd this on a white babe," she said under her breath.

Eliza stepped closer and drew her brows together. "Seen what?"

Chany shifted him to show Eliza and Caroline his back. "Does ya see that spot?"

Covering the baby's lower back was a large splotch of grayish-blue pigment—so large it bled over into part of his buttocks.

Caroline's heart stilled. What was wrong with her son?

"What is it?" Eliza's lips pulled so tightly they lost color.

"We calls it 'blue spot.'" Chany stared hard at Caroline. "I'z only see'd it on black babes." She laid him down and took hold of his tiny hand, examining his palm and then fingers, ignoring his wails. She held his hand up. His nails appeared darker than his skin, not the pink they should be. "Dark nail beds and groin."

His skin was slightly darker than Caroline's and John's, but it certainly wasn't as black as Chany's. What was she trying to say?

"I . . . I . . . ." Caroline stammered, her gaze flying from the baby to Chany to Eliza.

Eliza laughed uncomfortably. "I'm sure there's a reason. Perhaps the spot is similar to what you've seen on your kind, but I do hope you're not suggesting this child is Negro."

Chany ducked her head, more submissive than Caroline thought Chany could be. "No, Ma'am." She cut the cord with large shears Caroline had only seen used on animals.

The connection between mother and son severed. The sound of the snip, the rigors of childbirth, the babe's wails, and Eliza's furrowed brow contradicted what should have been contentment. Caroline sank into the pillows, wanting Mama. Wanting John. Wanting anyone but these two calloused women.

Surely nothing was seriously wrong with her little son? He was born early. Perhaps there were skin diseases on babes who didn't mature long enough in the womb?

Tired both physically and emotionally, Caroline needed to rest and concentrate on her baby's needs. She'd sort out what Chany suggested later. She pushed herself up against the headboard. "Bring the child to me."

Chany placed his still wet body in Caroline's arms. "There's my precious son," she spoke soothingly to him. "We've been waiting for you many years." She snuggled him against her and bounced him gently.

He immediately stopped wailing, closed his eyes, and breathed irregularly, the spasms of his tiny chest slowing. She looked him over closely, as did Eliza, who hovered above.

A beautiful baby with a perfect mouth and full lips, Caroline touched his tiny flat nose and kissed his forehead. She couldn't take her eyes off his darling face. Surprisingly, other than brown hair, the baby didn't resemble any of her family members. Both John and Caroline had brown hair, and Caroline's eyes were green to John's brown, her skin pale to his slightly darker complexion.

The bedchamber door closed behind Chany.

With cold fingers, Eliza pulled Caroline's chin toward her. Her frigid stare took all courage from Caroline. "Whose child is this?"

Caroline's mouth went dry.

Eliza bent closer. "I demand an explanation. What have you done? Are you trying to break John's heart?" Her voice cracked.

Flinching, Caroline searched for words to defend herself. "I've never had relations with any man other than your son. I'm as baffled by the child's appearance as you." She twisted away, weeping into her pillow. How could this be happening?

"I simply cannot believe you." Eliza's whisper was venom in Caroline's ear. "Whether it's John's or not—which I am more inclined to think not—you cannot keep this black bastard."

Caroline trembled. Eliza always made Caroline feel she wasn't good enough for her son. Anger moved through her body. She squinted bitterly at her mother-in-law. "You've no right to tell me what to do. He's our child." The fury pulsed in her head. "Of course, we'll keep him," she shrieked.

Chany stepped into the bedchamber toting a pitcher of water, which she poured into a washbasin next to the towels. There was no way she hadn't heard Caroline's outburst.

Eliza made room for Chany, turning to display her unyielding back and stepped away.

Chany washed the baby, who slept as she made quick work of removing the white substance covering his body.

"Ain't safe fo' a black chile to be raised by white folk," outspoken Chany stated.

"He's not black!" Caroline wailed, not caring who heard. The baby fussed and she bounced him to calm his troubles.

Eliza quickly turned and angrily shushed her.

Caroline said a little quieter, "He's mine and John's. He can't be black."

CHAPTER ONE

6 Years Earlier
December 30, 1859
Gibson House in Swansboro, Onslow County, North Carolina

Caroline sat in the parlor by the fire, working out a lacy pillow-cover design by rote as she intertwined a ring of thread with twelve curved picots separated by one double stitch. Holding the ivory tatting shuttle in her right hand while a piece of twisted, smooth white cotton thread wrapped around two fingers of her left, she thought about the upcoming new year, only days away. Another decade closing as 1860 approached. She had nothing but positive thoughts for her future.

The pillow cover would grace the bed she'd one day share with John in the home they'd provide for the children she hoped to have. The daydream warmed her as much as the fire. They'd have a grand home with beautiful furnishings and parties that others admired. He may not have money now, but she was sure he'd inherit his family's wealth soon enough, even if he didn't think so.

Papa strode into the room interrupting her dreams.

She hid her disappointment by putting on a smile. She'd dream later.

He sat close in a cushioned chair, the golden velvet lapels of his winter housecoat glimmering from the glow of the fireplace. He wasn't a large man, but his prominence in the community was great, and all admired him, including Caroline. She loved when he was home during the winters and missed him terribly when he sailed to the West Indies in the summer months to sell tar, turpentine, and rosin that his slaves had extracted from the pine trees that grew so readily on his nearby plantation. Gone for months at a time on the islands, he traded these products of the pine in exchange for sugar, molasses, honey, and fruits. Then his ships caught the Gulf Stream currents and sailed to Boston, New York, and Philadelphia where he sold the islands' commodities. His trade made Caroline's family quite comfortable.

Papa leaned toward her. "That's a lovely little thing you're working on."

"Thank you. It's to be a pillow cover for my trousseau." She smiled but found his brown eyes somber. Her heart skipped a beat. Perhaps he had bad news? "What is it, Papa?"

"John came to see me today," he answered without a change of expression.

Her heart leapt ahead of her thoughts. "Why?" her voice squeaked.

"He's asked for your hand in matrimony. Did you expect this proposal?"

She drew in a quick breath. "I've been hoping." Had he given John permission to be her husband? Her heart flip-flopped, her emotions and reasoning jumbling together.

He squinted. "Your sisters were courted by many beaus. I'd hoped it'd be the same for you. To be honest, I thought you'd find Reverend John Mattocks wasn't right for you because of his zeal for religion and little else. Appease your Papa. Tell me you'd like to be courted by others before you decide."

Caroline gathered her disordered thoughts. This was not a time to display her usual reticence toward expressing desires. "I've never felt this way about a man. Seems all that is on my mind lately is how to make a comfortable home for him." He'd only been a preacher for a year, but during that time she'd seen changes in him that made her admire him more and gave her the desire to become someone better.

Papa harrumphed and sat back. "I don't mean to crush your hopes, but I'd wanted more for you. Although he comes from a family of privilege, he has little now, and his occupation will always make that so. You do realize he can't offer the extravagances you're accustomed to."

"Things could change. His family has wealth. He's bound to inherit property and more." It's what Caroline had thought anyway. John had been raised as a gentleman and had attended university. Had Papa refused his offer on the condition of lack of wealth? She felt faint, as if the blood had drained from her head. "Can Spicey come live with me if you let us marry? If so, no matter his salary, I'll always have help." Although John had voiced his disapproval of slaves, Caroline was sure she could talk him into Spicey's relevance.

Papa again faced Caroline. "No matter who you marry, I'll give her as a wedding gift. As I've done for your sisters, I'll do for you. Your mother and I have always been pleased with Spicey's care of you. You'll also need slaves for the heavy work, gardening, care of animals, and such."

"Have you spoken with John of this?" Caroline leaned in. "Did you accept his proposal?"

"I told him I needed to think on it before I decided . . . and to hear your desires." He rubbed his face. "John and I spoke nothing of how many slaves I'll give you. It would've been premature—"

They both turned toward footsteps in the hall.

"Oh, there y'all are." Julia, Caroline's oldest sister, came into the parlor, her sapphire-blue silk gown much too formal for the middle of the afternoon. Her white gloved hand fiddled with a gold necklace over her ample bosom.

Papa stood. "To what do we owe the pleasure?"

Caroline pulled the thread from her fingers and leaned back in her chair, closing her eyes. Papa hadn't yet given his approval for the marriage and Julia had interrupted her attempts to convince him she wanted nothing more than to be John's wife.

"With Hiring Day almost upon us"—Julia pulled off a glove—"Daniel has brought to town the slaves he wants to hire out and sell. This morning, the mothers at their cabins gathered their little nothings, hoping to with their children. But these things rarely go their way, and they've been wailing ever since. I needed a distraction from their shrieks. They never learn." She shook her head, pulled the other glove off, and sat where Papa had been. "You look a bit pale, Carrie."

Before Caroline could steer Julia away from learning of John's proposal, Papa said, "She has every right to feel piqued. Reverend Mattocks has asked for her hand."

Julia gasped. "No!" She grabbed Caroline's arm. "He will never do. You aren't considering him, are you?" She glanced from Caroline to Papa with large brown eyes, her alluring arched eyebrows raised.

Caroline's throat felt like it was closing. She clenched her jaw. *Go away Julia!*

Papa frowned deeply. "I was about to convince her otherwise when you entered."

"He doesn't even own a decent home, much less a shack." Julia said in a high-pitched screech.

Caroline swallowed. "He—"

"John is staying in Abe Watson's home while Abe's in Florida." Papa's stare bore down on Caroline. "John said you both could live there for at least a year, as that's how long Mister Watson is expected to be away. I'm uneasy about the transient lifestyle you could have with John."

"What do you mean?" Caroline needed to stall for time as she gathered ideas of how John could better himself before she presented her case. She knew he could. She bit her lip. Or maybe if Papa understood she loved John for the way he treated her with care and for how considerate he always was of hers and others' feelings, then Papa would quickly give his approval for the marriage. "He grew up as a gentleman. It wasn't long ago that he lived on a plantation with servants. He will not always be poor."

With a head shake and wavering frown, he sighed. "Those were his parents' servants. I'm not a church-going man and don't clearly understand such things, but much of what John receives for a living is a limited salary from the Church and what is given to him by his congregation for his services. He has no farm or even a small garden. His food comes intermittently as people see fit to give. I suppose the life is suitable for him, but how will he support you, your children, and slaves?" He stared intently at her.

She didn't have the answers and knew she daydreamed too much about how it could all work out fine. Her family always complained about her overdramatic imagination and unassertiveness. She scrambled for what to say next. "In the same way, I suppose, from his congregation?"

"You can't live like a beggar!" Julia said.

Ignoring the comment, Caroline addressed Papa. "I've seen the house he's staying in. There's plenty of room in the backyard for a vegetable garden. Cannot a darkie work the soil?"

"It's possible." Papa's shoulders slumped. "Perhaps I should give you Moses? He has a fine wife and daughter to help with house chores. They could sleep in the same slave quarter they do now, here on my land, and walk to your home each morning." He shifted from one leg to the next. "That only solves the problem for this coming year. How will you house slaves when you move? John's not even sure he'll have a home for *you*." He drew his palm across his forehead and sighed heavily.

"You aren't really considering his proposal, are you Papa?" Julia sounded as if she couldn't believe any of this. "She's only eighteen."

"I turned nineteen a few weeks ago," Caroline said. "The same age as you at your marriage."

Julia shrugged nonchalantly, obviously disappointed she couldn't argue the point.

Caroline's emotions roiled like one of Papa's sea-going schooners. Up high on a wave of hope as Papa's positive comments seemed to signify he was considering the marriage, but then plunging down into the depths of the ocean as he and Julia voiced their concerns and asked questions to which Caroline gave weak answers. "Papa, think of what he's done with his life. His aspirations aren't the same as yours but hopefully as worthy. Without a father, he put himself through college at Trinity. At the age of eighteen, he travelled across the oceans to Israel by himself. He followed his convictions and became a preacher." Her heart pounded in her chest. Her abiding happiness depended on this conversation. "He has a great love for educating youth. If he can't rightly support us through his clerical duties, I dare say he can teach."

Papa squatted to her level and took her hand. "I love you, Carrie. This isn't easy for me. If I allow this marriage to take place, I'll feel responsible if you're unhappy. The slaves will help with physical duties, but I fear your life will turn out harder than what you're accustomed to—definitely harder than your sisters' lives, and they've married well."

John's brother Ned had married Caroline's sister Mary. Papa must have seen something more in Ned than in John. Ned had become a merchant and raised hogs. There was no need to worry about Mary's wealth.

Julia leaned over and grasped Caroline's other hand. "Listen to him, Carrie. Papa is wise and knows what's best for you."

Caroline yanked her hand from Julia's and put it to her brow. "Julia, please—"

"You were raised genteel. Don't you appreciate all Mama and Papa have done for you?"

Papa released Caroline's hand and pulled up a chair in front of her and sat. "You'll not have the fine dresses you love. Your life will be simpler."

They were rallying against her. "My sisters give me things now." Caroline hoped to reassure Papa. "Perhaps they'll still do so after I marry?" She turned to Julia, imploring her with her eyes, wishing she'd help her cause. "Yesterday, Julia gave me some lovely gloves she said she no longer needed since Daniel bought her lace ones from Paris."

Julia made a noise in her throat like she was fixing to say something condescending.

"Your sisters are good to you," Papa said, "but I wouldn't count on their generosity. John might not set store by it either. A man likes to feel he can take care of his wife. He might look at gifts as handouts."

"You just told me that's how John makes his living—by people in his fellowship supplying his food and necessities. Why would he care if my sisters gave me things?"

"Aye, I did say he lived off the generosity of others." Papa grinned slightly, but no humor reached his eyes. "I believe he looks at that as a payment for his services. I don't well understand . . . perhaps a minister is a different breed of man? All the men I know find pride in taking care of their womenfolk. I dare say I don't rightly understand your man." Then almost under his breath he added, "I've worked hard to rid us of the shame of others."

"You simply cannot consider the preacher's proposal." Julia's brown curls bounced as she shook her head. "You weren't raised to live in a shack like white trash. Let me introduce you to gentlemen in our circle of society."

"I know you'd approve of John if only you knew him like I do." Tears stung Caroline's eyes. She loved John and had been trying to convince herself ever since they started courting that no matter how much money he had or didn't have, she'd stick by him, stand up for him, and support him. "Papa, he's considerate of my feelings and has voiced his concerns about not being able to give me what you have. I can accept that and have told him I cannot live without him."

Papa's eyebrows shot up, and Julia gasped.

Caroline realized she'd spoken too boldly and looked away, wiping at her tears. She gulped in air. She needed to stay strong.

"You're young, and you don't yet understand how your feelings can change," Papa said sharply. "You can see nothing but goodness in this man you think you love. In real life, there are sacrifices we make for love. Some sacrifices help us become better people. Others we regret. Seeds of disappointment or resentment can easily grow into hate."

"What do you mean?" Was he talking about a specific sacrifice? There was no sacrifice too great to be John's wife, was there? Could she give up her life of ease and comfort for her love?

"Well . . ." Papa leaned forward, placing his forearms on his legs. "You need to make sure your expectations are the same as John's. If you're in agreement of what sacrifices need to be made, then there will be fewer problems. For instance, I would assume John is expecting you to have fewer gowns. If he is, then you need to know this ahead of time and be willing to sacrifice your love of new gowns. If you agree and *mean it*"—Papa said with conviction— "all will run smoothly. If you agree, but in your heart you're disappointed and new gowns mean more to you than you let him know, then the disappointment can grow into anger."

She could never be angry at John. Papa didn't understand.

He gently tilted her chin up. "It will drive a wedge in your love and soon you'll be blaming John for your unhappiness when in reality it's you who shirked on the bargain—if we can call it that." He released her chin but kept his gaze steady. "Marriage is made up of many such bargains. There're things you'll ask John to sacrifice, no doubt. Marriage is much like a business."

Despite herself, Caroline almost laughed at the statement.

"I can tell by the look on your face you think me a foolish old tradesman who compares marriage to business."

Caroline ducked her head to hide her grin.

"Perhaps these are considerations your mother should speak to you about. Your heart is full of love that's ruling your head." Papa cleared his throat and took Caroline's hand again. "Please, listen to me and think hard on this decision."

Caroline's mirth quickly left. She knew in her heart her father wanted her to hear and consider the seriousness of the matter.

"You'll be giving up too much to marry your penniless preacher." Julia scowled.

Papa nodded. "I need to know you understand exactly what you *are* giving up and be willing to do so."

Caroline gazed at the forgotten tatting in her lap. It almost sounded like Papa could be convinced. The fire at the hearth suddenly felt hot and her forehead moist. She searched her heart and mind for any doubts she might have about marrying John and found none. She pulled her shoulders back. "I understand you think I'll be giving up gowns, a big home, and several—but not all—slaves. What else do you think I'm giving up?"

"Your way of life in more ways than you'll understand until it's gone." Papa's eyes became tender. "If it's any consolation, I do believe John is a good man and will do all in his power to make you comfortable, but I fear that is much less than you're accustomed to."

"You talk as if I'm a fragile and spoiled." Caroline's back went straight. "Mama has never allowed me to be idle. I can work."

Julia puckered a sour look, shaking her head back and forth.

Caroline swallowed the lump in her throat.

"I meant no insult. You've more backbone than most of the belles in this town." He patted her hand. "I think that's the only reason why I can consider John's proposal. But I need you to know what you're getting into before I give permission." He smiled and his eyes shown with concern and devotion. "You will not be easy to give up, my pet. I need assurance you'll be happy."

Caroline stood. Her tatting fell to the floor in a mess of threads. The shuttle bounced along the hardwood.

Her father stood too and opened his arms.

She fell into them. He smoothed her hair and tears came to her eyes as her chest swelled with love for him. She thought of the other man in her life who waited for her, and her chest became even tighter. "Please Papa, tell John you'll agree to our marriage. Please make him feel welcomed into our family."

Papa heaved a sigh, but his body did not relax.

The logs in the fireplace popped, and she held her breath waiting for an answer.

"I see you'll have it no other way. In the end, we all make our own happiness." He held her at a distance and smiled sadly. "You'll be expected to keep your husband happy. Once out of this house, your Ma and I will not interfere in your decisions. Be wise, Carrie. You've grown into a lovely young woman. I'm proud to be your father."

"Don't do this, Carrie," Julia said as if she were warning her not to jump off a cliff.

"I love you, Papa. I will be a good wife to John. You'll see."

CHAPTER TWO

January 19, 1860 - Gibson House

With a dozen words, an inherited ruby ring, and the love of John, Caroline's life was about to change forever.

The Reverend James Brent, a man John admired, had come from New Bern to perform the wedding ceremony in Gibson House's extravagantly decorated great hall. She couldn't imagine anywhere else she'd rather get married than in her family home. "In the presence of God and before these witnesses and friends . . ." The reverend's voice rang clear and loud.

Caroline moistened her lips. Over a hundred people watched her and John, but he seemed not to notice as he looked at her with his warm brown eyes, as he had when they were alone. A flutter traveled from her chest to her stomach.

Out of his typical clergy garb, he'd dressed in a black vest, jacket, and trousers with a crisp white shirt, necktie, and alyssum on his lapel. Clean shaven and brown hair combed back, he looked her complement. His mother must have made sure his clothes were that of a refined gentleman.

Men didn't come better than John. The only time they'd fought was about his secret activities to free slaves. If Papa knew, she wouldn't be standing here now. But John loved her, and she loved him, and now nothing stood in their way. He was a man who carried compassion like southern gentlemen carried self-importance.

Reverend Brent's voice interrupted her thoughts. ". . . may God be in your union. I now pronounce you husband and wife. You may kiss the bride."

John brought her to him, his lips warm as they brushed over hers, and her breath caught. But it was over too quickly. He stepped back. She blinked. The guests stood and clapped.

Turning to them slowly, she smiled, tears gathering at the corners of her eyes. She hurriedly blinked them away as John was spun away by his mother, Eliza.

Caroline found herself in Mama's embrace. "I'm so happy for you. May all days find you surrounded by such love." Her spiral curls tickled Caroline's face. Mama pulled back and gently cupped Caroline's cheek in her hand. Her dark eyes showed the weariness of wedding preparations, but her servants had beautifully arranged her mahogany-colored hair and azure silk gown so skillfully that others probably wouldn't notice.

"Thank you, Mama."

"You're beautiful, my little lamb." Papa hugged her. Violin and harp music began to play, and the voices of the guests heightened. "Find joy with your preacher." His uncertainty showed in the squint of his eyes and press of his lips. He'd finally relented to her marriage if John would teach at the Male and Female Swansboro Academy. John got the job, and the deal was struck.

"Thank you, Papa." She fiddled with her new ring.

He kissed her on the cheek. "Enjoy your day, darlin'." He stepped away with Mama to greet guests as Caroline's sisters, Julia, Mary, and Hester gathered around her to effuse about her dress and hair.

After they wandered away, she moved closer to John, where his mother fawned over him. Caroline smiled weakly at Eliza, and she stepped aside with a frown.

Others moved forward to congratulate, compliment, and envy them. The house was packed with family, friends, and Onslow's leading citizens. Family from nearby counties had traveled in and would stay for a week or longer.

John pulled her closer. "Did I tell you how lovely you look?"

Her earbob swayed against her neck, and she shivered. She couldn't get enough of his nearness. It had not been allowed while they courted.

"You look quite elegant yourself. No one is more fortunate than I to have such a husband."

"I'll have to argue you on that. For it's me who is most blessed."

More people congratulated and separated them once again. For at least another hour, they visited with their guests until finally Mama came to the rescue and told them to eat. As they sat to dine on stewed rockfish, roasted duck with applesauce, and potato snow, visitors continually approached for conversation.

"You've done yourself well," James Mattocks said as he leaned over the table and clasped John's hand.

"You don't have to convince me." John laughed at his cousin and caressed Caroline's hand under the table.

His enthusiastic joy helped give Caroline reassurance she'd done the right thing by marrying him. She needed to stop fretting about Papa's concerns.

Music, guests, and brandy flowed freely throughout the day. Caroline's sister, Mary, played the piano with skill, and Julia's high spirits and calls to dance kept the occasion festive. Although Julia had never stopped trying to convince Caroline to call off the wedding, she loved parties and would always play the cheerful mistress of ceremonies. Besides, the deed was now done. There was no turning back. And Julia would never air the family's disappointment to others and give them something to gossip about.

Days before, every room in the house had been cleaned and decorated from top to bottom. Ivy and holly cascaded from candelabras and stair rails. China, crystal, and silver to serve the guests had been collected from Papa's White Oak Plantation and borrowed from Julia's and Mary's plantation and town homes.

Only rarely throughout the day did Caroline have a moment to survey the crowd drinking, eating, and dancing. Many servants, even those not normally house slaves, had been brought in. They moved through the rooms with large silver trays, serving sparkling drinks and candied fruits in crystal dessert dishes. As they came and went through the backdoor, smells of smoked pig wafted in from the cookhouse.

Big George, an outdoor slave who tended animals, stood out in the crowd in his black wool breeches and white shirt. His skin was blacker than most darkies. His apprehensive eyes darted about the room as he weaved through the crowd with a silver tray of oysters on the half shell. When he accidentally bumped John's brother Kit on the back of his head with the tray, Caroline gasped behind her hand.

A nearby guest turned on Big George. "Watch out, *boy!*"

Shuffling his feet, Big George lowered his eyes to the floor. She couldn't hear his words, but she was sure it was an apology.

Kit, in his usual good humor, seemed to make light of the incident and a bit of his laughter diffused the situation. Some men whipped slaves for such heedlessness. Was Kit a sympathizer of the black man's plight like John?

After dining, Caroline and John moved about the room.

Aunty Ann stepped forward as John was pulled into a conversation with some of his parishioners. He was much more personable than she.

"I remember when you were just a wee thing." Aunty Ann gestured to the guests and decorations. "And now this." Papa's sister was Caroline's oldest living relative. A widow for years, she always wore black, even to weddings. Her dark, high-collared dress was a stark contrast against her white-gray hair, styled in ringlets like a young girl's. A jet-studded hair comb bejeweled with diamonds, stood upright at the crown of her head declaring her wealth. "I wish to have a barbeque when you come to Lenoir County," she offered.

Most couples honeymooned for weeks, sometimes months, traveling throughout the countryside visiting family and friends, attending parties and balls in honor of the newly married couple. Caroline thought of Papa's warnings. This was just the beginning of accepting that things would be different for her.

"You're a sweet thing, but I must decline. John, um . . ." Caroline couldn't tell her John didn't have money for a honeymoon. "John has a busy work schedule. Did you know he's teaching Greek and Latin and other subjects at the Academy?"

"But no honeymoon?" Aunty Ann pursed her lips.

The disappointment at not having a honeymoon settled heavily in Caroline's heart. "Perhaps soon," she said with false conviction. She was tempted to share the real reason because if Aunty Ann knew, she'd probably offer to fund the entire honeymoon. Papa wouldn't have liked that though, and neither would John. In fact, it could bring shame on her whole family. So, she kept quiet and forced a smile instead.

Papa approached to speak with his sister, and Caroline quickly escaped.

Boyish in stature, her childhood friend Juju marched up to her as if she had something on her mind. "Knowing you as I do, I was surprised when I heard you were marrying a preacher man." She smiled, a teasing twinkle in her eye.

"Are you saying I'm a sinful creature, not worthy of a preacher?" Caroline tried to smile warmly but wondered if Juju honestly thought her not good enough for a man of God. Much of her and John's closeness came when he taught her the gospel—converted her to know there was something deeper in life. Or maybe it was the other way around and Juju thought Caroline too high in society.

"You don't seem the religious type is all." Juju giggled, her freckled nose wrinkling. "And marrying a preacher may be the end of looking pretty. How can he afford your gowns? Fashions change as often as Queen Victoria throws a ball."

Hurt inside, Caroline forced a laugh. "I don't fear my life will change much," she lied. Would she always feel the need to defend herself in this regard?

Juju shrugged. "Enjoy this lovely gown while you can." She took Caroline in with an approving gaze. "Sure wish I had a wisp of a figure like you." She pinched Caroline's waist. "I don't know how you eat, let alone breathe, while wearing that bodice though. All the same, the only people who benefit from overly tight corsets are doctors and undertakers." Her giggle ended with a shake of dull blonde curls that had fallen to become frizzy and contorted.

Hours later, as the sun began to set, slaves lit candles throughout the great hall, dining room and parlors. Each small flame kindled together into one radiant glow. The soft illusion pleased Caroline. The day was all she'd hoped for in splendor, but now she felt tuckered out. In front of her on the table, her sweet little bridal bouquet of winter pansies and violas had wilted. The alyssum on John's lapel was crushed beyond recognition.

John leaned toward her. A lock of his wavy brown hair fell over his forehead. "Dance with me?"

Caroline's feet ached. "I'd like nothing more."

Together they moved to the open expanse of the great hall.

Mary on the piano and the musicians on their violins were playing "Aileen Aroon," an Irish folk song, its slow melody perfect for the occasion.

Caroline was sure she was where she wanted to be—in the sweet comfort of John's arms. Having his love was all she needed.

"No regrets?" she teased, wondering if he questioned the union like Papa.

"Not on your life. Only pure joy." He pulled her close and kissed her temple. "Thank you for marrying me. I never thought I'd find a woman with such strength of character and goodness of heart. I love you."

Her body filled with pleasure. "I love you too." They'd always had easy companionship and she couldn't imagine that would ever change. John offered her kind care and a solid foundation. She wished Papa could see that. Her weariness forgotten, every sense and nerve became engaged with him so near. "When do you think it appropriate to leave?"

"Are you anxious to leave?"

She detected surprise in his voice and suddenly felt embarrassed.

"I'm anxious too," he whispered. "But I didn't want to appear so and make you feel uncomfortable." His eyes were fully upon her. "I'm glad you're ready." His face was so perfectly handsome with a strong square jaw and straight white teeth. There wasn't a more good-looking man in all of Onslow County.

"Johnny." Freddie, John's adorable, little half-brother, pulled on John's coattails. "Mama says she'd like to speak to you." His brown curls, so similar to John's, fell around his pudgy face.

John crouched in front of Freddie. "She did, did she?" He tickled the little boy on the ribs. "Tell her we'll come give our farewells."

Freddie ran off as John stood and took Caroline's hand. "Let's thank our families and leave."

CHAPTER THREE

January 20, 1860 - Watson House—"borrowed" home in Swansboro

Caroline awoke to the smell of lavender. She remembered Spicey shyly telling her how she'd ironed lavender water into the sheets. Entranced to awaken in the same bed as the man she loved, she looked over at John's dark, thick hair. It tumbled around his face, curlier than usual since it wasn't pushed back behind his ears, and she gently moved a section away from his closed eyes.

Remembering the night before, passion for him warmed her body. The man who would hold her night after night had been as gentle with her as she'd hoped he'd be. John had awakened desires she never realized she had. She touched his cheek.

He slowly opened his eyes and smiled, showing the dimples she loved so much. "Good morning, beautiful." He took a lock of her hair between his thumb and forefinger, rubbing it gently. "I love your hair down. And how beautiful your green eyes are with their flecks of blue." He kissed her tenderly and brought her to him.

They breakfasted late at a small table in their bedchamber. Papa's slaves, Keziah and Mahaly, brought them a meal of smoked fish on eggs, griddlecakes with buttermilk syrup, and sausage.

Caroline ate it all. "I didn't realize I was so hungry." She laughed nervously, her face warming.

"Looks like you worked up an appetite last night." John winked and stood, blushing a little himself. He kissed her on the forehead.

Heat moved across her cheeks and burned her ears.

He didn't remark on her high color. He'd told her last night he was as innocent as she. "I need to check repairs being made on the Academy roof. I'll be back before you're dressed for the day. Maybe we can open our gifts when I return?"

"I'd like that."

"Carrie, I love you," he spoke softly. "Again, I'm sorry we won't have a honeymoon." His eyes were sad with regret.

Trying to hide her disappointment with a smile, she remembered her conversation with Aunty Ann. "I know. Don't fret. I want to spend as much time as possible with you." Her breath hitched. "I don't care where we are as long as we're together." Perhaps if she said the words enough, she'd believe them.

"I don't know how I ever captured such a gracious and lovely woman for my wife." He stroked her arm.

After John left, Spicey performed her morning ministrations for Caroline. Spicey had been Caroline's servant as long as she could remember and knew just how to dress her and arrange her long hair.

"Your wedding was lovely, Miss Carrie." Giddy as a child, Spicey chattered as she went about her duties. She wore a hand-me-down day dress from one of Caroline's sisters. Sometimes she wore her gray uniform and it too displayed Papa's wealth. "You looked as rich as cream, you did." She sighed and looked off to the distant wall as if seeing Caroline there once again in her wedding gown. "And all those country folks! Lordy, was Gibson House crowded! I never see'd so many folks in one place."

"I think you're forgetting Julia's wedding. We were both so young, but surely there were more to hers than mine."

"That so? I don' rightly remember. I be too young to serve the folk back then." Spicey slipped a hair snood over the large chignon she'd created at Caroline's neck. "My feets still sore, but I happily do all you wishes of me today."

The house John rented from Mister Watson had already been prepared for Caroline's arrival, her bedchamber furniture brought from White Oak Plantation. Other than the winter's spent in Swansboro at Gibson House, she'd grown up there. Even now she sat at her own vanity.

What would she have Spicey do here? What was Caroline going to do with her days? She hadn't thought beyond the wedding.

She and Spicey found Keziah and Mahaly sitting at each end of a narrow table in the kitchen. Much smaller than Gibson House, the borrowed home had a modern convenience of a kitchen and not an outdoor cookhouse like most houses in Swansboro.

Keziah and Mahaly stood as Caroline entered. An old woman of small stature, Keziah was a caramel-colored Negro with hazel eyes and raised freckles. Mahaly, much taller and darker than the old woman, had delicate features and dark brown eyes that were almost impossible to see. The girl watched the floor as if she were intently studying the grain of the wood to decide what variety of tree it had come from.

"Mornin', Mistress Mattocks. Do ya hab chores for Mahaly and me, Ma'am?" The old woman fidgeted with her white apron, keeping her eyes down.

"Oh...aah...what did you do at White Oak Plantation?" Caroline should've been prepared for molding her slaves into the servants she wanted. She couldn't allow her own reticence to keep her from doing so.

"We's outdoor slaves dere. Yo' Pa says we yir indoor slaves now. Dat so?"

"Yes, if that's what Papa said, then that's what you should do. Is Moses your man?"

"Yessum, and Pa to Mahaly." She motioned her head toward the girl staring at the wooden planks.

Mahaly bent further toward the floor and curtsied. Parts of her face were pocked with scars, possibly from smallpox. The damage inflicted marked her for life, perhaps the reason for her sheepishness.

The opposite of her daughter, Keziah held her head high but did not look Caroline in the eyes. Papa never had a rule about slaves not looking their masters in the eyes. Keziah must have once worked a plantation where such a rule existed.

"I do recall Moses taking care of the animals. We only have one horse and one cow here. What else can he do?" Caroline asked.

"Yo' Pa tole him to plant a garden. Believe he out turnin' up de soil now. Not much he can plant in Janry, no ways."

"I suppose you're right."

Keziah fussed again with her apron. "Mistress Mattocks, iffen yo don' mind me sayin'. . . iffen we don' have work, Massa Mattocks might rent us out." Fear showed in her eyes as she ever so briefly shifted her glance to Caroline. "We powerful glad to be here and be togeder. Would hate to be separate." Keziah gave a slight curtsy, probably to soothe her boldness.

Caroline liked the small show of humility with the curtsy, but surmised Keziah was normally an outspoken slave. She'd have to curb the woman's courage, or she'd lose control of her new household. "Master Mattocks already has two slaves he'll rent out." She didn't want to explain to the woman how her brother-in-law, Ned, gave them slaves as a wedding gift.

She'd never thought about slave matters. Mama always took care of such things, and she didn't want to tell Keziah or the others she wasn't sure what jobs they should be doing.

In order to train these new slaves to her liking, she needed advice. "I need to visit Mistress Gibson." Glad she was the tallest, Caroline clasped her hands together and tried to feel the senior, although she was younger than Keziah and Mahaly. "Master Mattocks will be home directly. When he returns, you may ask for the use of the wagon. You and Moses will meet me at Gibson House and collect the wedding gifts then bring them here into the front parlor."

"Yessum." Keziah curtsied.

Caroline turned to Spicey who gazed at Mahaly with a frown on her face. "I'll ask Mama if you can help with laundering the wedding linens. Walk to Gibson House with me."

"Yessum, Miss Carrie." Spicey drew her attention away from Mahaly and pushed her long loose curls under a scrap of torn orange fabric loosely tied around her head. The crease on her brow gave Caroline the suspicion that Spicey was discontent with the changes in her life. She needn't fear—Caroline would always be closest to Spicey.

And although Caroline cared for Spicey, she wasn't fixing to let Spicey dampen her resolve to make a well-run home for John. "And Spicey, call me Mistress Mattocks." She couldn't have the girl making her appear young and inexperienced.

"Yessum, Miss Ca . . . Mistress Mattocks." Spicey curtsied, and her curls fell back over her bewildered expression.

Hurrying out with Spicey, Caroline hoped by the time John returned it would look like she had everything under control.

CHAPTER FOUR

January 31, 1860

A lmost asleep, Caroline lay in bed in John's arms.

"There's something I need to tell you." John exhaled and tightened his hold on her. "I should've told you a long time ago, but I didn't want you considered as having knowledge of my crime."

Crime? Her eyes flew open.

"When I was eighteen, I took my slaves to New York and freed them." The passion in his voice was something she couldn't understand. Although she'd been dreading the conversation, she'd also been wondering when it would take place.

The signs of something bothering him had been evident since their first week of marriage, escalating yesterday when he unexpectedly snapped at her after she'd asked Keziah to do a better job with cleaning the floor. Later in the day, he'd been impatient while Moses saddled his horse, finally taking over and doing it himself.

Long before they married, she'd heard rumors of him having sympathies with abolitionists. Then she caught Spicey helping John free a runaway slave. They'd come to an agreement that Caroline would look the other way if he continued the practice. Since he'd never discussed it again, she'd hoped he'd stopped for her sake. But there were plenty of clues she might be wrong. Probably the most obvious was his reaction to the wedding gifts given by Papa and Ned.

Papa had meant no harm, she was sure. In fact, on the slave deed he'd written, "a gift because of my love and affection toward my daughter." John's brother Ned, on the other hand, had laughed as he'd handed John the piece of paper. There was mischief in his eyes when he said, "I hope *these* slaves stay with you all your life." Shoulders sagging, John had stared at the deed gifting him two twenty-one-year-old male Negroes. Caroline had tried to recover his bad manners by thanking Ned for such a generous gift. John had just walked away.

As he held her in his arms now, telling his secrets, it all made sense. Although it was too dark to see his face, she knew he spoke from his heart. She didn't think he had the ability to lie.

"You were so poor. Why would you throw away your property?" she asked.

He tensed, and then sighed and relaxed. "I didn't consider them property."

"But of course, they were your property. Your father left them to you in his will. Even the law is on your side in that regard." She pushed herself onto one elbow, but she still couldn't see his features, so she laid back down with her head on his shoulder.

"I'm not arguing the point of property laws. My argument is with moral obligation." He kissed her on the top of the head, she supposed to show he didn't mean to be directly quarreling. "I need you to consider some things, my dove."

Her stomach churned. "Go on."

"We've spoken before of my feelings about the importance of family. Do you remember?"

"Yes." She remembered the conversation well. He spoke of it when they were courting, and it was one of the many sentiments that drew her to him. He'd told her he'd been impressed with her compassion toward her family and that he saw her as their calm peacemaker, something he hadn't seen in his own mother. Caroline's shyness never seemed to bother him. He always saw the good in her.

"I endeavored to tell you how I felt women's gentler virtues made them good mothers. Their hearts are with the children. Women shouldn't carry the brunt of the work but men should, so women can raise their babes."

"To be sure, but what does this have to do with the slaves you set free? Did one have a baby?"

"No, but she didn't grow up with her mother. In our southern society, the children of a Negro mother are not her own. They are considered the master's property. A slave owner can sell his property to the highest bidder. What do you think that does to a mother whose natural desires are to love and care for her children?"

"But I've always been told darkies aren't like us, but ignorant—like children. They're used to our ways." Her hands fisted. "They don't have the ability to support their own."

John was quiet a moment. "Have you ever thought about why so many women house slaves become attached to the white children? I've wondered if it's because they can freely have motherly feelings toward them since there's no threat of the white children being sold away."

She rolled onto her back, looking for answers in the darkness, not wanting to believe his statement. "I always imagined Mammy Abby loved me better than her own baby." Hot with embarrassment and frustration, she clenched her teeth. "You make me appear as if I'm a vain and selfish creature."

"I don't fault you. You only know what you've been raised to believe. I grew up with slaves too, remember. Slavery has been in both our families for generations." John gave her a squeeze, a peace token. "And what about male slaves? Unlike white men, they can't have the satisfaction of working to support their family or show their love for their own in this way. A black man has no legal or social fatherhood. No control of property. No land. He cannot dominate his household. And perhaps worst of all, he doesn't have a wife who is his and no other man's."

Caroline felt uncomfortable with the topic of the slaves' intimate lives.

"I've heard the slaves compare themselves to the Israelites in bondage who were carried away to many nations. Some of them believe their time will come to be set free and return to Africa," John said.

"Doesn't the Bible also teach the blacks are a cursed race? Mama said God created whites more intelligent. We're caring for them as God expects. Papa never flogged or beat them. He houses and feeds and clothes those under his protection. Is there anything wrong with that as long as we take care of them with kindness, as we would a child?" Caroline didn't tell John she sometimes heard the drivers crack whips out in the fields. She remembered seeing slaves in stocks on a few occasions. There had to be some kind of control over those who didn't obey, after all.

John pulled in his breath and let it out in a whoosh. "I personally believe white men are under a false pretense of superiority. No man has the *right* to control another's destiny. God wants us to depend on His word, not the arm of man. They should be able to make their own choices."

She hated arguing, but she thought him unrealistic. "Even if I come to agree with you and somehow let our slaves have freedom, what will they do? They have no means to get by. No one will hire them for pay. I don't think they can take care of themselves. They can't rightly learn as whites can." She felt ill just thinking of Spicey leaving her.

"You underestimate them," he said with disappointment. "If anything, they're hard workers. Some of them have been in the fields since they learned to walk. I've seen slave women plow and plant and perform work a white woman would never be expected to perform.

Has it ever occurred to you that we may have created a world where it's actually the wealthy white woman who cannot care for herself?"

She was stunned. Did he think her so weak? He must not know her strengths. Maybe she didn't *want* to do menial work. "This all seems too big for you to take on. You can't change things."

To her bewilderment, he chuckled.

"I guess I wouldn't have come back to the South if I didn't think I could make a difference. Education is the key to freedom. Slave owners know this. Why do you think they won't allow their slaves to learn to read?"

Fear gripped her stomach and she sat up. "Are you somehow educating the blackies at the Academy?"

"No." John was adamant in his answer. "That wouldn't be safe for them or me. I've been trying to figure out what I can do, though. I made the mistake of not educating the slaves I set free—to set them up for success. I believe if I can educate a slave, he'd do something with his life. Perhaps realize his potential."

"If what you say is true, then I'd have to think of myself, my family, and my neighbors as evil!" Her nails dug into her palms. "You're speaking of changes that would make our world fall apart. Our social ways are a means of survival."

"That makes sense, but it doesn't mean it's right." The impatience was evident in John's voice. "Ignorance is a prison for people who don't have an opportunity to be any other way."

John's comment stung. Was he suggesting her to be deliberately cruel and ignorant?

He pulled her down and kissed the top of her head. "I should've said that differently. I'm sorry." He stroked her rigid back. "What I meant was, it's a necessity for this society to believe these obtuse ideas in order to function. It's fear-based, I believe."

Caroline swallowed her anger. He'd pricked her conscience, and doubts hammered at her brain. No one had ever discussed these things with her before. While she understood what John told her, there was no hope he'd win his battle with her or anyone she knew. She appreciated the goodness in him, even if she may not be able to support his lofty dreams. To go against his desires would hurt their relationship, but she didn't want to go against her parents or her community either. She was afraid to give up her slaves and change her life so drastically. But did it scare her more not to have her husband's full devotion? John was right about one thing—the ownership of slaves was fear-based.

She moved, and he relaxed his hold on her. "I need to think this over. Your convictions are admirable. You must think very little of me, but I can't rightly agree to give up my slaves." Her heartbeat felt sluggish as she waited for his answer.

"There's nothing more important in my life than you. You have an eagerness to nurture, and I believe once you think this through it will make more sense." His voice was thick with emotion. "I love you. You'll always have my heart."

A wave of relief washed over her. She buried her face in his chest, amazed at her overwhelming need for him.

Two hours later, Caroline stared into the darkness while John breathed in slumber.

All her life, Papa had acquired more land and more slaves. She grew up believing a man desired to support his family in comfort. Why did John not have the same desires? She knew when she married him, they'd have little money, but despite Papa's warnings, her expectations were that John would slowly gain property. Inherit his mother's wealth one day, even. Didn't he want Caroline to be comfortable? What exactly were his goals for their marriage? For their life together?

The pit of her stomach tightened. He was a completely different man than her father. Would he care so little that he'd expect her to do all the cleaning, cooking, and running of the household when her father had made sure she wouldn't have to do those things? The more she thought over her conversation with John, the more her muscles stiffened. He must not love her as much as she loved him, or as much as her father loved her.

No. She wasn't going to give up her slaves. She'd just have to make John see reason.

CHAPTER FIVE

February 1, 1860

Caroline pulled the thread tight on her sampler, knotting it at the back of the fabric. She surveyed her work for imperfect stitches. There were none. *What therefore God has joined together, do not let man put asunder. Mark 10:9.* She touched the embroidered scripture and their names and marriage date beneath. The sampler was a sign of devotion to her husband that she wanted others to see. She'd hang it in the parlor.

Sitting up straighter, she stretched her sore back and closed her stinging eyes, remembering the lengthy conversation she'd had with John the previous evening. She wanted to justify herself and show him he was wrong. Her slaves were satisfied with their lives. Why wouldn't they be? She took good care of them.

She decided to approach Keziah on the subject and found her in the sitting room on the floor, legs tucked under a large braided wool rug. Her dry, cracked hands worked a needle and waxed thread into the outer loop where the rug had separated. Considering Keziah was probably older than Mama, Caroline was surprised to find her sitting in such an uncomfortable position.

She walked to the edge of the rug. "Keziah, I'd like a word with you."

"Yessum." Keziah poked the thick needle in the rug to mark her spot and worked her legs out from beneath the heavy braids.

"Oh no, you need not stop your task. I can speak to you just as well here." Caroline sat in a rocker.

Keziah scooted back to her previous position. Her overused and aged shoes were pushed against the wall.

Caroline made a mental note to ask Papa if he'd help with new ones. She couldn't see Keziah's feet under the rug. Was the old woman barefoot? If she had stockings, what semblance were they in? As mistress, she must pay more attention to such needs.

Despite her age, Keziah remained an attractive woman. Her skin a yellowish-brown, she was a mulatto. Her hair, more salt than pepper, had been pulled into a bun on top of her head with tight short curls escaping to create a bushy effect.

"Keziah, are you happy here?"

"Oh yessum, Mistress. You an' Massa Mattocks bes' Massas I ever had." Her fingers picked at a non-existent fleck on the rug.

"I'm not wanting to be pacified, Keziah. I'd like to know your state of contentedness."

"Is yo' goin' ta sell me?" Keziah's aged hands shook. She hid them under the lifted edge of the rug.

"Glory be, of course not! What would give you that impression?"

Keziah briefly glanced at Caroline, then at the rug. "Yo' axt iffen I happy here, as iffen maybe yo' have anoder place in mind for me." She brought her hands to the rug again.

Caroline calmed. "No, I've no other place in mind for you. What I should ask is if you'd leave if you could."

Keziah's distracted fingers froze their nervous picking. She looked at Caroline and then glanced away so quickly that if Caroline hadn't been studying her, she would've missed the flash of fear in her eyes.

The conversation was not going as Caroline had hoped.

"Maybe ya know'd I run once when young? He be a mean massa. I had many mean massas. Some good massas . . . Mattocks good massa. I not run!" Keziah's old, strong-willed nature returned. She looked Caroline in the eyes and held her head high.

Caroline sighed. "I'm not making my meaning clear. All I want to know is if there were no slave laws—if you were a free woman, let's say—where would you be? What would you do with yourself?"

Keziah gave her a long stare, as if she was wondering if it was a trick.

Caroline hoped Keziah would say she'd stay.

But fear remained in her eyes. "Kezzy happy. I not run."

Caroline sighed. How was she to convince the woman she wasn't trying to set a trap? "Tell me about yourself. Where were you born?"

Keziah squinted. "In Virginny . . . somewheres."

"Who were your parents?"

"I never know. Sold as a babe. Some say my pappy de ole massa." Keziah responded slowly, watching Caroline intently. "Back den it be a crime ta tell who be de daddy of a slave chile."

It saddened Caroline to think of Keziah having come from such a relationship. Papa never had relations with his slaves. "I remember hearing of such laws. What year were you born?"

"Not rightly know. Not even know de day or month."

"Did you ever hear a master speak of your age? It probably would've been on a bill of sale."

"Told I four and ten when I have my first chile. Same year dey bar slaves in Missoura. My massa plan on movin' der 'til he get de news. Dat hep some fo' de age?" Keziah visibly relaxed.

It was best to keep her questions simple. "That does give me an idea. Was Mahaly the child?"

"No."

"Where's the child you gave birth to?"

"Not know. Deys took her when still at de breast."

The idea sickened Caroline. It was as John had said. But not all slave owners were so cruel. She wouldn't be. "Did you have other children?"

Keziah nodded in confirmation. "All wid me short time."

"How many?"

"Don't know numbers."

A mother would know how many children she'd had. Caroline figured she was lying. Fieldhands knew enough numbers to plant so many rows of crops or drop so many seeds into a hole. Surely, she had fewer children than rows of crops. Caroline decided to let it go. "Has Moses always been your husband?"

"Never marry de uder pappys of chillins. Jump de broom wid Moses when firs' come to Car'liny. Befoe yo' daddy my massa." Keziah sat cross-legged under the rug and leaned forward, now looking more at Caroline than away, her hands still.

"You told me once Mahaly is your child with Moses." She'd seen Keziah watch Mahaly on many occasions, obviously proud of the girl.

Keziah finally smiled slightly. "She sho' be. Onliest chile I keep. Thought I pass de birthin' age." Keziah gazed off into the distance as if her mind had gone somewhere with her memories. "Good massa who sold us ta yo' daddy. Sold us as a family. Bless de name of Jesus. Bless yo' daddy to give us to ya."

Good. Keziah was happy. Caroline could now tell John that Keziah wanted to be with them. Grinning, Caroline hoped the woman kept speaking her feelings freely. "If you were a free woman and could move away from us legally—would you do it?"

Keziah's eyes narrowed and darted back to her. "Moses and Mahaly free likewise?"

"Yes, they'd be free also."

Keziah boldly looked her straight in the eyes. "Kezzy go without lookin' back."

Cringing inside, Caroline took in a sharp breath, her heart sinking. Was John right about the slaves not needing—or wanting—someone to care for them? "Is there nothing that binds you here then?" She needed Keziah to confirm her misgivings.

"Mattocks's best massas, but massa a massa." Keziah watched Caroline closely. "Iffen Kezzy not property, den Kezzy tell only herself what ta do. No massa hurt her. Iffen we'uns free, I'z love Moses an Mahaly wid no fear of dem leavin' 'cept when dey go ta de grave. I'z too old ta read, but Mahaly can learn her letters and read, write, and figger." Tears quickly gathered in her eyes as she spoke of what surely must be her dreams.

Caroline shifted uncomfortably.

"Ya whip me now?" Tears ran down her face. She bowed her head as if she waited for an axe to fall.

"Of course not!" Caroline's heart sank even further.

"Massas whip me fo' sayin' less." Keziah lowered her voice. "I mean no insult, but two dings I want most in life is freedom an' my chillins restored ta my bosom." She put her hands together as if to pray. "Twas my mouth dat got me sold sometime. I thought I learn my lesson. Now yo' axt me ta speak, and I'z said too much."

Keziah had experienced more suffering in her life than Caroline ever imagined in her own. Although the thought disturbed her, perhaps she could bring herself to grant the woman her freedom.

CHAPTER SIX

February 6, 1860

Caroline would always remember the bedchamber as the first she shared with John. It was a cozy room with deep-piled, floral carpets, and wallpaper of a botanical design in greens, oranges, blues, and yellows. Fire popped in the grate and glowed against furniture pieces of mahogany red.

The bed had feather ticking, a wedding present from Aunty Ann. Mary had made her an Irish chain quilt in cobalt blue and cream, Caroline's favorite.

Spicey brought in a lit kerosene lamp, placing it on the dressing table, and then went about her evening duties to prepare Caroline for bed.

The brush felt good against her scalp. She leaned farther back into her chair, relaxing as Spicey performed her nightly ministrations. Softly humming a tune Caroline had heard many times before. Spicey sprinkled rose water into Caroline's dark brown tresses and brushed it through. Her hair wasn't thick like Julia's, but it was long and needed to be braided each night before retiring.

She gazed at Spicey's reflection in the mirror. The girl was younger than she by almost a year, and a good foot shorter. She appeared to be twelve, not eighteen. Standing behind Caroline's chair, Spicey's head barely showed above Caroline's. Spicey's long, black-curly hair was swept back into a large twist and messily tied with a length of vibrant red cloth. Escaping spiraled curls framed her caramel-colored face. Caroline envied Spicey's lovely, thick hair.

The red haircloth contrasted against the gray homespun dress made by Spicey's own hands, closed at the neck with a small white collar and tied under the chin by a narrow black bow. The handsome dress was the same as all uniforms worn by Gibson House slaves. Spicey had inherited her uniforms, but Caroline wasn't able to give Keziah and Mahaly the same. They wore what they also inherited from Papa, the brown and cream striped dresses of fieldhands.

"Why do you hum the same tune each evening?" Caroline asked.

Spicey looked at Caroline's reflection with her kind, dark eyes. "My Mam learned it to me when we was little un's. Don'cha remember? It was when I's bein' taught to be your maid." She laughed.

Caroline held fast to the girl's cheerfulness and reactions to youthful memories. John was wrong, Spicey would never leave.

"Mam told me I was to brush your hair hun'red strokes and iffen I hum this here tune two times, it be same as countin' hun'red—see'z as I don't know how to count higher than ten."

Caroline had never thought to ask about the song before. Her nightly rituals were just that—rituals she knew as daily necessities and nothing more. She wanted to speak to Spicey about slavery as she had Keziah, but she wasn't sure where to start since she'd made such a mess of that conversation and brought fear to the poor old woman. Deciding to keep talking about their past, she said, "Tell me what you remember about your childhood."

Looking again at Caroline's reflection, Spicey grinned, a twinkle in her eye showing she'd instantly embraced the subject. "I do believe my first memory was of your Mama havin' a sit down with my Mam. With my Mam bein' your Mammy, I done rightly recollect ever bein' anywhere's but near your side, Miss Carrie . . . 'scusum, Mistress Mattocks."

She couldn't remember life without Spicey, either. She trusted her as much as she did her sisters. Spicey was her closest friend, even if she couldn't admit it to other whites.

Caroline nursed at her own mother's breast, as did all her siblings, but it was Mammy Abby, Spicey's mother, who slung Mama's babes to her back. "I remember Hester being carried on Mammy's back when an infant. Where were you?"

Spicey's hands stilled. She stopped humming and looked up, puzzled. "I disremember." Her brows crinkled. "'Spose I be's with Ole Pearl, who tended the young'uns while mams worked the fields and house chores." The question didn't seem to concern Spicey for long because she soon started humming and brushing Caroline's hair again.

A slave merely in name, Caroline considered Spicey more of a servant and part of the family. She cared for Caroline's room, body, hair, and made and cleaned her clothes. At Papa's, she was often found spinning cotton to be made into cloth for Caroline's linens and sheets.

"Spicey," Caroline said a little too loudly, making Spicey stop humming again. "If you weren't in my employ, what would you do with yourself?"

Spicey looked at the reflection of Caroline's eyes. "Scusum?"

"If you didn't live here, where would you want to live?"

Spicey crinkled her brows and pursed her lips. "You're all the family I have left. This be my home. I have no other."

It was the answer Caroline thought she wanted to hear, but something felt wrong. Was it thinking that Spicey was part of the family that helped justify the power Caroline had over her? Why did she feel an emptiness? John had said she was weak for letting slaves take care of her.

Forced to look at a deficiency in her character, she wanted to turn from it—wanted to believe it wasn't there. But at that moment, it gaped before her, and she faced it for no other reason than that she wanted John to see her as she saw him—a person worthy to love.

Suddenly sitting straighter, Caroline picked up the cloth next to the china washbasin, dipped it into the warm water, then squeezed the liquid out.

"Lordy, Miss Carrie! I do that." Spicey was visibly disturbed. She took the cloth from Caroline's hands. "Did I brush too long?"

Not looking Spicey in the eyes, she reached again for the wet cloth, but Spicey pulled away and wouldn't give it up. "You can keep brushing. I had a mind to wash myself tonight."

Spicey shook her head. "I always have washed you. Are you sore with me?"

Caroline dropped her arm. "No, I'm not angry. But I am a grown, married woman. It occurred to me that I should wash and dress myself for bed. I can't rightly explain why, exactly . . . but I need to. You're a devoted servant. Please don't feel slighted." She stood and reached out her hand, palm up.

Spicey brought her brows together in question but declined her head and gave Caroline the wet cloth.

"As I said, don't you fret. Now leave me be. I'll see you in the morning."

Spicey dropped a quick curtsy and left the bedchamber, closing the door soundlessly behind her.

Caroline stared at the closed door. What had gotten into her to treat a faithful servant in such a manner?

The fire in the grate popped. The clock on the bureau ticked. And Caroline stood staring at the closed door for a long time. Finally, she returned to the dressing table and dipped the cloth in the now cold water. Squeezing it until damp, she slowly wiped her face with a cloth that wasn't warm and comforting as when Spicey washed her. Selfishly, she hoped John would walk in and see her, finding the respect for her she feared was missing in their relationship.

Was he right that slave owners created a world where a wealthy white woman couldn't take care of herself, making her weaker than a slave? And if he were, could she wash away all she'd been taught by her parents? Did she even want to?

CHAPTER SEVEN

February 8, 1860

Firewood crackled, warming Caroline as she sat sewing in her bedchamber, embroidering little pink rosebuds on a silk hanky. The daily quiet and inactivity of the house was unlike living with her family, and she didn't like it. There was too little to do.

She used to enjoy visiting with her friends, but they were unmarried, and their conversations no longer interested her. And it may have been her imagination, but it seemed there were now expectations of her as a preacher's wife that she wasn't sure she could live up to. They counted upon her to serve the congregation or asked her to relay awkward messages to John. Consequently, she often stayed home during church activities other than Sunday services.

After her fiascos with Keziah and Spicey in trying to understand their contentedness, it was easier to let things be and concluded she couldn't participate in John's passion of *helping* slaves. Some dark nights he left and didn't return until just before dawn, telling her he was helping slaves, but saying no more. She didn't ask questions. She didn't want to know. The subject of slavery had become a raw sore between them that she wished to ignore. Although he'd tried, John hadn't changed her mind. She wanted to make him happy, but she also wanted to keep her slaves. Weren't both possible?

With Mama's help, it'd taken a few weeks to train the slaves and for Caroline to learn how to oversee they functioned efficiently. Things were running smoother, but she felt cheated of something. She stewed over her inadequacies. The slaves met all of her and John's needs, so how was she supposed to make *herself* useful?

She missed John during the day when he worked at the Academy. There were almost a hundred and fifty students who attended. John taught Greek, Latin, and theology, which he called "a moral as well as a mental training for the students." Living his passion to educate the youths, he came home each evening and enthusiastically shared the events of his day. He'd ask what she'd done, and she'd fumble over what to report. After the first week, he'd stopped asking. Instead of giving her relief, it made her feel dispirited. She was convinced each day should have a solid purpose to it. But what was her purpose?

"Mistress Mattocks, Ma'am?" Keziah stood at the bedchamber door.

"Yes, Keziah."

"Massa Mattocks's ma here for a visit, Mistress."

A sick feeling soured her stomach and made her hands tremble. She set her sewing aside. Her mother-in-law intimidated her. Consequently, Caroline spent little time with her. "I'll come right down . . . ah . . . Tell Moses to quickly get a fire burning in the parlor, and you make tea and scones prompt now."

"Yessum." Keziah curtsied and hurried away.

Caroline removed her duster. At the bureau mirror, she anxiously examined her appearance. She wished she'd known of her mother-in-law's visit so she could've properly prepared. John didn't have the wood needed to keep all rooms in the house warm. She had to ask Papa for the small amount they did have. Papa's slaves cut pine trees from his plantation forests and brought it to town seasonally. John had no forests in which to acquire wood, so they were at the mercy of family, friends, and parishioners to supply their needs. Which is exactly what Papa had told her would happen.

As she started down the steps, Moses entered the hall below, toting the precious wood into the parlor.

She smoothed her skirts and patted her chignon. She hadn't spent enough time with Eliza to say she truly knew her, but her own mama admired Eliza as "a woman of immaculate etiquette with an inherent sense of social elegance." Eliza was modest in looks and always seemed completely calm and composed. In the few visits to Eliza's home that Caroline had made, it was always impeccably clean, despite John's six young half-siblings. She could never match up to Eliza's capabilities or the command she had of her slaves.

Entering the parlor, Caroline found it cold and smelling of boiled crab, the scent of dinner coming from the kitchen.

Moses stacked wood in the grate as Eliza looked at sheet music on the square grand piano Papa had given Caroline as a recent gift.

"Good afternoon, Eliza. I apologize for the cold room. Moses shall have a fire shortly. Would you care to be seated?" She motioned to the settee near the fireplace.

Eliza stepped toward the settee. "My apologies for not warning you of my visit. I didn't know I'd be here myself until this morning when Philip . . . Dr. Koonce . . . asked me to come into town with him for medical supplies." She sat, carefully arranging her skirts.

Caroline settled on the edge of the settee, facing her.

How straight Eliza kept her back. For giving birth to nine children, she was remarkably slender. Her dreary, gray wool dress reminded Caroline of the few Quaker women she'd seen on trips to Jacksonville. Eliza certainly had the money for silks, but her taste in clothing was on the drab side. Her brown hair had been parted in the center and pulled back in a simple bun, making her look older and more severe than need be.

"I just saw John at the Academy," she said. "He seems immensely happy. He suggested I come visit you." She didn't smile.

Had she meant to compliment Caroline by telling her of John's happiness? Perhaps the visit wouldn't be so trying after all. "He does love his work educating the young."

"Yes." Eliza took off her gloves and laid them in her lap. "He expressed much admiration for you being the wife he'd hoped for."

Caroline breathed in relief. "I thank you for raising such a charitable man. I've found much happiness myself." She'd never let Eliza know her dissatisfaction.

Succeeding in getting the fire started, Moses stood, bowed, and left the room.

"I expect you'll be a good wife." It was a statement, not a question. "It's rewarding for me to see my children compatibly married." Eliza gazed toward the piano. "Do you play?"

"Yes. It's a pastime I enjoy."

"How else do you occupy your time?"

Caroline froze. Her mother-in-law had found right quick where she was most vulnerable. She smoothed her skirts. "Well, I . . ." Her face warmed as she picked at a loose thread at her cuff. "I enjoy all types of sewing and handwork."

Eliza didn't seem to notice her embarrassment. "Do you read much?"

Relieved to answer in the affirmative, she said, "Yes. I especially enjoy reading about other cultures and places to travel. Papa's library is always open to me. He's brought home books from the West Indies and his travels to New England."

"At what age did you stop attending school?" Eliza's bleak expression changed little.

Caroline's stomach curdled with the cross-examination. "Sixteen. There was a small school at White Oak, but most of my education was accomplished in town during the winter months under the tutelage of Captain Duffy."

"Did your parents bring educators or tutors into the home?"

"A few, but Papa couldn't find one old enough—or blind enough—to concentrate on lessons as he taught Julia."

Eliza gave no indication that the humor of the comment registered. "I've always believed in education, both for the male and female. Mothers who are educated have children who are successful. When John's father died, I had one stepson, Ned, and three of my own little boys to raise. It was two years before I married Dr. Koonce. Before him, many men courted me, but Philip was the only man who understood my desires to educate my boys and not expect them to be planters. He's a supportive stepfather."

Eliza's face showed emotion for the first time when she gave a half smile—probably more for her thoughts of her sons than for Caroline's benefit. "Ned, as you know, became a merchant. John attended university, and although a highly intelligent man, followed his heart and became a clergyman, an admirable profession if one believes in divinity." She cleared her throat. "Kit will soon be a doctor. He travels often with Dr. Koonce."

Mahaly entered with tea, scones, and jam on china plates, all beautifully presented upon an ornate silver tray, a wedding gift from Eliza. Caroline doubted it was a coincidence and needed to praise Mahaly later.

Caroline served, and Mahaly left.

Eliza held her steaming cup of tea near her lips and continued the inquisition. "John doesn't earn a lot of money, and I expect he never will." She tisked. "I tried to direct him otherwise." She took a sip of tea. "At any rate, you'll need to make sure your children are well educated." As though Eliza tried to see into Caroline's soul, her mother-in-law hadn't taken her eyes from Caroline's.

Wishing she were still upstairs in front of her warm fire, not in such an uncomfortable circumstance, she shifted her position on the settee. She'd need to speak to John about letting her know well in advance when her mother-in-law was to visit. Looking to her tea, she realized she'd been stirring in the sugar for some time. Taking the spoon out, she laid it on the saucer. "I do have dreams for my future children. I hope I'm as successful a mother as you've been."

Eliza didn't acknowledge the compliment. "Dreams are admirable as long as they can be transformed into reality. You have an ambitious man for a husband, who can help you achieve high objectives for your children."

Albeit uncomfortable, the conversation helped Caroline understand her mother-in-law. Based on today's conversation, and things John had previously mentioned, Eliza was a woman who reached the top of her mountain only by her husband and children being successful.

Caroline held the plate to offer Eliza a scone.

She showed the palm of her hand in refusal. "Although you must keep my son happy, don't concern yourself with what John expects. Decide what you'll expect of yourself. Presently, without children, you've much free time. Read and educate yourself. Become more accomplished on the piano, acquire skills that will someday help you direct your children to be disciplined and able to find their own interests that motivate them to have successful lives."

The room wasn't yet hot. Still, moisture trickled down Caroline's back. Tightening her grip on the saucer, she sipped her tea and glanced out the window, then finally looked at Eliza. "I appreciate your advice." She didn't mean the words. "I'll do my best." She shifted her gaze to her tea, hoping her mother-in-law couldn't read the uncertainty in her eyes.

Eliza sighed and placed her cup and saucer on her lap. "You're young. I don't aim to burden you, but it would do some good to realize your opportunities now. Your progression depends on how you choose—and you must choose."

"My own Ma—"

"Johnny is a good son, and I love him with all my heart. There's nothing more important than family. You'll see. Being a mother is the most rewarding undertaking there is. The feelings I have for my children are rooted deep within my soul."

Caroline was taken back by Eliza's words. A forthright woman, she spoke her mind, but with that last statement, Caroline wanted to hope her mother-in-law had a tender heart too.

She now understood where John received some of his traits. It was no wonder he was so knowledgeable and driven. She hadn't realized he was so much like his mother. She hoped someday she felt comfortable around Eliza, and that Eliza grew to like her. But Caroline also felt the great weight of so many expectations. What if she failed both John and her mother-in-law?

CHAPTER EIGHT

March 11, 1860 - Swansboro Church

On a quiet Sunday morning, Caroline and John were alone in the church. She was readying the hymnals when he approached. "Mrs. Tucker is home sick today. We won't have anyone to play the piano. I know I've asked before, but are your feelings still the same?"

He had asked before. And she'd always declined. Holding an armful of hymnals, she shifted from one foot to the other. "Oh John . . . I wish you hadn't asked. I want to please you. You know right well I do. But . . ." She sat on a hard pew and placed the books next to her, looking away from him toward the tall stain glass windows where early morning sun threw jeweled shafts of light into the chapel.

The social aspects of going to church were new to her. Some of the folks she used to see in town sitting on their porches—the ones she never socialized with—she now saw at church. She tried to visit with them after services. Gathering outside in groups, the women gossiped together while the men discussed their crops or trades. She speculated they expected her to be righteously flawless, and so she tried to play the part, which kept her saying little, as not to give away her ignorance or embarrass John. She was a newcomer who didn't fit in.

Papa had no need for religion and Mama tried to do what she could when they were young by reading the Bible and teaching them to pray. But God seemed distant and foreign, like a fairytale Mama might recite.

Caroline alleviated some of her feelings of inadequacy by helping John on Sunday mornings. But playing piano in front of all those people who judged her was more than she could bear. What if she made a mistake?

John moved closer. "Forget I asked. I want you comfortable here."

She wiped her brow. "It's hard to explain what my music is to me. It's emotional and private. When I play for others it's like I'm giving it away and can't rightly have it for myself." She shook her head, feeling guilty for not telling him the complete truth. "I'm talking nonsense. I dare say you don't understand me. You'd never hold back sharing any talent."

He sat on the other side of the hymnals. "People can sometimes feel God's presence more through music than through a sermon. What you play might very well be as important as what I say. I know I'm not helping to convince you to play today, but I think I do feel a little of your trepidation. Believe it or not, I sometimes get nervous before a sermon if I perceive it's what God needs the people to hear."

"Why do you preach?" A simple question. One she was surprised she hadn't thought to ask before. She was also glad to change the subject.

"I can't help it. I want to share my testimony and convictions. It's not just the teaching. I enjoy ministering to the sick and helping people in need."

She was far below this man on the ladder to Heaven. His illusive sense of spirituality is why she'd been attracted to him in the first place but also why she felt self-conscious. "When did you decide you wanted to be a preacher?"

John leaned into the bench, staring at the pulpit in front of him, but his eyes seemed to be seeing something distant. "I had an experience as a child when playing by the White Oak River. I think I was about two, almost three. Ned had made a boat from driftwood, and I was floating it along the shore. The current took it out farther than I could reach. By the time I took off my shoes and stockings, the boat was quite a distance away. Thinking I could retrieve it, I went into the water. I didn't know how to swim yet, and when I stepped off an underwater ledge, I slipped into water over my head. I still remember that experience as if it were in front of my eyes right now."

He turned to Caroline. "I remember being underwater with my eyes open. It was murky, but I could see a short distance. I wasn't afraid and waited for my brother to pull me out. Even though he was nowhere in sight when I was playing with the boat, somehow I *knew* he'd come. And he did. Ned reached in and pulled me onto the shore. Angry with me, he yelled until I cried. Years later, he told me the rest of the story. He said he was whittling by the barn when a man said to him, "Run and get your brother out of the river." He looked around and saw no one. Even though the voice was calm, he'd felt a sense of urgency. He ran as fast as he could to the river, which wasn't far. He couldn't see me in the water, but instinctively knew exactly where I was. The rest you know."

Goosebumps rose on her arms. "What an exceptional story." She wanted to hold him in her arms but thought better of it while in church. "How did that experience make you want to preach?"

"As the years went by, I became intrigued as to how that could've happened. Whose voice had Ned heard, how did I know he was coming, and where did my calm feeling come from? There's something bigger than us that is veiled from our eyes and from logic. The only answers I could find were in scripture. God sends His angels to help us and His Holy Spirit to guide us. I think I experienced both that day." He chuckled. "And I think I was baptized."

Caroline laughed softly, then sobered, remembering aspects of his miraculous tale. "Do you think it was your father's voice Ned heard? Do you think our family members are still near after they die?" She thought of her ten-year-old sister Sarah who'd died the year before, hoping she was close.

John reached over the hymnals and grasped her hand. "I don't know. There are still questions I need answered. Why, for instance, was it important for me to live? What am I to do with my life?"

"You seem to be on the right track and doing what you love. I imagine God is pleased with your occupation. Would you change anything if you could?"

"All roads led me to you. I wouldn't change a thing." His glorious dimples accented the love in his eyes.

Caroline blushed. "You're a far better person than I, yet you always make me feel as if I'm a queen." She leaned over the books and quickly kissed him on the cheek.

"You don't give yourself enough credit. I can't imagine it's easy to live with a poor preacher." He smiled sadly. "I don't know what's ahead for us, but if the Lord saw fit to keep me alive, I owe Him a great debt."

CHAPTER NINE

May 1, 1860 - Gibson House

Caroline watched her sister Hester and her new husband George Ward dance in front of their wedding guests.

"A bride at seventeen," Papa said to her and Mama, who sat on either side of him. He shook his head as he watched.

"Don't fret. It's a good match. Many girls marry younger." Caroline assured him but had the same apprehensions.

"Not my girls. I believed you too young at nineteen." Papa smiled and patted her hand where it rested on the white linen-covered table.

"And now, what do you think about my marriage?" She wanted to take the question back as soon as it left her lips.

"I think you did well after all. I just hope you can live on love, because you certainly don't have anything else." Papa chuckled good-naturedly.

"I haven't gone hungry a single day. And the slaves you gave us have kept me from any household drudgery." She felt guilt even without John hearing her words. "Stop teasing me, Papa. All's well in my home." She squeezed his hand for added reassurance that she didn't feel. Only the night before, John had been gone all night again. She lived in fear her family would find out about his unlawful activities.

"I'm sure I don't need to remind you it's not *your* home you're living in but a borrowed one."

That prick to her heart stung.

Mama gave Papa a sharp look. "William, leave the girl alone. You certainly didn't have all the land holdings you do now. And need I remind you of *my* age at marriage?"

Caroline laughed, hoping to squelch her small hurt. "Papa, you're as sour as bad cider. What makes you so ornery?"

"Apologies, little lamb. Feeling sorry for myself, I am. I just married off my last daughter, and I don't look forward to a home empty of my four delicate belles."

"Delicate belles?" Mama harrumphed a laugh. "Spoiled, to be sure, but I didn't raise delicate daughters. They're all headstrong women who can care for themselves, children, and a household." Mama raised her crystal goblet of wine and saluted Caroline.

She hoped Mama was right.

The music concluded, and people moved off the dance floor, skirts swishing as they passed. Many stopped to thank and congratulate the host and hostess.

As the evocative notes of a new song commenced, John approached with two crystal goblets of punch. "I heard talk over at the refreshment table that Stephen Douglas came out the front-runner as the nominee for president at the convention in Charleston last week." He sat in the chair between Papa and Caroline.

Papa replied, "Yes, I'd heard about that. I might throw my vote to William Yancey of Alabama. His idea is to let settlers in the territories decide for themselves whether slavery should be allowed."

John set goblets of punch in front of Caroline and himself. "I'm considering not supporting the Democratic Party at all. There's a new party forming called the Constitutional Union Party. They're talking about nominating either Sam Houston of Texas or John Bell of Tennessee. Their emphasis is the Constitution and not to take a firm stance on slavery either way." John spoke boldly, like an abolitionist.

Papa wasn't going to like it.

Caroline brought her hands to her lap, curling her fingers into her palms.

"Good luck to them!" Papa frowned. "I think the election will come down to slavery, no matter who you go with."

John stiffened. "I'm concerned the Northerners are trying to take away our right to decide many issues, not just slavery. We need to keep freedom to govern ourselves."

Papa looked at John. "I'd feel more comfortable voting for a Southerner than Douglas from Illinois, even if he seems to share our sympathies."

"I agree. When I was in the North, they talked about Southerners like we were a bunch of uneducated imbeciles." John caressed his glass at the stem and twirled the punch around and around.

The motion and the discussion put Caroline's nerves on edge. How covert could John keep his sympathies for the Negro?

Papa nodded affirmatively. "I heard similar talk in Boston when I was up there last year selling West Indies sugar. The Northerners see themselves as carrying us on their backs. They make good money from their fabric-producing factories, forgetting where the cotton for that fabric came from in the first place. Our agriculture is needed to support their livelihoods." Papa spoke calmly, but his temper had been known to flare when talking politics.

Caroline looked to Mama for interference, but she watched her guests and tapped her hand on the table to the beat of the music, seemingly not listening to the conversation. Caroline followed her gaze to Mary playing Hester's new piano—the last piano Papa would give to his daughters. Sarah was dead, and only Benny remained at home. Would Sarah's piano remain in his storehouse forever? He'd bought them all together on the same trip to Boston.

John still twirled his goblet by the stem. Condensation from the glass left a wet ring on the tablecloth. "Is there a candidate with a platform on education? We need more public schools to educate our youth."

If he didn't stop twirling his glass, she'd reach over and stop him herself.

"Vice President Breckinridge might be your man. They say he represents the Southern Democrats and is well educated. He has a pro-slavery platform."

John finally took a drink. He set the glass down and drew his hand into a fist. "I'd rather the vote didn't come to slavery." The tightness of his voice wasn't lost on Papa. "I've issue with a few things, such as the law for a slave not to be able to read the Bible."

Caroline shifted in her chair and bit her lip.

Papa sighed. "Yes, I can see how you would."

Exhaling slowly, she closed her eyes. *Please John, don't bait him.*

John didn't seem to consider who he was talking to. "Ironic that the Bible is taken to the black men in the Dark Continent, as if we're doing them a favor, yet I cannot preach it to the Negroes here."

Under the table Caroline gave John a tap on his leg. He glanced sideways at her, but then gave his full attention to Papa without acknowledging her warning.

Not noticing their exchange, Papa went on, "I can't agree with you on that account either. If you educate the Negroes, they'll get all kinds of ideas in their heads. Why do you need to teach them the Bible anyway? Most are taught religion by their own kind."

"There's a difference between Christianity and some of their ancient religions."

Papa clasped his hands. "No offense, John, but I'm not concerned with religion. Whites are naturally more intelligent than blacks. They can't learn like we can. That's why they need caregivers."

Caroline's stomach writhed in agony.

The music stopped, and people walked by the table to thank Papa and Mama for the party while others chatted about how beautiful Hester looked.

Caroline hoped the change in subject brought Papa and John's conversation to an end.

During the brief exchanges with guests, she glanced about the room. Spicey had a tray in her hands, engaged in conversation with a tall male slave Caroline didn't recognize. She'd need to remember to ask Spicey about it later.

A new song started, and the guests moved away.

"When I was in New York," John addressed Papa, "I heard the black man, Frederick Douglass, speak about education. He was no less intelligent than I."

Couldn't John let it lie? Why must he continue to goad Papa to converse about a subject he was cantankerous about?

Color rose on Papa's face. "I can't rightly judge by your word about one highly unusual man. I've witnessed fifty others on my own land who would live like Barbarians if I didn't clothe and feed them. I care well for my slaves—just as I do for a good horse." Papa's voice grew louder, and a few people turned to stare. "It's only good business to keep them healthy and strong. These slave owners who whip and abuse their darkies"—Papa's face became red—"and run them into the ground, are idiots!" His last word rang out into the room.

The music cutoff, and more people turned.

Caroline's face burned with embarrassment.

Papa waved his hand and forced a smile. "Forgive me. Please continue dancing."

Hester, on the dance floor with George, furrowed her brow and gave Papa a questioning stare.

Mama also frowned.

Caroline felt ill. "Papa . . ."

Papa moved closer to John. "I don't consider myself a Christian, yet I do give my slaves a civilizing influence of Christianity." He turned and touched Mama's arm. "Makes Susan here happy too."

"Oh, my bless-ed!" Mama finally joined in. "You fray my nerves talking about religion and politics on the joyous event of our daughter's wedding." She stood. "Come help me see to our guests."

Papa tilted his head in capitulation. "As you wish, my love." He passed John, frowning at his back.

Finally breathing normally, Caroline was no less angry at John. "You had me on pins and needles. You know Papa doesn't take kindly to abolitionist talk. What were you thinking?"

"I'm sorry, Carrie," he said sincerely. "Believe me, there was a lot I wasn't saying. I'd like for your family to know my feelings, but I didn't aim to upset you."

Suddenly curious about what his parents knew of his abolitionist ideas, she asked, "Do your mother and stepfather know how you feel?"

"Only my mother. We've had many discussions. Like you, she cautions me as to whom I should talk about it." He rubbed his face. "She certainly doesn't condone my sympathies. She's more akin to your father's point of view."

"I'm surprised she *allows* you to have differing views from her."

John showed his dimples and broke the tension. "She thinks the stars rotate around her sons, and they can do no wrong."

Caroline's irritation almost forgotten, she said, "I suppose I must be in the same orbit as those stars. Just mind yourself around Papa."

ର୍ଷେ

"Spicey?" Caroline asked later that evening. "Who was the slave boy I saw you talking with at Hester's wedding?"

Spicey stood behind Caroline in the bedchamber, taking her hair out of a chignon. "Who you mean, Miss?"

Even after five months of marriage, Spicey still called her "Miss" occasionally. Caroline had given up correcting her months ago. "As you were serving, I saw you speaking with another servant. Who was he?"

"'Haps you refer to Massa Kit's manslave, Junior?" Spicey looked away with a timid grin. "He was sayin' how he's growed up with Massa Kit, just as I growed with you."

"I see. Did you speak with him at length?"

"No, Miss Carrie. He made me feel flustery-like whenever he was near." She turned away to grab a brush.

"Well, seeing as he's living with Master Kit in Carteret County, perhaps you'll not see him again." She stared intently at the girl to make her meaning clear.

Spicey visibly uncomfortable with the conversation, began brushing Caroline's hair. "I sure that be the case." She hummed the hair brushing song.

Worry niggled at Caroline's heart, and she hoped they'd never have to speak of the Negro man again. She never wanted to lose Spicey—especially since the girl had been by Caroline's side ever since she could remember. Spicey knew Caroline better than anyone else. Before she married, Spicey slept beside her on a palette. On many occasions, when Caroline was upset, Spicey talked with her late into the night to calm her troubles. Spicey was the most gentle and kind person Caroline knew.

CHAPTER TEN

July 4, 1860 - Swansboro

Caroline opened the parasol to shade her face from the bright morning sun. White sails stood out starkly against the deep blue of a clear day and waters of Bogue Sound. Seagulls dipped to scout out any morsels of food left by the hundreds of people gathered around.

Two men on the pier scrambled to catch ropes from the docking paddle-wheel ferry. On its decks, the band from New Bern played "My Country 'Tis of Thee." After the gangplank came down, Captain George T. Duffy, marshal of the day, led the band off the boat. A cannon fired with a loud boom to usher in the beginning of patriotic festivities. People cheered.

Caroline linked her arm through John's. "Are you nervous about your speech?"

"No, I look forward—"

"Everyone follow the band to the Academy," Captain Duffy shouted to the gathering.

The people parted to make room for a cadet who carried a flag of rich and heavy blue silk with deep yellow, made by the Ladies of Onslow. On one side were the words "Onslow Cavalry" and the other an American Eagle with shield and the motto, "Pro Patria." The band followed the flag bearer and the Swansboro Cadets, who performed military maneuvers while they paraded up the street. After the cadets passed, Caroline and John filed in behind the procession, marching across Front Street toward Main.

The day hot, Caroline shifted her parasol, wishing she could take her gloves off, but dared not let the sun darken her ivory skin.

The smells of smoked pig, fish frying, and fresh scones filled her with nostalgia. She always loved the excitement of public holidays but could do without the crush of people.

The crowd continued to follow the band as it marched up Main, playing "Brothers, Will You Meet Me." Turning onto Water Street, they stopped in front of the Academy where a stage and podium had been set up.

"Good luck to you, John," she said.

"Thank you, my dove." He left her side and went up on stage.

After a brief introduction of the speakers, Captain Duffy sat, and John's brother Ned a member of the North Carolina State Convention, read the Mecklenburg Declaration of Independence. Written in 1775 in North Carolina, it was a document Carolinians were proud of. Caleb Hewitt then stood and read the National Declaration of Independence.

When John rose and walked to the podium, Caroline's stomach fluttered, and her knees weakened. Every Sunday she heard him preach without being nervous for him. Why was she now?

"Ladies and gentlemen," His strong voice carried through the crowd. Even people in the back wouldn't have difficulty hearing.

She hoped he'd show the same passion he demonstrated when he gave his Sunday sermons.

"You accord me a great honor by extending this invitation to address you on this Fourth of July—a celebration of our country's independence from tyranny."

Light applause flowed through the audience.

"God intended man to be free. Seventy-three years ago, in 1787, men formed a government which institutionalized safeguards to protect the freedom of its citizens. It's been said that 'life, liberty, and property do not exist because men made laws.' On the contrary, it was the fact that life, liberty, and property existed beforehand that caused men to make laws in the first place.

There's a divine origin to man's rights. If we accept that human rights are given by government, then we must accept that government can take them away. I say *God* instituted our government for the *benefit* of man. We must have free exercise of conscience. What are some of our freedoms?" John's voice boomed. "Freedom to worship," he shouted.

Most people in the audience applauded.

"Freedom to travel where we want in this great land."

More applause.

"Freedom to own property and enterprises."

Everyone joined in on the applause.

"Freedom to speak our mind."

"Hear, hear!" someone called out.

"Freedom to bear arms and serve in a militia."

The applause grew louder.

Caught up in the excitement, Caroline clapped her gloved hands as well as she could while holding her parasol and remaining genteel.

"Our government was established to protect these freedoms." John waited for the shouts and applause to die down. "I believe we cannot maintain these freedoms unless our political institutions are founded on faith in God, and we believe in the existence of moral law. If we reject God's law, then we must base a political system on human law. We'd then allow our elected officials to become our gods."

The audience no longer cheered but respectfully listened, and Caroline felt proud of John.

"If we accept the source of man's rights come from God, then we recognize the sanctity of the individual. The most crucial element of self-government is the family. The family is the foundation of society. Man's success will never be greater than what he attains with his own family. If we make the Union the source of law, then they can control our family, education, and religion."

"Boo," a citizen called out. "We want control!"

"Man does not exist to serve the Union." John ignored the outburst. "Man exists to serve, teach, and strengthen his family in an atmosphere of freedom. Once our freedom is lost, only human blood will win it back. If our nation keeps the commandments of God, we will not perish.

"Our spiritual foundation is the essence of our strength. If we do not accept the existence of a Supreme Being, on what basis can we morally resist tyranny? Freedom is a God-given principle."

"Amen," a few called.

"God intended men to be free." His voice became quieter, but he kept his tone of sincerity. "Let us teach our children this principle. Our youth are this nation's strength." He paused for a moment. "Let me say to our youth—God knows who you are. You are blessed to live in this Promised Land, and He expects much of you." He cast a sweeping glance encompassing the crowd, perhaps to make eye contact with the younger folks. "Be ready to defend the land of your birth. When you see an American flag unfurled, let it inspire your minds with those deeds and heroic values which are the legacy of our Revolutionary fathers." John covered his heart.

Caroline smiled.

"Thank you for this opportunity to speak. Now enjoy your celebrations of freedom this day." He took off his hat and held it in the air. "God bless America," he shouted.

Cheers went up throughout the crowd, and people jostled Caroline as they moved toward Front Street to continue their festivities.

Moving against the stream of bodies, she tried to squeeze her way through the throng toward her husband. She could no longer see him at the podium or on the stage. Where had he gone? Finally extricating herself from the array, she caught a glimpse of his long, black clergyman's coattails. He seemed to be quickly heading for home, away from the gathering and merrymaking.

"John! Wait!" He didn't stop. She hurried to follow him.

He walked swiftly up the steps and entered their house.

Leaving the celebration seemed an unusual thing. Her chest squeezed tight with anxiety. Something must be amiss. She entered the house. "John, where are you?"

Her parasol clattered when she dropped it in the umbrella rack.

Boot heels sounded overhead and moved across the upstairs floor. Then there was silence.

She rushed upstairs to find John sitting on their bed with his head in his hands.

"Are you unwell? I was worried about you leaving so suddenly."

"You don't want to be with me right now." He sounded both angry and sad.

"What's wrong? Are you ill?" She pulled off a glove, feeling his forehead, then ran her hand over his hair.

Jaw clenching, his body went rigid.

She sat beside him on the bed and rubbed his stiff back. "What's upset you? Are you worried about your speech? I think it was the finest Fourth of July speech I've ever heard," she said with conviction.

He shook his head. "It's not that I think it was a bad speech." His voice was constricted, as if his collar were too tight. "It's what I did not say that distresses me."

Surprised at his anguish she embraced him.

"How can you respect me? How can I respect myself? Here I am, preaching freedom, while in front of me I can see slaves holding parasols over the heads of women and fanning their faces. And more slaves in the back of the crowd, caring for the animals that pulled the carriages they drove to bring their masters to the festivities honoring our freedoms." He looked away, his eyes moistening.

She didn't know what to say. Spicey wasn't there to hold her parasol, although if she had been, it wouldn't have bothered Caroline. "I'm sorry you feel that way."

"I'm a hypocrite . . . citing freedoms when a whole group of people within earshot of my words have no freedoms at all. Many who were born in this country . . . should be considered Americans and should have the same freedoms enjoyed by every white man." He moaned. "Carrie, how am I going to resolve this conflict in my soul?"

How could she comfort a man with words she didn't feel? "I wish I had answers for you. Your anguish breaks my heart."

He sighed. "I don't expect you to have the answers. It's something I have to figure out for myself."

She nestled her chin on his shoulder and spoke into his ear, "You were right not to say anything in your speech about the darkies. It would have put us both in danger."

Going rigid in her arms, John stood, breaking her embrace, and stalked out of the room. He stomped down the stairs and slammed the door on his way out.

CHAPTER ELEVEN

August 1, 1860

It had been six days since John had left for a theological seminar in Raleigh. It was the first time Caroline had been separated from him since their marriage in January and she missed his companionship.

Lonely, she tried to keep herself busy with activities such as tatting, embroidery, and reading. Occasionally, she visited her sisters, cousins, or her friend Juju. She seldom saw her parents and Benny, who had returned to White Oak Plantation, a half-day's ride away, as they always did during the planting season.

Each hot evening, she played the piano for hours until her fingers could play no more, her soul wearied from emotions the music evoked. Worn out, she allowed Spicey to prepare her for bed and then fell into a fitful sleep.

Today, Spicey stood by Caroline's side in the front room, fanning her while she read *Jane Eyre* out loud when Mary burst through the door. "Caroline," her sister sobbed, her name a lament, distress etched on her normally refined and lovely face.

Dread ran through Caroline's veins. She stood, the book tumbling to the floor.

Mary fell into her arms.

"What is it?" Caroline said.

Mary gasped for breath. "It's Papa. He's ill. Mama has sent for us, and Ned's gone to get a doctor . . . Papa Koonce." She released Caroline to wipe her tears. "You know Mama never calls on doctors. I'm uncertain if she's lost her resolve since Sarah died . . . or if something worse . . ."

Caroline's heart constricted. Her most immediate thought was to get to White Oak Plantation. "Do you know what ails him?"

"Mama thinks malaria."

Spicey gasped, and Caroline collapsed onto her chair.

"Not only is Papa sick," Mary went on, "but so are many of his slaves."

"No!" Spicey whimpered.

"Two have died."

"Who?" Spicey's voice was barely above a whisper. White Oak Plantation had been her home too.

"I don't know." Mary shook her head and brought her gloved hands to her face. "We can't lose Papa!" She cried as though her heart would break.

ଔଔଔ

Caroline apprehensively entered her parents' bedchamber with Mary.

Mama sat slumped, asleep in a cushioned chair near an open window.

Papa lay on the bed, a thin white sheet draped his lower body, a yellowed, vinegar-stained kerchief on his chest, and a wet cloth upon his forehead. At the side of the bed, his favorite slave, Betsey, moved the hot, humid air with a square, brightly painted vellum fan—its colors oddly juxtaposing the pathetic scene. With her other hand, the servant shooed away flies as they landed on him.

Papa's pale, sweat-slickened skin frightened Caroline. Never had her strong father been in such a weak condition.

Betsey motioned them further into the stifling hot bedchamber that stunk of unwashed bodies and vinegar. Drapes had been pulled aside at the open windows, but no breeze stirred within.

Betsey set the fan on the bedside table and removed the cloth from Papa's head. She dipped it in a washbasin of water, wrung it out, and replaced it. "What I'd do fo' a little ice," she said more to herself than to anyone in the room. "Yo' Pa mighty sick." She spoke quietly so as not to wake Mama. "The worst of the pain and vomit seem to have passed." Obviously, she wasn't fixing to pacify the women. "Better when he sleeps, as his thirst cain't seem to be quenched none when he awake. And the liquid don't stay in him no how. We's been treatin' him with powdered dogwood, but 'spect it doin' no good. Yo' Ma hopin' the doc come wit' quinine."

Caroline pulled her eyes from her unconscious father to gaze at Betsey. Dark circles ringed her eyes, the worry evident on her light brown face. Stains of perspiration spread under her arms and breasts.

Mary stepped forward. "Ned should be here soon with Doctor Koonce. But quinine is never easy to come by this late in the season. Let's pray he has some."

Caroline touched Betsey's sleeve. "When was the last time you slept?"

She gave a weak smile. "Reckon it's been over a day now."

"Let me take the fan." Caroline reached for it. "You go get some rest."

Betsey inclined her head and stepped back. "Will ya be 'spectin' some nourishment?"

"No, Betsey. We'll make do. Go rest." Caroline tried to make direct eye contact with her, but Betsey kept her eyes lowered.

She couldn't help but feel sympathy for a woman who cared so gently for her father. She'd known Betsey her whole life, and suddenly, for the first time, desired to embrace her. Were John's convictions becoming her own? She pushed aside the impulse and turned to Papa, moving air over his still body with the fan.

Massaging her upper arm, Betsey walked away.

The oppressive and stagnant heat left Caroline breathless. She undid the first few buttons of her high neckline and opened her shirtwaist as much as she dared.

Mary did the same. "I'll find another fan, and we'll see if we can cool Papa some." She left the room.

Mama slept on. The last two days must've been horrific. If John were taken ill, Caroline would be out of her mind with worry.

Mary soon returned with a palm fan, and the women tried to do what they could to circulate the stagnant air around Papa. The sisters talked little, both lost in their own thoughts and rhythmic motion of the fans. Caroline had never been close to her older sister, Mary, but she was married to John's brother, Ned. They now had a mother-in-law in common and found equal ground in that regard, but it wasn't time to speak of such things. The only blessing that came to them that day was when the sun began its decline and the room cooled slightly.

Mama stirred and straightened. She laid her head against the chairback and stared with glazed eyes. "Praise be to the Lord, I'm glad to see you two." She wiped her hand across her wet forehead and closed her eyes again. Surprisingly, she fell back asleep. She must've been doctoring Papa day and night with no rest. Poor Mama!

Mary shrugged, her thoughts probably in the same vein as Caroline's.

The smells of the medicinal herbs and vinegar brought back her sister Sarah's suffering. How could that have been only nine months ago? The sorrow and angry feelings about why God hadn't saved her sister was what had drawn Caroline to John. She knew he'd comfort her, and he had. Their courtship started soon after.

As darkness fell, Papa awoke, still in a sweat, but shivering. "Cold." His voice sounded as if there was sand in his throat.

Caroline panicked. "Mary, what do we do? Do we cover him when he still perspires?"

It wasn't Mary who answered, but Mama. Papa's voice had brought her to her feet. "We must wipe the moisture completely from his skin and put dry linens on him."

She went to work, with Caroline and Mary helping. It took all three to move him to the side of the bed not soaked from his fever. Blood began to drip from his nose. His head dropped to one side, his mouth sagging open. He trembled, and his hands jerked spastically.

Mary wept, turning her back.

Horrified, Caroline's breath caught in her throat. "What shall we do?"

Mama slumped. "We try and comfort him as best we can."

At that moment, carriage wheels crunched toward the front drive below.

Mary wiped her eyes. "That must be Ned with Papa Koonce." She left the room.

Mama wiped the blood from Papa's face. He seemed oblivious to the ministrations, which Caroline counted as a blessing.

She stepped to her weeping mother and put her arm around her waist, giving her a slight squeeze. "I love you, Mama. I'm sorry I haven't told you in a long while."

Setting the bloody cloth on the bedside table, Mama turned to Caroline. Wrapping her arms around her, she sobbed. "A mother should be a rock for her child. Instead, you . . ." Her cries wracked her thin frame.

Mary led Ned and his stepfather into the room.

"Mama Gibson," Ned said gently, "let me take you downstairs for some rest and refreshment. Caroline, help me?"

ଔଔଔ

"Papa Koonce, we must get word to John." Caroline paced the dining hall.

Her family had gone upstairs after he'd advised them Papa definitely suffered from malaria. He'd administered the last available quinine—hopefully enough to comfort Papa through the night.

"I'll make sure someone starts out in the morning with a letter. Perhaps Kit could go?" He stopped her pacing and held her at arm's length, his face somber, eyes kind. "These will be hard days for you and your family. I'm sorry I can do no more. Your Ma is a smart woman when it comes to doctoring. She's done all she can. Sadly, there's little to stop the decline at this stage of the disease. Don't let her take it to heart." His imposing mustache almost covered his sad smile.

Moved by his compassion, his words sat heavy on her heart. He'd brought to mind how Mama blamed herself for not saving Sarah. How would she take Papa's death? "Thank you for your concern. I'll remember your advice."

Caroline had the kitchen slave, Cozy, pack a basket of food for her father-in-law, and he left with the promise of doing all he could to bring John home.

ରେ ରେ ରେ

One lamp softly lit the room. Caroline, Mary, and Benny had come to say their goodnights to Papa. He'd been in and out of consciousness, his breathing labored. When it was Caroline's turn, she put her hand on his. It felt cold. She laid her other hand on his cheek, anticipating warmth, but it was cold too.

Papa roused and whispered something she couldn't understand. She put her ear near his mouth. "Take care of your mother."

"Don't fret, I will. Now rest and get better." She kissed him goodnight, praying she'd find him well the following morning.

She retired to her old bedchamber filled with new furniture but couldn't sleep. In the quiet stillness of the night, she walked back and forth across the piazza outside her room before finally, close to exhaustion, she had to lie down.

Sleep came in fits. Throughout the night, she arose to kneel and plead with God to spare her father. Each time she asked, her chest tightened with the anguished plea. She needed John's prayers. She was sure he had a personal relationship with God. Toward morning, a sense of comfort came as she prayed. The hard knot of emotion in her chest dissipated, and her mind became clear. Her prayers changed, and she asked for calmness and strength for Mama's sake.

CHAPTER TWELVE

August 2, 1860 - White Oak Plantation

Papa had said nothing more since his plea the previous evening for Caroline to take care of her mother. He lay motionless on the bed, his rattled breathing a dreadful sound. Caroline feared each exhale would release his soul. Her nerves and emotions screamed to collapse, but she forced herself to remain strong for Benny and Mama.

It was late in the afternoon, and Julia and Hester had recently arrived with their husbands, bringing more slaves, including Spicey. The family gathered around Papa's bed.

"Here Papa, drink this." Julia held the liquid quinine in a silver spoon.

How and where Julia got more quinine, Caroline didn't know. Most people thought Julia could raise her arms and part the White Oak River. But perhaps the quinine had more to do with her money than her beguiling personality. Caroline appreciated Julia's forthright, positive attitude and was happy to step back and let her older sister try to control the situation.

Caroline could hardly breathe the hot, stagnant air in the crowded bedchamber. Too early to light lamps, the late day cast shadows onto the bedchamber walls.

Julia sighed and placed the still full spoon on a plate.

Mama tenderly wiped Papa's brow, whispered something in his ear, then sat in a chair. Frowning deeply, she fixed her gaze on his immobile body. Earlier in the day, Caroline had tried to get her to eat and drink something, but her arms appeared too weak to lift food to her mouth.

All but Caroline and Benny had their spouses to hold and comfort them. In the hallway, Betsey peeked into the room, her eyes swollen and red. The house was quiet with the hush of evening coming on, the slaves seemingly as apprehensive as the rest of them as the thread of Papa's life stretched thin.

Suddenly a shriek and moaning came from the direction of the slaves' cabins.

Caroline closed her eyes. Malaria was claiming more lives than just Papa's.

Pulling Benny to her, Caroline kissed the top of his head, grateful to have him by her side. He'd little to say the last two days. She'd tried to persuade him to talk, but each time she explained what was happening to Papa, he'd walked away. Benny spent little time in Papa's room. She knew not where he went, but assumed he was with his manslave, Jess, whom he hadn't known a day without. Other than Jess, there were no other eight-year-old boys at White Oak Plantation. Jess was considered Benny's companion, as Spicey was Caroline's.

Suddenly Papa's throat gurgled. His body twitched, and he let out a long breath.

Caroline held her own breath, watching his chest. It did not rise. Her heart slowed. Her stomach clenched.

"No!" Mama screamed and broke from her chair, throwing herself on the bed, burying her face in Papa's neck. "William, don't leave me!"

Julia went to her mother.

Looking away from the scene, Caroline held Benny tightly. Sobs pulsed in her ears—her own among them.

"I need my Papa!" Benny cried loudly. "I need my Papa!"

ରଃରଃରଃ

Caroline stared out her bedchamber window at a huge, ancient oak—one of many that gave White Oak Plantation its name. If anyone had told her Papa would be laid in the ground next to Sarah nine months ago, how hard that would've been to believe. Now there was a hollowness in her soul she didn't know how to fill. Even though she'd felt God strengthen her to help Benny and Mama, she still grieved deeply. Roused from her thoughts by footsteps, she hadn't the strength nor desire to turn.

Within moments she was embraced from behind, John's lips on her neck, and then at her ear. "When I received the news, I rode through the night and pushed the horse as hard as I dared."

She leaned back and gave him her weight. No longer did she need to carry the sadness on her own. He held her and her breaking heart securely.

"Will you ever be able to forgive my absence?" he asked, his anguish evident.

She wanted to console him, but her throat constricted. She couldn't make her mouth move.

"As I rode, my mind kept replaying your distress over Sarah's death. I prayed for nothing but your comfort." His love was almost painful.

Hot tears coursed down her cheeks. She forced words through her tight throat. "Your prayers were answered. The experience was unlike Sarah's. I felt comfort, as if a blanket were wrapped around me warm and tight."

To her astonishment, his chest heaved in sobs.

CHAPTER THIRTEEN

August 4, 1860

Exhausted, Caroline looked down into the dark, rectangular hole in the family cemetery. She expected the coffin to open at any moment and Papa to climb out, alive and breathing, as healthy as he'd always been. Cold reality told her his body was instead blue and rigid in that oak box with the black crepe draped over it. Soon he'd be beneath a blanket of earth, forever sleeping outside, worms consuming his flesh. She shook her head to remove such thoughts.

Her sisters were again securely held and comforted by their husbands, white kerchiefs with black laced edges held to their faces.

John stood alone at the head of the deep chasm, not at her side, as he petitioned God to comfort those still bound to earth. "I am the resurrection and the life…"

A chill ran through her. Glancing at John, she tried to induce herself to listen and be soothed by his words, not his arms. After all, no other preacher would have given services for an unbaptized man.

Mama and Benny sagged against her like limp dolls. Mama was now a widow in her forty-seventh year of life—still a lovely lady to behold with dark brown hair and no gray. Too young to be left alone. But Caroline couldn't imagine her with another man. None could compare to Papa.

A fly landed on Mama's black crepe head cap. She didn't seem to notice.

Caroline thought to shoo it off, but her arms were heavy in defeat. She watched it climb along the black folds and finally fly away.

John said something about not feeling hopeless and forsaken.

She wanted to listen, but her mind wandered and couldn't embrace the teachings. She couldn't grasp the idea of never seeing Papa again. Never touching him. Never hearing his voice.

Papa had not been a member of any church, which resulted in his graveside interment. From where they stood, Caroline could see the white walls of the White Oak Plantation home through the trees. She knew the cemetery well. Many generations of Gibsons were buried here. She vaguely remembered her grandparents' funerals. She'd been a young child at their passing. Too clear in her memory was Sarah's burial.

Almost fifty people stood listening to John.

When he paused, the woods were so quiet she heard Gibson Branch Creek tinkling along its path and birds in song. The worst of the heat had finally passed, a lovely morning, if not for the gloomy occasion.

Dear, sweet Aunty Ann stood across the pit from Caroline. How must it feel to be the last of your family to live? To watch parents, siblings, spouses, and children pass into eternity, leaving you alone on earth. Another chill passed through Caroline. She chided herself for her drifting thoughts and tried once again to make herself listen to John's message.

He stood tall in his black clergyman's garb, hat in hand, his face shaven as always, his thick dark hair swept back but for the escaping curls near his neck. He was an animated man, which usually encouraged his audience to stay alert. His eyes burned with passion when he preached. Today, he was subdued. He wanted to comfort, not excite. "God is the Father of our spirits. William has gone home to his Father." His gentle voice tried to sooth the grieving. "There he was greeted with open arms. He's in the company of his children, parents, and siblings, and all those who have gone before him."

Caroline pictured the reunion of Papa with Sarah and Willie, a son lost before Caroline was two. Discerning John's gaze upon her, she looked up.

He sent her his love, keeping his eyes on hers, as if he spoke to her alone. "We are physically separated from God during this life, but He wants us to find peace. A fullness of joy will only come after this life when we're in His presence. Let your hearts be lightened. William is in a better place, experiencing this joy." He ran his hand through his hair and looked to the assembled family and a few friends. "This life is for us to gain experience and progress to become better people. It's a time of testing and trials."

She didn't find comfort in those words.

"We must walk by faith and choose between good and evil. Jesus Christ is our redeemer. Through the Savior's grace and mercy, we can become clean from sin. We can be filled with joy, peace, and consolation. All that is unfair about life can be made right through the suffering of Jesus Christ. Amen."

"Amen," was repeated in unison.

The slaves in the back under the shade of an ancient oak added another two or three repines.

Ned offered a prayer.

Mama threw a handful of dirt on the coffin.

All Papa's children and Aunty Ann also performed the ritual. The thuds of dirt clods echoed on the coffin lid while the slaves in the back sung "Lay This Body Down," the beat a march to somber finality.

Fatigued in both mind and body, Caroline thought she had no more tears, but when John came and held her in his arms, she sobbed out her desperate desire to have her father back. The pain of loss weighed down her soul as if light would never penetrate it again.

CHAPTER FOURTEEN

August 4, 1860

That evening, gardenia fragrance hung heavy in the warm night air. Snippets of conversation floated through the open door to where Caroline sat alone on the back-porch swing, but she paid little attention. Her thoughts had taken her back to childhood and Papa sitting tall on the buggy seat as he drove her across the boundaries of his beloved land.

"Your Gibson ancestors lost this land through bad management," he'd said, then proudly pronounced, "Through sound business practices I was able to buy it back." And when he'd smiled, his perfectly groomed mustache had stretched across his cheeks.

They'd passed the headwaters of the White Oak River that day, barely a trickle in the swampy grasslands. "Life springs up at the head." His contented expression had shown his pleasure in his fertile lands, creeks, and forests. His hair had been a thicker brown then that matched eyes that held love for not only his land but for Caroline too.

He'd stopped the buggy at the edge of unplanted acreage and left her to go into the field. Squatting, he'd set both hands flat on the ground. When he came back, he'd said, "The earth's warm enough to start planting."

Caroline treasured the memory of those times alone with Papa. She hadn't realized their importance until his death a few days ago.

Staring into the shadows of the porch, she pictured her sister's face. She imagined Sarah sitting next to her, chattering about how life in Heaven was better since Papa's arrival.

"There you are, dove." John stepped from the open doorway. At the crack of his boots on wood crickets stopped their music. He stood before her in his best black pants and loosely fitted linen shirt. The steady love in his brown eyes warmed her. Having taken his clergyman's coat off, he was hers again, and she marveled for the thousandth time at how she'd managed to marry such a gentle man. She smiled, hoping he hadn't felt abandoned. "Forgive me for leaving. I needed a little solitude."

"Am I interrupting that solitude?" He offered a questioning smile.

"No. Sit here by my side." They continued to swing in quiet for a few moments until the crickets sang their chorus again.

"Can I do anything for you?" John put his arm around her shoulders, pulling her close.

She inhaled the familiar scent of his rosemary and lemon shaving soap and laid her head on his shoulder. "I have many joyful memories of Papa and Sarah, yet so many memories of suffering too. How do I pull the joy to the forefront? I so want it to be the lasting memory."

"Time will help." John gently squeezed her. "You always expect too much from yourself."

A twig cracked, and footsteps approached on the hard earth.

Out of the dark, Betsey appeared, shoulders slumped, nose red, and eyelids so swollen she looked out through slits. She held no burning pine knot to light her way from the slave quarter. "Massa an' Mistress Mattocks." She stopped a couple steps from the porch, bowed her head and curtsied. "May I speaks with thee?"

"Of course, Betsey." John brought his hands to his lap. "What can we help you with?"

John knew her name?

"My sympathies for yo' Pa's passin'." She wept openly, drawing up her apron to wipe her tears.

Caroline hadn't noticed which slaves had attended the funeral and which hadn't. Surely Betsey had been there. She remembered Betsey's affection toward Papa as she tirelessly cared for him when he was ill.

"Thank you." Caroline swallowed grief. "We appreciate your ministrations to Papa. You're a good servant."

John made a funny noise in his throat and shifted slightly.

Betsey's shoulders shook with quiet sobs, and she covered her face with her apron again.

Caroline looked to John for an answer.

He leaned toward Betsey. "Can we help you with something?"

Caroline had never observed a white man speaking so tenderly to a black woman. Confusion stilled her thoughts.

Removing her apron from her face, Betsey forced in gulps of air. Pulling her shoulders back, she stood straighter but kept her eyes lowered. "I comed to ya 'cause it said amongst the slaves that you, Massa Mattocks, has symp'thies towards my kind."

Caroline choked on her next breath. If the slaves knew John's feelings, perhaps her family and others did too? *They will ridicule him and perhaps shun us both.* She looked toward the open door, hoping no one overheard.

John took Caroline's hand. "What are you worried about?" he asked Betsey, the way he would any white person in his congregation.

Caroline's heart thudded in her chest, and she couldn't help checking the door again.

"Massa Gibson dead, and those in the quarter tis worried what happen nex'." Betsey glanced toward the door too and lowered her voice. "They say he left no will. We who is his property now belongs to who?" She sniffled. "Please don' sep'rate our kin." She cried louder.

John sat back, moving the swing gently back and forth. He stopped it by planting his feet flat on the porch. "I don't know how much power I'll have over these decisions, but my older brother, Ned, will most likely be assigned as the administrator of the estate. I'll talk to him."

"Bless ya." Betsey stepped closer, her worried eyes darting to-and-fro. "If he needs to know . . ." She looked into the darkness, then at John. "Massa Daniel Gibson be my pappy."

Currents of shock crashed through Caroline's core. She moved to the edge of the seat. "Betsey, no! How could you say such a thing about my granddaddy?" Her voice sounded strangled—not her own. She wanted to say more. Scream even.

"Carrie, hush now." John squeezed her hand. "All will be well. We'll talk about this in private."

She yanked her hand from his. "Are you going to let her say such scandalous things about my family? Do you love these people more than you love me?" Tears burned her eyes. A pressure in her ribs caught her breath.

"You're overwrought. This needs to be settled in another place." He turned to Betsey; whose features held fear. "I understand your concerns. We'll talk again soon. Please tell the others not to worry."

Betsey curtsied and hurried away, disappearing back into the darkness.

"This has gone too far." Caroline's voice sounded louder than she meant it to.

John pulled her close. "Your family will hear. Let's talk about it at home."

"I thought Betsey loved us." She did lower her voice—to a quiet and bitter insinuation. "How could she say such terrible things about my family? She was always so good to Papa. She cared for him as if . . ." Realization struck. Could it be? Could she have been tender because Papa was her brother? *Family*? "No!" Caroline wrapped her arms around her waist and bent over. "No, John, no! How could it be true?" She sobbed into her lap. "Did you know? Did Papa know? Am I the only one who didn't know this dirty secret?"

"Please don't get so agitated." Bringing both arms around her, he tried to hug her in her slumped position.

Caroline wanted to run from her grandfather's betrayal. From John's foolish acceptance. She tried to stand, but John held tight. She squirmed and cried out, but he wouldn't let go. The tightness in her chest released into a sob. "No!"

"We can work through this." He loosened his grip slightly. "Your pain has been great today. If you must leave, let me take you up to our room."

It had been a horrible day. The worst of her life. Giving up the fight, she calmed, suddenly so weary she didn't know if she could get herself up the stairs.

John stood. "Here, my love, lean on me." He gently pulled her to her feet, wrapping an arm around her waist.

As they started their ascent up the stairs inside, male voices rose from the parlor. The smell of tobacco made her think again of Papa. Why would he have kept such a secret from her? And what other secrets had been buried with him?

CHAPTER FIFTEEN

August 5, 1860

*B*etsey *is my aunt*. The thought floated before Caroline as she roused from slumber, seeing in her mind Betsey's light brown features. "Betsey is family," she whispered into the still dark morning, as if it were a curse.

John moved. She stilled, her back to him, waiting to see if he'd say something. He did not.

A black fog hovered in her mind. If she could fall asleep, perhaps she'd re-awaken to sunshine and clear, carefree thoughts? She wished she were home in Swansboro and away from the sadness of White Oak Plantation.

She tried to slide back into slumber. But as soon as her eyes closed, she pictured her deceased granddaddy—his thick gray eyebrows, his strict demeanor. She replayed the back-porch scene. Why had John believed Betsey so easily? Couldn't she be making it up to insure she wouldn't be sold? After all, was there any way to substantiate her claim? She had no right to *choose* who she could live with.

Caroline needed to make sure Betsey didn't tell anyone else. If she did, perhaps it would entail discussing the matter with Caroline's sisters and their husbands. She was sure that would lead to more embarrassment and shame.

"Are you awake?" John asked in a hushed tone.

"Yes." The answer came callous and impatient.

He gathered her in his arms. "What are you thinking about?"

She loved the tender mornings with John. But on this morning, she wanted to be left alone. "I'm wondering what to do about Betsey's claim. Do you think Mama knows?"

John slid his warm feet under hers. "I guess it'd surprise me if she didn't. Your parents seemed close. I can't imagine your father keeping such information from her."

"You think Papa knew too?" She wasn't surprised by John's statement but wanted it confirmed.

"Yes. Betsey could probably validate that if you wanted her to."

Caroline stiffened. "Why did Papa not sign his will? If he had, this could've been avoided."

"Your father's priority was always to provide for his family. Perhaps there was a transaction that needed to be added or corrections or additions of some other kind. Besides, he was always strong and healthy. Why would he think death was near at fifty-five?" He sighed. "We humans tend to think we're immortal."

"If Ned is the intestate administrator, can we approach *only him* with the information about Betsey? Being your brother, might could he be sensitive to the secrecy of the matter."

"Telling Ned might be all we need do. He'll be the one to decide how the estate will be distributed after the assets and debts are accounted for. But Carrie, you'll always know. Secrets never stay buried. They have a tendency to unearth sometime later in life—and usually when least expected."

"I guess I'll deal with it then." She ground her teeth. "I'm worn out. Whatever strength I have, I need to give to Mama and help her get through the loss of Papa."

"How can I help?" John tenderly asked.

His kindness lessened her distress. "I realize it's the Sabbath and the fieldhands won't be working, but yesterday it was decided George and Hester will move here with Mama. George needs to direct the slaves on finishing the cotton harvest. Can you talk with him and see how best to help? I'll tend to Mama's needs."

"Yes. But Carrie . . . can I say one more thing about Betsey?"

"If you must." Her throat grabbed tight with irritation.

She figured John sensed her dismissal because he kissed the back of her head, then cleared his throat, his arms tense around her. "Betsey's been raised with the knowledge of who her father was, yet never told you before. I think she told because she trusts us and truly does love you all. She doesn't want to be separated from her family."

Caroline groaned. "Do you expect me to treat her as my kin?" Anger spread from the knot in her stomach up to her throat. "You're asking too much." She pulled away from his embrace and slid across the tick, getting out of bed, keeping her back to John. "I've tried to understand your beliefs and have given way on many things regarding our own slaves, but treating Betsey as family I cannot do." She wrapped her arms around herself and stared at a painted landscape hanging on the wall.

"We need to be sensitive to her needs." John's voice sounded sad. The sheets rustled. "My greatest joys have been experienced since I married you, and I can only imagine they'll be greater when we have children. The most important people in my life are you and my family. I think God put us in families for a reason. I also believe these relationships will endure beyond this earthly life. I've asked myself, where does this leave Betsey? Because she was conceived in sin, does that place the sin on her head?"

Caroline hated to distance herself from John but asking her to accept Betsey was too much. She swallowed to try to release the tightness in her throat.

John came up behind her and rubbed her back. "I don't believe Betsey should suffer for the sin. We can treat her with respect and make sure her needs are met."

He'd voiced his beliefs with such conviction Caroline didn't want to argue anymore. If he knew her lack of belief in all things good, then he'd have no respect for her. Even with that, she couldn't fathom how he expected her to treat Betsey. *With respect,* he'd said. What exactly did that entail for the slave owner? She was afraid for herself and her family. She didn't want them branded lovers of the Negro. They'd be ridiculed and shunned from society. John grew up amongst the same people she did. He knew the risks. Did he not love her enough to protect her? "Do you want people to treat us poorly?"

"If you're asking if I care what people think of us, I think you know the answer." He brought her to him.

She held her body rigid.

"In time, you might find you can love Betsey. I think I know your heart, and if you search it, I believe you'll find that you already do have love for her."

The pain in Caroline's chest expanded. When she opened her mouth to protest, a sob escaped before she could stop it. She covered her face and cried over the loss of Papa and that he was tied to the secret about Betsey. She cried in anger, resentment, and fear.

John held her and said no more.

Later that day, Caroline stepped off the wooden catwalk into the old cookhouse. Mama had started using the building as her medical remedies room after an indoor kitchen had been added onto the main house. Caroline liked coming here. It smelled of the earthy fragrances of aromatic vinegars, dried plants and fruits and balsam.

Bundled upside down, flowers and herbs hung drying from the rafters. Baskets filled with tree barks, nuts, and dried fruits lined the walls. The shelves held jars of powdered roots and herbs, salves, ointments, and poultices, each labeled and neatly alphabetized—such as garlic, ginger, and ginseng. Leather-bound books about various medicinal cures occupied one shelf—a few printed in the eighteenth century. On the windowsill, fresh herbs grew out of chipped and discarded pottery. No breeze ruffled the curtains at an open window. It was another hot and humid day.

Dressed in a black crepe mourning dress, Mama stood at a worktable. With a pestle, she ground what looked to be dried herbs in a mortar.

"Mama, what are you doing? Everyone's looking for you."

"I'm sorry if I worried you. I couldn't lie in bed another instant." Tears slipped down her cheeks, and she wiped them with the back of her hand. Dark circles ringed her puffy eyes. "I need to get my mind off the sadness, even if my body cannot seem to shed its grip." She looked briefly at Caroline and then continued her grinding.

Caroline moved to the other side of the worktable. It was a sturdy, thick-legged table where slaves used to knead dough but was now used for the purpose of Mama's remedy preparations. Spread across its top were small branches, bark, and leaves of many varieties. "What are you making?"

"It's for Betsey."

Caroline's back tensed.

"I noticed this morning how she had white swelling of her hands." Mama kept talking in a gentle voice, unaware of Caroline's discomfort. "She hasn't complained a minute, but I know her arthritic swellings are painful."

"You don't need to fret over Betsey at a time like this," Caroline clipped.

Mama sent her a questioning glance, then blinked. Her face drawn and empty from sorrow.

Caroline looked away with a pang of guilt. "Why do you not come into the house? It's deplorably hot out here. If Betsey's hands are aching, Cozy can fan you." Moisture trickled down Caroline's back. She inwardly cursed all her layers of clothing.

Sprinkling something into the mortar, Mama started grinding again, releasing the heavy smell of herbs and fruit. "I prefer my work. After I grind these elderflowers and peach leaves, I need to make it into a poultice with wheat bran and milk. Run along. I won't be long."

When her mother was this determined, it was fruitless to try to persuade her to do what she didn't care to do. Mama had a mission. Someone needed her doctoring.

Caroline walked to the open door, but instead of leaving, she closed the door and turned back. "Has Betsey approached you about her fears of being sold?"

"I'd never sell Betsey." Mama suddenly stopped her work, her eyes concerned. "Why? Is this her fear?"

"She came to us last night as John and I sat on the back porch." Caroline's fingers twitched with the memory. "She's worried we'll lose our holdings because of Papa's death. She doesn't want to be sold."

Mama's eyes softened and she sighed. "Oh, I see. I can't rightly bring myself to think about what the future holds regarding our property. I'll trust in Ned to make all well. But rest assured, Betsey I will never sell."

"But why, Mama?" The words came out shrill.

"Why so much concern?" Mama's brows drew together. "I don't recall your ever having an opinion about plantation matters."

Caroline wiped moisture from her forehead, turned and walked toward the pump sink against the wall. She gripped its edge. With her back to Mama, she sucked in her breath. "Is Betsey Papa's sister?" she asked in a rush, then held her breath.

Hot, motionless air made the room feel small.

Mama's skirts crinkled. "Come sit by me."

Caroline's stomach did a flip-flop.

Mama had moved to a small wooden chair between the worktable and gaping mouth of the blackened fireplace, unused in August. Her black-hooped skirt rose before her. She patted an empty chair.

Caroline sat, and Mama took her hand. The cold ash in the fireplace smelled of decay. Distant voices came from the direction of the barn, but she couldn't decipher their words, nor did she care to.

Mama rubbed Caroline's palm with her thumb. "Betsey is the daughter of your Granddaddy Daniel and one of his slaves."

Tears fell to Caroline's skirts. The tears came from fear and anger, not sadness. "What would happen to us if others found out?"

"Oh, Carrie! These kinds of secrets are kept on every plantation. It's a fact we don't discuss, but it's the way of things."

She clenched Mama's hand tighter. "The way of things?" She finally looked her mother in the eyes. "My husband doesn't mate with slaves." She pulled her hand away, turning in her chair so Mama couldn't see her face. "Did Papa conceive children with slaves?"

Mama squeezed Caroline's shoulder. "Of course not. I didn't intend to make it sound like all slave owners were heartless and unable to control themselves." She stroked Caroline's hair and sighed heavily. "It's more common than you realize, though. Have you ever wondered at the entries in the Simmons family Bible?"

"What do you mean?" Wiping her tears, she braced herself for more horrors.

"There are handwritten entries recording the births of my grandparents, parents, and sister. Even an entry for you, along with my other children." Mama's hand stilled. "But also listed are the births of Manda, Pleasant, and George—all children born to slaves." She cleared her throat. "And my father." She stood and walked away from Caroline, her face pale.

Caroline wrapped her arms around her ribs. "I don't want to know these things." She shook her head vigorously. "I've grown up in a world of ignorance. What must people think of us? How will I go out in society again?"

"You'll move amongst others as you always have. Nothing's changed, other than your knowledge. Keep it to yourself as I have." Wiping her face, Mama stepped to her worktable. "As heartless an act as it is, some slave owners mate with their slaves to produce a larger work force. It's a way to not have to purchase slaves."

Bile rose in Caroline's throat.

"What did John say when he learned of Betsey's parentage?" Mama asked.

Thoughts reeling, Caroline remained in the chair with her arms wrapped around herself, as if that could keep her from plunging into despair. "He actually had the gall to tell me Betsey probably loves us as her family, and I should accept her as such." She flung both arms out. "He thinks I should make sure her needs are met when the whole thing disgusts me!"

Mama looked quickly toward the window. "Caroline, please . . . lower your voice."

"Yes, Mama."

"I understand your feelings, child, but I don't agree with them. You've a husband with a heart that flows as wide as the great White Oak River. He's right—"

"But Mama!"

"Hush, Carrie. Give yourself some time to digest this information. I recall the revulsion I felt when I found out I had Negro siblings. I hated my father for such treachery toward Ma."

Time wouldn't change anything. Mama was wrong.

Picking up the pestle, she banged it into the mortar. Bits of dried leaves jumped from the bowl and drifted to the table. "The knowledge of my father's infidelity still leaves a hole in my heart." She kept banging. "I realized back when the pain was so great I thought I'd die that I was the only one suffering. Papa wasn't affected. Mama was an empty shell by then. Life is made of heartaches, some more painful than others. You have to find the sweetness in life and hang onto it." She stopped banging. "Carrie?"

Caroline tried to look her in the eyes but failed.

"Learn to find room in your heart for compassion and mercy. John could teach us both about forgiveness."

CHAPTER SIXTEEN

August 6, 1860 - Leaving White Oak Plantation

Caroline leaned against the seat in the borrowed coach. Physical and mental exhaustion had taken its toll. Her world had changed the moment she'd discovered the tangled roots of her family tree. The fabric of her beloved family had unraveled, and she didn't know how to mend the separation.

"Are you comfortable, dove?" John asked.

"This heat." She furiously fanned herself. "I can scarce take a breath."

John moved from beside her to the seat opposite to give her some air. He slipped off his coat and rolled up his sleeves. His forehead glistened with moisture. "I fear that probably has more to do with your corset than the heat. I don't understand how women can wear such contraptions."

Caroline tapped him on the arm with her fan. "We must abide by convention. But honestly, I cannot wait to be home and out of it."

John smiled.

Caroline gazed blankly out the window as they traveled past the turn-off to Pollocksville and then farther into the countryside.

"Your father will be missed. I hope you know I'll try to do all I can for your comfort and well-being."

Touched by his humble assurance, she could only hope he meant it. Her father and Julia had warned her otherwise. Now who was going to help them with their needs?

"I can see you're troubled. Will you let me attempt to comfort?"

She stilled her fan, not ready to hear any more of his opinions about Betsey. She hadn't told him of her conversation with Mama because she was embarrassed and tired of the chaotic emotions the discovery had created. How could she tell him that she had yet three more mulatto relatives? He would probably tell her she should care for and love them too.

He leaned forward and grasped her hand. "What is it?"

His voice was so tender, her resolve slipped a little. "I don't want to talk about it."

The window curtain had been pulled back to allow a breeze, but the humidity held the air stagnant.

John sat back with a sigh. "I've hurt you in some way, have I not? Please tell me what I did so I can make amends."

"It's a difference in opinion is all. I don't want to discuss it further." She fanned, the carriage interior sweltered, and she envied Moses and Spicey on the seat outside.

"I'd like to know what opinions you refer to. Do you think me such a cad as not to be able to allow you yours?"

The coach wheel hit a rut. They shifted against the wall and then righted themselves.

Guilt got the best of her. "If you must know, I've exhausted myself fretting over Betsey. You need not concern yourself. It's a family matter between Mama and me."

"I see." Hurt filled his voice. "I realize I've no legal claim or persuasion on Betsey or any of your mama's property, but I do care about anything that may cause you distress. Have I made that distress worse in some way?"

"I feel we're always at opposite ends when it comes to slavery. And now that it concerns my family, I'm absolutely alone in the matter." She lifted her chin in anger. She didn't want to feel anger, or *any* emotion, at the moment. Why must John go on?

"I see your point. I'll try and be more understanding." He reached for her hand again.

She pulled away. She wasn't going to let him comfort her. Her family had betrayed her with the deceit they'd thrown in her face. He wouldn't understand.

"Dare I say have mercy and understanding?"

He was so self-righteous. She wanted to hurt him for it. "You are not my preacher!" Her anger exploded, erupting in words she quickly pushed past her constricted throat. "Mercy and understanding? You don't see my side of things. I feel like all my life I've had a version of what I thought was truth, and now that version has been taken away like a chapter ripped out of a book. Nothing makes sense to me anymore, and your words give me *no* comfort."

His eyes widened. "Your family tree has always been there, whether you observed all the branches or not. The past is always present. It just hides from us sometimes."

What an exasperating man. "You're talking in riddles." She was tempted to knock on the carriage ceiling and have Moses stop the coach. She'd do better to walk home than be stuck in this conversation with John.

"I'll try and be plainer in my speech." He wiped perspiration from his brow. "I think there are things to be learned from your ancestors. Although they are no longer with you, their existence has now intersected with yours. You're a part of them. Their choices are affecting your life."

"Well, that's the first piece of truth you've uttered. What, pray tell, am I to do about that?" Tears stung her eyes, and she quickly looked out the window, blinking them away. She hated herself for fighting with him, but she needed to stand her ground.

"Mercy and understanding are where you'll find peace."

"That's exactly what Mama said. But what good will that do? It will not change anything. My grandfathers aren't left with the embarrassment and troubles—I am!" Those last two words hung in the air loud and clear.

"You can't change the past, as the saying goes. You can change the future, though. It's up to you as to what you'll do with the result of their decisions. Choice plays into destiny. If God doesn't allow us to have a choice, He ceases to be God."

"What does that mean?" She folded her arms across her chest and glared at him.

He calmly leaned toward her again. "It's choice that makes us human. We have to work out our own salvation through Christ. I suggested you have mercy for your ancestors, not for their well-being, but for *yours*."

She sighed and let her arms fall to her side. Religion was strong in John, always directing his thoughts. Fighting with him wasn't going to change him. "Mama did say she hated her father and had to put that anger aside to find peace for herself."

"Why did your mother hate her father?" His brow lowered.

She stiffened at the slip. She wanted to lie, but she couldn't. "When I approached Mama yesterday about Betsey, she told me the same was true for her own family. Even worse, my Granddaddy Simmons fathered three children by slaves." She glanced quickly to John to see his reaction.

John's expression didn't change.

"He cared so little about others that he recorded his sins in the family Bible by naming those children. What a selfish man."

"I don't condone his behavior, but by recording the names of his children in the Bible, he was in a sense accepting them and perhaps giving them a better life. Did he free them?"

"I didn't ask. Why should you care about such things?"

"You're hurt and angry. I thought you knew why I cared. Have you forgotten?"

"I can't rightly accept your love toward Negroes."

"It's my love toward mankind."

"I suppose you think me a wretch?" She cared too deeply about John's opinion of her.

He moved back beside her, taking her in his arms.

She stiffened but allowed the embrace.

"I love you with all my heart and consider myself bound to you eternally." He kissed her forehead. "You're too hard on yourself. I've watched beauty unfold as you showed compassion to your mother in her time of need. I've seen your growth from accepting your father's death with an understanding you didn't have when Sarah died. You're the peacemaker in your family, and your strength and determination to help them is something few people have."

She nudged her elbow in his side. "I didn't intend to draw out compliments."

"I know, but I wish you could see yourself from my eyes. It's our values that make us who we are. As you mentioned earlier, people can have a version of what they think is the truth. You've been taught all your life to deride the Negro. I hope someday you can see them differently. With your good heart, I believe it will be so."

They didn't mention Granddaddy Simmons or her newly acquired family members again, but they were all that filled Caroline's thoughts on the suffocating trip home.

Why had her grandfathers betrayed their family's dignity? Family dignity had always given her strength. Were they so selfish as to not see past their pleasures? And as for John's sentiments, she had no idea how to forgive someone who was dead, nor did she want to.

CHAPTER SEVENTEEN

September 7, 1860 - Harget Town House, Swansboro

Of the eight women sitting around the colorful quilt, four wore black bombazine mourning dresses. Caroline wasn't comfortable socializing so soon after Papa's death, but Julia was adamant all her sisters attend the quilting bee. Their friend Nancy was soon to marry, and the album quilt needed to be finished. The patchwork was a beautiful array of appliqued floral blocks incorporating reds, greens, and blues, the colors clean and fresh against the women's black clothing.

They were in Julia's morning room because it had the most windows and gave good light for their work. The scorching temperatures of August had raged on into September making Caroline damp and pinched in her corset and heavy black dress. But silently, she stitched while Julia carried the conversation.

"Good Lord! Daddy dead only a month, and his property already being looked over by those vulture assessors in Jacksonville." Julia spoke in a loud whisper, as if she were telling secrets she should not. "Mama's worried they'll take the house right out from under her. She's afraid to move into Swansboro for the winter in fear they think the plantation house abandoned and make it their own." Julia huffed. "What is this world coming to? I hear Mister Barbour might be buying the land. To think how Daddy loved that land and spent his life acquiring it after Granddaddy lost it through bad business. It's Gibson land and will always be Gibson land, no matter who gets their filthy hands on it."

Caroline shifted in her chair. Julia talked nonsense to save face. Papa died with mortgages and without signing his will. The recent state of events was his fault, but Julia wasn't fixing to lay blame at his feet when she could make others look hungry with greed.

Mary sat wrapped in silence, her clenched jaw the only indication of her annoyance. Mary's husband, Ned, had been assigned administrator of Papa's estate, and she most likely knew more details than Julia about the whole business.

Hester also sat quietly with her head bowed. She'd come into town for the quilting bee, but still lived at White Oak Plantation with her husband, George, Mama, and Benny. Caroline expected Hester to make some comment, but none was forthcoming, perhaps because she still grieved.

Caroline tried to pay close attention to her tiny stitches, ten to an inch.

Two male slaves stood on either end of the quilt, fanning the women but hardly creating enough cool air to shoo a fly. Two more female house slaves, dressed in dark blue uniforms with crisp white aprons, stood erect against the wall closest to the main hall. Their eyes stayed trained on the floor, and they gave no indication they heard the conversation. But if Julia gave a command, they'd be quick to respond.

The other four women at the quilt were cousins, related in one way or another. In fact, most of Swansboro's residents could trace many of the same bloodlines. It was common conversation at social gatherings to talk of who was on your mama's or daddy's side. There was hardly a body in Swansboro who wasn't born there or somewhere nearby within Onslow County's borders.

Caroline was pleased when Julia finally changed the subject from Papa, even if it was to politics.

"Saints preserve us!" Julia went up an octave. "Have you heard about that ugly Lincoln man running for president? He has taken the stage for the Negro."

Caroline cringed. Would Julia speak differently if she knew Betsey was her aunt? In all probability, if Julia learned the truth, she'd likely deny it to her dying day.

Julia sighed. "We need not concern ourselves with him. He'll never win anyway. Daniel says Breckenridge is our man. Caroline, who is your preacher voting for?"

Surprised to be called upon, she stammered, "He . . . he hasn't made a decision as yet. I know he feels Douglas is not concerned with our agricultural and business needs."

"Phewy on Douglas. He's a Northerner. Why would he care about us?" Julia turned to Hester. "Are you wool collecting, Hester? What does your man say?"

"I'm surprised at you, Julia." Hester's sweet voice was all sugar. "George doesn't talk politics around Mama and me. He feels women shouldn't fret over such things."

"I suppose he doesn't let you read the newspaper either." Before Hester could respond, Julia went on. "George needs to learn women make this world go 'round, whether we can vote or not. We're not fragile flowers who wilt at the first sign of power. But it's better our men don't know just how cunning and smart we are." Her laugh tinkled like silver on china. "If they knew we had brains, they might not spoil and pamper us."

The cousins laughed.

Caroline bit her lip. She needed to champion her husband. "John talks to me about all subjects. I feel his equal. He believes all humans should have the same rights, including the right to education and to vote."

"*All* humans have the same rights? I hope he means all *white* humans." Julia scrutinized Caroline.

Caroline hadn't considered darkies in her statement, and she certainly didn't want Julia thinking she had, but she couldn't lie either. "He believes we should all be taught Christian ways and be caregivers of one another." Shame for not fully representing John's beliefs crept through her.

"Sounds like you've gone religious on us, Carrie. But I do reckon you're right. It's the Christian way to be a caregiver. I know I care for many under this roof. Humph!" Julia stood. "Ladies, shall we have tea?"

The four slaves quietly withdrew, and all the guests followed Julia to the dining room.

A hand-embroidered white linen tablecloth lay beneath china edged with lovely lavender flowers. Opulently crafted silver dining utensils were positioned in the appropriate places. Cousin Cassy complimented Julia on her exquisite taste.

As the women were being seated, two muscular male slaves carried in a silver tea set on a tray so large it would have plumb covered Caroline's dining table, but it fit nicely in the center on Julia's. Female slaves brought miniature cakes, biscuits with layers of currants inside, raspberry and scuppernong jams, and platters of red, juicy watermelon cut lengthwise into sections in true southern fashion.

"Bless Papa," Julia announced, "for shipping in barrels of sugar that will last us years. I hear the Abolitionists are boycotting sugar from the West Indies because slaves grew and harvested it. Those Abolitionists deserve to suffer. I would simply die without my sweets."

Julia's house slave, Esther, placed a platter of poached mackerel on the table near Caroline. The aroma almost visible, it gave her a wave of nausea. She shook her head to try and clear the sensation.

"You're as green as a frog, Carrie. What ails you?" Julia inquired.

"Just a passing dizzy spell. Go on with your conversation. I'll be fine in a moment."

Julia turned toward her guests. "I was just saying how Miss Burton is so tacky she doesn't know the difference between a shrimp fork and a pickle fork."

The cousins laughed.

"What lovely butter molds," Cousin Charlotte commented.

"Yes, are they not? The butter brings to mind ole' Mrs. Newton. There is plenty of cream and butter on her table." Julia laughed. "Did y'all notice how she's always looking a little hungry? Her maid needs a commendation for getting all that surplus flesh into her corset."

Perspiration covered Caroline's upper lip, and the boning in her corset dug into her ribs.

"Warm milk for yu'z tea, Missuz Mattocks?" One of Julia's kitchen slaves stood at Caroline's left, holding a small pitcher of cream. A streak of blood floated at the edge of the cream, not uncommon for fresh milk straight from the cow.

Caroline's stomach suddenly lurched. She promptly stood and hurried toward the back door.

"What is it, sister?" Mary called.

If Caroline opened her mouth to answer, whatever was in her stomach would leave. She hurried out the back door and down the steps. The fresh air on her face revive her a bit. Staggering to the side of the house, she leaned against it, gulping air. Wanting the world to stop spinning, she closed her eyes.

The door opened behind her, and someone descended the steps.

Esther stood a step behind and to Caroline's side. "Mistress Harget sent me. I wonder iffen I be of he'p?"

"No Esther, I needed some air for a moment. I think I'll walk home. Please tell my sister to excuse my sudden departure."

"Ya come up caught?"

"Pardon?"

"Ya be wid chile?"

She let out a gasp. "I don't know. Is this what it's like?"

"Smells and certain foods make ya feel like losin' yo' inners?"

"Yes."

"Esther say ya come up caught."

The nearby cellar door opened, and a large manslave came out with an armload of sweet potatoes. A mildew smell seeped up from the cellar floor. Caroline had no choice but to double over and vomit at the edge of her hooped skirts.

Esther ran off, and soon Mary was at Caroline's side, rubbing her back as she vomited until nothing remained.

"Let me take you home, Carrie. I think you have some news for John."

CHAPTER EIGHTEEN

December 24, 1860 - Kit Mattocks's Plantation Home

K it, John, and Caroline were the only whites who sat among their slaves in the great hall of Kit's new home. They weren't far from the Koonce Plantation, with Kit's inherited ancestral Mattocks lands bordering his stepfather's lands.

"Spicey, do ya promise to do yo' best each day to love Junior and honor 'im?" The black preacher's broad smile showed a mouthful of large white teeth.

Positioned next to Junior, joined by their wrists with a string of cowrie shells, Spicey affirmed her commitment to become his wife. The ceremony was a mixture of Christian and African beliefs.

Why Kit allowed a black preacher to marry the couple, Caroline couldn't fathom. In fact, the whole situation went against her principles. Why would a slave ever love and marry? Having no control over their bonds, she thought them foolish to think they could develop deep ties. Spicey had never expressed love for Junior.

Spicey and Junior could only have met on the few trips John and Caroline made to the Koonce home, where Junior had lived, or at the occasional gatherings of the Mattocks, Koonce, and Gibson families. There wouldn't have been time to develop a relationship strong enough to consider marriage unless one of them had been sneaking out. Spicey's secrets wounded Caroline's trust.

Only a year ago, a young, single Caroline had danced with John at the Harget Plantation home. Now here she sat, married, pregnant, and in a house decorated more for Christmas than for a wedding.

Fresh evergreen garland draped across the door and window frames and laced through the curved arms of two candelabras. A large wreath made of sugared fruits and nuts rested upon the mantle. Oranges, pierced in various designs with whole cloves, hung by ribbons from the ceiling.

Even with a wedding and the decorations, this Christmas didn't offer the joy and excitement of last year's holiday. The gloomy weather meant candles already burned at ten in the morning. A watery, coastal sun shined at a slant through the window, creating a low-filtered light, which contributed to a sense of foreboding. A storm was coming. The black cloud of trouble had moved from the North to the South. Within the blowing winter wind were whispers of war.

Abraham Lincoln had won the presidential election with only forty percent of the popular vote. Ten southern states, North Carolina included, had voted for someone other than him. The South took offense to the outcome. Although Caroline feared the election could hurt her household, she resolved not to let it happen.

She examined the couple in front of her, then the other brown faces watching the ceremony with great interest. The cold sting of anxiety left her distracted.

Kit's household was unusual in that his six slaves considered themselves a complete family. Caroline felt anxious about Spicey marrying into such a situation and hoped the girl didn't expect to live with them some day.

Kit had set up his new home as a step toward adulthood. Soon to be twenty-one, unmarried, and with a growing medical practice, he was anxious to be independent of his mother and stepfather. He'd tended toward a solitary lifestyle even when he'd lived in the Koonce home.

Spicey could visit Junior on holidays. Caroline would keep her as a personal maid, figuring the more she kept them apart, the less likely Spicey would present with child. She'd told Spicey if Junior came into Swansboro, she'd refuse to let him stay under her roof. Kit and John were unhappy with her decision, but they didn't try and coerce her otherwise. Spicey was her property.

A young black child sitting across the aisle from Caroline rolled onto her belly and slid to the floor. She toddled toward Caroline, but the old slave, Alsey, quickly came after her, bowed her head to Caroline in forgiveness, then brought the child back to sit on her lap and whispered something to the girl. With fearful eyes, the child met Caroline's stare.

Junior, a large man with broad shoulders, stood over a foot taller than Spicey. Eliza had explained to Caroline that Junior's true name was John, but she wasn't going to have a slave by the same name as her son, so they called him Junior. The same was true for Junior's father, who went by Jack.

When the preacher completed the ceremony, the couple performed the traditional jump over the broom to represent their superstitious beliefs that past problems would now be swept away.

John gently nudged Caroline. "Let's go give our congratulations to the couple."

The slaves stood back as Caroline and John approached. Seeing Spicey's face lit with joy, sent a stab of foreboding through Caroline. "Congratulations. May your union bring you much happiness," she said gracefully, without truly meaning it.

Spicey beamed and looked as if she'd cry.

Caroline quickly stepped away, not wanting the girl to do something foolish like hug her.

John came forward and shook Junior's hand, pronouncing upon him his good wishes. Kit followed and then the wedded couple joined the black folk in the room. Junior was instantly swallowed in out-stretched arms and congratulatory hand thumps on his back. Short, petite Spicey, not looking old enough to be a wife, smiled shyly as her new mother-in-law, Alsey, scooped her into the group.

"Let's retire to the parlor," Kit suggested.

"And leave these fieldhands alone in your home?" Caroline was aghast.

"I won't send them out to the barn in this weather." Kit drew his brows together.

John patted Caroline's back. The patronizing gesture irritated her.

"I trust them in my home," Kit added.

If Caroline said anymore, she'd be rudely questioning a master in his own household.

She, John, and Kit made their escape to the parlor and closed the door. Kit brought out a crystal decanter of brandy and poured two drinks.

As he was fixing to pour the third, Caroline raised her hand. "None for me." Being in her fifth month of pregnancy, she still felt poorly, and spirits didn't sit well.

"May I bring you some other kind of refreshment?"

"No, thank you, I'm agreeable."

Kit handed John his drink. "So, big brother, what're your thoughts about the events of our once blessed nation? Do you think North Carolina will secede from the Union as South Carolina has?"

John sipped his drink. "I hope not. I don't like the aggression displayed by the North, yet I can't imagine going to war with my fellow Americans. Let's pray it won't come to that."

Kit reclined into his chair and crossed his legs. "There will be enormous pressure on us to change our society. Just how much will we surrender, I wonder?"

"Every American should be free to worship, travel, own property and enterprise, and bear arms," John answered like a politician. "If the North is going to infringe on those freedoms, then let's hope there are enough of us to resist without war. I'm not sure our government can abolish slavery through the courts, but if they can, I think you know I'd be all for it."

"There's no law against slavery." Caroline sat straighter in her chair. "I've the right to own property, as you say. If someone tries to take my property away, are they not infringing on *my* rights?"

Kit's eyes grew wide, and he looked to his brother with a silly half-grin, which he tried to cover by sipping from his glass of brandy.

John didn't join his brother's mirth. His quizzical gaze met Caroline's. "You aren't breaking any *law* by having people as your property. It's more of a moral issue—hence the improbability that it will be solved by our elected officials, especially considering the largest planters hold the most political power." He tilted his head and squinted his eyes in thought. "Consider this—to more than three-quarters of the white people in our state, slavery is not central to their economic concerns. Dare I say there are even many who regard slavery as an impediment to their progress?"

"The economics of slavery have nothing to do with the distress I feel about Spicey's marriage," Caroline said. "She's been by my side my whole life. It's unrealistic to think our arrangement will end through force or the change of a law."

Kit wisely kept silent.

"Friendship isn't held together by ownership," John said. "Spicey's feelings for you wouldn't change if she were no longer by your side as your servant. In fact, you might be surprised at how much stronger the relationship could be if those ownership ties were broken."

Caroline shifted in her chair. A slave shouldn't be a friend to an owner. Yet, Spicey was exactly that to Caroline. In some ways, she felt as close to Spicey as a sister. They shared the same childhood memories as sisters sometimes do. But it certainly wouldn't be right to call her family. After all, even knowing Betsey to be her aunt didn't make Caroline want to acknowledge her as such. These thoughts and feelings were disconcerting. She doubted John truly understood. "I'm not certain how to answer the what-if's right now." Turning to Kit, she said, "I do need a drink. Would you happen to have something without alcohol?"

Kit quickly stood. "Would you care for wedding punch?"

"That would be lovely, thank you."

When he opened the door, music and laughter floated in from the adjoining room. Stepping out, he closed the door behind him.

"Are you feeling poorly?" John leaned toward Caroline. "I hope I didn't overstimulate your sensitivities."

Caroline hated when John showed concern for her when she was angry at him. "This conversation and the wedding are to blame for my anxiety," she said with an edge to her voice. "I wish I wouldn't have let you talk me into Spicey marrying. And unlike you, I fear emancipation would be irresponsible and wreak havoc on our society."

"You may be right. I'm not sure what the South is ready for. I'm afraid we'll be forced into situations we won't like or understand with Lincoln as our president." John leaned forward and placed his hand on top of hers. "Let's stop this talk. You're with child and shouldn't have such great worries. Let us enjoy our first Christmas as man and wife and surprise Kit with some genuine cheer when he returns."

How this man always made her feel guilty, she wasn't sure. She turned over her hand to accept his, but her anxieties pulled at her. She couldn't lose Spicey. She'd soon need help with the baby.

CHAPTER NINETEEN

April 13, 1861 - Swansboro

Caroline missed her father's smile, his easy-going nature, his gentle touch on her shoulder as he passed by, his advice and concern for her well-being. Although she'd discarded her mourning clothes in February, the dull ache in her heart remained.

In her last month of pregnancy, she was uncomfortably heavy as she stood before her mirror, frowning at her girth. She sat in a chair and presented her foot to Spicey, who placed a slipper on it.

Spicey had dressed Caroline in a simple lavender day gown. Appropriate for the spring weather, it was a hand-me-down belonging to last season and one of only three dresses that fit her. Papa was right after all—she missed her stylish gowns and finery. At this moment, she also missed her slim figure. She had more questions than answers about what to expect in the weeks to come. Above all, she was sad she wouldn't be sharing her child's life with Papa.

And what would Papa say about the turn in national events? The spread of hatred between North and South flowed like a rising tide of poison. Since each state initially joined the Union voluntarily, they could leave the Union if their rights were no longer protected. Consequently, more states seceded in South Carolina's wake. They created a new government, declaring themselves the Confederate States of America. Conventions took place all over the south—North Carolina included—as states tried to decide what their next move would be.

That morning, Caroline had read in yesterday's New Bern newspaper that throughout the South, only about fourteen percent of its population were slaves, but North Carolina's percentage was over thirty, with Onslow County having almost fifty. The adjoining Jones County had more slaves than whites. Even so, North Carolina's delegates urged a wait-and-see policy. Zeb Vance, a congressman, proposed the same caution. Some eyes were focused on Virginia's conventions. Many felt whichever way Virginia went, North Carolina would follow.

In March, Lincoln had promised not to interfere with the slave states. His emphasis, he insisted, was to preserve the Union. Caroline didn't believe him. He was a Republican, and Republicans were bent on abolishing slavery. It was clear he didn't want slavery to spread to other states. He thought the slave states were bluffing when they first threatened secession. She sighed.

Spicey glanced up from trying to squeeze Caroline's swollen foot into her slipper. "Did I pinch ya some?"

"No, Spicey. I'm thinking about our state of affairs and missing my Papa's advice."

Petite Spicey stood and braced herself, leaning back to pull Caroline up. Then she helped her into her duster, tying it on in back.

John burst into the bedchamber.

Caroline gasped, and Spicey let out a yelp, jumping away.

"What is it, John?" Caroline asked.

"Forgive my intrusion." He nodded toward Spicey. "You may leave us."

She curtsied and hurried from the bedchamber, closing the door behind her.

John's dark eyes frightened Caroline. He gently took her arm, helping her back onto the chair.

"What is it?" she repeated. Her heart fluttered despite not knowing what brought on his agitation.

His gaze locked with Caroline's, clearly trying to decide how to proceed. "A ferry from New Bern brought people with news of events in South Carolina." His face grew ashen.

Caroline held her breath and waited.

"There's a fort on a small island that guards Charleston Harbor. The South Carolina militia at the fort fired on Union troops." John knelt before her. "Perhaps they're over-reacting, but it's almost as if the people downtown are celebrating the event. It's possible this will mean war." John's eyes deepened in concern. "Lincoln promised that while he'd never be the first to attack, any use of arms against the United States would be regarded as rebellion." He creased his brow. "That is one promise I hope he won't keep."

Hair lifted on the nape of Caroline's neck. "Perhaps he won't want to anger the South by appearing the aggressor?"

A knock sounded at the door.

"You may enter," Caroline called out.

Keziah opened the door but remained in the hall. "Mistress Harget in the parlor and axts for ya, Mistress Mattocks."

Caroline glanced at John.

"You best go to her. I suspect your sister has heard the news."

Caroline descended the stairs at a slow pace, holding her dress up a few inches with one hand, grasping the rail with the other, bringing her belly before her. She was surprised when John followed. She hoped he wasn't planning on visiting with Julia. The two were dissimilar in personality and could be antagonistic when they conversed. Caroline usually went out of her way to keep them apart.

Wearing a luxurious ivory satin-hooped dress, Julia dominated the parlor with her silhouette of beauty and poise, extravagant in what was supposed to be a day gown. Her jewelry consisted of a small chain of seed pearl earbobs. Caroline's face warmed in jealousy.

Julia quickly walked to Caroline in her confident way and took her bare hands in her gloved ones. "Did you hear the news of events in South Carolina?" She spoke with a broad smile on her face, her eyes wide with glee.

"Yes, John was just telling me." A shiver went up Caroline's spine. *Was this news good or bad?*

Dropping her smile, Julia briefly eyed John, then returned her attention to her sister. She pulled her away from him toward the settee where they sat facing one another.

John moved farther into the room and sat in a chair across from them.

Julia watched him out of the corner of her eye. "I was at our store when a group rushed to the flagpole out front." She grinned with an overly pleased smile. "They pulled the flag down, threw it to a crowd in the street who tore it to shreds. Then they replaced it with a flag with a red star on a white background." She giggled behind her silk-gloved hand. "I asked Danny what that flag was, and he said, 'That be a secesh flag, darlin.' Well, I'll be, I felt so proud when he told me that." Julia's exuberance was contagious.

"What do you think it all means?" Caroline couldn't help but feel a little titillated. "North Carolina hasn't seceded. Do you think we'll go to war?"

Julia pouted. "I cannot imagine we'd stand by while our sister-state fights the Yankees." Her eyes twinkled. "We'll join Jeff Davis's Confederacy, you'll see." Julia had a satisfied look on her face as if she had just been given a diamond brooch.

Uncertainty crept into Caroline's chest.

"A Southern republic would not only be freer but economically superior to the North." Julia brought up her chin, her nose so high she could drown in a rainstorm.

John's jaw flexed.

Caroline dropped any pretense of delight. "The North has a much larger population. Doesn't that alarm you?"

Julia shook her head as if Caroline were a foolish child. "Every southern village has a militia in case Federal soldiers are harebrained enough to come here. If we do nothing more than secede, we need not invade the North to stay independent. Besides, we have the agriculture they need."

"We cannot eat cotton or tobacco," John finally spoke.

Julia leaned toward him with fire in her eyes. "And what's that supposed to imply?"

He sat back and crossed one leg over the other, calm in the wake of her high drama. "Most of our planters are growing cotton and tobacco, which they sell to the North. We don't have the means to manufacture cotton into a usable commodity nor sell the amount of tobacco needed to keep our planters solvent."

"Well, then we'll have to start doing that," Julia clipped. "Next year, we can plant our fields with more food stuffs."

"Perhaps," John replied. "Do you happen to know how much of what your husband sells in his store is shipped in from the North?"

Julia's mouth pinched tight.

John said, "Almost all of the nation's wheat comes from the North. And not only food goods, but things like clothes, shoes, boots, farming implements, and vehicles."

Caroline wanted to steer the two away from disagreeing, but she couldn't think of what to say. She blamed it on the pregnancy. As if on cue, the baby stretched within her and pushed a body part into her already cramped rib cage. She gently massaged the area.

"We can develop more commerce with England and France. England needs our cotton," Julia said with her head still posed a little too high.

"Perhaps," John replied again.

The vague answer seemed to frustrate Julia's optimistic stage performance. She persevered and declared a little too loudly, "Why must you pick on all of Dixie's faults? Do you want us to be taken over by the damn Yankees?"

Caroline jumped at the curse. Mama would've slapped Julia's face for speaking so crudely. Caroline was sorely tempted to do just that.

"I most certainly do not," John said calmly, but clenched his hand at his side. "I also don't want to go to war with my own country. The North has over two hundred arms manufacturers. We have less than a dozen, and only one cannon foundry. The Union has a Navy that could control the sea as well as many of our rivers and inlets. How would those ships from England get our cotton or France bring us food stores and commodities if our ports are blockaded?"

Julia acted as if John's comments weren't reputable enough to consider and turned her face away.

"Our Southern railroads run east-west, respectively, but the Union could control those that run north-south." John spoke with more emphasis. "They could close the doors to us for our means of travel and business."

Julia narrowed her eyes. *Her* perfect and strong Southern homeland knew no weaknesses. "Well John, if you aren't with the South, then you must be against it."

"Julia!" Caroline straightened. "Why say such a horrid—"

"I'm only trying to be practical and supply information you perhaps weren't aware of," John said. "I certainly have no desire to fight with you . . . or my fellow Southerners." Color rose on his neck, and he spoke louder than usual. "In the end, we may not have a choice but to join the Confederacy." John brought his volume down to a normal level but kept his fist clenched. "I love my home and certainly would fight for mine and my family's freedoms. But I also believe in being prepared and practical. If North Carolina becomes a battleground, I wouldn't hesitate to take Caroline and our child west to avoid harm."

Caroline's stomach flopped. "You'd take me from my home and family?"

John looked to her with a softness in his demeanor that he didn't hold for Julia. "Only for a time, dove. My cousin Sarah Barry is married to a Texas Ranger, and I'm sure you could stay with them in relative safety until it was free of danger here."

"God forbid such a thing would ever have to happen," Caroline said, shaken by the turn in conversation.

"Come see me later and we'll talk some more, Carrie." Julia rose and left the parlor without a nod or goodbye to John.

Collapsing onto the settee, Caroline let out a slow, long breath. "I apologize for my sister's high spirits. Let's pray these national conflicts can be solved without war." She shook her head. "Why have you not spoken to me of going to Texas?" She crossed her arms and stared hard at John.

"I didn't want to worry you unnecessarily. It's an idea I've had in the back of my mind."

"I set store by your concern, but there will never be a reason to leave you, my home, or my family."

CHAPTER TWENTY

April 27, 1861

A s each labor pain peaked, Caroline engrossed herself in the sound and comfort of Mama's voice.

"All is as it should be. You're doing so well, Carrie." Mama gently massaged Caroline's lower back. "I'll bring you through this. You aren't alone, love." Her compassionate voice was an anchor in a tempest-tossed sea. Caroline wanted to sink into the oblivion of those deep waters, and escape from what was happening to her body, but Mama's peaceful words went on slow, clear, strong.

When another pain swept Caroline away, she closed her eyes, telling herself over and over that labor in childbed only lasted for a short time compared to the rest of her life with her child and John. After a couple minutes, the pain ebbed.

Mary attended Mama to learn the craft of midwifery, although it seemed she could no longer bear any more children of her own. Mary was most like Mama in her interest of the human body. "There are men doctors who will tell you nature does the whole business for you." She shook her head. "It's not completely true, but if you'd merely release your fears and relax your muscles as Mama is encouraging you to do, you'll sometimes find the birth process easier."

Spicey quietly fanned Caroline with one hand and held Caroline's hand with the other, her brows furrowed in concern.

Hours passed. A great pressure filled Caroline's lower abdomen. She was so tired she doubted she'd have the strength to continue, but her body seemed to be progressing on its own to an end she both feared and wondered at.

Mama excused Spicey, but Caroline hardly noticed her absence as she was being split in two. She lost track of time. Had it been minutes or hours? She wanted to stop the process, but every muscle and nerve of her body screamed that there was nothing left to do but push.

The pain rose and threatened to take her into darkness, but Mama wouldn't allow that to happen. Her soothing voice guided her through waves of agony. The pain ripped and tore until Caroline finally delivered her baby into Mama's waiting arms.

"My darling girl, it's all over." Mama giggled. Had Caroline lost her senses or had her mother? She'd never heard Mama giggle. Ever. She didn't even know her mother could giggle. "It's a girl. And a healthy one at that."

Caroline heard a short bleat like a newly born lamb, not a long and loud wail. Shouldn't a healthy baby be crying harder? She pushed herself up on her elbows.

Mama tied off the cord and washed the tiny body. The baby's skin pink and wrinkled, she squirmed as Mama cleaned, but she didn't cry out.

A peace entered Caroline's heart like she'd never felt before.

Mama handed the baby to a smiling Mary, who cooed to her.

"It's best to put her to the breast immediately." Mama tenderly unbuttoned Caroline's chemise to expose her breast and then turned to Mary, taking the naked child from her arms and laying her on Caroline's bare torso.

The sensation of skin against skin was magical. She touched the baby's cheek, softer than anything she'd ever felt before, and her heart entwined with her child's.

The baby stared as if she were taking in the sight of her mother with great interest.

A miracle! Tears blurred Caroline's vision. It was the single most spiritual moment of her life.

When she'd imagined childbirth, she thought she'd spend hours screaming in pain and then collapse into unconsciousness once the baby was delivered. Instead, through her mother's skill and gentle coaxing, Caroline delivered in an atmosphere of love. Yes, the pain was by far the worst she'd ever endured, but she was already losing the awful memory in light of her lovely newborn, perfect daughter. She couldn't take her eyes off the infant. Never had she witnessed anything as precious as this small child in her arms.

The baby turned her face toward Caroline's breast, her tiny mouth open.

Mama coaxed Caroline's nipple into the baby's mouth and surprisingly, she sucked as if she'd done it a hundred times before.

Caroline drew in her breath at the wonder of it.

"It's the miracle of our young, and I'll never tire in seeing it. They know what to do to keep themselves alive." Mama patted Caroline on the shoulder. "Those who have their slaves as wet nurses are missing a tender experience." She stepped away to clean up.

Caroline marveled at the gentle pull on her breast. As the baby nursed, her tiny chest rose and fell. She smelled fresh and new, like nothing Caroline had ever smelled before.

She touched every part of her daughter's small body.

Her fingers and toes seemed too long to belong to a newborn. Perhaps she'd have Caroline's hands—with fingers long enough to play the piano with ease. The baby had thick dark hair, like John's, her pink skin a darker hue than Caroline's, also like John's. Her ears were delicately small and her nose short with a little pudge on the end. Her eyes were such a dark gray that Caroline was sure they'd turn brown. And certainly, the baby had John's chin. This daughter of hers appeared excessively like her father. She smiled at the realization.

Another pain pulled her back to the business of her body's need to expel the afterbirth.

Spicey was called back in, and twenty minutes later Caroline was clean, dressed in a fresh nightgown, and nursing her daughter again.

Spicey stroked the baby's head. "All that love wrapped into a wee body. Sweet baby girl, a gift from God."

Mama took Spicey and left to tend to household instructions for the servants.

Mary brought John into the room and then left them alone.

Caroline smiled as he cautiously sat on the edge of the bed, his wordless expression of awe touching her heart. He cupped the back of the baby's wee head in his large hand. The baby didn't respond to his touch or presence and contentedly continued her suckling. There was an intimacy in Caroline and the baby's nakedness that John was naturally a part of. She suddenly found herself with a lump in her throat.

John kissed Caroline on the cheek. "This is more than I imagined and prayed for." His eyes glistened. "She's divine." He lightly touched the baby's small back and trailed his hand down her leg. "Such perfection." He smiled. "Now I have two lovely women to light up my life."

"What shall we name her?" Caroline asked.

"*Light* describes her so well, but that's probably an inappropriate name." John thought a minute. "Ora means light in Hebrew. And since she is divine, what do you say to Ora Divine?"

CHAPTER TWENTY-ONE

May 22, 1861

After Ora's early morning feeding, Caroline couldn't fall back asleep and arose to a quiet house. She found the day-old New Bern newspaper where Moses left it every morning, on the sideboard in the hallway. Settling into a chair, she read the disturbing news about North Carolina's delegates voting unanimously for the state to secede from the Union. Grief and confusion made her head pound. She squeezed her eyes shut, startled when John touched her shoulder.

"Is something wrong?"

All she could do was hand him the paper.

Reading while walking, he sat in a chair near a window. His eyes widened as if in surprise and then deepened into sorrow. "Listen to this," he said. "'We do further declare and ordain, that the union now subsisting between the State of North Carolina and the other States under the title of the United States of America, is hereby dissolved, and that the State of North Carolina is in the full possession and exercise of all those rights of sovereignty which belong and appertain to a free and independent State.'"

He lowered the paper. "We're the last southern state to join the Confederacy. How could we choose otherwise?" He shook his head. "We cannot fight against our own. As much as I hate to see it happen, we must join the South."

She crossed her arms around her chest, hugging herself. "We suspected this, yet it feels unreal."

"The resolution goes on to give the Confederate central government jurisdiction over some North Carolina land for military use. I wonder if they'll use Swansboro's Port?"

She swallowed hard. "I've had the same concern." How involved would they be in this war? She massaged her temples.

He tossed the paper on the side table and stepped to the window, his back rigid.

Going to him, she gently placed her hand on his shoulder. "Will you join the fighting?" How would the war change their lives? Some said it would be over by July 4th. Let them be right!

"No, I can't take up arms against a human being. Perhaps I can offer ecclesiastical services somehow?"

Relief washed through her like rain off a slick rock. She wasn't surprised John felt as he did about fighting, but it was comforting to hear.

He pulled her to him, and they stood looking out the window upon a glorious new spring day, the street eerily quiet. Perhaps the whole town felt the blow of secession.

"I wish there were an answer other than force when two factions want inconsistent worlds," he said.

"Is that not one of the functions of our government—to solve such problems by vote, not force?"

"They've tried to seek a solution for years." He sighed heavily.

"Many of us have family with our same values and beliefs who live in the Northern States. Are they now our enemies? It astounds my thinking to see it clearly. This war doesn't make sense. I keep thinking I'll awaken tomorrow and it will all have been a dream."

John absently rubbed her arm. "The problem is the South feels that its rights of freedom and property are being threatened. I feel it myself."

"But to kill each other for it?" Caroline faced his profile.

"We're living in an evil time." He stared out the window. "I pray our leaders come to their senses soon."

"How much of this is really about slavery?"

"For a few men, it's all about slavery. But this conflict is about much more."

She clenched her fists.

"The North isn't willing to destroy us because they're morally better, and I don't think they're on a holy crusade to abolish slavery. Their virtue is no greater than ours." He faced her. "I've lived among these men in the North. In many ways, their prejudices are as strong as many slaveholders here in the South. Most Northerners refuse to integrate free Africans, and they don't want to pay for the independence of hundreds of thousands of slaves. They profit from slavery, whether they want to admit it or not."

"What does this war have to do with, if not slavery?"

"Slavery is certainly a part of it, but there's also long-standing constitutional, political, and economic conflicts."

"So, what's to be done?"

"The morally right thing to do would be to fund a liberation program for the slaves, compensate slave owners for their loss, and start integrating the black people into our society. It wouldn't happen overnight, *but* it wouldn't entail war and bloodshed. Our government doesn't want power over the institution of slavery. Besides, it would take an amendment to the Constitution to do that. I don't believe we could get every state to step-up to such a program, anyway."

He frowned. "We've found ourselves in a great mess. I suppose what's to be done is whatever does the most good with the least amount of harm. I fear there'll be an invasion by the North to wield power over us. Power is a dangerous thing to give men with guns."

Caroline shuddered.

"Our social structure may go through great changes. For that, I'd be glad." John's features softened.

"Why?"

"Slavery may likely be abolished. You're aware of my sentiments in this regard."

She was more than aware.

"Carrie, I'd like to make a proposition."

Her back went rigid. "And that is?"

He looked toward the ceiling. "I'd like to find other homes for your slaves."

Her body swayed. "No—"

"Listen." He turned and clasped her upper arms. "I have strong feelings about where our nation is heading."

"Feelings? Let us deal with facts!" She glared at him, resentment growing in her heart. She wasn't going to change her life for his idealistic dreams.

"The *facts* are we could lose all we have. I'm saying this as much for your safety as I am for your slaves' futures." John's voice strained under the stress of his words. He grasped her harder, and she shrugged to get him to release her arms. He loosened his grip but didn't let go. "I'll not force you to do anything, but please consider my ideas."

"If you must, tell me, but know I can scarce stand here and consider what I think you're fixing to say."

"Then come sit." He released his grip and motioned her to the settee.

"That's not what I meant," she said, angry at his lack of empathy. She followed him to the settee, but not in defeat.

They sat facing each other as if to fight their own war.

"We should let Spicey move to Kit's place. It's only appropriate we allow her to live with her husband. I think if you'd truly consider it, you'd agree," John said.

Caroline clenched her jaw. John didn't know the ramifications of what he asked. She needed Spicey. She was Caroline's dearest friend and she believed Spicey felt the same about her. Spicey had never complained about not being able to live with Junior. It was because she didn't want to leave. "Have a care, John." Her voice was hardly above a whisper. She cleared her throat and said louder, "Do you think your own wife heartless? Spicey has spent her life by my side. She doesn't mind the work. I don't believe she'd leave me if you asked her to." She glared and deepened her tone. "Do you expect me to iron, scrub, and do my own hair like white-trash women? I was raised genteel. You knew that when you married me. Can you not accept me as I am?"

John put his face within inches of hers. "You're getting carried away with your emotions, but yes, I think you can care for yourself—and Ora, for that matter. I'll help you." He clasped her fingers in his. "If necessary, perhaps we can hire a white girl to help."

She pulled her hands away. "You know as well as I that we have no money for servants." He was patronizing her.

"Give me time to think on it. Perhaps there's something we can sell to pay for her?"

"We have so little. Please don't consider selling my china or silver. They were wedding gifts. Would you sell our wedding gifts?" How could he consider it?

He shook his head. "We seldom use the wagon . . . perhaps I can sell the wagon?"

Did he know so little about the household activities? His days spent at the Academy had kept him from interacting with the slaves. She suspected it was intentional. "Moses uses it often to haul firewood, horse feed, and much more. It's bad enough those things are donated to us. Need we borrow a wagon too? Or maybe you expect Moses to tote them on his back?" She sounded ridiculous, but his unrealistic suggestions frustrated her.

"That's another matter . . . I think we should give Moses and his family to your mother."

"Lord-a-mighty! This is downright foolishness." Her throat tightened, and her mouth went dry.

"It's not a permanent solution, but that way they wouldn't be separated. If I could get them north, I would."

"Hush now!" She lowered her voice. "I don't want the slaves hearing you." Truth be told, she didn't want to hear him either.

"Listen, Carrie, I don't want slaves. I never did." He spoke quietly but fiercely. "Before I married you, I took my slaves north and gave them freedom. I'd do the same again if I could."

"I don't doubt it." She wanted to say more, but her anger left her tongue-tied.

"Your mother needs more help at White Oak Plantation. If you find after living without slaves for a month or so that you simply cannot get by, then we'll bring them back. It will be a stipulation we make with your mother when we give them to her."

"What of the slaves Ned gifted us, which you hire out? We need the income they bring us." She felt tears prick her eyes.

"Well, I figure if we have four less mouths to feed, we can do without that income."

Caroline jerked her head up, her mouth falling open. "Good Lord! Are you of unsound mind?"

John's smile seemed forced and out of place. "I've been accused of worse." He chuckled sadly.

Caroline let her tears fall at their impalpable situation.

"I can garden," he added. "At this point, Moses has planted this year's summer vegetables. I'll take over from here. There's only the three of us. Think of it, Carrie. We could care for ourselves—depend on each other and grow closer."

"Closer?" Her mind felt like shutting down. "Do you not feel close to me now? What have I done for you to treat me so poorly?"

"That's not what I meant."

He put his warm hands on her clenched, cold fists and rubbed them gently. He tried to get her to open her hands.

She refused to let him comfort her and floundered as if in the ocean without a boat, her past life slipping away.

"I'm not asking for you to do this to hurt you," John said as if offended. "If I thought it would truly hurt you, I'd never consider it."

"It already has." She hastily stood and walked out of the room.

CHAPTER TWENTY-TWO

July 4, 1861 - Koonce Plantation Home, Carteret County

Caroline tried to capture what breeze she could from the open window while nursing Ora in one of the many guestrooms of the Koonce Plantation home. They'd come early that morning in celebration of Independence Day. The day was now spent, the sun low behind distant sycamore trees.

As Ora suckled, Caroline watched a group of about fifty slaves on the wide grassy yard. A pile of corn at least four feet high by ten feet wide was laid out in a semicircle, as to suggest a fortification—a breastwork against the attacks of hunger until harvest came again. Men had divided into teams on either side of the recently cut corn still in husks.

Today was for corn shucking. Papa once explained to Caroline that white people husked corn, Negroes shucked it—just as the white man played a violin and the Negro a fiddle. The two great high feasts for slaves on a plantation were the Christmas hog killing and the July corn shucking, with a barbeque to follow. Some said the corn was far more valuable than cotton, sugar, rice, or tobacco. The darkies had a saying: "Nigga make de co'n, hog eat de co'n, and Nigga eat de hog."

The slave women sat on blankets, laughing and visiting with one another while their youngsters ran in all directions playing with David and Freddy, Eliza's youngest children. Spicey was among those on the blankets. Caroline felt a pang of jealousy seeing Spicey in animated conversation with another slave. How much of Spicey's life would change if Caroline let her leave? Would she like her new life of freedom better?

John wouldn't win that battle. She wouldn't let him.

Every time she thought of the consequences of having to do all the housework herself, and losing the companionship of Spicey, Caroline knew she could not allow it.

She leaned closer to the window's opening, hoping for a better view of the activities below.

A few elderly slave men sat on stools near the corn, shouting out wagers on who would win. A bell rang, and two slaves acting as captains came forward and shook hands. The crowd quieted, and some of the children ran over to grab rakes leaning against the wall of the corn house. Both captains drew a cross in the grass with the sides of their bare feet, and spat on it for luck, then walked back to their teams.

"Begin de co'n shuckin," an old man sitting to the side yelled out.

Both teams converged on the corn. Green husks and golden silks flew in the air, raining on laughing children who caught it mid-air or raked it up. They scampered over to baskets and barrels, where they stuffed the fibrous skins.

"Do me proud, Junior," Spicey called amidst other women shouting for their men.

Each shucker wore a shucking peg—a sharpened spike about five inches in length fastened at the center to the forefinger by a bit of buckskin. With this, they ripped open the husk from the ear of corn. Hands moved almost faster than the eye could see. Once shucked, the men threw the ear of corn onto their team's corn pile.

Caroline couldn't help but enjoy the intensity of the competition. Her heart beating fast, she squeezed Ora a little too tightly, and the baby squirmed. "Oh, sorry little one."

Caroline leaned back in her chair and took several deep breaths, trying to slow her heart. She was missing out by not being on the blankets with the women cheering for their men. For just an instant she could see the benefits of not having society judge her reputation.

The huge green pile of corn was soon plumb gone, and ears of yellow corn lay in two mounds. A cry went up, and the win was claimed for the team with the largest pile. Children threw corn husks in the air in token of the victory.

The joyous crowd grew quiet as they moved the mounds of corn to the corn house where it would be dried and made into hominy or feed for the animals. The children started up the song "Ole Dan Tucker" as they carried away the baskets and barrels of the leafy green matter to be dried and used for slave ticking and winter feed for cattle. The adults joined in the song. When it ended, Eliza's children ran off.

John's voice, not too far distant, traveled through the silence. She listened more closely and realized he was in the room next to hers, speaking to Kit. Their voices carried out the open window.

Ora's sucking slowed. She'd soon be asleep.

Caroline listened to the timbre of her husband's deep and controlled voice in response to Kit's young and eager one.

When Caroline first met Kit, she thought him quiet and unsociable. The more she came to know him, the more she admired him and found he had plenty to say. He just didn't talk of trivial matters.

In most ways, he was nothing like John. In appearance, Kit had a much lighter complexion. His eyes were set close together, and his eyelids drooped as if he were half asleep. His high arched eyebrows juxtaposed the droopy eyes. Like John, his mouth was wide and lips full, with a smile of beautifully straight, white teeth.

Where John enjoyed teaching from the pulpit, Kit was reserved and preferred to be alone. John admired art but would never allow himself to take the time to create it, whereas Kit reworked his schedule to find the opportunity to paint or write poetry. John was organized and fastidious, Kit indifferent.

Kit had a room in his home he wouldn't let his slaves enter or clean. At Spicey's wedding, Caroline had been greeted by the sharp, piney smell of turpentine coming from that room. Her curiosity had gotten the best of her, and she'd peeked in. Tables had been covered in bird nests, branches, and books. Flowers, probably once used in a still life painting, had stood dried and crisp in their vase. Pictures of botanicals ripped from books had hung crookedly from pins pressed into the wall. Easels and canvases had leaned against the lower part of each wall. Brushes of many sizes had been upright in jars with colored smudges of dried paint on their handles. Caroline had surmised Kit must be self-indulgent, whereas John never gave a thought to allowing himself such pleasures.

Yet through both men ran the blood of Eliza. Whether Eliza taught them, or it came naturally, both John and Kit were idealistic and driven toward their goals. Both seemed to want to please their mother. Both had the best tutors as children and went to university.

Earlier in the day, Caroline had found John napping in a chair on the porch. He'd been tuckered out from the day prior when he'd helped a family bury their young daughter who'd died of a bilious fever.

Caroline had tiptoed away from him and walked alone toward a harvested field. Grasshoppers jumped from the drying cornstalks as she waded through in her wide skirts. She walked into a small cluster of beech trees. The bark on the trees smooth and pale gray, lovely against the bright green of the heavily veined and toothed-edges of the leaves. The canopy of leaves let little sun through, consequently leaving the ground barren.

Coming from an opening into a dry, grassy area, she came upon Kit standing at the banks of Cale's Creek in front of a canvas on easel. His back was to her, his right hand poised, holding a paintbrush in the air. He stood uncommonly still.

Caroline couldn't see what he was looking at but stood still too, not wanting to startle away a raccoon or rabbit or whatever it might be.

After many minutes of waiting, she became restless, imagining chiggers climbing onto her stockings. She couldn't stand still another second. She thought to sneak away, but when she turned, the fabrics of her skirts rustled against the dried grass.

Kit lowered his brush and turned. "Oh, Caroline! How be the fair wife of the preacher?" he called with a half-smile, much like John's, dimple and all.

"I didn't aim to interrupt your concentration." She moved toward him. "What were you looking at, pray tell?"

Kit shrugged slightly and smiled broader. "I was watching the light on the water and trying to decide what colors to mix to accurately portray such sparkle in motion." He sheepishly lowered his head. "It can be challenging to give a painting the illusion of life and movement."

She studied his painting. In its beginning stages, it had no detail, only blocks of color. "Coincidentally, last night I was trying to form notes on a piano to sound like running water. I never did get it right. I wish you more luck."

Her memory of Kit at the river was interrupted by his voice in the present. If a person's tone could show love, his was doing so now, which made her even more interested in what the men discussed. She turned her ear toward the window.

"What would Father want me to do?" Kit asked.

"I can't guess at Father's politics and ethical leanings. I was three when he died, and my only memory of him was being lifted by his large hands onto a mule. I was scared and wanted down, but he soothed me by talking in my ear. He kept his hand on my back the whole time he walked that old mule in circles."

Kit sighed. "I think I should go." He sounded as if he didn't believe what he was saying.

With a start, she realized they were discussing the war. Was he saying he thought he should join the war? Her heart sank. She couldn't imagine sensitive and artistic Kit firing a gun at another human being—she shuddered—or them firing at him.

"Although I'd hate to see you leave, I won't try and keep you here," John said. "Have you told Mother yet?"

"You're the first I've spoken to. I'd hoped you'd tell me the best way to approach the subject. You remember how she acted when you wanted to go to Jerusalem. How did you ever get away?" Kit gave a short laugh that wasn't a laugh at all.

"I told her I felt God wanted me to go. It didn't convince her. In the end, I sold my land and left in the middle of the night, sneaking out like a thief."

"Do you suggest I leave in that manner?"

"I was a young and insensitive lout. Don't follow in my crooked path. Perhaps you should tell her while I'm here so I can be a mediator."

"That's not a bad idea." There was silence for a moment. "Tell me, do you think we can win?"

"I don't know," John said. "The numbers are certainly not in our favor. I heard, for every soldier we have, they have four."

"When I read Lee didn't want to live in 'a union held together by bayonets,' I knew I had to join the fight. Someday I hope to marry. I want my children to have what I had and grow up in peace where they aren't threatened by someone in the North taking away their land and rights."

"I fear for our rights and lifestyle too. As you heard in our Freemasons' meeting a few nights ago, they advised the Brothers without wife and children to fight if they must."

"Well, if by my going you can stay home, then I must."

A few heavy steps sounded and then silence. A moment more and then what sounded like a pat on the back.

"A man couldn't have a better brother." John's voice was muffled.

Kit murmured something Caroline couldn't hear.

"We best go and approach Mother," John said.

Caroline took a few moments getting Ora settled into her bassinet. She found the men with Eliza and Papa Koonce in the parlor.

Unlike her usual straight-backed stature, Eliza drooped in a chair, looking pale, and Papa Koonce stood tight-lipped at her side, a hand on her shoulder.

Kit bent on one knee in front of her. "Mother, I'll enlist as a hospital steward. I may not fight at all." His reassurance sounded hollow.

Eliza vacantly gazed at him, as if gathering her wits. Tears glistened in her eyes. Caroline surmised she wasn't fixing to let them fall in front of everyone. "Take Junior with you so I know you're cared for." She seemed to want to say more but instead covered her eyes with one hand and turned from Kit. "You will come back," she demanded.

CHAPTER TWENTY-THREE

July 23, 1861 - Camp Green, North Carolina

The day was one where the heavy mood should've lifted with a smell of the fresh air and sight of the clear blue sky—a day for a picnic, not a day to send men to war. Grassy fields which should have held blankets, baskets, and young lovers were instead covered with piles of weapons, ammunition, and other military supplies for the men of the 27th Infantry Regiment.

Somber families and loved ones held off as long as they could with their farewells. A few called out positive wishes despite their tense faces. A band played "Battle Cry of Freedom," elevating Caroline's emotions, if only for a moment.

She stood with John and their families, feigning happiness for Kit and Hester's husband, George, who'd both enlisted in the 27th that morning, giving their oaths to bear true allegiance to the Confederate States of America and serve them honestly and faithfully against all enemies. Their parents, not wanting to come into the crowds today, had already said their goodbyes the night before at a small send-off party.

John was expected to present a speech. Caroline couldn't imagine how he'd give comfort at such an occasion. She was torn with fear for her brothers-in-law, relief that John wouldn't leave with them, and guilt for not wanting her husband to fight.

"Reverend Mattocks, can you please come to the stand?" an officer called from the porch of the old farmhouse, newly turned into enlistment headquarters.

John waved to Caroline as he headed toward the farmhouse.

She moved closer along with Mary, Ned, Hester, George, and Kit. The crowd hushed when the officer introduced John, Caroline's palms sweating with anticipation of him saying just the right words to so many bewildered people.

At the porch railing, he removed his hat and loudly called out, "Today is a day many of us will never forget, and I hope I can provide comfort to your souls, as well as mine. For you see, I too have a brother and brother-in-law going to war."

Caroline watched with trepidation as he stood tall in his black clergyman's coat. It was a warm day, yet he wouldn't take it off. To him, his garb represented his religion. It wasn't something he wore just on Sunday. He wore it proudly whenever he was about the Lord's work. And he didn't use written notes. He wouldn't need them.

"Psalms 27:3, tells us that 'though an host should encamp against me, my heart shall not fear: though war should rise against me, in this will I be confident,'" John said. "Circumstances are before us that we would not have chosen. Warfare is a conflict between right and wrong, between beliefs and false principles. In this we stand in need of good counsel. Proverbs 24:6 reads 'For by wise counsel thou shalt make thy war: and in multitude of counselors there is safety.'"

As John spoke, Kit stood with his hands clasped, looking at the ground, making Caroline wonder what was going through his mind.

"With whom do we counsel?" John asked. "Depend on God for guidance and strength to enable you to perform as He would have you do. We are facing a great calamity of evil. Our state's freedoms are at stake. When we're on the Lord's errand, we are entitled to the Lord's help." John's voice was loud, but kind.

Mary grasped Caroline's gloved hand and whispered in her ear, "He does give a good speech, does he not?"

Caroline nodded.

"Poor Hester!" Mary said. "I pray it will never be us bidding farewell to our husbands."

Caroline nodded again. If she spoke, she'd cry.

"I know you wouldn't have chosen war," John continued. "War was chosen for you. We must cleanse the earth of evil. Some of you will come out of this trial purified and refined. Have Christian hope. What do I suggest by Christian hope? Christ conquers all. Be on his side. Go with God's strength."

A small flock of starlings settled onto the upper point of the farmhouse roof. Somehow, they seemed out of place—in order—when all around her was in confused disorder. Caroline supposed she should be comforted by John's words, but a dismal foreboding troubled her soul.

"But I say unto you, love your enemies, bless them that curse you, do good to them that hate you, and pray for them which despitefully use you and persecute you." John quoted more scripture. "The command may seem impractical, but it's not. By loving your enemies, you'll be guided by Christian thought and behavior."

Was God on their side? She couldn't recall how He ever tolerated war.

"Fight in self-defense, not as blood-thirsty men. Defend our homes and freedoms. Keep our families' safe from invasion. Psalms 68:30 says, '…scatter thou the people that delight in war.' Make them run back to their homes and forget their nonsensical ideals. We ask only to be left alone. Let's end this war quickly and pray we come home better men." John's voice sounded raw.

Mary wiped away a tear. People bowed their heads and wives and mothers held tight to their men, probably feeling the unease of their unknown futures. Caroline hoped her husband's words gave courage.

"It's my prayer this war of northern aggression will soon be in the past and our people can once again live in peace. I, your families, friends, and community will pray daily for your safe return to your loving homes. God be with you!" he called out, his voice breaking along with something in Caroline's heart.

A shout went up from the crowd. The startled starlings took flight. Men threw hats in the air. Clapping and Rebel yells went on for many minutes as the leading officer tried to regain control.

Caroline didn't feel it in her to clap or call out.

At last, the officer quieted the crowd and directed the new Confederate soldiers to say their goodbyes and line up as commanded.

The air filled with clanking weaponry and shouts of "hoorah" for the departing men. A gun report shot into the sky and reverberated, spooking horses who whinnied and stomped. Young and old, gentlemen and workmen, all dressed in the same gray clothing—some homespun, others skillfully made into uniforms—moved to line up with their companies, trampling a once lovely farmhouse yard.

John joined Caroline and their group. With tears in his eyes, he embraced Kit.

"Do you think God will punish me if I kill others?" he asked John.

John held him at arm's length. "I know you well enough to know your allegiance is to God, and I don't think He would want you, or us, to sacrifice our rights and freedoms. Remember, you aren't out there alone." He squeezed Kit's arms. "I don't claim to know what's in the hearts of men nor how God will judge them or you." He embraced Kit again. "Depend on God for guidance. I'll pray for you, brother."

"I'll miss you and will write as often as possible," Kit said.

John released him and turned to George to wish him farewell.

Kit grasped both Caroline's hands. "Take care of the preacher." He smiled sadly as he looked into her eyes. "He might seem like he can carry the world, but don't let him fool you. He needs you as much as you need him."

Caroline couldn't help but let the tears fall. "I pray the war will be over before you reach a battlefield."

"If luck is with me, I'll be working in a hospital."

Caroline embraced Kit, then he turned to Ned.

Hester, face red and swollen, buried herself in Caroline's arms. The women watched George pack his haversack and Caroline worried about his departure for many reasons. Hester was pregnant. But also, under George's direction, what land remained at White Oak Plantation produced enough to keep Mama solvent. With George gone, harvest would fall fully on Mama and the few slaves she had left.

"It cannot be helped," George had said. "There is no good time to go to war."

Curse this war. The entire situation was unreal. She couldn't let herself consider the possibility that she may not ever see her brothers-in-law again.

Kit's slave Junior knelt on the ground a few yards away, wrapping Kit's bedroll with rope and tying a makeshift handle. Junior would accompany Kit as his servant. When he was finished with the bedroll, Spicey stepped away with him, her head bowed, hands clasped as if in prayer.

Perhaps she was praying. She'd often led Caroline in prayer when they were young. She wouldn't be surprised if John's teachings had also influenced the girl. Caroline's heart softened, and she wanted to take Spicey in her arms. Then she noticed fullness to the front of Spicey's skirt. She must be with child. Dread welled from within, and then came anger at Spicey for not telling Caroline.

George called out, waving his last farewell as he trotted off to join his unit. Kit soon followed, Junior toting his gear.

Caroline lost sight of Spicey. Women everywhere cried, hanging onto the arm of a loved one as long as they could. Some stood alone, weeping quietly into their hands.

John ran after Junior, saying something Caroline couldn't hear. Junior turned, nodded and to Caroline's shock, John embraced him as he had his brother. The large, black man didn't hesitate in hugging back.

John jogged back to Caroline and put his arm around her waist.

She knew better than to ask. Instead, she breathed relief that her husband remained with her. Leaning against him, she watched the men depart, wanting to remember how brave the young men in gray appeared as they stood tall with their compatriots.

The crowd sang "Dixie" with gusto.

"God be with you all," Caroline whispered, hoping He truly could hear her, for there was no one else to ask the favor. Silently she continued the prayer, *Please, come back to us as whole as you are now.* There was no way a just God would let Hester be a widowed young mother, would He?

Turning to leave, she saw Spicey's face streaked with tears. She looked so alone. Would her unborn infant become a fatherless child?

John approached her and spoke quiet words, but her sobbing did not lessen.

CHAPTER TWENTY-FOUR

August 14, 1861 - Swansboro to Pollocksville

Spicey helped Caroline with her stockings, chemise, and drawers, then pulled the strings of her corset until she was barely able to draw breath into her lungs.

"I'll miss makin' you look purty." Spicey smiled a sad smile and Caroline doubted her words. If Junior weren't at war, Spicey would choose him over Caroline. She suspected Spicey longed to be with his family. The thought stung.

Since Junior had gone to war, Caroline had distanced herself from Spicey. The betrayal hurt less that way.

Spicey stepped upon a stool, dropped Caroline's hoops past her raised arms, and pulled them to her waist. She moved off the stool and tied the crinolines at the back. Spicey retrieved Caroline's petticoats from the cupboard. Stepping back up, she manipulated them over Caroline's head and then over her hoops.

"Once the war is over, you can live with me again." Caroline could only hope her words were true. Her life had come to a bitter detour, leaving her apprehensive about the future. War had separated her family and threatened to devour her lifestyle. She *had* to believe the future wouldn't be much different than the past. Glancing around the empty bedchamber, she sighed and dropped her arms. Her furniture had already been loaded onto the wagon for Pollocksville, though she wanted to move to the country about as much as she wanted to lose Spicey.

Spicey smiled and shrugged, going to the cupboard once again.

"Bring me the yellow cotton gown. I'm much too hot already."

"Yessum." Before mounting the stool, Spicey gathered the yards of fabric into her small hands to better maneuver it over Caroline's head. She stepped up and brought the dress down while Caroline placed her arms through the sleeves. Spicey pulled the dress into place, left her stool once more, and stood in front of Caroline to button her bodice.

"How you gonna dress yourself?" Spicey asked with eyes lowered to her task, some of her long curls draping her right shoulder.

Caroline sighed heavily. "John says there will be no need for corsets and hoops in the country. I wore them at White Oak, I don't know why he thinks it will be any different in Pollocksville." She recalled seeing other preachers' wives wearing simple dresses, always gray, black, or some other dull color. Surely John wouldn't expect her to look like that.

She pulled in as much breath as her corset allowed. "He assures me he'll take care of my needs. You just remember your living arrangements are temporary, you hear?"

Spicey nodded.

For three months, John had worked at convincing Caroline to give up her slaves. When he received an assignment by the Church to be a circuit rider for Jones and Carteret Counties, the decision came down to logistics and finances.

After many young men went to fight in the War of Northern Aggression, the Academy had closed. Without John's teacher income, their finances were meager, so he wrote the bishop for another assignment. Along with the circuit rider salary, each church on the circuit paid toward room and board. The only home offered them had one bedchamber and not enough land for slaves' cabins.

Caroline had spent many nights wrestling with her conscience. She'd never told John of her conversations with Keziah and Spicey, but the memory of them still played in her mind. Her heart said one thing and her mind another. She finally accepted John would be happier without them, but she didn't know how to get by without her servants, yet she didn't want John to see her lack of competence.

She would never look at the darkies as her equal as John did. But she wanted him to see her as compassionate. She had to make sure he never had a reason not to love her. She could start by pretending she believed in equality and then eventually, at some time in the future, she hoped she *would* believe in it. But for it to be so, the Negroes needed to prove they could be educated and conduct their own affairs. It all seemed too farfetched to believe.

She sighed and sat on the stool, her gown flowing around her, while Spicey fastened her slippers using a buttonhook. Caroline looked ridiculously perched, but her dressing table had already been removed as had her chair.

Spicey pulled a box out of a satchel on the floor. It held Caroline's dressing kit—a silver mirror, brush, and comb. Spicey quickly did Caroline's hair in a simple chignon and covered it with a snood, then set Caroline's bonnet upon her head and handed her a handkerchief and parasol.

A knock came at the door.

Spicey opened it and turned to Caroline. "Moses and your Ma's slave here to tote the cupboard."

"Yes, well, let's be on our way then." Caroline glanced around the room one last time. This was the first home she and John had shared. Even though it had never been theirs to keep, she'd miss the floral wallpaper and colorful carpets. And she couldn't shake the apprehension she felt toward their new abode, which was also temporary.

Before embarking, they left Keziah and Mahaly with Mama and borrowed Mama's carriage and a hired driver. Moses and Spicey sat atop the wagon full of furniture and a crated hog and chickens. Tied at the back of the wagon, Fat Chance, the dairy cow, lumbered along.

Moses and the driver would return in the carriage, and Moses would live with his wife and daughter at Mama's slave quarter. Caroline tried to satisfy herself that it was for the best, because Mama only had Cozy and Betsey to care for her needs along with an occasional male slave hired for heavy work. All of Papa's slaves had been sold to cover debts.

With Ora in a basket at her feet, Caroline leaned against the carriage interior and feigned sleep so she wouldn't need to converse with John. She feared once she started crying, she'd never be able to stop.

On the way to Pollocksville, they detoured to Kit's plantation where he'd left his cousin James as overseer. Spicey was to live with Junior's parents in their cabin until Junior returned from the war.

Trapped in John's choices, Caroline dreaded parting with Spicey. As the carriage came to a stop at Kit's, her breaths caught in her chest. She wanted to believe her misgivings were only because she needed Spicey's help, but the truth was that she also felt a great loss, as if a sister were being taken from her. Yet she couldn't show her feelings toward a slave lest someone misinterpret.

John gave Caroline a hand out of the carriage.

Moses helped Spicey from the wagon about twelve feet behind them. Unease showed in her face. With her arms wrapped tightly around herself, she would look like a lost child if it weren't for the obvious swell of pregnancy. She stared at the ground and stayed close to the wagon.

Caroline had never talked to Spicey about the child growing within—it was evidence of her betrayal. Proof she'd picked Junior over Caroline. Perhaps Spicey was fortunate to have her mother-in-law, who could help her with the birth and infant care.

Spicey had always been a house slave and had never lived in a cabin. She'd abided a protected life in the big house, her decisions made for her. A personal lady's maid wasn't needed in Kit's household. Her tiny body not meant for fieldwork, it was decided between James and John that she'd help with the kitchen garden and necessary food preparation and cleanup.

Junior's mother, Alsey, stood by the barn, back straight, body firm. She was a blue-black darkie with hair turbaned in a white cotton cloth. She watched Spicey with gentle eyes and waited on an order from James to approach the girl.

Spicey inclined her head toward Caroline, and their eyes met, Spicey's glistening with moisture. Caroline's muscles tensed, tears stinging her own eyes. Her throat constricted. She glanced at John, but he had his back to her as he talked with James.

She sucked in her breath, her corset boning digging into her ribs, and as if some unseen force pulled her, she slowly walked toward Spicey, who again gave a fleeting glance. Not being able to stop herself, Caroline moved faster.

Astonished, Spicey left her spot and ran. They fell into each other's arms.

For the first time since childhood, Caroline held Spicey close, and the girl sobbed onto Caroline's chest. She caressed Spicey's head, bewildered at how soft her long curls felt. Her body no bigger than a child's, Caroline felt the distinct bump of Spicey's belly.

Warm tears ran down Caroline's cheeks. It was only then that she acknowledged she truly loved Spicey. If not for Caroline's deep love for John, she'd never give up the girl. Unable to tell her, Caroline held her tighter.

Spicey wasn't so assured of impropriety. "I dunno how to live without 'cha." She sounded like a child crying for a lost toy.

"We'll be back together again someday." Caroline gulped down a lump in her throat, wanting it to be true. But it probably wasn't. John would undoubtedly never agree to have slaves again. "You let me know if you're treated poorly or need anything, you hear?"

"Yessum, Miss Carrie." Spicey sniffled.

Caroline motioned her head to Alsey, and she hurried over and put an arm around Spicey's shoulders. "Come girl, you's wid us now. We's gonna take real good care of ya." She wiped at Spicey's tears with her apron. "Lemme show ya our home."

Spicey stared dejectedly at Caroline, then turned with Alsey and followed her to their cabin.

Caroline watched the girl's retreating figure, and a great pain filled her heart. Her life altered, she longed for the way things used to be. Wiping her tears, she turned away.

John regarded her with a relieved smile while James looked like he was in shock.

It took the rest of the day to get to Pollocksville. A quiet afternoon, they passed few homes as they traveled farther into the country. Caroline kept her arms wrapped around herself and chewed at her lower lip, swallowing back a giant lump in her throat.

The sun sat low as they pulled off the main road into a large opening. Back about ten wagon lengths was an unpainted clapboard, single-story house with dense woods a short distance behind. A graying barn stood to the right of the home, a privy a little farther past that. The house had a hipped roof coming out over a deep porch covered in mossy roof shingles.

"That's our new home." John observed her.

She scowled, still too upset about leaving Spicey and her old home to give him satisfaction. He'd seemed watchful of her all day and had said little. Perhaps he felt as apprehensive as she about this move.

"It has no piazzas," she said.

John frowned at her. "Although it's unlike any home you've ever lived in, it looks inviting, doesn't it?

Out of guilt and for John's sake, she tried to imagine wild pink roses lining the front of the house and rockers on the porch, perhaps even a porch swing, but she doubted any of it would happen.

The driver steered them closer and stopped.

John alighted, and Caroline handed him a sleeping Ora. Cradling her in one arm, he helped Caroline down, and they entered the house together. The last rays of the setting sun lit the still and dust-covered room, lonely and forgotten. The floorboards—obviously cared for over the years by someone but probably never waxed by slaves—were at least twelve inches wide and needed rugs.

John handed Ora to Caroline. "I'll go find a lamp in the wagon."

She walked slowly around the front room, her yellow gown gathering dust at the hem. There was no morning room, sitting room, or parlor. Only one spacious room to do the day's work or visiting. A large rock fireplace gaped like a hole in the wall, yet its hand-hewn stone had been carefully laid. The small amount of twilight coming into the room entered through a sizeable front window, looking out toward the covered porch and bare dirt yard. If she put her square grand piano in front of the window, would it give the room distinction?

There was not a flight of stairs, and she felt the loss of a second story. There would be no squeaking of floorboards overhead. Unless rats scurried up there. Caroline shuddered.

Open to the front room was a built-in kitchen. As she passed it, her heart beat faster. She should've swallowed her pride and asked Keziah how to cook.

She stepped through the only door off the front room and into a shadowed bedchamber. A solitary window faced east. Although in darkness now, they would surely be awakened by the sun each morning.

Caroline moved back to the front room. The only room, really. Empty and dusty, there was still something pleasant about the tiny house. She imagined it was once well lived-in and loved. Built tight and sturdy, it was a home that would shelter them for, perhaps, many years. The impression helped calm her trepidation about living alone with John and Ora and attending to all their needs.

John entered and knelt in front of a kerosene lamp he'd placed on the floor, striking a lucifer to light it. Once lit, the soft glow highlighted his wary face and pursed lips.

"It's a nice little house. I think we can be happy here," she said, trying to relieve some of his worry.

Standing, he searched her face. She smiled at him, and his shoulders dropped—his face washed clean of concern. "I'm so happy to hear you say that."

CHAPTER TWENTY-FIVE

August 15, 1861 - Pollocksville, Jones County, North Carolina

Sitting at a small dining table in the front room, Caroline and John ate cold ham and biscuits for breakfast, brought from their Swansboro home the day before. Right after, fearing the lateness of getting in a fall garden, John hurried outside to start the soil preparation.

It had taken only an hour for John, Moses, and Mama's driver to unload all their belongings last night. The piano now sat in front of the window, moved away from the wall at a diagonal.

With Ora on her hip, Caroline ran her hand along its polished surface. The wood felt as smooth as a wakeless sea. The intricate wooden lattice music rack had been set upright, waiting to hold her music. The legs of the piano were as round as barrels but ornately carved. Across the front, the maker's names, Hallet and Davis, were embossed in gold. The piano always reminded her of Papa. He'd given it to her for her nineteenth birthday instead of making it a wedding gift, hoping it would bring joy back to their family where so much sadness had lingered after Sarah's death. Sadness snatched at Caroline now at the memory, but she couldn't let herself dwell on it. She was starting a new chapter in her life, and she needed to try and feel cheerful.

John's writing desk stood to the side of the piano, against the wall, with at least a dozen large theology books on the floor leaning against the desk's legs. It'd be nice if they could somehow earn extra money for a bookshelf.

Caroline put Ora, who was still too young to roll over, on a blanket on the floor so Caroline could start unpacking her dishes from a crate into a china cabinet Mama had given her. John had set it against the wall between the bedchamber and kitchen doorways. She unpacked their wedding gifts of silver pieces, blue and white Pearlware Staffordshire china plates, bowls, platters, teacups and saucers, and a few odds and ends, loving the luxury of the china, but knowing it appeared just as out of place as the piano in their rustic home. Just as out of place as her. She sat on the settee, facing two empty rocking chairs in front of the fireplace, missing her family.

Considering her new home simple—Julia would say "meager"— Caroline reasoned she could be satisfied. Maybe. Everything was John's and hers, after all. There was something special in that.

She rose with a sigh and cleared the breakfast dishes, then took Ora in her arms and stepped out to watch John for a while, not knowing what else to do with herself. The garden sat about ten yards past a well behind the house, fenced to keep animals out. As Ora played with a gold heirloom necklace at Caroline's neck, John cleared weeds and shriveled, dry plant remains from a long dead garden. After that task, he prepared the dark earth by spading about six inches deep.

He stopped to wipe his brow, then looked at Caroline. It was fixing to be another hot and humid day. "Planting by seed this late in the season might be a waste, but we need to try. If we're lucky, the carrots, beets, and greens will produce good flavor when they mature during cool weather. However, the seedlings need to have adequate moisture to keep them actively growing during germination. We can keep the soil moist and cool by covering it with damp burlap cloth. I'll need your help with this on days I'm on the circuit. Do you think you can do it?"

"Yes." Caroline leaned against the fence. "If you show me how." Apprehension pinched her neck muscles.

By noon, Ora fussed for a nap.

Caroline took her in and put her to bed. Stepping back into the front room, she glanced around. What should she do next? John would want dinner, and she wasn't sure what was expected of her in that regard. He'd been patient with her lack of skills thus far. She walked into the kitchen and stared at the pots and skillets in horror, biting her lip. She'd never cooked anything in her life. How was she to learn when there was no one to teach?

That morning, John had given her *Mackenzie's Five Thousand Receipts in All the Useful and Domestic Arts*. She brought the book to the table. It described everything from gardening to pastry baking, medicine, and how to make soap and varnish. She closed her eyes, trying to picture herself doing such things. Tears burned behind her lids, but she refused to let them fall. It would take some time, but perhaps she could do it—if it meant making a comfortable home for him and Ora.

A quick, light *tap tap* at the door startled Caroline.

Before she could stand, a woman opened the door and stepped inside. "Well, hallo and welcome," she said with a genuine smile.

Shouldn't those have been Caroline's words of greeting?

"My name's Molly Hill." She stepped to Caroline and embraced her as she rose from her chair.

Pulling away, Caroline was too taken aback at the woman's forwardness to speak.

Molly smelled like fresh bread. Strange. Her thick gray hair may have once been piled high on her head, but now a large bun lay lopsided with wisps of frizzy hair falling around her narrow face. Probably in her late forties, her wrinkles weren't yet deep. "My, you're young, ain't 'cha." She held Caroline's shoulders, examining her from toe to head. "That's to be expected, I 'spose. The old preachers' wives never let their husbands ride the circuit—that is, if their husbands were still alive."

What did she imply?

Molly moved away and scanned the room. "Looks cozy here, and I'm wondering how we'll fit everyone. It's mighty hot to be outside, but I think that's what we'll need to do." She turned and waited.

Was Caroline supposed to answer? "Excuse me?"

"For the Donation Party." Molly stared at Caroline with raised eyebrows. Her friendly brown eyes creased in kindness. "Didn't anyone tell you?"

Caroline shook her head. The strangeness of her new life closed in around her. She had no idea what was expected of her, but she was sure whatever it was, she wouldn't be successful.

Molly grasped Caroline's hand. "When a new preacher comes to these parts, we welcome him and his missus with a dinner and party." Molly squeezed her hand. "Church members will be bringing you gifts for your home. We want you to feel welcomed, and it's a way we can all introduce ourselves."

"That sounds lovely." Caroline finally found her voice. "You're very kind." She swallowed her anxiety and squared her shoulders. "How many do you think will be attending?"

Molly pushed some of her fly-away hair from her eyes, but it immediately floated back. "Including the young'uns, I guess forty or there 'bouts. Come outside and I'll introduce you to my family."

Family?

John stood by a wagon near the barn, speaking with a man Caroline surmised was Molly's husband. Standing around the wagon were four young men and three younger girls, most of them redheads.

"These are my seven—Benjamin, David, Joseph, Joshua, Faith, Hope, and Charity." As she named them, they tipped their heads.

"And this is my husband, Ben senior." She motioned to the tall redheaded man next to John.

Ben came forward. Taking Caroline's hand, he tipped his head, the hair thinning on top. "Nice to meet you, Sister Mattocks."

"The pleasure's mine." Caroline made herself smile. "Please come in and make yourselves at home."

"Oh no, we won't bother your home none." Molly waved a hand. "We brought a table and chairs, and we'll set-up outside." She motioned to her sons. "You boys, get that furniture off the wagon. Girls, bring the food." She turned back to Caroline. "Would you like the boys to bring your table and chairs out?"

John moved to help the boys at the wagon. "Yes, thank you kindly."

Within minutes, more wagons and people arrived. The dusty yard was soon full of country folk and a buffet of fried chicken, ham, corn on the cob, fresh bread, deviled eggs, and many other homemade delights laid out on tables. The neighbors came from miles around.

Caroline tried to concentrate on which names went with whom. Presented with gifts of quilts, smoked ham, jams, chair tidies, cucumber pickles, and flower bulbs, her anxiety lessened with the offerings of friendship.

And at least dinner was one meal she needn't fret about making.

CHAPTER TWENTY-SIX

November 12, 1861

Caroline smiled at the three loaves of plump, brown bread cooling on the worktable. She'd studied *Mackenzies Five Thousand Receipts* like John studied the Bible. And finally, the reward sat in front of her. Three loaves would last four days. There were plenty of other recipes to try before she needed to bake bread again.

They'd settled into a routine. Each morning, John lit the stove and went to milk the cow and muck the barn. She figured out how to cook eggs, warm ham, and eventually bake biscuits. Making gravy was a skill she hadn't quite mastered. Sometimes the gravy looked good but tasted bad, and then others looked bad but tasted good. More food went into the hog's slop than she cared to explain to John.

As time went by, she discovered a warmth in their home she hadn't felt in Swansboro. She found joy in what her own hands prepared. She remembered how inadequate she'd felt in her first weeks of marriage, but now her life finally had real purpose. Her work showed her husband and child were well cared for.

Molly visited often and happily taught Caroline how to cook, churn butter, make cheese and light the stove. Educated in needlework as a child, Caroline figured out most mending jobs, but Molly taught her how to darn socks and patchwork britches. Caroline suspected Molly spread the word to other church ladies about her domestic ineptness, because occasionally they stopped by with household tips and a homemade meal. Their visits were pleasant, and she loved having an excuse to serve tea in her seldom-used china.

Contentment with her home didn't change her longing to be stylish. The days of wearing her corset and hoops were fewer. She couldn't put them on by herself and hated to ask John when he had more important things to do. When her friend Juju had told her marrying a preacher was the end of looking pretty, she turned out to be right.

The corset gave Caroline's thin frame a more feminine shape, but how could she wear it and bend to pick vegetables from the garden? The garden kept them from hunger and gave her a way to demonstrate care for those she loved. She enjoyed seeing the vegetables grow in their neat little rows. She'd already harvested lettuce, collards, and Brussels sprouts. The first frost was coming, and she was anxious to pick the carrots and beets, but each one she pulled in hopes of maturity proved to be too small. John laughed good-naturedly at her haste.

In the evenings they played games, or she played the piano for him once Ora was in bed. She'd let her anger at him for giving away her slaves dissolve before it created a wall too immense to tear down. She loved him too much to have disharmony. As hard as the jobs were, caring for him had become her aim. He did the same for her when he wasn't on the circuit. They'd never been closer.

"Smells like heaven in here." John entered wearing a loose-fitting work shirt with sleeves rolled to the elbows and brown faded trousers. Functional, not the sober black suit. He looked like a farmer.

Somehow it cheered her.

"What will it take to claim a slice of warm bread with butter?" he asked.

"Oh, I don't know. How about an hour of you and me on the porch swing later?"

"I win twice. Doesn't seem fair to you." He took her in his arms. "In case I haven't mentioned it recently, I love you."

"And I love you." She laid her cheek against his chest. His shirt smelled of hay and sweat. "I'd love you more if you smelled sweeter."

His laughter warmed her.

That night after supper, she put Ora to bed. When she came from the bedchamber, John took her by the hand. "I'd like to take you up on that promise of an hour in the swing."

The nights had been getting chilly, so they nestled together under a quilt on the swing he'd made for her. The air smelled of damp autumn leaves. A few crickets chirped, but Caroline suspected they'd be gone within the week.

John pulled her closer and kissed her head. "There was something missing in my life before we married. You're the other half of my soul and you make me feel complete."

Caroline's heart twisted. "How can you overlook my faults and the selfish, spoiled belle I am?"

He sat straighter and gently brought her face to his, surprise in his eyes. "You're an amazing woman. I've asked you to live in a home with scarcely any comforts, and you've done it with few complaints. I've asked you to change your lifestyle and adjust to the activities of a minister's life, and you've worked hard so I can serve my parishioners."

She never told him she felt a sting of jealousy when he left to perform his circuit duties. Sometimes it seemed he cared more for *his people* than for her or Ora. Not tonight, of course, as he held her in the swing, but the times he rode up to thirty miles to cover his circuit and was gone for days. Over the past months, she'd learned the most important duties of a circuit rider were to pilot the dying through death's experiences, perform marriages and baptisms, help troubled souls, listen to confessions, and bring those who'd gone wayward back into the fold.

She laid her head back on his shoulder, thinking about how her mind was as much in the world as John's was in Heaven. She prayed only after she'd worn herself out trying to think of every other way to solve a problem, while John prayed before the problem existed.

She tried to make him a home, but he didn't completely belong to it or to her. He belonged to God—something Caroline wasn't sure she could ever really understand or get used to.

As much as this new life brought a fulfillment she'd never known, she still missed her old life of comforts and folly. As in her younger years, she could no longer drum up her imagination to dream of better things. She missed Spicey's smiling face and gentle touch. Sometimes she ached not just for the help Spicey offered, but the contentment of having her companion with her daily.

All these things were of the past, yet she couldn't help thinking about them when John was gone for days on end. Sadly, she couldn't have her old life *and* the man she loved. She remembered Papa trying to help her realize what life with a preacher would be like. At the time, she thought she knew, but she hadn't truly understood how difficult it would be. Yet if she had, she'd still have chosen John. He completed her also.

She snuggled closer, the warmth and solidness of his body her gauge of contentment. "I do what I do to please you, I admit. I never want you to regret marrying me."

"Never in my lifetime would I regret that."

ଞଞଞ

Later that night, from the bedroom, Caroline rolled over and heard John in the front room, speaking in low, urgent tones.

She couldn't make out his words, yet goosebumps surfaced along her arms. "Who's there, John?" she whispered into the darkness.

"Don't fret." His hushed tone was strained. "I'm taking care of it. Go back to sleep."

She wondered if someone from his circuit needed his services, but something felt wrong. A draft came through the house from the open door. John hadn't invited whoever it was in.

The next morning, she asked, "Who came to our home last night?"

John looked like he hadn't slept well, and her question made his appearance sink further into gloom. "The less you know, the better."

The sting of betrayal pierced her heart. "What do you insinuate?" On the other hand, because of the nature of his church work there were probably many secrets he kept from her.

John rubbed his face and pushed his half-eaten plate of eggs and pork sausage away. He locked gazes with her for a moment, seemingly considering his words. "They were runaway slaves."

Caroline gasped. "What—?"

"They were never supposed to come here. I'll make sure it won't happen again. I need to talk to some people."

She was speechless.

"There's a cabin far into the woods they're supposed to go to. Our home is too close to the main road. Slave patrols still operate at night."

Her breakfast turned to stone in her stomach. Were his activities making them unsafe? "What are you involved in?"

He stood and walked to the window, his back stiff. "Like I said, the less you know the better."

"Have you put us in danger?"

"I'll make sure I didn't." He turned. "I'll be back by supper." He took his coat and hat from pegs and left the house.

CHAPTER TWENTY-SEVEN

January 29, 1862

Caroline sat in the rocker by the barely warm hearth, feeding Ora her one-a.m. meal. Time alone with her child, giving her sustenance, brought fulfillment and a little understanding into John's world of serving others.

With closed eyes, Ora sucked slowly, almost dreamily.

Caroline ran her finger across her baby's pudgy cheek.

She didn't stir, almost ready to go back to bed.

For the most part, life had been peaceful in their secluded little home in the woods. Yet the quiet was a reminder of just how much Caroline missed her friends and family. Some days she longed for the parties and balls and seeing the new fashions women wore.

When John traveled his circuit, he didn't bring her reports of society. Instead, he brought news of the war raging and battles won and lost. Since the Confederate victory at Bull Run, the first notable Union conquest had taken place only a hundred miles from Pollocksville, when coastal Forts Hatteras and Clark were captured after a bombardment by seven Union warships.

She shuddered at the possibility of the Union blockade extending farther down the coast and the Federals trying to gain entry into other North Carolina sounds, like nearby New Bern and Swansboro.

North Carolina had raised and equipped twenty-two infantry regiments since the beginning of the war. Sixteen of those fought in campaigns in Virginia, which left only the remaining six to defend North Carolina. To Caroline's relief, Kit and George were safe in the 27th Regiment defending the coastline. They'd been assigned to the District of Pamlico, not seventy miles from Pollocksville.

Ned had enlisted with the 3rd Cavalry, the Gatlin Dragoons, who were charged to guard Swansboro and protect the surrounding coast. The Dragoons shelled an old, empty British ship and another sloop loaded with tons of wrought iron, then burned and sank them at Bear Inlet to make entry into the sound surrounding Swansboro harder for Union ships. A fort had been constructed with six cannons on Huggins Island to protect the waterways.

Ned had told John if they all put forth the effort now, the war would be over in no more than ninety days.

Caroline sighed. Let Ned be right! At least her cellar was now full, and they had plenty to get them through winter. The vegetables she'd grown were bottled. With help from Joshua Hill, Molly's twelve-year-old redheaded son, John had slaughtered the hog, giving them slabs of smoked and salted pork. Finding a recipe in her *Mackenzie's Five Thousand Receipts*, she made soap with the hog fat. She now also milked the cow. Learning that chore ended the last of her hopes to one day be a lady of society.

When John traveled his circuit, Joshua often came by, milked the cow and performed other outside chores, giving her some relief. Molly's other sons had enlisted in the war, while her husband Ben raised bay horses, which he sold to the troops. Ben tried to sell John a packhorse he'd raised from a colt, but John refused to replace his mount. He loved his horse, Sammy, like a person. Probably because of how much time he spent with the animal. He sometimes slept out in the open with only Sammy for company. John said the horse was as much in the service of God as he was.

Coincidently, she thought she heard a horse galloping. She listened more intently. Why would anyone come at this late hour? Suddenly fearful it had something to do with John's involvement with escaping slaves, tingles surfaced along her arms. "John, someone's out front," she softly called, trying to keep fear from her voice and not wake Ora.

Rap, rap, rap. An urgent knock sounded on the door.

John got out of bed and put on his britches, passing her.

She stopped nursing and covered herself as he opened the door and cold air blew in.

Brother Meadows stood in the doorway. "I'm sorry to bother you at such a time."

"How can I serve you?" John's voice was kind and patient.

Brother Meadows stepped in, removing his hat. His hands worked its brim. "My wife's ill, and I fear for her life. She's asking for you."

"I'll come immediately."

Brother Meadows was out the door and back on his mount within moments.

John knelt before Caroline. "Sister Meadows has four young children. Would you mind coming to help me?" His brown eyes were troubled. "If their mother passes, they'll need your strength." He moved to the bedchamber to get himself ready.

Caroline swallowed hard. She didn't believe she had "strength" to give to the poor little strangers. But how could she say no to John or helpless children?

After dressing, she quickly gathered provisions for the family. She didn't know how long Sister Meadows had been ill or in what situation they'd find her house.

They drove in silence through the cold night, the waning moon giving little light, Ora sleeping soundly in a basket at their feet. After a long while, they left the main road and followed smaller roads she hadn't realized even existed. Sammy blew loudly, pulling the wagon up an incline.

As they traveled, her inadequacy at being a preacher's wife haunted her. Afraid she'd make a mistake at the Meadows and embarrass John, her insides churned.

Perhaps Sister Meadows would die. Otherwise why would she have asked John to come? People didn't want to die without the witness of the spirit. The duty of a circuit rider was to make the dying process a gentle transition from this world to the spirit world.

John had once confessed he didn't care to officiate over death because he often received ignoble secrets from the dying person. In Caroline's view, he usually came through stronger in his faith. He never seemed to hold the sins of a man against him. He knew his parishioners' weaknesses and faults better than anyone else and, in spite of his knowledge, he loved them more. She hoped he did the same with her sins.

They arrived at the cabin and found Sister Meadows gravely ill. John and Brother Meadows stayed at her bedside. Ora slept, and Caroline made herself busy washing dishes. Just before sunrise, Brother Meadows went to the barn to care for his animals, but soon returned to his wife's side.

Caroline cleaned the kitchen and took stock of what food was in the house, and how she could supplement it with what she'd brought.

"Who are you?" a child's voice asked.

Caroline turned and found a girl of no more than four, standing at her skirts and wrapped in bedcovers, her hair mussed, sleep still in her eyes.

"I'm Sister Mattocks, the preacher's wife."

"Why is you here?"

Caroline wrapped the blanket more snuggly around the child. "Your Mama is sick and my husband is with her."

"Oh." She seemed not to need any further explanation. "I'm hungry."

"I have breakfast. Would you like to wake the others?"

"Bobby can't rightly come until you tote him. His legs don't work since they was runned over."

Caroline caught her breath but tried not to show shock. How much had this young family endured? How could they survive with a crippled child if their mother died? Why hadn't Caroline realized her own blessings of a healthy child and husband? "Show me where Bobby sleeps."

The child took her to a room in the back of the house, no bigger than five square feet. Three children slept on ticks on the floor, a fourth tick empty, likely the girl's. Only one child was a boy.

Caroline knelt at his bedding, trying not to bump the other tiny bodies sleeping nearby. She stroked little Bobby's arm, worried about his reaction to being awakened by a stranger. "Bobby, I'm here to help you come to breakfast."

The child awakened. He looked about six. His bright, intelligent eyes showed understanding. His dirt streaked face was another indication of his mother's illness keeping her from caring for her young. He pushed himself up on his elbows. "You here 'cause Ma died?"

The little girl gasped.

Caroline tried to give her a reassuring smile. "Your mother's not dead." She looked back to Bobby. "My husband's a preacher, and he's comforting your mother in her illness." She bent closer to him. "Can I carry you to the table for breakfast?"

Bobby looked away.

Her heart felt as if it were being squeezed.

The other children woke at the commotion of Caroline lifting him. The youngest, no more than one and barely walking, fussed a bit before her older sister took her hand and walked alongside.

Once the children were at the table, Caroline quickly fed them the cold ham and bread she'd brought and heated some cider.

John approached and whispered in her ear. "Her passing was peaceful. Her husband asked that you prepare her for viewing while we dig a grave."

"I wouldn't know how." Caroline swayed, and he grasped her waist. His arm did nothing to calm her fear. What a nightmare they'd stepped into. Visions returned of her sister Sarah's dead body on the table in the parlor at White Oak.

"All you need do is undress and wash her body," he whispered. "Her husband will give you the garment she's to be buried in."

She drew in her breath. She needed to look brave for the children, who couldn't hear their conversation and didn't yet know their mother had died. "Take me to her."

Sister Meadows lay on her bed—face gray, eyes sunken. Caroline wished she'd take a breath, open her eyes, and save her family their oncoming grief.

Brother Meadows knelt at the bedside, his face buried in his hands.

John stepped forward and clasped his shoulder. "My wife's here to prepare her."

Brother Meadows stood and wiped his face. There was so much pain in his expression, she quickly shifted her eyes to the floor.

John put his arm around Brother Meadows' shoulders. "She's with the Lord and out of pain. Let us praise God for his mercy in not letting her suffer longer."

Brother Meadows nodded.

"Can you direct my wife to an appropriate garment so the children's last vision of their mother may be kind?"

Brother Meadows went to a small cupboard and removed one of only two dresses hanging on pegs. It was a simple, blue cotton that buttoned up the front. He handed it to Caroline and walked out of the room.

John touched her shoulder. "I need to help him explain to the children. I'll bring you water in a moment."

He closed the door on his way out, leaving her with a dead stranger. She shivered, wrapping her arms around herself. Of all she endured as a preacher's wife, this had to be the worst.

Laying the dress over a chair, she kept her eyes from the woman's face as she pulled back the covers, trying not to feel the impact of what she was doing. Unbuttoning the nightgown, she slowly worked it off one shoulder at a time. When she saw the swell of Sister Meadows' belly, she could no longer hold back her tears. A child, certainly now dead, must lie inches below the skin. Was this the cause of death? Caroline observed no blood as she continued to remove the undergarments.

A knock sounded. She opened the door a few inches as to not expose the naked woman on the bed.

John handed her a pitcher of warm water.

The heat of the water was for *her* benefit, as Sister Meadows surely wouldn't feel it. She said nothing, closed the door and went back to work by first pouring the water into the washbasin.

So as not to let her actions of washing a cold, dead body enter her thoughts, she imagined playing a piano concerto by Anton Rubinstein, which she'd been practicing the day before. She saw in her mind's eye what keys she'd play as she remembered the tune—repeating its melody over and over. Over and over—as she washed the woman gently.

Caroline finished with the woman's oily hair, then dried and styled it to frame her face. Once she was clothed in her blue dress, Caroline found a light blue ribbon draped over the mirror on the bureau and tied it around Sister Meadows' head. What was her name? Caroline wished she knew.

She couldn't help then but to look closely at the woman's face. She looked so young. Not much older than Caroline.

"Rest in peace, young mother," she whispered, then turned her mind to God and prayed for peace and comfort for the Meadows family.

It was almost dark by the time she and John left. Not wanting to have to come so far again for the burial, they'd done it this day. As Sammy pulled them away in the wagon, Caroline's body sagged in weariness. She laid her head on John's shoulder. "My heart breaks for that family. How do you see such things time and again?"

He looked to Ora sitting in her basket on the wagon floor.

The innocent child knew nothing of the day's events. She babbled a song between chewing on a rattle.

He smiled at her with the love of a father. "I remember my own blessings, and it helps get me through. I also believe the Meadows' reward will come in Heaven. God is just."

She wished she believed as John, but his statement struck her as naïve. "You'll think the worst of me, but I can't rightly feel God as you do. I do try, and I pray, but I can't tell if He's any part of my life."

"Keep searching. Trust you'll get answers. It doesn't come as easily to some as others. Look at your blessings and find gratitude in your heart. When you open your eyes to your blessings, you'll see the evidence of God's hand in your life."

She slid her arm into the crook of John's and squeezed. "One of my greatest blessings is you. Your goodness is the closest I can get to believing there *must* be a God. You're wise and gentle, which I trust comes from your own faith."

He put the reins in his left hand and set his right arm around Caroline's shoulders, pulling her to him. "Faith is an individual thing. I'd give you mine if I could, but you must build your own. Your heart is as good and kind as you think mine is. You'll be blessed with a testimony of God's presence someday, I'm sure of it."

CHAPTER TWENTY-EIGHT

March 11, 1862

Toting an armload of food, Caroline approached John as he packed his saddlebags with socks she'd knitted for Kit and George. He took the food and added it to the bags.

"Do you need to be gone so long?" she asked.

"With it being three days ride to Roanoke, it may even be longer than two weeks."

"Are you sure it's safe?" She was apprehensive about him going into Yankee territory.

"From everything I've heard, the Yankees want no more trouble there." He smiled reassuringly, tightening the bag's straps. "I'll go in the capacity of acting chaplain and see if there are needs I can attend. I've also heard there's a thriving colony of former slaves established on Roanoke Island. I'm curious if their colony is successful." John finished and turned. His eyes seemed eager for a positive comment from her.

Her stomach turned. What if those former slaves rose up and helped other slaves establish their own colonies? Which was the worst threat—freed Negroes or Yankees? "Are you sure you should go?" She couldn't shake the unease. "What if a band of Negroes come through this area and find me alone?"

"That won't happen. White men patrol, and if there were escaping slaves, they wouldn't be using the public road. They'd be hiding out in the woods, far from here." John rubbed her arm. "I wouldn't leave if I thought you'd be in danger. Besides, I'm anxious to see Kit and George along the way."

There was no use in arguing. "Please ask if there's anything else they may need other than socks. I do hope they have enough food."

"You're fretting too much." He hugged her briefly then double-checked the horse's straps.

"Promise you'll be careful." Her legs felt weak and she had a sudden need to sit down. "Wear your clergy garb at all times so there'll be no doubt who you are." She clenched her fists. "If the people back home hear of you helping former slaves, they'll shun us for sure." He often told her he didn't care what others thought. Well, she cared, and she wished that meant something to him.

"All will be fine." He smiled with one-dimple. "Josh will come mornings and evenings to milk the cow when he can and do some of the outside chores. Can you feed the chickens, tend to the garden, and finish what he can't?"

John's belief in no person being owned by another had repercussions. It meant each for his own—including his wife. She hated milking the cow. To make matters worse, she felt guilty about Joshua helping since his older brothers had gone off to war. He was now expected to milk his own family's cows and assist his mother with the horse ranch. Joshua often reassured her he was happy to help. He was a kind boy, raised in a good family. But she wished she could pay him for his services.

"I'll just have to be all right." She turned, anger bringing her chin up.

He caught her arm, pulling her to him. "I love you, dove. I'll be back before you know it." He kissed her head, and she relented, wrapping her arms tightly around him.

Rain had drummed constantly on the roof for three days after John left. The night before had brought even heavier rainstorms, but this afternoon was beautiful with brilliant, clear blue skies. A light breeze transported the scent of pine from the woods. How nice to have the front door open and the outbuildings and wooded areas washed clean.

After putting Ora down for a nap, Caroline found herself with little to do. Joshua had come and gone—the gardening done, dishes cleaned, and floors swept—which left her with a rare moment to read. In hopes of understanding John's convictions better, she picked up one of his books, *The Way of Holiness*, written by a woman. She had a hard time concentrating on the improbable idea of people obtaining perfection, the focus of the book, and her head kept nodding. Finally, she set the book aside and reclined into the rocker.

She awoke with a start to an unfamiliar, distant rumble vibrating the floor. Through the open front door, no storm clouds gathered, and the sky remained crystal blue. The sound couldn't have been thunder.

She listened intently.

It soon became obvious the rumble was the reverberation of galloping horses. That many horses meant . . . an army!

The hairs on the back of her neck rose as she walked out to the porch, her heartbeat matching the thudding horses' hooves.

A Confederate soldier on horseback, covered in mud up to his thighs, came into view—and then another and another—on the main road, only a hundred feet from her home.

The soldiers, now numbering six, reigned in their mounts and looked her way. The rumble of more horses grew louder.

Although she wanted to run back into the house, these men were her Southern soldiers, so she planted her feet and did what came naturally—she waved and meekly grinned.

Most took off their light blue or gray kepis and waved them back. The lead rider turned his horse toward his fellow soldiers and briefly spoke. She couldn't hear his words, but several soldiers nodded in affirmation. Five of them rode into the yard. One soldier remained on the road.

She grasped the porch railing.

The five rode close, almost into her flowerbed.

"Howdy, Ma'am." The lead soldier took off his hat again, his blue eyes dull with fatigue. When had he last slept? His blond hair, matted with sweat, was in need of a barber. Black smudges crossed his forehead and right cheek. "I'm Quartermaster Sergeant Abram Lane of the 26th North Carolina Regiment," the blue-eyed soldier informed her. "You probably haven't heard but New Bern's been taken by the enemy."

Caroline took a sharp breath, her midsection clenching. She knew so many people in New Bern. How could she find out if they were unharmed? She'd been told the 27th Regiment was in Pamlico. Could they have gone to New Bern to participate in the battle? Were Kit and George harmed? John would have never gone through New Bern to get to Roanoke, so she *had* to believe he was safe. Yet he said he'd stop to see Kit and George. She tightened her fingers on the rail. "I didn't know. Tell me more."

"They sailed up the Neuse River last night and attacked at about half past seven this morning." He pushed himself up by the saddle horn, practically standing in his saddle. "Also attacked along the railroad. After four hours of fighting we retreated. They had us outnumbered four to one. I'm sorry to tell you this, Ma'am, but most of us left in a hurry without food and supplies." He again shifted in his saddle.

He must be sore from the quick retreat from New Bern, fourteen miles distant.

Could she help these men?

"We need to rest and to water our horses. I see you have a well." He tilted his head toward the side yard. "The rest of our company is behind me and will be here any moment." He now yelled over the rumble of horse's hooves. "There could be as many as ninety of us, commanded by Colonel Zebulon Vance. Would you happen to have food to feed us?"

Stunned for a moment, her mouth went dry. "Yes . . . of course." She let go of the rail, her fingers tingling. She flexed them and called out, "I have a smoked ham and can make biscuits and—"

The rest was drowned in deafening hoof beats as the first of the 26th entered the clearing. Clumps of wet earth flew into the air with the approaching horses. Mud, gray uniformed soldiers, and horses filled her front yard.

It became obvious who Colonel Vance was. He came at the lead, flanked by two officers. Sergeant Lane nodded to him, and Colonel Vance brought his horse to a stop next to the first five riders. The men saluted each other.

"Colonel Vance, this kind woman has offered us ham and biscuits. Would you like to rest here for a meal, sir?" the sergeant asked.

"Thank you, Sergeant Lane. Yes, call a dismount, but keep the boys and their horses in the woods over yonder. The officers will retire in the house." He turned to Caroline. "Mighty kind of you, Ma'am. To whom do I owe thanks?"

"My name's Caroline Mattocks. I'm here alone with my baby while my husband, Reverend Mattocks, is acting as chaplain on Roanoke Island."

Colonel Vance dismounted, as did four officers near him. Sergeant Lane rode to the rest of the troops, calling out commands. Some of the men were injured, dried blood caked on their heads, limbs, and uniforms along with thick layers of mud. They looked to drop out of their saddles with weariness.

The officers entered her house, and she followed, listening for any noise alerting her to Ora's needs. Surprisingly, she'd slept through the arrival of Regiment 26. "Please, make yourselves at home, gentlemen."

The smell of wet wool and sweat emanated from uniforms.

Colonel Vance approached her. She'd read newspaper articles about him and admired his accomplishments. In 1858, at twenty-eight, he'd been the youngest member of Congress. She'd never seen him in person. His eyes a striking green, he was a big man with a full face, his dark brown hair amazingly thick—thicker even than John's. Considering his youth, his face displayed years of crucial decision-making. Four pronounced lines etched between his low eyebrows, giving him a scowling appearance, which his green eyes softened.

"I'm sorry to rush you, but we need to eat directly. We fear the Yankees are close behind."

Caroline tensed.

"I apologize if Sergeant Lane didn't alert you. We'll only take time to rest our horses and eat. Please, may we eat the ham cold?" Vance smiled slightly. "I'll call on my Commissary Sergeant, Mister Ferguson, to help you make the biscuits quickly."

She nodded and got to work.

The officers never sat. They conferred together in a circle by the window, continually looking toward the road.

As she worked in the kitchen, she listened for another rumble of an approaching army. She couldn't imagine they could sneak up on them, considering how loud the 26th had been in coming. She took deep breaths to calm her nerves.

She also kept an ear open to what the officers said.

They seemed to be trying to decide if it best to ride the main road to Kinston as quickly as possible or take slower, inconspicuous side roads. They talked about New Bern. She gleaned several prisoners were taken during battle. They tallied their wounded, dead, and missing. Often Sergeant Lane came to the door with more information. The name General Burnside was discussed more than once, and descriptions were exchanged about the Confederates blowing up their own military supplies and the Trent River Bridge.

Her heart dropped. What must New Bern look like? Surely citizens suffered. Such destruction and death she couldn't fathom. She prayed John was safe in Roanoke, far from New Bern.

Ora woke before Caroline had the biscuits completely rolled and cut.

"I can take it from here." The commissary sergeant tipped his head toward the crying baby. "I'm used to providing food for all these men."

In her bedchamber, Caroline had trouble nursing. She couldn't relax enough to let her milk drop. She wanted to believe they weren't in any immediate danger. After all, this was her opportunity to help the cause and show her loyalty to her southern soldiers. But what if the Yankees did follow Vance's regiment? How could she keep Ora safe if the battle landed at her front door?

Even though Ora didn't get much milk, sucking seemed to soothe her.

Caroline put her with small toys on the floor, out of the way in the kitchen corner.

The cook had already pulled biscuits from the oven and had gravy bubbling in a pan. "May we move your table outside?"

"Certainly. Let me get platters and a large bowl." Caroline arranged the cut meat and biscuits on her Staffordshire platters—which seemed ridiculous—but it was all she had big enough to serve the group. She poured the gravy into a large tureen.

The cook rang the dinner bell.

Men came out of the woods covered in dried mud, obviously tired as they moved toward the food. Some wore bandages on their heads, arms, or legs. Others limped or came in with the support of another. Only that morning they'd experienced bloodshed. Some perhaps had killed another human being. Maybe others had lost their comrades.

What would it entail to have Yankees living in New Bern? Would they soon have control over Pollocksville? Since the Confederate Army had retreated from New Bern, who would stand in the Union Army's way?

She picked up the plate of ham as two men came into the kitchen and carried out the rest of the food. The officers in the house ate standing at the piano, constantly watching out the window. Colonel Vance sat at John's desk, writing a letter.

Outside, she asked a few soldiers whether they knew if the 27th had fought in the battle. No one knew.

Only a little more than an hour passed from the time the army arrived until the time they left. Caroline stood once again on her porch, this time with Ora in her arms. Her yard and the road were strewn with mud clods. It would be a bumpy mess when it dried. She was too tired to do anything about it. The stress of the situation had frazzled her nerves and left her weary.

The war had made it home. To her home. And for the first time, Caroline understood what it meant to be alone and vulnerable. She wrapped her arms tightly around Ora. She needed John home. She needed to know he was safe and unharmed. And she needed him to keep her and Ora safe too.

CHAPTER TWENTY-NINE

March 15, 1862

The Union troops never came, but Caroline still didn't sleep well. She hoped Colonel Vance and his men were far from enemy hands. She anticipated Joshua would bring her news, but he didn't appear in the morning. Weary of the cow mooing in discomfort, she milked it.

Later that morning, sitting in the rocker darning John's sock, Caroline poked her finger with the needle for the third time. "Oh, Jehoshaphat!"

Ora crawled over, seemingly curious about the yarn balls in the basket. As she played with them, her soft baby sounds blended nicely with the birds singing in the yard. Other than "Mama" and a few simple words, she couldn't talk, but her smiles and cooing were enough to lighten Caroline's heart.

The moments of contentment weren't lost on her. She sent a prayer of thanksgiving to God as John kept reminding her to do.

As she darned, she sang "The Old North State." Her chest swelled with patriotic loyalty.

Ora clapped her hands and wiggled to the melody. She crawled to Caroline's skirts and pulled herself to standing, patting Caroline's knees. "Up, Mama."

"Of course, my sweet baby." The two rocked until Ora fell asleep, then Caroline laid her daughter in the infant bed John had made.

It appeared Joshua wouldn't be coming at all, so she tied on her bonnet and went to do chores. Although there'd been a lot of recent rain, a smattering of dogwood blooms still hung on the trees, the white blossoms against the distant green woods a sign of spring. Descending the porch steps, she delighted in the pinks and purples of the azaleas and rhododendrons she'd planted, wishing this country house was hers.

In the garden, tiny green shoots of vegetables peeked above ground. Proud of her hard work, she still had a twinge of embarrassment about doing the gardening herself. Unlatching the gate, she pulled a few small weeds. The roots easily released their hold from the soft ground. The pleasant smell of damp earth promised life. She stared at the mud on her hands, knowing it would have never been there before she married John.

Loud, sharp tweets from the chickens told Caroline they were hungry. Retrieving the feedbag from the barn, the smell of fresh hay and warm cow dung stung her nose. Fat Chance looked her way and mooed her acceptance of the intrusion.

"I'll see to you in a moment," she said, hoping if she waited long enough Joshua would come muck the barn.

About twenty feet past the garden, the old, raised chicken coop leaned to one side. She supposed it had once been painted white, but there were few patches of paint left. The wood had splintered and peeled. She couldn't figure out why the previous owners had put it so close to the edge of the woods, vulnerable to wild animals. She didn't want to give her own feast to a fox, so one of the first things she was fixing to buy in town were materials to build a new coop. If they could spare the money, she wanted to buy more chicks from Mr. Watson too. She'd heard he had the best Rhode Island Reds, yielding seven eggs a week. She only hoped he still had chicks to sell. She'd heard they'd become scarcer and more expensive since the war started.

After feeding the chickens, she noticed flowers on the wild strawberry plants behind the house. Removing her bonnet, she bent closer. Tiny yellowish-green starts of fruit poked from their centers.

A rustling noise from the distant woods a few hundred yards past the front of the house caught her attention. Before she could fully straighten, a rifle shot rang out.

Ora! Caroline dropped her bonnet and ran around the house, toward the front door, which also was in the direction of the repercussion. She hardly took three steps before a tall boy in Yankee blues backed out of the woods. He hadn't yet seen her.

Another soldier in blue, not far behind the first, moved toward the house.

She changed course and ran toward the well and its high walls, where she dropped to the ground. Crouched behind the moist rock, she peeked out.

The men, with rifles pointed forward, ran toward her home.

She lost sight of them as they thumped up the steps. "I'm a Federal soldier, and you're all under house arrest," one of them shouted.

The thought of Ora alone with armed Yankees nearly made Caroline faint. Her mind foggy, she shook her head to clear it. With a wave of nausea, bile came to her throat. *Please God, don't let them harm my baby.* Swallowing the bitter bile, she thought hard and quickly about what to do.

She stood and lifted her skirts high, running as soundlessly as she could around the strawberry bushes. She stopped at the back corner of the house and looked out at the front yard. Seeing no one, she ran toward the barn.

With heartbeats pounding in her ears, sweat collected under her arms and down her back. Breathing hard, it took a moment to adjust her eyes to the darkness of the barn.

Fat Chance mooed her complaint at having yet another intrusion.

Caroline whispered, "Hush!"

Her hand shook as she snatched an axe leaning against the wall by a shovel. It felt heavier than she'd expected. When had John sharpened it last?

Heart flying as fast as hummingbird wings, she tiptoed back to the barn's opening. Were those men even now taking Ora from her bed?

Holding her breath, she kept her body behind the partially open barn door, leaning out enough to get a view of the side of the house, part of the porch, and what she could see of the front yard.

No one in sight. No sound.

I'm coming Ora. Caroline brought the axe flat against her chest as she quietly ran toward the side steps of the porch. She stopped, lifted the blade over her head and soundlessly placed her foot on the first step, then the next.

"Aah!" A stinging, sharp puncture into the flesh of her back brought her to a standstill.

"Drop the axe, or I'll gore you like a pig."

Caroline nearly fell to the ground with fear as the bayonet tip pushed farther in, burying itself into layers of flesh. The pain seared. A warm trickle of blood oozed down her back. The axe fell with a thud.

"Don't turn 'round. Let's git ourselves into your cozy little home. I bet you know how to make a man comfortable." He laughed a high snicker. "I've heard you Southern Belles are very hospitable."

The man sliced down her back another fraction and then backed the bayonet tip out of her flesh. She gasped at the sting. With the bloody and menacing bayonet now near her face, she somehow willed her legs to move.

"How come I always git the slow, stupid women?"

She gritted her teeth. The door, ten paces away, seemed to be a mile. She briefly registered the birds still sang their songs, the flowers held their blooms, and the sun was as bright and warm as when she first stepped outside moments before. How could the world turn up-side-down so quickly? She was in some kind of nightmare. Her body trembled uncontrollably.

"Hey Nate, I found the mother of that babe." They stepped into the house, he threw her bonnet at the feet of the man he called Nate, who stood by her rocker.

Nate's dark hair was plastered to his sweaty forehead, his face young, maybe only sixteen or seventeen. His startling blue eyes were fixed on Caroline. "Where'd you find her, Frank?"

Frank lowered the bayonet and stepped to her side. His sour stench stung her nostrils. He looked down at her like she was a woman of the streets. As ugly as the hog Mister Frazar used to parade around town, his face and uniform were brown with filth. "Spied her coming out of the barn with an axe. She ain't no genteel southern lady like we been hearin' 'bout. 'Speck she would have chopped you into pieces if I didn't have your back." He laughed another high snicker and spit tobacco juice onto Caroline's hand-tied Persian rug, a wedding gift from Julia, and one of the few nice things she had in the house. "You need a spittoon in this dump, lady."

Nate sneered at Frank. She surmised the two weren't the best of friends.

"Did you kill that Reb in the woods?" Nate asked.

"I did." Frank stood a little taller, sticking out his chest. Underneath his filth lurked something restless and dangerous. "Easier than spit. You know I can't miss. Stop jabberin'. We need to make a plan. Let's say you stay here and have tea and cakes with the missus while I go find our troops. This place looks as good as any to set for a spell." Frank brought his gun upright, examining Caroline's blood on the bayonet. He wiped it across his thigh. The bright red mixed with grime of who knows how many days of battle and living outdoors.

The sight of her blood weakened her knees.

Nate instantly stepped forward to offer a hand.

Frank roughly pushed her sideways. "Sit on that sofa and don't move a muscle. Nate may be sweet on the ladies, but he'll kill Confederate baby-makers if he has a mind to."

Caroline crumpled sideways onto the settee and stared at Nate, fearful the boy would kill her. She suddenly realized he may have hurt Ora. "Is my baby all right?"

Nate's eyebrows rose in surprise. "We didn't touch the sleeping babe."

"Quit bein' all-fired worked up." Frank took a step toward Nate. "I'll gather the horses and bring yours in before goin' for the troops. You sit tight and guard our prisoner."

Nate scowled at Frank. "Just hurry up. Captain ain't gonna be singing your praises while waiting on us. He's hoping to catch up with them Rebs before sundown."

Frank turned to Caroline. "Where's your man?"

Caroline's midsection constricted. Should she tell them the truth? If they knew he was over a hundred miles away, they may feel inclined to take advantage of her and kill Ora. If she told them he was close by, working the turpentine stills, they might leave and go hunting for him, only to discover she'd lied and come back to kill her.

Frank pinched up his face in impatience, and looked even uglier, his wide nostrils flaring. "Well? Is he a Reb out killin' my brothers?"

"He left yesterday to purchase supplies in town," she lied, tucking her shaking hands under her skirt.

"That buys us most the day then. I'm outta here." Frank stomped out the open door and down the steps.

Nate walked to the rocker, removed his blue hat and sat, placing his hat on his lap.

Caroline wished she knew his thoughts as he gazed at her. They said nothing for a good five minutes while she glanced about the room, looking at everything but him. She slowly brought her breathing to normal.

Had this young boy enlisted in the war to save the slaves, as the Yankees were claiming, but John didn't believe? "Would you kill me to save a black man?"

Nate's eyes widened with surprise. He leaned back in the rocker and crossed his legs. His expression became friendly, quizzical. Had he been raised by a mother who loved him? "I never entered the army to kill women—nor men for that matter, although I knew I'd probably have to someday. A friend persuaded me to join. He said they needed trackers, and he knew I was the best in Franklin County. Plus, I needed the pay."

Still leaning forward to keep her injury from the settee, she shifted her weight and sat slowly upright. Her back burned where the bayonet had sliced her flesh.

"Frank's too stupid, but even at a run, I noticed many horse and boot tracks in your front yard. Want to explain those to me?"

Not about to put her southern men in danger, she shifted her eyes toward his rifle leaning against the fireplace hearth. "My husband was working to tame a wild horse yesterday."

Nate's eyes never left her. "I s'pose I'd want my wife, if I had one, to lie for me."

Caroline stared at the space between them and clasped her hands on her lap.

"How many hours ahead of us are they?" he asked.

"I don't know what you mean." She moved her eyes to her lap.

"I told you, I'm a tracker. I followed the signs to your house. The tracks weren't just in your yard, I saw remnants of small campfires inside the tree line. I also noticed plenty of horse manure. I know the Rebs were here. All you need to tell me is how many hours ago they left."

"You must be mistaken."

Nate harrumphed. "Makes no difference anyway. I know which way they went, and I know we'll eventually catch 'em."

The room fell silent, and she shifted to remove pressure off her back.

"Did he wound you deeply?"

His question seemed sincere, but she wasn't about to give him reason to see her wound, even though she had no idea how she'd attend to it herself. "The blood feels like its drying."

"Good. I can't let you out of my sight." His words weren't spoken harshly.

"How long do you think your friend will be gone?"

Nate grimaced. "He's not my friend. The horses are close . . . in the woods. He'll bring mine in and then go for the regiment . . . about forty minutes away, outside Pollocksville."

What horrors was she to experience with enemy soldiers in her home? She didn't suspect herself in danger with Nate, but Frank would be coming back with perhaps many more of his sleazy breed.

Last time she'd been in town at Harget's Store, she'd overheard women whispering about Yankees who were probably much like Frank. The ladies had shared stories of what they'd heard happened to some women in Virginia—how they'd been treated as women of the town. The ravished women were afraid to report that Yankees physically knew them because a woman's virtue represented her most valued asset. Carnal assault to them was a fate worse than death, so they'd kept it hidden from their own men.

Caroline's heart quickened with the memory. *Dear Lord, please protect me.*

Nate stretched, pushed his legs out straight, boot tips up, head tilted back. He obviously didn't see Caroline as a threat, and it was hard for her at that moment to see him as intimidating.

She glanced again at the rifle leaning against the hearth. If she moved quickly enough, she could grab it before he got to his feet. She dismissed the thought. She couldn't shoot a man—not to mention she'd never handled a rifle in her life. She resigned herself to the fact this day would be a repeat of the day before but much worse. She needed to focus on keeping herself and Ora out of the way of the soldiers. "How long will your regiment be here? I don't have much food."

Without changing his reclined position, Nate answered, "They'll likely want your well to water themselves and the horses. We'll help ourselves to whatever hay you might have. If your husband's been workin' with horses, *as you say*, I'm sure you'll have plenty. I did hear your cow awhile back. Some fresh milk in coffee would be mighty nice. What's in your cellar?"

It would do no good to lie. No matter what she said, he or another soldier would inspect her cellar soon enough. "I have about a dozen jars of peaches and various vegetables, a small barrel of pecans, wheat, small bag of coffee, some dried corn, a few onions."

"No meat?"

She sighed, fearing it all but gone once the soldiers arrived. "Slabs of salted pork."

Hooves sounded in the yard. Nate sat up, put on his hat, and stood. "That you, Frank?" His loud voice awakened Ora, who cried out.

"It's me. Just stay put. I'll stable your horse with some feed and be on my way to fetch the Cap'n and the men."

Caroline stood. "I need to get my baby."

"I'll come with you." He walked to the hearth, picked up his gun, cradling it in the crook of his arm then followed her into the bedchamber.

A stranger entering her room seemed too intimate—wrong in sense and propriety. Her shoulders tightened, the hairs on her neck rose, but she could think of no excuse to keep him out. She walked to the small infant bed in the corner, her hands shaking as she picked up Ora. She turned quickly to leave, but found herself within inches of Nate, close enough to feel his breath. He was taller than John and young enough to hardly have whiskers.

His mouth pinched. "No need to be in a rush. Your babe won't calm her cryin' if you get all worked up."

"Excuse me, but I need to change the baby's nappy." When Nate stepped away, she took a deep breath and tried to calm her trembling.

"'Spose I'll just wait right here by the door."

An hour later, the earth pounding with horses' hooves. The mud now dry, rose into the air as they arrived. Metal clanking of canteens, swords, and rifle bayonets mixed with the sounds of horses and men's voices. A wagon rattled by and stopped in the backyard. Commands were barked, men dismounted, and the enemy surrounded her house.

CHAPTER THIRTY

Holding Ora on her hip, Caroline watched the soldiers from the front window.

Nate had gone to meet with his superiors. Dust floated from the recent arrival of what she guessed to be more than eighty men in blue. Soldiers moved through the trees at the edge of the woods. She assumed they were collecting evidence from where the Confederates had camped the day before or looking for the body of the man Frank had shot. She prayed it wasn't anyone she knew. As much as she hated having Yankees in and around her home, she hoped it gave the Southern Army more time to evade them.

The insanity of the war struck her again. Men hunting each other like animals. Americans killing Americans. For years, Southerners felt pressured and threatened by Northern control to give up their lifestyles. Distrust for the Yankees hadn't started with the war. But to kill them for it? She shifted Ora from her right hip to her left. The muscles in her back twinged with pain from her wound.

Boots sounded on the steps then across her porch.

She stiffened with anticipation.

Four men in well-decorated blue uniforms entered. The enemy looked remarkably similar to the soldiers she'd seen yesterday. Whiskered faces and weary eyes.

Ora whimpered and clung tightly to Caroline's neck.

The highest-ranked officer brazenly stared into her face. Young, a dark beard blanketed only his jaw, and his immaculately combed hair fell in curls covering his ears. Two rows of large, brightly shining gold buttons ran all the way from his slender waist to his high collared neck. A dandy. He gave his name and rank. "I serve under the command of General Ambrose Burnside. My scout reported your husband is in town getting supplies. Is this the truth?"

Caroline's throat felt as dry as sawdust. "Yes."

Two of the officers moved to either side of her. Although she didn't take her eyes from the captain, she was well aware of how close they stood. Did they think she'd do harm to their officer? Or run?

"What kind of supplies is he buying?"

"Feed for the horse." As much as she hated lying, she wouldn't tell him the truth no matter how high ranking or intimidating he may be.

"When do you expect him home?" The captain stood extraordinarily stiff.

Did they plan to wait for John's return?

"I'm not sure." She looked to the door and hesitated too long. "Today . . . or tomorrow sometime."

The captain narrowed his eyes. "I was under the impression the town was only a few hours ride."

Her heart sped up. "It's half a day's ride. He went to Swansboro. He also had clerical duties to attend to while in town." Her stomach roiled, but she kept her face expressionless.

"He's a preacher?"

Had she said too much? "Yes."

"A chaplain for the South?" The captain didn't relax his regal pose, looking as if he should be entertaining important guests on a veranda rather than standing in Caroline's small home, interrogating a mother holding a babe.

"No."

"Do you expect anyone else to arrive at your home today?"

"No." *Please God, don't let Josh come.*

His shoulders dropped a fraction. He looked at Ora. It was the first time he took his eyes from Caroline since entering the room, but he just as quickly looked back. "We'll bind you if you try to leave. My men fought at New Bern and need to rest and be fed. We have some food but need more. We'll help ourselves to your cellar and camp here tonight."

Worry about feeding her family made her want to beg him to leave the food alone. But she couldn't bring herself to beseech this highborn. Right now, she needed to get through this. She'd fret about food later.

"The officers will sleep in your home. I'll use your bedchamber. We can move your baby's needs into the kitchen where you'll sleep on a cot. We'll not hurt you—if you do as *I say.*"

She considered bringing up the fact that Frank had already hurt her but had no desire to further the conversation.

"My scout tells me there are signs that an army camped here as recently as last night. Who were they?"

His intense stare made her wonder how many lies she could get away with. Would he read the truth on her face? Sweat trickled down her back. "I don't know." She gazed again at his rows of gold buttons, each one embossed with an eagle, wings outstretched.

"This would be a lot easier for both of us if you'd be honest. It surprises me how easily a preacher's wife can lie."

The statement stung, but she refused to let her guilt put her husband and soldiers in the way of danger. She stood taller. "There may have been men in the forest last night, I don't rightly know. I retired early and heard not a sound."

His mouth pulled back and eyes narrowed. "How long has your husband been away?"

"He left yesterday afternoon."

"Not a wise man, this preacher of yours, leaving his wife and babe alone with war at his doorstep."

"I dare say he wouldn't have left if he'd realized the war had actually come to his doorstep." She didn't like the man's banter and his speech was so foreign—fast and not as relaxed as the men she knew who drew out their vowels.

"I have an idea he's been gone a lot longer than a day. If my men discover he's a Rebel, I cannot be responsible for what happens to you."

Hate welling inside, she narrowed her eyes and brought Ora into a protective embrace. "I'm telling the truth. He's a preacher and has gone to town for his duties and supplies."

The captain shook his head and looked at her as if she were a child. "Do you own slaves?"

She didn't expect the question, relieved she could give a truthful answer. "No. My husband's beliefs include that no man should be bound to another."

"Ah, that's right. He's a man of the Bible. I'm glad to hear it. We'll consider that in our treatment of you." Blessedly, he walked away with his entourage.

A bang against the house alerted her to soldiers opening the cellar door. A joyous shout of, "Soap! She's got soap!" Then cheers hollered around the camp.

Soon four men brought two large wooden tubs into the kitchen and directed Caroline to wash their laundry. She used her stove to heat water. Men stood guard at the kitchen doorway as she stirred the clothes with a wooden paddle in the tub of hot, soapy water. She kneeled and scrubbed their filthy garments. After washing the clothes, she used the paddle to lift them into another tub of clear water. Once she had as much soap rinsed out as possible, she wrung and laid them in a heap on the floor. The caustic soap created raw sores on her hands. Her cuticles broke open and bled. Julia would have swooned at the sight. In exhaustion, she collapsed to the floor.

"Get up, here comes more." A guard motioned with his gun for her to rise.

Five soldiers walked in, one dumping a mound of begrimed clothes at her feet. The others took the heavy tubs outside and dumped the filthy water off the side of the porch into her flowerbeds. She cringed. The new spring flowers would be destroyed.

She repeated the process. The piles of clean, wet garments were occasionally gathered by Yankees and taken outside to hang on lines haphazardly strung from her porch posts across the yard to the barn door hinges.

She hadn't been allowed to rest or leave the house. She felt the work of the day in every muscle, and still her wound hadn't been tended. No one even commented on the blood that surely must show on her back. Her movements sometimes pulled the fabric from the laceration, tearing open the cut, causing fresh, warm blood to trickle down.

Silent, she listened to what fragments of conversation she could as soldiers walked near her window or stood in her front room.

They complained of their conditions or reminisced of home. Some talked of what kind of food they'd eat once the war was over. Mostly they exulted in their victory at New Bern.

There was resentment in their voices as they discussed having suffered one embarrassing defeat after another, starting at Bull Run the year before. Puffed-up with his invincibility, the captain bragged how he'd make the South bow to his threats.

For the most part, other than the soldiers who helped with the laundry or brought in wood for the stove's fire, they kept their distance, and she did the same.

Eventually she needed to use the privy and approached the nearest soldier standing guard at the kitchen door. He was older than most the soldiers and stood with a sway to his back.

"I need to use the privy."

"Come with us." He swung his rifle off his shoulder and nodded to another Yank, who did the same. Escorted, they marched her across the yard.

"Ain't she a beaut?" A man leered at her.

Others turned away, unconcerned, while still others whistled and made snide remarks.

Her privy had been used by so many men, she feared she'd swoon at the stench. She covered her nose with her sleeve and did her business privately, then was marched back to her kitchen.

On her knees, she peered into the front room as she scrubbed clothes along the washboard.

The officers seemed hypersensitive, rarely sitting, and often huddled quietly, making plans. They wouldn't sit to eat their meals, but stood at the piano, just as Colonel Vance and his officers had done. It took all her willpower to not walk over and place doilies under their drinks, saving her lovely piano top from water rings. Instead, she scrubbed, tears mixing with the filthy laundry water.

Although the officers claimed to be in pursuit of their enemies, they acted as if they were being pursued themselves. More than once she heard the words "ambush" and "trap." Did Confederates follow them after all? The question alarmed her. If they caught up with the Yankees at her home, how would she keep Ora safe? There was no place to hide. Would her Southern men know she and Ora were inside and vulnerable? The thoughts of bloodshed, brutality, and murder in her home and on her land heightened her hearing as she listened for an approaching army—her nerves on edge.

How far into the countryside had the Yankees gone? Could her family be suffering the same kind of ordeal? Was John safe? She became so agitated with worries that she feared she'd vomit. Her head throbbed in pain, as did her hands. With a wet hand, she brushed hair from her eyes and looked at Ora.

Although now crawling, she'd stayed near Caroline's side throughout the day, seemingly fearful of the loud men.

"How's my baby?" She hoped that talking in quiet, comforting tones she could comfort them both.

With a ragdoll's arm in her mouth, using it as a teether, she smiled, softening Caroline's heart, and she chided herself for fretting over the piano and home. Ora and John were the real possessions of her heart.

Near dusk, the soldiers cooked food outside, bringing her a bowl of bland and tasteless mush. Although men took what was left in her cellar, it wasn't served that evening. Was it to later satisfy the officers?

Would she and Ora starve before anyone came to help them?

CHAPTER THIRTY-ONE

That night, Caroline lay in her filthy dress on a cot near the kitchen window, listening to the snores, vaporous gases, and groans of sleeping men. By her side, Ora slept in her infant bed.

The heavy smells of perspiration, dirt, and gunpowder permeated her home. No one visibly guarded her, but sentries stood somewhere nearby. If she snuck out with Ora and ran, she'd be putting them in more danger.

The officers had stopped their pacing late in the evening and were now sound asleep. There was probably something she didn't understand—perhaps it was safe enough for her to sleep too? Had they received word there was no evidence of a pursuing army? She finally took her weary body into consideration and tried to get comfortable on the cot that had a fetid odor of filthy men.

She must have slept because her eyes were closed when she became aware of sounds from outside. Pans thumped, tin cups clanged, and people moved about the yard. She quickly sat up and immediately regretted the action. Her dress tore from her wound and opened a fresh split in her flesh. She slumped, breathing deeply until the worst of the pain subsided, then went to stand at her kitchen doorway.

In the first light of early morning, she watched the sleeping men. Two were on cots, one on her settee with his legs dangling off the end, two others on blanket rolls on the floor.

Turning back into the kitchen, she peered into the infant bed, surprised Ora was awake with a smile.

Caroline's heart constricted, and she breathed a sigh of relief that some things were constant. Ora reached up and babbled, and Caroline envied her innocence as she turned her back to the room and nursed her baby without interruption.

To her amazement, the soldiers were fed, packing, and leaving by the time the clock struck seven. Unwashed stacks of dishes towered next to the basin. Glancing out the window, she didn't see Nate amongst the soldiers. She hadn't seen him since the morning before.

Ora fussed at her feet, and she handed her a clean wooden bowl and spoon to play with. Her baby noises became melodic. If Caroline stayed in Ora's sights, she held up well.

Boots sounded on the steps. The captain stood stiffly in full uniform, hat in hand, his face expressionless. "We'll be leaving. Don't try to get to your neighbors or warn anyone of our whereabouts. We'll find your cowardly Rebs, you can be sure."

She sensed hollowness to his character. What a sorry man. Who knew what deaths he'd caused among her friends in New Bern. For the first time she wanted to spit on someone. "I understand."

He tipped his head, put his hat on, and walked out the front door without closing it.

With her hands in soapy water, she watched from her window as privates held the officers' horses ready, and they mounted and rode off. Most of the regiment followed, but some soldiers milled about the yard, took down tents, folded small wooden chairs, and loaded everything onto their backs or the few horses that remained.

After another twenty minutes, the dishes were done, and the cook gathered his pans and utensils, loading them onto his wagon.

It was then she saw Fat Chance tied to the back and her chickens in crates on the wagon bed. Her heart sank, tears coming to her eyes. She swiped them away, chiding herself for crying over farm animals.

The wagon swayed out of her yard in the same direction the others had gone. Fat Chance gave no resistance.

A group of five men talked with their heads close together, occasionally glancing about. One of the men was Frank.

She flinched. Why had he not gone on ahead as a scout? The wound on her back ached where his sword had entered.

The soldiers nodded and dispersed, three walking toward her house, two toward the barn.

She clutched the rim of the basin, her mind blank as to a plan of escape. With no one to call out to for help, she turned to God. *Don't let these evil men hurt us.*

Frank's smell entered the kitchen before he did. The sour stench of his body odor and chewing tobacco nauseated her. "You been playin' housemaid for the Cap. How does it feel to have a Massa?"

Forcing herself to let go of the sink's edge, she turned to face him.

He sneered, his cheek bulging from tobacco.

Adrenaline pulsed through her veins, giving her an unexpected sense of power. "Get out of my house."

Frank snorted.

"Shouldn't you be scouting ahead of your regiment?"

He took a step closer. "It's someone else's turn today." He winked and took another step. "Come now. Fairs, fair. I jus' wanna git a little piece of ya." He sniggered, his yellow teeth in various forms of decay. Tobacco juice squeezed out of his mouth, running down his chin.

Fear pushed her back against the sink. "Leave me alone." The confidence in her voice wavered. She quickly glanced to Ora, relieved she lay asleep in the opposite corner of the kitchen.

"This will be a lot easier if ya hold still." Frank slid his arm around Caroline, pinning her arms to her sides. The fingers of his other hand grasped her neck.

She tried to scream, but he pushed his thumb hard into her throat. She couldn't breathe. She twisted, trying to free herself.

He held her tight against his hard body and moaned in pleasure.

She brought her knee up with as much force as she could but missed and hit him in the thigh. Her teeth, however, found their mark as she bit his ear. The metallic, salty taste of blood made her gag.

Frank howled and pushed her away.

She fell hard onto her backside, narrowly missing Ora, who woke and wailed.

Caroline expected Frank to jump on her and rolled left, away from the baby, spitting his blood on the floor, struggling to get up—her skirts tangling around her legs. Turning to face him once again, she discovered Nate had entered and had Frank in a chokehold, a knife at his side. Blood ran from his ear onto Nate's sleeve.

With rage in his eyes, Frank pulled at Nate's arm. He couldn't free himself. Face red, his bloodshot eyes watered. Tobacco fell from his gaping mouth in a clump on the floor. Reddish-brown juice trickled from his chin onto Nate's shirtsleeve, mixing with the blood.

"You're killing him," Caroline screamed.

Nate pulled Frank backward, dragging him out of the house, still holding the knife to his side. "Stop struggling," he told Frank. "Or *I will* kill you."

She followed.

Frank stilled—his face blue, eyes bulging. Was he dead?

Before Nate could pull him down the steps, two soldiers ran from behind. One put a bayonet to Nate's back. "Release him."

Nate dropped Frank, who slumped to the porch with a thud.

"Is he breathing, Hank?" the man with the bayonet asked.

Hank laid his head on Frank's tobacco stained chest. "Yeah, he's breathin'."

"Drag him out to the yard and git him on his horse. We better git outta here."

Hank dragged the unconscious Frank down the steps, and Nate inclined his head toward the soldier who held him. "You kill me, and the Captain will kill you. You know I'm his best tracker."

"And how's the Cap'n gonna know who killed ya if he can't find a body?"

"Frank's not worth killing over," Nate said calmly, as if he wasn't seconds away from being gored.

"Now that might be the truth." The soldier grunted. "But maybe I want to kill you just to kill."

Nate shrugged. "It's your neck that'll hang."

"Stop talkin' and start walkin' toward the barn."

With the bayonet at his back, Nate did as he was told.

Startled by Ora's cry, Caroline ran back into the house.

Two men came out of her bedchamber with feathers drifting in the air around them, stuck on their hair and uniforms. They looked at one another and laughed.

"What are you doing?" she asked, confused.

Their laughter cut short. "Hey, where's Frank? We expected you two to be havin' a little fun." One laughed again, the other picked feathers off his comrade. "You ain't gonna have a soft bed to sleep on no more lady." They both guffawed.

Caroline's mind reeled. She wasn't sure if she was in danger with these buffoons and suspected their fun was anything but humorous. All the while Ora howled her discomfort.

"What have you done to my bed?" Caroline's fright was evident in her shrill words.

"We figured, why should Rebs have a feather bed to sleep on when we're sleepin' on the ground."

She wanted to crumple to the floor and cry. Instead, she threw them a look of disgust and left to get Ora.

The poor baby had wailed so hard she was gulping in breaths, her little body shaking.

As Caroline picked her up, she glimpsed the lump of tobacco and blood on the floor. Dizziness overtook her. She faltered with Ora in her arms and leaned against the wall. As much as she hated to interact with the two soldiers still in her home, she had no place to sit but the front room. She staggered into the room and sat in her rocker, her entire body trembling.

The soldiers had moved to her china cabinet.

Pressing her cheek against Ora's head, she closed her eyes and rocked. *Please God, help us survive this madness. And if I can help Nate, put it clearly in my mind what to do.*

"Hey, lady. Ya wouldn't mind us takin' your purty china, would'cha?" They collected dishes and vases, caring little that she was in the room, and stepped out the front door.

She felt no attachment to any of her previously cherished china. If the men left Ora and her in peace, she'd gladly give it away.

Another soldier entered her home and rolled-up the Persian rug at her feet. "This will make dandy saddle blankets."

Gunshots and shattering china made Caroline jump.

Ora screamed.

And the Yankee hefted the rug on his shoulder and walked out.

She rocked and prayed while the men outside hollered and laughed as time and again, they played target practice with her china.

The soldier who'd taken the rug returned and left again with her nicest gowns. She realized her jewelry and silver brush set had probably also disappeared. From her collar, she unpinned the gold brooch John had given her as an engagement gift and quietly slipped it into her pocket.

After about ten minutes, the gunshots stopped. Men talked, but she couldn't make out what they said over Ora's whimpering. Something was dragged through the yard, then the horsemen rode off.

She sat another five minutes or so, waiting to hear any other sounds. Could they have left? Was it over? Ora had stopped crying, her breathing returned to normal, but Caroline still quaked. Her throat hurt where Frank had squeezed. Taking a few deep breaths, she placed Ora on the floor and walked slowly to the open door.

The yard was empty of soldiers and their gear. Her flowers were limp or crushed, the ground covered in sparkling blue and white china shards. Downy feathers stuck in deep horse hoof and wagon track indentations. Her china vases sat on the edge of the porch, picked full of holes.

Tears flooded Caroline's eyes and she collapsed onto the porch. She sobbed deep, throat-scratching laments. It was madness. She'd lost her mind—with no one to help her find sanity.

She laid on the hard, wooden planks a long time before Ora crawled onto her back, putting pressure on the wound. She didn't bother to move the baby. The pain seemed meaningless.

"Mama." Ora's little arms tried to reach around her.

Caroline's heart swelled with love, and her tears became quieter. Rolling gently to her side, she let Ora slide slowly to the porch, where she pushed herself up by using Caroline's shoulder.

Too weak to stand, Caroline sat and reached for Ora. "Come here, baby."

Ora willingly went into her arms.

"What are we going to do now?" she asked Ora, who had no answers.

CHAPTER THIRTY-TWO

March 16, 1862

Caroline's raw hands stung as she washed off as much blood as she could reach on her back. Holding a hand mirror, she looked in its reflection in the bureau mirror, grimacing at the sight of her back covered in dried blood and the straight, open cut at least three inches long, swollen and oozing a yellow liquid. She couldn't quite touch the wound, but the skin near it felt hot.

Years ago, when Benny fell off a wagon onto a plow blade, he'd had a similar wound. Mama had made him a poultice of garlic, purple coneflower, and goldenseal. But it was too early in the year for any of the ingredients to be harvested.

Dressed in an old but clean chemise, skirt, and shirtwaist, she dumped the bloodied water from her bedchamber window, then refilled the washbasin with warm water. Lifting Ora from the pile of feathers she played in, she bathed and dressed her.

The Yankees had left nothing in her cellar. Needing help and food, she started her trek to Ben and Molly Hill's horse ranch with Ora in her arms. She'd visited them on a few occasions but had always traveled by wagon roads. She estimated their home a few hour's walk if she were to avoid the main road and any Yankee armies. Ora's weight added to her exhaustion from lack of sleep, manual labor, and worry. Yet she stopped to rest for only short periods, hoping to get to the Hill's and back before dark.

Ora slept more than usual, but occasionally whimpered, "Hungwee, Mama." Caroline tried to nurse her, but she had little milk. She needed food.

Sunlight filtered through tree branches. The damp smell of fallen pine needles reminded her of White Oak Plantation. Was her family safe? They were far from New Bern, but she had no way of knowing how distant the battles of occupation had reached. She wasn't sure if her mother was at the country plantation or in town.

She heard the Hill children long before she saw them. When she came into the clearing of their horse ranch, two blonde sisters played at tossing stones into a bucket. A redhead girl stood by the smokehouse, and Joshua worked at a distance in one of the horse corrals, the copper tones of his hair glowing in the sun.

The two girls stopped their game and ran to Caroline, their faces clean, hair pulled into braids, hems dusty. "How-do, Sister Mattocks. Did you come to visit Ma?" the oldest girl asked.

"Is she home?"

"She's over yonder in the barn." She pointed toward the massive brown building on the far side of the property. Further from the barn were paddocks with a few grazing horses.

"Is your father here abouts?"

"He and Uncle Dan took horses to Jacksonville and won't be back 'til to'mora," the smallest girl answered. Ben wasn't an enlisted soldier but was often away from home supplying troops with fresh horses.

Caroline gazed toward the barn and hesitated, apprehensive about asking for food and medical attention.

The oldest girl cocked her head. "Can we help you some?"

Caroline quelled her misgivings. "Would one of you mind getting your Ma? Could might another take Ora and me into the house. We need to sit a spell."

"Charity, ya run and git Ma."

The smaller girl ran off toward the barn while the bigger one took the baby.

As they walked toward the house, Caroline's stomach rumbled so loudly she was sure the girl heard.

Moments later, Caroline held a cold glass of water as she sat facing the open door.

The sun behind silhouetted Molly in the doorframe. "Caroline, nice to have you visit. What brings you to us today?" Stray pieces of hay covered her brown work dress. As usual, the bun on her head flopped to the side. Strands of gray hair had pulled themselves free, hanging around her face, while others floated in the air. Raised with all brothers, Molly never learned feminine ways, and was a hard laborer. "You look piqued!"

Caroline swallowed hard. "I'm sorry to intrude, but . . . Yankees encamped. They took my food and animals."

Molly took in a sharp breath and quickly rushed to Caroline. "Did they hurt you?" She squatted, putting her hand on Caroline's knee.

Pressing her palms to her eyes, Caroline slumped forward. "I've a cut on my back that needs tending. I'm sorry to be a burden, but I can't reach it." Embarrassed to come to this kind woman with troubles, tears gathered and fell.

Molly's eyes grew wide. "Let's get you in my bedchamber." She called out, "Hope, fetch me a pitcher of warm water. Faith, come help your Ma." Standing, she gently helped Caroline to the bedchamber. "Sit here on the rocker while I give my girls instruction."

Molly told the girls to tend Ora and make a plate of food. While she was out of the room, Caroline dried her tears and took deep breaths.

Entering the bedchamber, Molly placed a washbasin and pitcher of water on a small table next to the bed. She briefly left and returned with torn strips of muslin. When she turned to shut the door, a few stray pieces of hay floated from her dress, settling on the wooden floor. "Let's take your shirtwaist off so I can get a look at your injury."

Trembling, Caroline stood, turned her back to Molly, and undressed from the waist up.

"Come lay on the bed, I need to wash it. Might hurt a bit."

Caroline had no doubt it would.

Molly poured water into the washbasin and then sat beside her. She laid a moist, warm cloth across the wound. "I'm fixing to let this soften what's crusted before I wash further." She stood. "My, my, Caroline, the war has visited your home. Who would've thunk? My brother stopped in yesterday to tell me the Yankees were in New Bern. I dropped to my knees right then and there, praying the horror would end."

Caroline squeezed her eyes shut, willing her emotions to subside. Once in control, she said, "I fear for John and my kin. If this can happen to me, what must they be enduring? If the troops are heading for Swansboro, my Mama and sisters may be in their path."

Molly applied slight pressure to the cloth making Caroline wince. "Lordy, here you are with a nasty wound, hands cracked and red, no food, and who knows what state your home's in, and you're frettin' over others. It's the way of us women, ain't it?" Molly clicked her tongue and pulled the cloth from Caroline's back, submerging it once again in the bowl.

Molly wrung the cloth a second time and laid it on Caroline's back. "Sorry, child, but this time I need to scrub a bit." She applied slight pressure over the wound.

With the bite of pain, Caroline sucked in her breath and gritted her teeth. The stinging torment took all other thoughts out of her head.

"I'm sorry to hurt you, child." The soft squishing noises of cloth in water gave Caroline a slight reprieve, but Molly soon returned to washing the wound. Caroline gathered the bedclothes tightly in her fists. Her toes curled in her shoes. Molly kept chatting, but Caroline couldn't concentrate on her words. After a few moments, Molly told her, "I'm finished. Sit up so I can bandage."

Dizzy from throbbing pain, she pushed herself to sitting. Taking a deep breath then letting it out slowly to clear her head, she said, "When wounds weep yellow, my Mama made a poultice of garlic, purple coneflower, and goldenseal. Do you have these things?"

"I do. Let me go fetch 'em, and I'll be right back."

ଔଔଔ

As Caroline rode home later in Molly's wagon, she estimated the sun would be setting within thirty minutes. Ora asleep in her arms and Joshua by her side, she dreaded returning home.

Molly had loaded the wagon with enough food to last them at least a week. The milk would last only a day or two before it soured. Caroline hoped the baby would be fine eating more table food than being nursed.

Near to her cabin, she scanned the yard for evidence of any changes or visitors. She saw none, but her heart raced with the memories of the past thirty-six hours.

Joshua pulled the horses to a stop and jumped down. "Hand me the babe." He reached up. Molly had raised good mannered children.

Scooting across the wagon bench, she gently handed Ora to him, feeling the pull to her wound. "Her bed's in the kitchen."

After he left, she began unloading the food. What sounded like a man's voice coming from far away startled her. *Please no, Lord*! Stopping, she listened intently.

"Help," came a weak plea.

She whirled around but saw no one in the dusky darkness of the porch. "Who's there?" Her voice was hardly above a whisper.

"Help," came another weak plea.

Now sure the entreaty came from under the porch steps, she called out, "Josh, I need you. Now!"

Joshua came running, his boots hitting the porch with a crack.

She jumped and pointed to the steps. "There's a man under there. I think he's hurt."

Joshua's green eyes grew wide, and it occurred to her how young he truly was. He didn't want to look under there either. "Dang, Sister Mattocks. Let me get my gun." He ran to the front of the wagon and pulled his rifle from under its seat. Walking slowly to the side of the porch, he positioned it to his shoulder and squatted at the side of the steps. "Who's in there?"

"I'm Nate. Help me, boy," came an almost inaudible, raspy answer.

Caroline couldn't believe what she'd heard. "Nate?" She rushed to Joshua's side and peered into the dark cavity under the steps. "I know him. He helped me. Let's get him out."

Joshua set his gun down and crawled to the step's opening. "You hurt bad, Mister?"

"Yeah."

"Just me and Sister Mattocks here." Joshua stuck his head in the opening. "Can you crawl out?"

"No. I think my leg's broke."

Caroline peered in.

Nate took a deep breath and let it out slowly.

She imagined him near unconsciousness.

Joshua moved to his belly, dragging himself closer.

"Nate, there's a young boy here with me. We'll try and get you out without hurting you further. Are you injured anywhere besides your leg?"

"Yes. They stabbed me. My head's a hurtin' too."

"I'm going to get a blanket." Caroline backed away. "We'll try to get it under him and drag him out," she called to Joshua as she ran into the house.

Once back, it took Caroline and Joshua a good ten minutes to get the blanket under Nate.

He tried to help by rolling onto it, but he blacked out with the exertion.

By the time they pulled him from under the stairs, the sun had disappeared. In the faint moonlight, Caroline gazed down at an unconscious soldier. Her back ached, but Molly's tight bindings kept the wound from opening. "Got any ideas on how to get him into the house?"

"No, Ma'am. Reckon we might could drag him up?"

"I fear we'd hurt his head and leg more. I think I can lift the blanket edge by his legs if you could lift the end at his upper body."

"Let's try that."

They lifted, and Nate's limp body bent in the center. His upper left leg had a slight sag. His head flopped like a dead man's.

Caroline shuddered. What would she do if he died? They carried him sideways up the steps, taking the same step at the same time. He was heavier than expected, her arms ached with the strain, and her wound re-opened. Warm blood spread to the bandages. She gritted her teeth until her eyes watered.

Finally, at the top, she was spent. "I need to set him down for a spell."

"You rest. I think I can drag him into the house." Joshua walked backwards, pulling Nate on the blanket into the front room.

She followed and tried to decide where Joshua should put him. Her feather bed destroyed, left just the intertwined ropes. He'd probably be more comfortable on some folded blankets on the floor.

"Let me lay out blankets." She gratefully found her extra blankets untouched in the cupboard, putting one on top of another in front of the fireplace.

Joshua pulled Nate's upper body on the blankets, then cautiously moved his legs and lower body onto them.

Caroline lit three candles in the room, frustrated that her glass lamps had all been stolen. She brought the candles close to discern Nate's injuries. "Josh, can you get some firewood? I need more light."

Nate's hair was matted black with dried blood, but she was relieved to see no fresh blood. Both his eyes were puffy, the skin around them deep blue. His cheek had a gash which needed stitches, and his jaw was swollen and bruised. Although his uniform sleeve had ripped, she could discern no serious injury, but there was fresh blood on his left side.

She pushed him slightly onto his right to examine his back. His coat was soaked in blood. She should've realized the problem before laying him on clean blankets. Letting him roll back, she picked up a candle to shine it across the floor where Joshua had dragged him. Sure enough, a large streak of blood stretched along the wooden planks.

She sighed, overwhelmed with what was before her. "John, I need you." She squeezed her eyes shut and imagined her words flying on the air out the door, traveling to wherever he camped.

"Sister Mattocks, you all right?" Joshua stood in the doorway with an armload of firewood, his green eyes full of concern.

"Just weary. Have you ever treated wounds before?"

Joshua moved toward the fireplace and stepped around Nate to put the logs in place. "Yes, Ma'am. Mostly on horses, but I 'spose they're similar." He glanced at her, then looked away, hesitating.

"What, Josh?"

"Well . . ." He cleared his throat and looked down at the floor. "He's got Yankee blues on, Ma'am. Ain't I hurtin' the cause by helping the enemy? My brothers are likely putting bullets into Yankees just like this here fella."

She hadn't considered the dilemma she'd put him in. "I don't want to make you do anything you aren't feeling right about." She shifted her gaze to look him in the eyes. "All I know is I can look past the uniform. This man saved my life this morning. I don't think he considered me the enemy."

Joshua shuffled his feet and inched his head in a slight nod but still appeared troubled.

Caroline stood and put her hand on his arm. "I feel it inappropriate to undress him. If you're comfortable with cleaning and wrapping his wounds, I'll ask no more of you. In the morning, you can fetch the doctor, then go on home. Is that acceptable?"

Joshua flattened his mouth. "Yes, I can do that. I believe Ma would ask me to do the same."

Caroline withdrew a long match from a box on the mantle. Handing it to Joshua she said, "You're a good man, Joshua Hill."

CHAPTER THIRTY-THREE

March 17-22, 1862

Caroline watched the elderly, forthright doctor pack the unused wooden splints into a brown leather satchel.

"This man shouldn't be in your home, Mrs. Mattocks," he told her again. He'd arrived that morning with a level head and thankfully took immediate control of the situation. "But at this point, he could die if he had to travel." He wrapped surgical scissors in cloth, then placed them in the bag. "I'll stop in town and let the sheriff know he's here. I wouldn't leave if I thought he could move enough to harm you. Considering the seriousness of his injuries, he may be unconscious for a day or more. Even when he wakes, he's not going anywhere with that broken leg."

Exhausted and vulnerable, all Caroline could do was nod.

"He has a compound fracture above the knee. He's lost a lot of blood, but I've stitched his stab wounds. No serious damage to his organs." He clasped his satchel shut and looked her in the eyes. "He'll probably have quite a headache from the blow to his head. I'm leaving you laudanum for that and his other complaints."

She nodded.

The doctor pulled a cobalt blue bottle from his coat pocket, handed it to her, then put a hand on her arm. "And as for your stitches, they'll sting for a few days, but you'll soon be good as new. Mrs. Hill's poultice likely prevented infection." He lifted his mouth in a kind, closed-lipped smile. "Which reminds me—there's a chance of infection for the Yankee." He dropped his arm and gazed at her closely, his gray brows knit tightly together. "I don't approve of you touching the soldier. I'm going to insist the boy—you said his name is Josh—lives here day and night. I'll school him on caring for the soldier's wounds."

She swallowed down the tightness in her throat. "Thank you, doctor. I apologize for not having the money for your services. Please leave a bill. I'm sure my husband will pay upon his return." Her face warmed with embarrassment and doubts of John being able to follow through.

"I can't rightly charge you for being an innocent victim of war—and certainly not for a Yankee soldier's injuries. There will be no bill."

Caroline's shoulders dropped with relief. "Thank you for your kindness. I wish I could at least send you with some food, but the Yankees took all I had, and the Hills are supplying me with theirs." Heat once again moved onto her cheeks.

"Don't worry yourself with me. You've plenty on your hands here." He moved toward the door.

"May you be blessed for your services," she said.

He stopped with his hand on the latch. "I'll be back in a few days to check on the patient."

Nate was unconscious for the rest of that day and the next. Late the third night, he groaned and cried out, and she heard Joshua tending to his needs.

Joshua had told her Nate never woke enough to do more than take sips of water or his medicine. She wished she had something stronger in the house, but John wasn't a drinker, and even brandy was rarely in the cupboard. And if there had been spirits, the Yankees would've taken it along with everything else they'd stolen.

Each afternoon, Molly brought food. On the fourth day, she stepped in after a quick knock, as was her custom. "Hey there y'all. I've carried over elderberry flowers I stewed with hog fat for a liniment Josh can put on Nate's festering sores."

Joshua looked up from where he sat playing on the floor with Ora. "Thanks, Ma." He went back to bouncing the ball—to Ora's pleasure.

Caroline took the liniment from Molly's hands. "You're kind to fret over a Yankee's ills."

"The only reason I'm doctorin' the man is to get him out of here."

"I'm not a welcomed guest?" The weak reply came from the patient on the floor by the fireplace. They were the first coherent words Nate had spoken since the day they found him under the porch.

Joshua caught the ball and froze, staring at Nate.

Caroline rushed to him, as did Molly. "You're awake!" Caroline squeaked in surprise.

Nate smiled as if they were old friends, then grimaced in pain. "I believe I owe you folks thanks."

Through the next two days, Nate's strength improved. With Joshua's help, Nate was able to be moved to the settee and elevate his leg on an upturned trunk.

Caroline discovered him to be quite talkative by nature, and his disarming personality freed her speech as well. She probably was much too friendly, but she enjoyed having an adult to talk to. When Nate spoke of his Pennsylvania home, he brought something of an unknown world. It reminded her of when John used to tell of his travels.

They talked of his war experiences, Nate telling about the campaign to Roanoke and Hatteras in February.

She coaxed details from him since it was where John had gone, although she didn't tell him that.

"They put thousands of us land soldiers aboard more than a hundred floating vessels. Some of 'em were freight boats fitted with guns and painted black to look formidable." Nate grunted a laugh. "You should've seen us—most crammed into the boats had never been off land before. Some hadn't even been more than thirty miles from home in their whole dang lives." He wiped his hand across his eyes.

She was glad they were no longer swollen.

"The ships rolled and pitched, makin' us sick. Then we hit terrible storms. Almost every minute I thought we'd capsize. Waves rushed into cabins. Chairs and tables were thrown about and broken. The sea dashed forward, rushing through the ship and then out aft." He shook his head. "You'd think with all that water we wouldn't be thirsty, but we were parched for clean, fresh water. The barrels of water we had onboard were casks once used for kerosene oil and camphene. Men couldn't drink it without gettin' sick. We all wondered when the nightmare would end." Nate paused, as if remembering what he'd endured. "Many ships were lost to the sea, taking with 'em gun powder, rifles, large guns, and bombs. Troops were rescued for the most part, but one ship took down over a hundred horses."

Caroline shuddered at the thought.

"Finally, we got to Hatteras. High tides washed over the beach, preventing us from landing. Eventually, we landed on the southwestern side of Roanoke Island. We embarked 7,500 men and had us a fight—my first," he said the last two words quietly.

"We drove back and outmaneuvered the enemy." He glanced at Caroline, then cleared his throat, as if he just realized he was talking *to* the enemy. "After losing fewer than a hundred men, the Confederate commander, Colonel Shaw, surrendered about 2,500 soldiers. With that victory, Burnside secured the Atlantic Coastal outpost." He abruptly ended his tale.

She needed to pull more information from him to determine if John was safe, and she also wanted details regarding the battle at New

Bern. "You don't need to fret over my sensitivities. Can you tell me if Roanoke is a safe place to live?"

"Yes, the Federals have let the citizens establish their commerce again—which is mostly fishing."

"You said you enlisted in the war for the pay. Is it the same for others? I was of the impression the North wants to free the slaves."

"I don't care so much about freein' the slaves. They won't be sitting at my table anytime soon, but I do believe the Union must be preserved. I 'spose others take offense to the South saying they don't need the North, and still others feel they are up-holdin' Constitutional principles, which to some is to protect the rights of all, including darkies."

Caroline nodded, not sure yet of her own feelings on exactly what the Union had ever done for her.

"Most Federals ain't like Frank, you know."

She bristled at the memory of Frank. "Explain all his ruffians damaging my property. They took every fine possession I had and destroyed some as if it were a game."

Nate's blue eyes were kind. "I can't explain men like Frank. Their manhood seems to lie in their guns. Chance he was reactin' to his best friend being shot in New Bern."

"Why did your commander allow the destruction in my home?"

"If I remember correctly, our captain had already left."

Nate was right. The captain had left. She suddenly felt she needed to defend her side. "Most citizens in North Carolina didn't want secession but rather fight for States' Rights. Our forefathers developed this country just as your forefathers." Her words came out harsher than she'd meant.

Nate didn't respond immediately. "I believe you . . . but you must know the Confederates will never win this war, no matter what they feel they're fightin' for."

Shocked, she looked away.

"Your armies are much smaller and weaker than ours. Not only do we have the manpower, but we also have the foundries to make weapons."

John had said literally the same thing to Julia. "I prefer to leave the fighting on the battlefield and not bring it again into my home."

Nate appeared sheepish. "I apologize, Ma'am."

"There is one thing I'd like to know. Tell me of New Bern. You told me you didn't know if the 27th fought, but do you know if any citizens were injured?"

"I didn't hear of any. Do you know people who live there?"

"Yes, many friends, but no family. It's possible my brothers-in-law fought, if the 27th was involved."

"I don't know what Confederate regiments fought, so I can't relieve your mind none on that account. But there were actually more Federals killed than Confederates—close to a hundred of ours, and a little more than half that, yours. Many more Unionists were injured but over 400 Confederates were captured."

"Land sakes!" The numbers surprised Caroline. She must figure a way to discover Kit's and George's situation.

Joshua came through the door toting firewood. Looking tuckered, he placed it in the wood box by the fireplace.

Caroline went to him. "Can I get you anything before retiring?"

Joshua sat on his cot, rubbing at his eyes. "No, Ma'am. I'll just settle in for the night."

"Very well. Thank you for your help. I couldn't get along without you."

The boy beamed at the compliment. "My pleasure."

Saying her goodnights, she carried a candlestick into her dark bedchamber.

Asleep in her bed, Ora stirred.

Days before, Caroline and Ora had made a game of collecting all the feathers they could find in the house and front yard. They didn't collect enough to refill the ticking but were able to fill two pillows. Ora slept on one, Caroline the other. She had layered two quilts across the rope bed. It wasn't comfortable, but it was better than sleeping on the floor.

She set the candlestick on her bureau and picked up the brooch John had given her. It was gold-framed and contained a photo of him. When he'd given it to her, he'd said, "When you look at this, let it remind you that you have my heart forever." She ran her thumb over the glass of the brooch. "Come back to me, love."

Nate grew stronger each day. He couldn't bear weight on his leg but often sat up-right now. Joshua tended to his wounds and seemed to have become comfortable with "the enemy."

On the night of the sixth day after Nate's injuries, the weather became stormy. When Joshua opened the door to leave for the night's chores, a cold gust blew in and almost put out the low-burning fire in the fireplace.

Caroline gathered the still damp blanket she'd washed that day and draped it over the rocker by the fire, hoping to dry it before retiring.

Under Nate's watchful eyes, she took small logs from the box and added them to the fire. Wind howled down the chimney, making it sputter. She shifted the wood with a fireiron causing a brighter, fuller flame, bathing the room in a warm light.

Nate said to her back, "My Ma used to have a sayin'—she'd say, 'the person you encounter is more than the person you see.'"

Caroline put the poker in its holder and sat in the rocker farthest from the fire. "And what's that supposed to mean?"

"I was thinking 'bout how when I first saw you, I was reminded of all the tales I'd heard of fragile Southern Belles. As I've received your care and kindness, I've noticed you work hard and place others' desires and needs before your own. I'd be lucky if I could find such a wife as you."

Heat moved up Caroline's neck onto her cheeks. Perhaps she put too much wood on the fire? She stood, not wanting Nate to see the flush on her face and again stoked the fire. He'd not have said that if he'd known her a year ago.

Nate cleared his throat. "Did I say somethin' wrong?"

"No." Her dress hot against her legs, she couldn't stand there much longer. She moved back to the rocker.

"Have you always lived here?" he asked.

She shook her head. "I grew up in two homes. My daddy had an 800-acre plantation at the head of the White Oak River in Onslow County. We lived in a beautiful, white home with many rooms and comforts. Papa has passed." She stared at her hands in her lap. "My mother has dowager rights to the plantation home, but the land has all been sold. Seasonally, I lived in our town home in Swansboro, a port city."

"You had wealth. Was marryin' a preacher acceptable to your family?"

She shifted. Perhaps Northern men didn't know how to have proper conversation with a lady. But his face displayed innocent curiosity, and his smile disarmed her.

"Papa was a caring father. He supported my decision in the end." She didn't want to tell Nate Papa deeded her slaves to ensure her comfort. "Papa was generous, and we were comfortable when I first married."

He smiled. "Another of my Ma's sayin's is, 'True happiness is bein' content with what we have.'"

"Your mother sounds like a woman of many words, like her offspring." She grinned at him. "She has certainly raised a kind son."

Nate's smile grew, and she feared she'd said too much. She was overly comfortable with this young man in her front room, against respectable decorum making his bed on her settee.

"Are you content with what you have? Your prosperous plantation days seem to be over. Did it hurt to lose your status as a Southern Belle?" He smiled a sly grin, probably trying to get her back for teasing him.

Playing along, she laughingly answered, "Oh, being a Southern Belle has nothing to do with money. My doting Mama and Grandmamas taught me from birth all the rules of gentility, charm, etiquette, and manners. Southern Belles have endured for generations. Actually, that's what we're best at—enduring and surviving when times get tough." She became serious. "So, the answer is yes, I'm content with what I have." She didn't realize the truth of the statement until she'd said it out loud.

With mischief in his eyes, Nate said, "So, then it's true, that a Southern Belle is as strong as a tigress *disguised* as a kitten."

Caroline laughed. It felt good. Nate's laughter was loud, young, and innocent, hardly the chest-vibrating bass of a man. The sound made her laugh harder.

The front door opened, and a gust of wind blew through the room.

Caroline expected to see Joshua on the threshold but beheld her husband. "John!"

Nate's and her laughter still echoed off the walls.

John stepped into the house. Water dripped from his long black coat and flowed rivulets onto the floor. His hat in hand, thick hair lay plastered to his forehead, but it was his face that startled her. With jaw clenched he glared at a reclined Nate, John's usually expressive eyes flat and hard. She'd never seen the look before. He then turned and stared at her in uncertainty—almost pain.

She rushed toward him, but he raised his hand and stopped her embrace. "I'm wet."

Hurt grabbed at her chest. After all she'd been through the past weeks and fretting about him, they weren't the first words she'd imagined he'd say at their reunion.

CHAPTER THIRTY-FOUR

John stared again at the man in his home.

Caroline gestured Nate's way. "This is . . . Nate." Heat moved up her face. She'd never learned his surname. John would think it too familiar to introduce him by his Christian name. She swallowed. "He was injured . . . the doctor said he wasn't to travel . . . and . . ."

John looked so hard at Nate, she wasn't sure he even heard her words.

"John?"

He shut the door, then strode into the room, water sprinkling the floor in his path. He smelled of campfire. Stopping at Nate's raised feet, he surveyed the man's splinted leg and freshly laundered and repaired Union coat thrown over the back of the settee. "I see." His face relaxed then a neck muscle jump. "You're Union."

Nate found his voice, "Yes, sir."

"What brought you to *my* home?"

"I'm a scout. We followed Confederate tracks here. My regiment was here a week past."

John straightened suddenly at Nate's words and looked to Caroline, who still stood near the door. She had a lot to tell, and this wasn't the way she wanted John to find out details. She moved forward.

His expression finally softened. "Were you harmed?" He quickly scanned the room and back to Caroline, his eyes hooded. "Where's Ora?"

Caroline stepped closer and grasped his arm through his wet coat. "She's unharmed and in her bed asleep. I've much to tell you."

John fastened his gaze on Nate but addressed Caroline. "Can he be trusted if we talk elsewhere?"

Nate suddenly appeared his age again—a young man who knew more about tracking people than understanding them.

"Yes, he can't walk yet. Here, let me take your coat."

He handed her his wet hat and unbuttoned his coat.

She lifted the now dry blanket off the rocker and replaced it with John's hat and coat. With the blanket draped on her arm, they walked into their bedchamber.

John closed the door.

Caroline desired to wrap him in the warm blanket and hold him close, but now that she'd discovered he was alive and well, she resented him for deserting her, part of her wanting to lash out at his not being home when she'd needed him.

She placed the warm blanket on the chair.

They stood facing one another for a moment. She didn't know where to start. She brushed wet hair off his forehead.

He suddenly grasped her in an embrace that threatened to take the breath from her. He smelled of rainwater and his rosemary and lemon shaving soap.

At last safety. Her anger forgotten, she wrapped her arms around his neck. "I pled with God to bring you back to me," she whispered so as not to awaken Ora.

"I told you He listens to your prayers." He laughed tightly and moved his hands up her back.

She gasped and pulled away.

"What is it?" He held her at arm's length. His eyes belonging to the husband she knew—kind and full of love.

"As I said, I've much to tell you." She gave him a sad smile, her frustration at him tightening her chest again. She stepped away. "The Yankees were here. Nate and another man came first—both scouts. They followed the Confederate tracks because a regiment came before them. They were retreating from a battle in New Bern."

"I heard about the battle and discovered Kit and George may have been involved, but I couldn't question them because they'd retreated to Kinston. I've been told they're both unharmed."

She sagged with relief. "I'm so happy to hear it." She moved farther away and sat on the rope bed.

He sat too. "What happened to our bed?"

"Some Yankee soldiers sliced the tick and let the feathers fly to the wind," she said with less emotion than she truly felt.

He shook his head then took her hand in both his. "How badly are you hurt?" His eyes suddenly clouded, and his brow lowered. "Did anyone *touch* you?" The tension at the corner of his eyes deepened.

"No . . . but . . ." Just how much should she tell him? Could she make him see what a poor decision he'd made by leaving her? She wanted him to feel guilt for not being there. She gazed deeply into his eyes to try and anchor him to her. "Someone tried to take advantage of me."

John leapt to his feet. "What!"

Ora stirred and whimpered in her sleep.

Caroline talked fast and quiet. "A wretched man laid his filthy hands on me. He stabbed me in the back."

"Stabbed you?" John covered his eyes. "Oh, Carrie!" he said, tenderness evident in his voice.

"I was fighting him in the kitchen . . ."

John's face registered horror.

"Nate came and dragged the man outside at knife point. But his friends jumped Nate. They took him to the barn, and I didn't realize the extent of his injuries until much later when Josh and I found him under the porch." Talking about it made her relive it, and she felt worse trying to make John assume guilt when in reality he'd never want those terrible things to happen. All she really needed was for him to comfort her.

Instead, he gazed at her in bewilderment.

She wished he'd say something. The rain drummed a beat over their heads. "The Yankees had left, leaving him to die, I suppose." Her lips trembled. "Oh, John! I was so scared." She covered her face with her hands and wept.

John pulled her hands away and sat close, holding her hands. "This is my fault. I should have never left you alone with a war going on." He glanced up to the ceiling. "What was I thinking?" He brought her into an embrace.

She felt both relief and guilt for bringing out his regret. "I suppose I'm getting used to you not being here."

"That statement tears at my soul. I don't think I can forgive myself for not protecting you." He stood and paced. "Now that New Bern is held by the Yankees, I need to take you away. I'll resign my circuit. You and Ora mean more to me than my occupation or anything else on earth."

She should've felt relief. She'd thought he loved his job more than her. "You can't resign."

"I can. And I will. We'll talk more of it later. I think right now I need to speak to Nate." He kneeled and took her hands in his, kissing each one, then kissing her gently on the lips. "And thank him for saving my wife."

CHAPTER THIRTY-FIVE

March 28, 1862

The sum of their belongings in the wagon filled half of what it had when they first came to Pollocksville, eight months before. Even not knowing what was ahead, Caroline didn't feel anxious. She had John by her side and hoped he meant what he said about not leaving her alone anymore. They'd created a home filled with love and could do so somewhere else. She'd accomplished something of worth. She wanted to believe her future held the happiness she'd enjoyed in Pollocksville because it saddened her to let go of her dreams. She wouldn't be harvesting the garden, planting fruit trees, or fixing the chicken coop.

Closing her eyes, she tried to shut her heart to the memory of her destroyed and stolen treasures. Reaching into her pocket, she felt the small box she'd placed there that morning. Earlier, John had packed the china cabinet into the wagon and found the box containing a wedding gift of silver salt and pepper shakers in the far corner of a drawer. When he'd handed it to her, she'd cried for all that had been lost. It would be the last time she'd shed tears over earthly objects.

As the wagon wheels crunched along the dirt road, startled birds took flight. The morning's weather was ideal. A canopy of trees shaded the road and kept the sun off their faces. Occasionally, they passed apple trees in bloom. The heavenly fragrance cheered her.

John loosened the reins to give Sammy his lead and leaned back into the wagon seat. "I think that boy took a shine toward you."

She acted like she didn't know what he meant. "What boy?"

"Nate. All the way to New Bern, he kept apologizing for being an inconvenience. When I dropped him at the Union hospital, the last thing he said was to give you his thanks."

"That doesn't sound so love struck."

"No, it wasn't what he said, it was the quiet way he spoke without looking me in the eyes, and the color that rose on his ears."

Caroline laughed in spite of herself. "You best stay close to your wife's side. You wouldn't want someone to snatch her away."

"I plan to," he said in all seriousness.

Disappointed he didn't banter back, she said, "Surely you know I'm teasing."

He glanced at her sideways. "I know."

"Then why so austere? You don't think I have feelings for Nate?"

John was quiet longer than was comfortable. He sighed. "I suppose not." He took her hand. "I can't stop blaming myself for what you went through." He kissed her knuckles. "Forgive me, my dove?"

"I must admit, I'm happy and relieved you'll be with us more."

"I've sent a letter of inquiry to the Church regarding any temporary positions in Hillsborough that might be had."

Ora dropped her ragdoll onto the wagon floor and wiggled off Caroline's lap. The child was rarely still. She'd soon be walking. As she slid to the floor of the wagon, her patchwork dress gathered around her waist.

Caroline pulled it down. "Where's Hillsborough?"

"Northern North Carolina. Orange County. Many refugees are traveling there, trying to avoid Yankees here in the Southeast. It's well into Confederate lines."

"How long do you expect us to live there?"

"My hopes are until the war is over."

Ora inched her way to her father's leg.

John released Caroline's hand and pulled Ora to him with one arm. She clung to his neck, and he kissed her fat cheek. There was always such a look of delight in his eyes when he held his child. She didn't stay put long, sliding off his lap to duck under the wagon's seat.

"Please don't let her go under there."

Caroline pulled Ora out by her legs.

"I bought a gun after hearing of the battle in New Bern. It's loaded and under the seat."

Caroline snatched Ora back onto her lap. She'd never known John to carry a gun. "Do you think we'll need it?" Her pulse sped with the possibility.

"A preacher with his wife and baby shouldn't be of interest to the Yankees, but after your recent experience, I can't be sure of anything. Best to be safe."

"Did you have any troubles during your travels?"

"No, but I did learn a number of things in Roanoke when I spoke to both citizens and Yankees. I've been trying to come to terms with my loyalty to state and country. I've always felt this war was about the right to decide what goes on in the states and not letting the government impinge on my freedoms, but I'm learning there's more to it."

"Nate believes we don't have the manpower or weapons to win the war."

"He's right."

Caroline stiffened.

"Don't get me wrong. I'm a Southerner, and I'll not go against my Confederate soldiers, however, people thought Congress would end the war last year. They didn't, nor do I think they can. I see no end until one side is weakened enough to surrender."

John picked up Ora's ragdoll and handed it to her. "It's not worth all those innocent lives. The Yankees captured Roanoke and New Bern, and soon they may be the victors of all our towns in North Carolina. When I took Nate to New Bern, I saw firsthand how the Yankees aren't just camped around the city—they're living in the citizens' homes and running commerce and the newspaper." He shook his head.

"I know too well what that's like. Those poor people!" Gratefully, Caroline got word Swansboro remained untouched by Union Troops.

"The Yankees aren't anywhere near ending this war until they are the victors over every city in the South. Yet we don't have enough military in the state to get them out of New Bern or keep them from overtaking all our ports. If we bring more troops in and regain New Bern, there'll likely be many citizens caught in the conflict. The North is not going to let the South alone until they can control our way of life. To accomplish that, I'm afraid tens of thousands will die."

Other than Nate, Caroline's experience with Northerners wasn't good. If the citizens in the North were like Frank and the men who destroyed her home's comforts, then their future looked bleak.

Sammy neighed, and his ears pricked up.

In the distance, a lone rider came toward them at a fast pace.

John instinctively bent toward the gun beneath the seat.

The rider quickly came close enough to distinguish a gray cap on his head.

John straightened and reined in Sammy.

As the soldier neared, Caroline realized he was a dwarf from Swansboro—a seaman, William Jones, who'd sailed on her father's ships.

John raised his hand in hopes the rider would stop, which he did, but seemed reluctant to do so. His horse's flanks, lathered white, twitched.

John addressed him, "Good morning, Private Jones. Is the road safe ahead?"

"Good morning, Reverend . . . Sister Mattocks." Private Jones took off his hat and wiped his brow with his sleeve. "This road is safe as far as I could tell at a fast run. I've been assigned to Fort Macon. Late yesterday, the Yankees advanced on the fort while a buddy and I were out gathering firewood. We watched the northern road all night and couldn't get past Yanks to get help. We decided we'd better take the long way and rode west this morning. I followed Emerald Isle and ferried to Swansboro and then rode Belgrade. I'm riding to Kinston for help. My buddy went to Jacksonville for the same. Without backup, I fear the fort will be lost."

John's grip on the reins tightened. "Don't let us keep you. May God be with you and keep you safe."

"Thanks, Reverend. Hopefully, I'll be seeing you in church soon. I've missed your sermons. Good day." He kicked his short legs into his horse and whipped the reins. Dust flew up around the wagon, and he was soon out of sight.

As they neared Swansboro, the road became sandy.

Caroline inhaled the salty sea air she'd missed over the past eight months. To her relief, Swansboro hadn't seen the war's horrors and all seemed as usual.

Caroline and John rode directly to Gibson House to ask if they could stay with Mama until their plans to move to Hillsborough were confirmed. Caroline found Mama in the backyard working her beehives, with a netted hat covering her head and face.

Years before, Mama had her slaves construct a straw hive which supported four large glass jars. It now produced the purest virgin honey. Not wanting to be stung or disturb Mama in her work, Caroline stayed by the house and watched as Mama gradually removed a top board to allow the forager bees to ascend.

Many quickly flew up, while some slowly flew in scattered patterns. Usually not flying far for food, the bees covered the sloping yard of gooseberry, white clover, and hyssop bushes.

With a paddle, Mama carefully lifted one of the jars. It was partly filled with combs. Using a knife, she removed a piece of comb, placing it on a plate, and then slowly replaced the jar and top board. She picked up her tools and plate and headed toward the house.

Curiously, the front of Mama's skirt was covered in dirt. She had always been clean and well appointed. As she came closer, with some bees still hovering, she looked to Caroline and called out, "What a nice surprise to see your lovely face."

"We've come for a visit. I hope you don't mind."

"Of course not, child. Where's that granddaughter of mine?" Her eyes danced with expectation.

"She's in the house with John. He saw George recently and is telling Hester about his visit."

Mama pulled the netting from her face, folding it back over her straw hat. Bees moved along the comb on the plate. "Did you hear about New Bern?"

Caroline kissed Mama's cheek. "That's why we're here. Yankees visited our house after the battle."

Mama's eyes grew wide. "All is well, I pray?"

"We're fine." Caroline wouldn't distress Mama with the worst of the details. "But John's worried we aren't safe in Pollocksville. He wants to take us to Hillsborough until the war's over."

"Oh, dear! So far away? But he's right in wanting to protect you."

"Did you fall? Your gown is dusty."

Mama looked down and *tsk'd*. She handed the tools and plate to Caroline and brushed at the dirt on her dress. She laughed a short chuckle. "I buried my jewelry under the beehive."

Caroline handed the honeycomb back and pulled from her pocket the salt and pepper shakers. "Can we add these to the stash? They're all I have left of anything valuable. Other than my piano, the Yankees either stole or destroyed everything else."

"Oh, Carrie!" Mama placed a hand on Caroline's arm. "Come inside and tell me what happened."

The women walked toward the house.

"Why didn't you have Benny bury the valuables?" Caroline asked. "I'm sure it would've been like hiding pirate's bounty for him. He'd probably even draw you a treasure map."

Mama laughed. "I sent Benny to school in Wilmington. With the Academy closing here, and seeing all the young men go off to war, he seemed restless. I pray he's safer there."

"We saw Will Jones on our way here. He said the Yankees have advanced on Fort Macon, and John thinks they're soon to capture all the port cities. Come to Hillsborough with us."

"No. I wouldn't want to travel so far from home. I can always go to White Oak if Swansboro is unsafe."

Unease settled in the pit of Caroline's stomach and she wrapped her arm around her mother's shoulders, giving her a squeeze.

CHAPTER THIRTY-SIX

April 13, 1862 - Gibson House, Swansboro

Sunday morning, Caroline stepped onto the porch.

On the road, a woman dressed in a plain brown work dress stood with Julia, her hands on her hips. "Well, if you ask me, it's a rich man's war and a poor man's fight. Your husband should be fightin' the Yanks like my man, Isaac."

Almost nine months pregnant and wearing a buttery yellow gown, Julia held her shoulders back and head high. "My husband is needed here. How would you buy your food supplies if not for the store he operates?"

"Who has money for food? Your husband would do us better to serve the Confederacy in battle."

Julia stepped closer to the woman, who backed away.

The argument was common in the little town of Swansboro, and Caroline assumed elsewhere. Other than a few merchants and old men, the male population had dropped tremendously since the war. With no one to care for the women, they became more outspoken and desperate.

"Being a plantation owner and employing more than twenty slaves, my husband has every right to be exempt from military service." Julia answered louder than was genteel.

Caroline guessed Julia hoped the whole neighborhood could hear her defend Daniel's decision.

"The Twenty Negro Law is a disgrace to our state, and you should be ashamed!" The woman in brown stepped toward Julia again, but Julia stood her ground.

"You shrew!" She put her face close to the woman's. "You have no idea what a gentleman is, much less how he takes care of his wife. Your shiftless man always left you to fend for yourself. This time, he at least had a good excuse."

Caroline shrank inside. Julia had gone too far with insulting the woman's husband—a man who had joined the Confederacy to fight for their rights.

The woman swung her hand to slap Julia's face, but she deflected the blow.

Racing off the steps, Caroline approached just as another woman screamed somewhere down Elm Street. Caroline stopped in her tracks. Dogs barked. She ran toward the corner of Elm to determine what the disturbance was about. Julia and the woman in brown arrived at the same time.

About six houses down, four soldiers in blue entered a home without knocking. More caterwauling came from the house. Soldiers yelled profanities, and a baby cried. Additional Union soldiers ran up the street toward them.

Julia seized Caroline's arm. "Run and get the others someplace safe."

"Will you be all right?"

"I'm pregnant, not lame. Now go!"

Shots rang out, and Caroline almost lost her step as someone in heavy boots gained on her. She climbed the stairs, glancing over her shoulder. A Yankee only yards away, with another close behind, followed her.

"Mama!" she yelled as she entered the house.

The soldier nearest her entered at her heels.

Caroline turned to a pistol pointed in her face. Her stomach turned to stone.

"Are there any men here?" he said, catching his breath.

"No! Please, don't hurt us. It's just women and babies." Her eyes stung. *Please God, don't let him shoot me.* Legs trembling, she swayed and backed against the wall by the parlor.

A second soldier barged inside.

Mama and Hester rushed into the wide passageway and stopped short. "Oh, my dear Lord!" Mama threw her arm in front of Hester.

Hester paled, and her eyes grew large. She clutched Mama around the shoulders. "Please, don't kill us!"

"Don't cause any trouble, and no one gets shot." The soldier with the gun didn't take his fixed glare from Caroline.

Lightheaded, she sucked in air. Swansboro was obviously being taken over by Union soldiers. John was at the church. Was he safe? Where was Ned's cavalry? Were they not supposed to protect the citizens?

The second soldier's boots clomped against the floor. "Is there anyone else in the house?"

Caroline's mouth went dry. Fear kept her from speaking.

After a second slipped by, Hester stammered, "Just two babies upstairs."

"Leave them be," the first soldier commanded.

Caroline exhaled sharply.

A whimper came from the parlor. Betsey and Cozy stood clutched in each other's arms, eyes wide with fear.

"Who's in there?" the soldier with the gun yelled.

No answer.

Caroline found her voice. "Two servants."

He pushed the gun into Caroline's ribs while looking into the parlor. "Servants, you call them? Ha! They're slaves, lady. That's why we're here. To make sure they no longer have to do your bidding."

"Are there more slaves?" the other one asked.

"One upstairs with the babies, and two out back," Mama answered.

The man with the gun swung around and aimed it at Hester. Her eyes grew wider, and lips pressed together until they turned white.

"Please, no," Mama pleaded.

With a sneer, the soldier stepped closer to Hester with his finger on the trigger.

Caroline's blood ran cold to the icy pit of her stomach. One quick squeeze or flinch of his finger and her sister would be dead.

"My comrade asked you what people were in the house and you tell him only the white folks. Do you see anything wrong with that? 'Haps you don't consider the coloreds to be people? What are they to you, huh?" He put the gun to her forehead.

Fear vivid on her face, Hester paled further.

Mama made a noise in her throat like she'd be sick.

Caroline stayed frozen against the wall.

The second soldier entered the parlor.

"We're here to give your slaves freedom and take them to New Bern," the man with the gun said.

A squeak came from the floorboards above.

The soldier swiftly swung his gun up the stairwell. "Who's up there? Show yourself."

"Jus' me," came a small voice. Face streaked with tears, Mahaly took the first few steps down. "Jus' me," she said again.

"You come on down here," the soldier said kindly, as if he were inviting her to tea. He motioned with the gun for her to come, then backed up and pointed the gun at Hester again.

Mahaly descended the stairs.

"That's five slaves." He lowered his brows at Hester. "Ike," he called over his shoulder, "Gather these folks, and fetch the two out back."

Ike motioned for Mahaly to follow while he pulled Betsey by the arm, with Cozy still attached at Betsey's waist.

Betsey resisted Ike. "Do I hab a choice whethers I leaves or goes?"

Ike swiveled back to stare at her. "Why in hell wouldn't you leave?"

Betsey shrugged a shoulder.

"Of course, you've a choice. That's what this damn war is all about, giving you the choice."

Betsey stopped. "I choose to stay."

Cozy released her and blinked in unbelief.

"Suit yourself, ol' woman, but you must be addled. There's hundreds of thousands of men fighting for your freedom and when asked, you say, 'No, thank ya,' like there weren't people dying over the decision."

Cozy stared at Betsey as if she'd lost her mind.

"Go now, Cozy. You'z free, chile," Betsey quietly said.

With tears in her eyes, Cozy kissed Betsey and followed Ike and Mahaly through the center passage and out to the backyard.

"Now you just tell them folks in New Bern it was the 103rd New York who set you free," Ike called to them proudly.

Betsey sadly gazed out the open back door.

Caroline felt surprised but relieved that Betsey decided to stay. She pictured Moses and Keziah outside hearing the news of their freedom and remembered back to Keziah telling her about her children being left somewhere in Virginia. Would her freedom give her the opportunity to find them? Caroline hoped so.

With both front and back doors left open, a smoke-laden breeze moved through the passageway. And as if suddenly awakened to sounds around her, she heard many voices.

Soldiers ran down Main toward Front Street.

Was John aware of what was happening? She couldn't imagine him missing the chaos of gunshots, women screaming, breaking glass, and men yelling. She prayed he'd come to help them.

"You three move over here." The soldier waved the gun toward Caroline.

Mama, Hester, and Betsey backed against the wall by Caroline.

"I'm not here to kill women, but if you move away from that wall, I'll shoot cha'."

A whoop came from the backyard. A stocky soldier entered. "I found dinner." He turned and backed in, dragging John's new calf, throat recently cut, still spurting blood. Pulling it by its back legs, the man dragged it through the passageway. Blood flowed freely onto the floor. He towed the calf out the front door, down the steps, its body thumping as it hit each one.

Two Union soldiers in front of the house tried to bring the neighbor, Caleb Hewitt, to the ground. Although he put up a good fight, he wasn't a big man, and they soon had him tied with ropes. His children in the distance bawled, "Daddy! Daddy!"

Caleb, past forty and a recent widower, had chosen not to join the Confederacy and stay home to care for his five children.

Caroline prayed. *Don't let them lose their father too.*

The scene was blocked from view as three more soldiers entered the home. "Apart from a lot of blood, what have we got here, Josiah?" one of them asked.

Josiah kept the gun trained on the women. "Some high and mighty Southern belles just said a lovin' farewell to their slaves, who they don't even consider people." He gestured the gun toward Betsey. "This one must be addled. She doesn't want freedom." He made a noise of disgust in his throat.

"Who would've thunk?" The soldier snorted. "All right men, I want all food, animals, wagons, jewelry, silver, and firearms removed from the home. If you find any men, bring them to me in irons." He strode out of the house, leaving the two soldiers he'd brought.

Caroline couldn't stop trembling. How much longer would her legs hold?

The soldiers began their search. One went into the parlor, the other headed toward the stairs.

"There's babies up there," Hester called after him.

"I ain't here to hurt babies." He stomped up the stairs and could be heard moving between rooms.

The soldier in the parlor came out carrying two silver candlesticks in each of his huge hands. He stepped onto the bloody floor, slipped, catching himself before he fell. He put the candlesticks at Josiah's feet. "You come with me." He gestured toward Betsey. "Show me your dining room."

Outside, Yankee riders galloped up Main, and a group of soldiers walked the same direction. At the center of the group, chained together, were some of Swansboro's oldest male citizens.

The soldiers guarding the men stopped briefly. A familiar black hat lay on the ground, getting trampled underfoot.

Lord, please, no!

With John's hands cuffed in irons behind his back, Union soldiers bent on either side of him, lifting him off the dirt road where he'd fallen, his coat covered in dust.

As Caroline felt a scream move to her throat, he turned to face her. Their eyes met. His showed no fear, only love and concern. He slightly jerked his head to the left, telling her to not make a scene.

⋘⋘⋘

Toward evening, on her hands and knees, Caroline scrubbed the dried calf blood off the floor. Between the wooden planks, it was still wet and sticky, smelling foul. Her stomach roiled. She tried to take shallower breaths. She hated the job but needed to stay busy to keep her mind from fretting about where John might be.

Once the Union soldiers left with their food and valuables—and everyone else's in Swansboro—she'd quickly checked on Julia and Mary and their children. All were shaken but unharmed. Julia said she'd come by later—once she figured out where Daniel was.

"Mistress Mattocks, Ma'am!" Betsey squealed, "Git off dat floor. I do dat!"

Caroline sighed. "You and I both know your knees are too rheumatic to kneel." She dropped the blood-soaked towel into the water and began rinsing and squeezing, rinsing and squeezing. The water quickly grew red.

"Yo' Ma would turn me out if she knowed 'twas you, not I cleanin' dat floor." Betsey's deep wrinkles creased around her gentle brown eyes.

Caroline dropped the rag into the water and leaned back on her heels. "Then we best not tell her." She cocked her head. "Why didn't you leave with the other slaves?"

Betsy fidgeted fingers, crooked from arthritis. "Y'all are my family." She backed away, as if expecting Caroline to lash out.

Betsey truly considered herself family? Somehow it touched Caroline's heart—unlike the time Betsey had first told her she was her father's sister. "How could you sacrifice your freedom? We've never treated you like family." Full of shame, she lowered her eyes to the blood-stained floor.

"Ya mus' not have noticed what yo' parents done for me. Dey gave me a room off the kitchen not in the slaves' quarter. Yo' Ma always watchin' affer me in my ole age." She smoothed at her apron nervously. "I watched all yous grow from tiny babes. If I ain't wid y'all, I be frettin' how y'all doin' and if'n the husbands be survivin' the war."

"But if you were free, you wouldn't have to do anyone's bidding."

"Don't bodder me none to work. The good Lord don't condone laziness." She wrung her hands and glanced at the ceiling. "'Sides, dis place and da plantation always been my home. I don't want no udder."

"Land sakes, Caroline! Get off your knees," Julia shrieked. She stood at the front door in all her pregnancy, filling the open space. "Betsey, what is going on here?" she said as she entered the house.

"I dun tole her, Mistress."

"Carrie . . ." As if suddenly realizing there was still a slave in the house, Julia stopped her exclamation and turned to Betsey. "Why are you still here?" Her tone showed surprise, not concern.

Before Betsey could answer, Caroline blurted, "She chose to stay." She understood Betsey's feelings and knew her origins, but Julia knew nothing and if she did, she'd never accept Betsey as family.

"Well, I'll be! You must be the smartest darkie in Carolina. You know right well when you've got a good thing. My senseless slaves couldn't leave fast enough. That no good Esther walked out grinning like a possum. Good thing I have plenty more slaves on the plantation." Julia pulled her dress up a couple inches and tiptoed around the blood to come stand by Caroline. "Sister, it's shocking that you've lowered yourself to scrubbing floors. Is this what you learned in Pollocksville? Now get yourself up and come into the parlor. We need to talk."

Caroline pushed herself up and followed Julia.

"Daniel rode in a half hour ago." Julia settled on the settee next to Caroline. "He talked with the Gatlin Dragoons, and they told him they're working on negotiations to free the prisoners." She patted Caroline's shoulder. "They have every hope the Union will release John, seeing as he's a preacher who has nothing to do with the war effort." Julia sighed. "The Yankees burned Daniel's steam sawmill down on the waterfront." She clicked her tongue. "I 'spose they took all your valuables as they did mine. You know, they even took my ornamental portiere pullbacks."

"I'm sorry, Julia," Caroline murmured.

"Daniel said they raided Palo Alto Plantation on their way to New Bern. My heart wept to hear it. Remember the fine balls they used to have there? Good Lord! I'm glad my plantation sits well off the main road." Julia prattled on.

But Caroline hardly heard what Julia said after she'd told Caroline that John could be released. She dared not believe it.

CHAPTER THIRTY-SEVEN

April 15, 1862 - Gibson House

Sleep stayed distant. Even in exhaustion, Caroline couldn't relax on another bed of woven ropes with no feather tick. Slumber also wasn't going to come as long as she worried about John—and she couldn't stop worrying.

The raid on the town had been thorough, but remarkably no one was hurt. Swansboro was emptied of food and even their kitchen gardens filched. Thankfully, Daniel brought them provisions from his plantation home.

Many of the women in town had gone to stay with someone in the country. Mama, Hester, and Caroline considered going to White Oak Plantation, but Daniel felt they wouldn't be safe without a man. And besides, they had only Betsey to do chores and take care of the young, whereas Harget Plantation had many slaves to do their bidding. Daniel convinced the women they should come home with him. They were to leave in the morning.

Finally giving up on sleep, Caroline arose and opened the window. The cool air coming off the water smelled of azaleas. The river below was quiet and dark, but who knew what lurked in a land at war. She sighed and sat in a chair, massaging her tight shoulders and neck.

What would she do if she lost John? She bowed her head and prayed he'd be released unharmed. Two times she'd survived Union soldiers in her home. She added to her prayer, hoping there wouldn't be a third.

A noise scratched downstairs.

Her pulse quickened. Were the soldiers back? Why now? There was nothing left to take.

She tiptoed to the door.

The stairs creaked.

Her heart dropped to the pit of her stomach. She moved against the wall. Perhaps she'd been too quick to think there'd be no molestations. She quickly scanned the semi-dark room for something she could hit the intruder with and spied the fireirons on the hearth.

The door opened.

Caroline's blood flowed to her feet.

In stepped her husband.

"John!" She released her breath in a gasp.

He whirled around, his arms around her in an instant. "I'm so relieved to find you unharmed. My prayers have truly been answered." He pulled away and gazed at her. "Did I startle you, dove?" He pulled her close again. Her trembling likely gave him the answer, because he held her tighter. "I'm sorry to come in the middle of the night but when they released me, they gave no transportation home. I've been walking for hours and just want to sink into bed."

The calming effect of being in John's arms helped her take slow, easy breaths. "The Yankees took all of Mama's feather beds. We're sleeping on ropes again."

John's coat smelled of campfire. She unbuttoned it and he shrugged it off and threw it over a chair. "I'm mighty sorry to hear it." He rubbed his lower back.

"Did they treat you poorly?"

"I'm unharmed." He showed one dimple. "Since the prisoners were citizens and not Confederate soldiers, they didn't know what to do with us. I believe they only hoped to keep us away from our homes in Swansboro while they were being ransacked. Those who ranked highest disagreed about a preacher being arrested. They let me go first. They were still trying to decide a legitimate way to release the others when I left. I believe all the men will be home by tomorrow." He took her hand. "Come here."

He brought her to the chair, pulling her onto his lap.

She laid her head on his shoulder, wrapping her arms around him.

He softly touched her cheek and brought her face to his, kissing her on the lips.

Fearing she'd lost him, and then suddenly having him in her arms, made her long to show him her love.

They came apart. "When last I saw you, a soldier had you up against a wall with a gun aimed at your heart. I couldn't get the image out of my mind. I've endured a long and miserable two days worrying about your and Ora's well-being. The contrast between where I was and where I am right now is like hell and heaven." He pulled her arm from around him, clasping her hand, kissing her fingers. "You're my heaven."

A shiver ran through her. "And you, mine." She embraced his cheek, finding his usually soft face covered in stubble. "Do you think there's a place in this war-torn country for us to have a happy life?"

Her eyes suddenly burned with tears she didn't want to shed. But they fell anyway.

He gently wiped them away. "We must make it so."

CHAPTER THIRTY-EIGHT

April 16, 1862 - Harget Plantation Home, Onslow County

The savory roast beef tasted sumptuously sinful. Caroline let it sit on her tongue for a moment to capture a flavor she'd long since forgotten. With the way they feasted tonight, you'd never know there were hungry people within a mile of the Harget Plantation.

By the grace of God, the plantation hadn't been touched by the Federals. Sadly, Daniel lost his business ventures in town, but his grocery store stood, albeit with empty shelves. He was still wealthy enough to recover from his losses.

Set with the finest china and crystal, Julia's table displayed her silver monogrammed seven-piece tableware, including a fruit fork and tiny salt spoon with a saltcellar at the head of each place setting.

Slaves came and went with soups, roast beef, baked goose, creamed carrots, and cold asparagus vinaigrette. A feast which made Caroline feel she was at home again, before the war, before John.

Considering the hardships she'd recently suffered, would similar trials have come without the war? Papa tried to warn her life would be hard and frugal as a preacher's wife. Yet if the only way to have John was with hardship, she'd still take him. He satisfied her in ways money could not.

Julia leaned toward Caroline. "You seem to be dreaming, sister. Tell us your thoughts."

The roast beef suddenly felt like a lump in Caroline's mouth. She wasn't fixing to tell Julia her thoughts, yet she couldn't seem to come up with a lie.

Under the table, John took her hand. "I'm sure she's enjoying her supper. My compliments to your cook."

"I'm delighted Beulah wasn't with us in Swansboro. The Yanks would have taken her and her culinary talent." Julia wore a sapphire blue evening gown. Her pregnancy kept her from sitting close to the table. Wanting to keep the posture of a well-bred lady, she sat a good foot away from the edge and ate slowly, careful not to drop any food on its way to her mouth.

Daniel sat across from her at the other end of the large table, with Mama and Hester ensconced across from John and Caroline.

"If it's appropriate conversation for the women to hear . . ." Daniel cleared his throat. "Tell us about your experience as a Yankee prisoner, John."

"There's not much to tell." John wiped his mouth with a fine cloth napkin. "Other than binding or chaining us, they didn't hurt us in any way. Not that the ride in the back of a wagon to New Bern was pleasant."

"Ha! I would think not." Daniel shook his head.

John took a sip of wine. "We stopped for hours at Palo Alto, never unshackled or permitted to leave the wagon. They forced us to watch needless destruction of property as they ransacked the plantation."

Caroline remembered well the recently deceased owner of Palo Alto Plantation. A good friend of Papa's and generous with his fortune, David Sanders had died only three weeks after Papa. In David's will, he left a Negro slave to young Benny and a thousand dollars to David Koonce, John's half-brother. He owned almost ten thousand acres and two hundred and eighty-eight slaves. His widow still lived on the estate.

"It's a shame the plantation sits along the main road to New Bern," John said. "I'm surprised it wasn't destroyed weeks ago."

Daniel set down his fork. "It's also a good thing Sanders wasn't alive to see it ruined. He spent much of his life developing that estate."

"His widow was there when the Federals arrived. She put up a good fight with her orations. After watching acres of crops burned, her furniture carted off, countless valuables stolen, and her livestock commandeered away, she was more than shaken. Hundreds of slaves ran into the woods, and some followed us to New Bern. Mrs. Sanders begged the soldiers to leave one horse and buggy, but they wouldn't."

Julia stopped eating. "Land sakes! All those beautiful jewels she had. What a shame to let them go to a bunch of thieving cowards who steal from women and destroy homes."

John's expression became distant. "It was hard to watch Mister Sanders' extensive library being taken apart. Some books were pitched on the ground, while others were packed into pockets, satchels, and barrels—whatever the men could get their hands on to cart them off."

"Poor Mrs. Sanders!" Mama's expression was troubled. "I wonder where she's staying now?"

"I heard she fled to her family in Wilmington and vows to never return to Palo Alto," John answered.

"Well, God be with her." Mama looked to Daniel with weary hopelessness. "Someone must check on White Oak Plantation."

Daniel nodded. "I'll send someone tomorrow."

The dinner plates were removed, and a butler and five maids entered, each toting silver trays with finger bowls placed upon doilies and napkins at their side. Each diner dipped their fingers in the bowl of warm water and then wiped them dry with the napkin. The slaves left and soon brought in desserts of plum pudding, hummingbird cake, and sweet potato cobbler.

Caroline put a hand on John's arm. "Are there no northern gentlemen? How could they have a clear conscience while stealing, destroying property, and frightening women? If they're honorable people who claim to care about the Negroes in bondage, why steal and threaten women and children?"

"Our men have honor," Julia said. "We raise them that way." She smiled sweetly at Mama. "Good Southern women train their sons right."

Caroline was sure she wasn't only complimenting Mama, but herself and her own two sons.

"I can't answer for their conscience," John said. "Only God can be their judge. Their acts of destruction are evil. I believe they're trying to weaken us so we can't survive without them."

"They've been burning courthouses throughout the south to destroy our land records," Daniel said. "If we can't prove it's our land, then we have nothing. They're stripping us of property and valuables in hopes we'll be weak enough to bend at the knees and allow them to be our victors."

"Oh dear!" said Hester. "George would never do the same to Yankee women, I'm sure."

"Nor would Kit," John said. "I believe the Yankees are also having a hard time getting enough supplies. By stealing silver and jewels, or any other valuables for that matter, they can sell them for money, food, or weapons. And of course, they're eating our animals and riding our vehicles and horses."

"What have you heard from Ned?" Daniel asked John. "I heard the Gatlin Dragoons caught up with the Yankees who ransacked Swansboro that very same night."

"Yes, there was a skirmish at Thomas Gillett's farm with about two hundred Union soldiers. Three charges were made on the Federals who were encamped around the farm. Colonel Robinson, of Ned's cavalry, led a charge with only thirty men. The colonel was wounded and captured, and the Dragoons withdrew. Ned didn't sustain any injuries."

Daniel nodded. "Good to hear he's well."

"He's sore about the fact that the Dragoons weren't there to defend Swansboro," John said.

"Aren't we all. I dare say Mary soothed his pride. I invited her here, but she wouldn't hear of it because Ned often comes home when not on duty. No insult to females present, but she does seem to have a steel resolve. Once I saw Mary get kicked by a mule, and she kicked him right back." Daniel laughed. "She doesn't say much, but she sure can stand her ground. You raised some spirited belles, Mama Gibson."

Caroline hid her smile behind her napkin.

Mama shook her head.

Daniel finished his meal and leaned back. "So, John, when do you depart to Hillsborough?"

"Next week. I need to be there by Sunday the 27th. The journey should take only three days, but the railroad out of Kinston hasn't been running consistently because of blockades."

"And how long will you be gone?"

"As long as I feel it necessary to keep Caroline and Ora out of danger. Many refugees are living there. Their minister recently passed away. I'll be taking over his responsibilities."

Caroline was glad he didn't mention she'd be helping a blind widow with her household. Julia would have never approved.

Caroline twisted her wedding ring. Was she right to let John take her hundreds of miles from her family?

CHAPTER THIRTY-NINE

April 25, 1862 - Hillsborough, Orange County, North Carolina

The train brought Caroline, John, and Ora to the Hillsborough depot, where they hired a coach to take them to their new home. With the window shades rolled up, Caroline could see and smell the lush green beauty of the hilly town surrounded by great pine forests. They traveled uphill along the Eno River, taking a turn onto Churton Street, and then entered the busy commercial district. The town was bigger than Swansboro, with three prominent church buildings and a courthouse.

People milled about on the streets, in shops, or stood in clusters visiting. The refugees escaping Yankee occupied territories in the South overcrowded the town. Like the other places they'd traveled through, most were women.

Turning onto Tryon Street, into a partially residential neighborhood, the horses stopped in front of a two-story white house built of battenboard siding with a green metal roof. Next door sat the fourth church, the one John would serve.

He pointed to the church, which stood out with its unfinished pilaster red brick walls. "The building was started in 1860, but the War interrupted its completion. Even without its steeple, it's a lovely Greek Revival building."

Across the front pediment were modillions. Caroline wondered, if when completed, they might run along the sides of the church cornice overhang as well. The tall, narrow sash windows made its two stories look majestic.

"The church is supposed to be finished enough for meetings," John added.

The door of their intended new home opened, and a corpulent woman stepped out. Caroline didn't think she'd ever seen such large bosoms and hips. The woman tottered, reached for the porch post, missed it, then tried again with a wider swing of her arm, finally finding and leaning heavily on the post. "Does that be the new rev'ren and his gal?" Her voice, gravelly and crude had a backwoods twang.

"Yes, it's us. Please stay where you are, and we'll greet you presently." John alighted and held out his hands for Ora. Caroline handed her to him, and the driver helped Caroline down.

Caroline and Ora walked toward the large woman. John had told Caroline the old reverend's widow was blind, but other than that, they knew nothing about her. Judging from her coarse language and clothing, she was obviously poor and uneducated. Now closer, Caroline could see the high and wide expanse of her forehead. Her greasy hair was pulled into a tight bun with no snood, bonnet, or hair doily.

The woman smiled. "Welcome trav'lers. I feared ya'd never git here."

The widow's eyes drew Caroline's attention. The pupils and part of the irises were covered with something that reminded her of white custard. It was so repulsive, she didn't want to look, yet she couldn't help but stare. Life might as well be over for Caroline if she ever appeared so grotesque.

"Thank you for greeting us so kindly." She reached to touch the woman's oily sleeve to show social graces, but then decided against it and withdrew her hand.

John placed a trunk on the porch. "We're pleased to be here. I presume you're the Widow Julip?"

"Francine's my name, but ever'one calls me Fanny." Her smile revealed two gaped upper front teeth and red, angry blisters on her gums. She reached out blindly to no one.

John took her hand like he would a woman of high standing. "I'm Reverend Mattocks, and this is my wife Caroline and daughter Ora. Thank you for your hospitality. If you'll kindly tell me where to put our trunks, I'll take care of the business and then we can sit and visit." He dropped her hand. "I heard your son lives with you. Is he at home?"

"He be along by 'n by. When he heerd y'all be comin' to live with me, he done wint and enlisted." She frowned. "He out tryin' to buy a gun and said he be back shortly to git his victuals." She motioned toward the door and let them move inside before she followed.

"I 'spect he on his way to the War just as fast as his feet will take 'im. Don'na understand it me self. A boy raised in a preacher's home, wantin' to go kill 'nuther like they was a possum or some-such." She shook her head. "Please, make you'selves comfy. I not much of a hostess, seein' as I can'na see nuthin'."

Little light came through windows covered by drawn curtains. Settees, chairs, and tables were all set firmly against every wall.

Caroline assumed the arrangement helped Fanny not trip over anything. There were no carpets on the bare wooden floors. She moved toward a window, dust swishing into the air. "May I pull some curtains?"

"Cert'nly, cert'nly. I 'pologize fir the state the room must be. Rev'ren Julip had a servant come once a week to clean, but with 'im gone, so be the money. My son not one fir women's work." She shook her head sadly. "I hope I not too much of a burden fir ya, Sister Mattocks."

"Of course not." A bit overwhelmed, Caroline tried to hide her feelings. "All will be fine. If you'll direct me, I'd be happy to put on some tea."

"Ain't ya a sugar? The Lord dun bless me when He sent ya." She smiled her grotesque smile. "Ain't no tea to be found fir months back, now. We be drinkin' parched grits fir coffee."

Caroline heard the *clunk* of another trunk on the porch, and the coach pulling away. "May I tell my husband where to put the luggage?"

"Glory be, I firgit." She laughed like she had sticky mucus in her throat. "Have 'im take 'em upstairs to the bedchamber on the right. My son, Buck, sleeps in the other one up theres, and I sleeps down here in the parlor. Can'na sleep prone, or I stops my breathin'."

Caroline took Ora's hand and went outside, closing the door behind her.

John folded the oilcloth which had covered the trunks on the coach.

"Fanny asked that you put the trunks in the upstairs bedchamber on the right." Whispering, she added, "I'm not sure this arrangement is going to work. I don't rightly know if I can care for a child *and* a feeble, blind woman."

John looked toward the closed door with concern. "I hope I've not placed you in an impossible situation. I'm sorry, dove."

Caroline sighed. He sometimes seemed oblivious to her daily struggles. She turned away from him. The neighborhood in front of her was unfamiliar. She missed her coastal home already.

They entered the house and Fanny stood. "Oh, I almost firgit— Buck said to tell ya straight ways, that two letters come here yesterdee, Rev'ren Mattocks." She motioned toward a table where they laid. "He said he left 'em on the front table. Are they there?"

"Yes." John picked them up, stopping in his tracks. He quickly glanced at Caroline, then back to the letters.

"What is it?" The hairs on the back of her neck rose.

"One is from the Confederate States Government. The other from Church headquarters."

"Oh no!" Caroline dropped into the nearest chair.

Ora, in her innocence, toddled about the room touching all the furniture, happy to no longer be confined in a train or coach.

"There ain't no hidin' from the war," Fanny said.

John sat near Caroline and opened the letter from the government first and quickly scanned its contents. "I'm being asked to serve a minimum of three months as a Confederate Chaplain, starting May 1."

Bile filled Caroline's mouth. She swallowed the bitter information, laying her head back against the chair.

John read aloud. "'You will hold no rank . . . and be paid $85 a month . . . you will bear no arms. If you do so, you will not be guaranteed the immunity granted under the rules of war.'"

Caroline squeezed her eyes shut. *God hear my plea! End the war before John has to serve.*

John continued reading, "Your main duties will be to tend to the spiritual needs of the soldiers, hear confessions, instruct in ecclesiastical matters, conduct worship services, pray, preach, and counsel men. Other duties may include correspondence to families of troops, care for the wounded and burial services for the deceased."

John stared at Caroline, but when she couldn't find words, he kept reading. "If you choose to wear a military uniform, it shall not have any insignia. The uniform should not set you apart from civilian clergy. You will have no official standing and no recognized authority within the military organization you serve."

John opened the letter from the church next. "We have received word of your chaplaincy assignment and are aware you may have recently arrived in Hillsborough for service. This letter is to absolve you from your duties in Hillsborough so you may serve the Confederate States of America. We trust you will serve with honor and go with the full mantle of our Lord. We will send a clergyman to take your place in Hillsborough, but it may take effort to get him there in these trying times of war. Please allow your kind wife to stay with Sister Julip until we may find a replacement."

John read on, but Caroline heard no more. Her mind filled with visions of John living amongst dead and dying soldiers and the ever-moving battlefields encroaching upon him.

Hours later, all the unpacking had been done, and Ora finally fell asleep.

Buck had arrived before dinner, toting a new gun and haversack. To Caroline's relief, he'd retired to his bedchamber early. He was a dirty, lazy, and loud young man who constantly clawed at his beard when he talked.

John moved to sit beside Caroline on their bed. The humid air smelled of the kerosene lamp that threw a soft glow on his face.

"How did the Confederate government know where to find you?" she asked.

"I wrote them of my willingness to serve as chaplain. I didn't expect a response so quickly." He grasped Caroline's hand.

But she looked away, the heat of her anger burning her face. Maybe he did love his job more than her after all. "You resigned your circuit post to be with Ora and me. You said you wouldn't leave us alone again." She hoped if he felt guilty enough, he wouldn't go. She turned toward the wall, hating herself for being selfish and not wanting him to serve the South. She wasn't vulnerable in Hillsborough, like in Pollocksville, and she really didn't have a good reason to make him stay. Except she wanted him to.

"I resigned my post to get you someplace safer. That, I've done. I'm not doing this because I want to leave you. When the Yankees invaded us in Swansboro, I was compelled to do my part." He stood and ran his hand through his hair. "It's now clear that I need to defend my family by serving in the War. I don't expect you to understand, and I really am sorry to leave you." He knelt before her.

Caroline wouldn't look at him.

"I promise I'll come back, and we'll set up a home near your family."

"I cannot believe your promises."

"Oh Carrie, come on!" John sat and wrapped an arm around her shoulders, bringing her to him.

A tear escaped.

"I love you, dove. You know I do." He kissed her cheek. "This might not be the ideal place to live, but you'll be safe. The fighting is far from here. I'll help you get this house in order, and after I buy a horse and tent, I'll use what money we have left for your food. I won't need my full salary, and I'll send you money every month. You'll be fine."

She swallowed hard. The perfect man she'd thought she'd married was not so perfect after all. Good, yes. But he left her alone more than she thought necessary, always following his heart without a thought for her and Ora. "When I married you, I never expected I'd spend most of my life alone."

CHAPTER FORTY

April 26, 1862

Caroline awoke to a dim room, rain drizzling down the window. With a lit kerosene lamp at his elbow, John sat writing at a desk. Ora still slept.

Caroline dressed and left. She didn't know what to do with her anger. Most married women her age had husbands in the war. Why should she be any different? Still, she clenched her fists in anguish.

Off the upstairs landing, Buck's bedchamber door stood ajar. Inside the room were a dresser and a stripped, yellow-stained tick. She could only surmise he'd left for the war. She would clean the bedchamber for Ora, giving John and herself a room of their own for the few days they had together. But the first tasks of the day were to make breakfast, clean the kitchen and parlor—which she'd given a good start on the evening before—and teach Ora to climb down the stairs backwards. She'd already fallen or cried for help a few steps up.

"That you, Sister Mattocks?" Fanny called from the parlor.

"Yes, I'm here." Caroline entered the room. "Reverend Mattocks will be down shortly. He's making notes for his new congregation, which it seems he'll meet with only this one Sunday." She cleared her tight throat. "What do we have to make for breakfast?"

"Don'na fret you's self 'bout that yit. Come sit by me fir a spell." She made a wide motion toward the chair near her. "I may be blind, but some things I see."

"I don't take your meaning." Caroline sat in the chair, trying not to look at Fanny. Would she ever get used to those eyes?

"That husband of yer'n loves you. I knowed it hard ta watch 'im leave, but he's got goodness in his soul and needs to he'p others, and iffen his heart's needs ain't seen to, he'll only be half the man he meant to be."

Caroline felt reprimanded like a child. "You assume to know my husband after just one day?"

"I've lived a long life of listenin' to people chawin' on what they wanna spend their energies doin'. Iffen I had my druthers, Buck would'na have left no-ways. Rev'ren Mattocks is gonna serve in the war 'cause he have true compassion fir his fellow men. Buck jus' might be feelin' the opposite. Yer man needs to serve God like he needs to breathe air and drink water. Mark me words, you'll always be sharin' 'im with others. But don'na fret none, his faith will sustain 'im. He'll come back to ya."

Caroline flicked her gaze upward and decided not to discuss the matter further with an uneducated woman who professed to understand people's ambitions.

The smell of slimy, old tobacco seeped up from a spittoon on the floor by Fanny. Caroline stood and gingerly grasped it with both hands around its middle, pulling her nose as far from it as possible.

"Whatcha doin'?" Fanny asked.

"Now that Buck no longer lives here, I had a mind to rid us of this spittoon."

"That's mine."

Caroline rolled her eyes in disgust. "Fine, I'll clean it then."

She left Fanny mumbling under her breath about so few comforts and walked through the narrow kitchen and out the backdoor onto a sloping porch worn gray with age. The boards creaked, and she wasn't sure it wouldn't collapse under her weight. Her shoes squished into the mud in the yard where she set down the spittoon to let it fill with rainwater. She swore not to touch it again until nature washed it clean.

Smelling of mold, the foreign rain-rotted woods blurred through the drizzling rain. John had brought her to this place, cutting her off from family, and now he would leave her stranded here.

☓☓☓

Caroline discovered horses were hard to find. Which made sense, seeing as most were needed for the war, and that more horses had been killed than men.

John found an eight-year-old sorrel, rather thin, with a rough gait.

"It's better than a mule," he said, which was his second choice. "I'll be missing Sammy, for sure." He packed his saddlebags with extra Bibles, church periodicals, and miscellaneous publications, one change of clothing, mess kit, and some food. No gun. He strapped a tent behind the saddle, then faced Caroline. "Please don't be angry with me anymore." He dimpled a lopsided grin, and playfully flicked the brooch at her neck, which framed a photo of him. "I'll be back before you know it."

"I doubt that." She battled frayed nerves. She didn't want the last thing John remembered to be an embittered and angry wife, so she tried to smile. But she couldn't stop the tears. She laid her hands on his chest. "Just make sure you come home. Keep away from the fighting."

"I plan to." He took her in his arms and held her until she stopped crying.

CHAPTER FORTY-ONE

Friday 16 May 1862   *Kinston North Carolina*
My Darling Carrie,

My health is good as I pray are yours and Ora's. I miss you both already. I hope you are no longer angry with me. I possess only deep love for you.

I am serving with Company I, 27th Regiment, as I had requested. The 27th is assigned to Ransom's Brigade and have not seen combat since I have been with them. We are camped near Kinston.

Other than ecclesiastical duties, I have been asked to act as courier and carpenter. Occasionally, I find time to teach the more learned soldier who seeks a distraction the subjects of Greek and Latin. I have taught some men their letters so they may write home and written correspondence for those unwilling to learn.

Faith gives the men refuge. I am trying to guard and guide their spiritual well-being. For most of the troops, it is their first time away from home. I feel I serve as a surrogate father to these young lads.

I am sorry to say, although the Confederate Congress authorized $85 salary per month, they have amended it to $50. Considering rations and feed for my horse, I am enclosing the $30 I have left for your use. I ask your kind indulgence and pray this sustains until I can send more next month.

Mother told me in a letter that my cousin James Mattocks enlisted. He is a genius for inventions. It would be a horrible waste of a brilliant mind if he does not survive. His seventeen-year-old brother George is here serving in the 27th. Aunt Kitty must be devastated to have both her sons gone so soon after the death of her husband. I am told she heads a committee to care for the soldiers' wives in Onslow County. Let us hope this war does not last long enough for her youngest, thirteen-year-old Nash, to enlist since he is now the man of the house.

What men are left at home I wonder? I worry about Mother having all three sons in the war. How grateful I am to watch over my brother and brother-in-law. They are doing well. In case you hadn't heard, George Ward has been made 2nd Lieutenant.

Write and tell me the goings on in Hillsborough. Please know my last thoughts before retiring are of you only.
I am as ever your affectionate husband, John
***

Sunday evening 22 June 1862   Near Petersburg Virginia
My Dearest Love,

With Walker's Brigade, the 27th traveled to Petersburg where we arrived yesterday. I believe we will be in Richmond before week's end, for the fear is she will be taken. Thousands are gathering to defend the capital city. For miles, the landscape is dotted with white tents.

We have had six long days of hard marching through severely muddy roads. The buzzing and stinging of mosquitoes is enough to drive a man mad.

I received your kind and most affectionate letter before leaving Kinston. It does my heart good to hear you have settled well with Fanny. I am glad all the work has paid off. I miss being by your side and watching our beloved daughter learn to talk. I'm sorry I missed hearing her say daddy for the first time. She must wonder where I am.

To answer your inquiries—Food has been harder to find than it was in Kinston. Sutlers, civilian merchants, follow the armies and for a fee provide some food and wares from the backs of their wagons. Coffee and sugar are commodities I can no longer afford because of their unreasonable prices. My clothes are holding up well, however I do wish I had brought an extra belt.

Kit has become full hospital steward, transferred to Company S. They camp near us and I still see him daily.

I have witnessed some of the soldiers performing their duties with a self-sacrificing spirit and am encouraging others to do the same. It is the ones who prefer to drink and play cards that I discourage over. As soon as the paymaster visits, the gambling begins.

Most men attend services, but some troops are merely too exhausted from traveling so quickly and building bridges for our company to cross.

I heard Lincoln signed a bill forbidding slavery. Those in camp feel that since he is not the president of our Confederate States, the bill does not pertain to the South.

I will someday be glad to see Ora's little red cheeks. I hold your lovely face in memory always and miss you daily.
All my love to you and Ora and kindest regards to Fanny. John
***

Sunday Evening 29 June 1862   *Malvern Cliff*
Dearest Wife,

    We are camped by the Chickahominy River and have joined Lee's columns. In three days, the troops have battled in Mechanicsville, Gaines Mill, and today Savages Station. Each day we follow the withdrawing Yankees and battle again. I can't find the words to write regarding the atrocities I have witnessed. It is only through my Heavenly Father that I have found the strength to face the injured and dying brought off the battlefields by the thousands.

    The terrain is swampy here and thickly wooded with a horrible stench because of inadequate waste disposal. The mosquitoes are constantly at our skin, and the struggles and slaughter continue. Today the men cleared the slopes of timber for better visibility of the enemy. The Union occupies the hill. They have ground advantage.

    Every hour of every day I am awake, I comfort and console those who face death and sometimes act as orderly and administer pain-killing drugs that are rubbed or dusted into wounds. If available, we use morphine and other opiates. The field hospitals are overcrowded, and we try to separate the soldiers based on their particular wounds. The majority need limbs amputated. There isn't enough chloroform and sometimes the patient only receives a couple shots of whiskey before surgery.

    The last few nights, I have taught crowds of the blessed who were not wounded. The problem with me having preached to the men on the eve of battles is that death was imminent, and I told them God watched over them, yet I knew many would be slain. Is what they are fighting for just? Is it right for me to say their deaths are for God's purpose? I cannot justify in my own mind whether this war was started by men or God. I tend to believe it is men. If so, is it war or murder? Self-preservation or the course of justice? I pray for understanding so I may direct my fellow men.

    Your letters sustain me. Oh, how I miss holding you in my arms. Keep praying for us.
Your devoted husband, John

***

Thursday 3 July 1862   *Drewry's Bluff, Virginia*
Dearest Carrie,

    I never knew a man could miss a woman so much. What I would give to be sitting with you before the hearth with Ora at our feet and this war in the past. God intended families to be together, I am sure of it. *I pray for your safety daily. Please know all is well with me and I am blessed to be your husband.*

The battle of Malvern Hill was a bloody attempt to take by assault an elevated plateau on which the enemy had planted all its artillery. Our men charged straight into cannon fire. Three gunboats also lobbed huge shells. By nightfall we sustained heavy losses in the thousands. They estimate it will be the worst loss of life since the war began, and in only a few hours. It was unfortunate that victory was not taken here, but the final retreat of the enemy was assured during a torrent of rainfall the night after battle and the Confederate Capital has been visibly saved.

Union cannon and gunfire even came to the field hospital. Kit tirelessly held his ground as he dug bullets out of flesh and administered to the injured and dying. There are few men like my brother. If he is not on his feet performing surgery, he is out on the fields finding the injured. We have few discussions as we daily pass one another while fulfilling our duties. I seldom see him asleep in his tent. I worry for him.

I am reluctant to share with you all I have seen and experienced. Not telling you is like not being true to myself, for you are my other self, yet I must protect you. See how I wrestle with my heart and thoughts?

I would give up my life to protect you from the evils of this war. It is as the gaping jaws of hell on the battlefield and in the hospital. I would not be surprised if the Lord Himself came down to stop the carnage. How He must thrash about to see His children behave in such a manner. Although I see I can do good by bringing His comfort to the soldiers, I am not sure how much I can endure in the flesh. I must bite my tongue several times a day to not condemn the bloodshed and unnecessary loss of life. I am on my knees privately asking for the Spirit to give me compassion toward the enemy.

There is little time for preaching now. Occasionally I offer a prayer meeting in the evening, but most of my time is spent ministering to the injured and suffering.

Sometimes I write letters for the wounded who no longer have their arm or hand. The letters I dread most are condolence letters to parents of the deceased, but no task is below me. Somehow love lightens labor. When I am expected to be helpful, God stands by me.

Forgive me. Enough rambling. I know you want to hear a little cheer so let me at least say George Ward came through the fighting with only a bullet grazing his shoulder. He misses Hester greatly. If you write, please tell her he sends his love. He is unsure of his correspondence reaching her because he hasn't heard from her in many weeks.

Cousin George is also safe. He was promoted to Full Corporal and sometimes does scout work and is gone in the mask of night.

If you are able, I need you to send food that may travel in a concealed package.

Kiss baby Ora for me and tell her Papa will return. I am feeling particularly blessed that we have her and each other. I hope to someday renew the affections and love of marriage and ask God's kindest blessings to rest upon you and dear Ora.

Remember me as your most affectionate husband, John

CHAPTER FORTY-TWO

August 4, 1862 - Hillsborough

In Caroline's new life of servitude, the clicking of Fanny's knitting needles had become the constant background noise. Fanny made socks and gloves for soldiers, which Caroline regularly delivered to the Hillsborough Soldiers Aid Society.

"Can I bring you dinner?" Caroline asked.

"I'm hankerin' fir some o' that fried okra ya made last night. Is there any left?" Fanny answered without missing a purl-two-slip-one, then dislodged a wad of tobacco from her cheek into the spittoon.

Caroline put her hand over her nose. She'd become accustomed to many of Fanny's crass ways but never got used to the spitting. She'd put her foot down about cleaning the pot when she realized Fanny could maneuver quite well through the house and yard and could clean her own mess. Fanny knew exactly how many steps it was to the kitchen and larder and how to find her way to the privy.

"Yes, and I picked the last of the blackberries this morning. We have a little cream I could serve with them. Does that sound agreeable?"

"That'd be right nice, honey. Ya treat me like a queen."

After dinner, Caroline put Ora down for a nap.

Fanny sat knitting. "I be tickled if ya'd tell me nuther story of yer kin at the waterways."

Over the months, Caroline had found Fanny to be unusually focused on people's activities, especially the church members' lives and needs. She also did what she could regarding the needs of the soldiers. Living under the same roof made Caroline the main target of her interests, and Fanny *always* wanted to know more.

Once Caroline understood Fanny's honest and warm desires of affability, she'd shared herself completely and found the widow to be compassionate and intuitive. Caroline had shared her childhood, the deaths of Sarah and Papa, the hardships in Pollocksville, and nursing Nate back to health. She read and reread John's letters out loud almost as many times as she read them alone. "Ora's asleep, and I think it best if I go to the post office. Do you mind waiting a bit for a story?"

"Nah, that'd be dandy fir ya to git out. 'Fore ya go, if ya'd hand me the basket of beans, I'll string 'em while yer away."

Caroline came home with letters from John and Julia. Sadly, nothing from Buck, although he did write his mother occasionally. She opened John's letter first and read it quietly and then aloud to Fanny.

Monday 28 July 1862   *Virginia*
My Sweet Dove,

How much I would enjoy the quiet and peace of home. Thoughts of you and Ora are always with me.

We've been ordered to Petersburg again. I'm not sure I can move Kit, who has been recuperating in my tent these past two weeks. I fear he suffers from malaria. I've prayed over him night and day, but he seldom regains consciousness. I spoon feed him broth and administer quinine as regularly as I am able. His steadfast servant Junior is with him when I cannot be.

More soldiers have died from sickness than battle. But even with the horrendous hardships faced, men find ways to feel peace. Often they read books, perform plays, sing at night or have rituals like watching the sun set. Regularly they ask me for guidance and comfort. Religion seems to be the greatest sustainer of morale in this Godforsaken war.

I sense your worry in your letters. I have not been sick in body, only of heart. I eat two small meals a day, which sustain me. They consist primarily of coarse cornmeal baked into a cornbread of sorts and occasionally sowbelly and beans. If I can find meat to buy from the sutler, it's usually smoked, dried, or salted and keeps well in my bag. Coffee is in short supply, but it can infrequently be found for a price. Fresh fruits and vegetables have not been present in my diet for weeks. I was able to forage for wild onions yesterday and fried them with a thinly sliced potato. It sufficed. Without a gun I cannot hunt, but others who hunt occasionally share their spoils. Yes, my tent keeps me dry and my horse is still with me. Please don't worry over my situation. Heavy artillery has always been at a distance.

Thank you for the canned salmon. Wherever did you find it? It was a delicacy. I am now writing upon the paper you sent. Thank you also for the candles.

The day I see you will be a day of rejoicing. May I never leave your side again. Knowing you are someplace safe is my touchstone and sanity when around me are only pain, bloodshed, and trauma.

And now I must bid you farewell. Forgive me for serving my God and being about the Master's work. Pray for Kit. Love to all.
Your devoted husband, John

"Good heavens!" Fanny stopped her knitting. "We must pray fir poor Kit. I knowed ya have a special place in yer heart fir 'im.'"

"That I do." Caroline shivered in dread. "John's the strongest man I know, yet I'm not sure how he'd take the death of his brother."

"Bless his heart. We must trust in the Lord to make all things right. As I always say, yer preacher will come back to ya."

Caroline excused herself and went to her room. She sat on her soft bed and read the letter again. She had no right to be in a comfortable home with food in her stomach while Kit suffered and John ate two small meals a day and slept in a tent. Each day in Virginia, life and death was fought in battles or sickness, with thousands of young men missing their homes or dying away from the arms of a loved one.

An ache fed upon her insides when she thought of John near those battles and moving among the wounded and sick. What if *he* got malaria? A hard knot of emotion lodged in her throat. Being alone right now wasn't such a good idea.

She went back to Fanny and sat. "I also received a letter from Julia. Would you like to hear it?"

"Surely," Fanny said, laying her knitting in her lap.

Dearest Sister,   *July 16, 1862*
  I pray this letter finds you better off than I. For you see, I have been stripped of all distinction. No more do I own silk and lace. How will people know I am special? But forgive me, I am getting ahead of myself. Let me back up so you may better understand my horrific circumstances.
  The Yankees found our lovely plantation and decided we should no longer own fine things. The cowards came when Daniel was absent. They started their destruction in the library by chopping the beautiful mahogany desk Daniel bought in the West Indies. All his letters, deeds, and important business documents were strewn throughout the room. They smashed windows and threw books into the yard.
  I entreated them to stop, but they waved my words away as if fanning flies. They forced the children and me from the house and held us at gunpoint by the barn, where we witnessed every manner of wickedness. My children clung to my skirts crying out for their Papa, but I could not comfort them for I was quaking myself and may have let a tear fall.

The scoundrels killed every hog we owned and threw them down the well making our water putrid and unfit for human consumption. They killed all livestock, took some with them, and left others half butchered and rotting in the yard.

As for the house, they did not leave one window intact. They sliced my lovely dresses to shreds and threw them from windows. What may I ask does destroying a woman's fine clothing have to do with a man's war? Are they such cowards that they can only conquer women and children? One soldier even ran off with my silver brush and mirror. I can picture him now in his tent at night, primping and brushing his hair this way and that.

The destruction of my exquisite home went on for hours. I could not see what they were doing, but I could hear as axes struck armoires, chests of drawers, and settees.

My slaves ran hither and yon. The Yankees told them they were free, but many didn't seem to know where to go. I called to two big fieldhands and begged them to get my piano out of the house. They refused to help. And to think only an hour before they would have done my bidding with a bow at the waist! With tears on my face, I pleaded and explained it was all I had from my dear dead Daddy. They took pity on me and brought it out intact and put it in the shade of a big pecan tree.

And still dear sister, I leave the worst for last. After the thieves and butchers destroyed every piece of furniture, mirrors and paintings hanging on the walls, sliced the bedding and clothing, and carted off food and valuables, they set fire to my lovely home. The children and I moved farther away, for the flames were too hot to withstand. All the out buildings were burned down too. The smell of a well-built and comfortable home going up in flames is the smell of evil. The smoke clings to me still.

So, you see, we are left with nothing in the country. Even the crops were trampled and partially burned. I now reside in our town home in Swansboro. The piano sat under that pecan tree for days before Daniel could borrow a wagon and bring it here.

I have a few of last season's dresses in my wardrobe here in Swansboro. But little good it does me. I have no servant to help with corset and crinolines.

Good heavens! I've been raveling a thread. I will end here. I pray you are not as forlorn as I. If you are safe there, then stay. No need to put yourself in harm's way down here where Yankees slither like snakes. I know I do not get on well with your husband, but he was

right to take you away from all this, even if you still have to endure the widowhood of your marriage.
Your most loving and despairing sister, Julia

CHAPTER FORTY-THREE

August 7, 1862 - Hillsborough

With no well on Fanny's land, Caroline made daily trips to the river with a yoke and two cedar buckets—one for her kitchen garden and the other for drinking and personal needs. On Saturdays she made two runs to the river for bath water. She instituted a weekly habit of cleaning Fanny's clothes and making sure she bathed. Fanny smelled and looked much cleaner, but there was little Caroline could do for the corrosive effects of tobacco in the woman's mouth.

Glad to keep out of the sun's rays, Caroline strolled along a broad path on her way to the river under a shadowy archway of old red cedar trees. The heat had been blistering for weeks. She eventually left the protective shade, climbed a hill, and crossed a bridge. The pink, white, and purple blooms of crepe myrtles were in abundance throughout town. She walked down an incline to the south side of the river, an area the locals called Dark Walk because of the low hanging, thick tree canopies, where she stopped to rest and cool down.

Later, as she neared the river, she picked up a stick and whacked at the grasses to frighten away snakes. The east flowing river ran low because of drought. Dragonflies with lacy iridescent wings skidded along the water's shimmering green surface. She splashed some cool water on her face, then scooped water in her bucket.

Filling the second bucket, she glanced at other women in the stream's low currents, doing the same as she, and farther downstream others washing their clothes. They beat the garments against a rock. Their faces had become familiar, but Caroline never visited with them. Most were black but not all. Hillsborough had fewer slaves than Southeastern North Carolina. Many of the black folk in Orange County were free and owned their own enterprises.

"Mornin'," a black woman, as dark as Caroline's inkwell, smiled and tilted her head.

"Good morning," Caroline said. She probably would have conversed more if she wasn't so shocked at being spoken to first. She hurried and attached the buckets on either side of the yoke.

The woman stepped forward and helped her bring the yoke to her shoulders. "Have a pleasant afternoon." She smiled, picked up her own bucket, and walked up the hill.

A fog cleared from Caroline's mind. The woman probably hadn't chosen to be a servant any more than Caroline. As the woman left, Caroline suddenly missed Spicey. She remembered them playing outside together as children on a winter's day. It was so cold their breaths had come out in wisps of fog, and Spicey's eyes had grown large. Her superstitious beliefs taught her the smoky moisture was ghosts escaping their bodies. Caroline had laughed so hard she fell to the ground. Now smiling at the memory, she thought about another time when she and Spicey stacked old corncobs like building blocks and made a whole village of the dried things.

How was Spicey now? Had she safely had her baby? Truth be told, she missed her more than she missed her own sisters.

On the walk back, Caroline was filled with longings for home. She missed the smell of cotton and hearing the slaves sing the song of the harvest in the fields. She worried about Julia and the loss of her magnificent plantation home—the splendor of parties there buried in the past.

Caroline belonged to the coastal lands, hungry for fish and clams and the sweet watermelon grown out on Cedar Point. She wanted to look down Main Street to the water's edge and watch the bustle of workers on the docks with seagulls swooping for a chance to grab a stray fish.

Rounding the corner to Fanny's home, she skidded to a stop.

In front of the house, John descended from his horse, which pulled a cart behind it. Junior was also there, bent over the cart.

She ran, but the yoke dug into her shoulders and the buckets sloshed water. She shifted the yoke a little higher, but it did little to balance her load. She walked as quickly as she could. "John!" she called.

He turned and ran to her. His gaunt face had dark whiskery stubble, but his eyes were alive with love for her. "Let me take that from you." He lifted the load, placing it on his own shoulders, then kissed her on the mouth.

Love embraced her body.

He gazed at her as if nothing else was worth his attention. "How I've missed you."

"But you're home!" She threw her arms around his waist. He was so thin. "You're home." She kissed him again. Not wanting to lose a physical connection, she wrapped her arm around his waist, and they walked to the cart where Kit lay.

His body trembled. Hollow, deep-set eyes gazed at her with little recognition, and parchment skin stretched tight across his bony face.

She reluctantly let go of John and laid a hand on Kit's prominent cheekbone. "Dear Kit."

He visibly swallowed, his Adam's apple moving up then down on his thin neck.

John set the yoke in the street and gently lifted Kit from his makeshift bed with Junior's help.

Kit moaned.

Caroline ran ahead into the house to prop the door open.

Fanny sat in her customary chair, shaking a jar of cream into butter, chattering away to Ora, who sat at her feet, playing with a wooden horse on wheels. Fanny's way of knowing where the girl was in the room was to talk to her and have her jabber back.

"John's here with his brother." Caroline stopped to catch her breath. "They're carrying him in."

"Glory be! If they can git 'im up the stairs, put 'im in the child's room."

Once they had Kit settled on the bed, Caroline brought up a pitcher of water and a glass. She pulled the drapes closed while John helped Kit drink, then laid him down on a pillow. Kit immediately closed his eyes and slept.

John, Caroline, and Junior quietly went downstairs where John scooped up Ora and hugged her to him.

She babbled in pleasure.

He stepped toward Fanny. "Fanny, I'd like to introduce Junior, Kit's manservant."

Junior crinkled his brow, fingering the brim of his hat. His once great bulk had diminished to a thinness that lacked muscle.

"Pleasure, and welcome to me home." Fanny held out her hand. "Ya mus' be weary to the bone from all yer travelin'."

Junior shuffled his feet, his expression twisting. "Pleez'd to meet 'cha, Ma'am." He hesitantly took Fanny's hand in his, cocoa surrounding cream.

Caroline sat stunned. Fanny couldn't see color.

ରେ ରେ ରେ

For weeks before John came, the scorching heat of summer had driven Fanny, Ora, and Caroline to sleep on the porches at night—Fanny on the front, Caroline and Ora on the back. The situation didn't help Caroline in her fight against dirt, mice, or vermin, but it was the only way to catch a cool breeze.

Sitting on the tick, Ora squealed her delight at the air around the bushes blinking with lightning bugs. When the lights eventually drifted away, she calmed down enough to let Caroline rock her to sleep.

Caroline laid her on the bed, then went into the house and up the stairs to where John talked in low tones to Kit. She stopped at the partially open bedchamber door and listened.

"Do you think the violence of the memories will ever leave us?" Kit weakly asked.

"In time." John's voice sounded terribly sad. "The noise of the thundering guns boomed for so long, it stays with me even in my dreams."

"It has soaked into me like water into sand." Kit was silent for a moment. "It's the visions of the mangled bodies and amputations that keep me from truly resting."

"Try to forget, brother. You're already much stronger than a few days ago. We'll all be on the train tomorrow, and I'll take you to Mother's."

CHAPTER FORTY-FOUR

August 14, 1862 - Gibson House

Caroline stood on the second-story piazza, skirts swirling around her, bonnet ties flapping in the hot wind. Her stomach grumbled as John fished on the distant dock. A bad day for fishing, the wind high and sea rough, but they yearned to put something in their stomachs other than cornmeal and eggs. John had spent all their money on train tickets home and hiring a wagon to get Kit to Koonce Plantation. John and Caroline had once again come as beggars to Mama's door at Gibson House.

After the Yankees had destroyed the first garden in the spring, Mama and Betsey weren't able to plant much before the season was over. With the added mouths of John, Caroline, and Ora, they had eaten the last of the contents of the small kitchen garden two days before.

Even with hunger, Caroline was happy to be home, but sad to have left Fanny with a member of her congregation. Perhaps Buck would survive the war and care for his mother upon his return.

The Union Army in New Bern set up and enforced a blockade of imports into Swansboro. For three months, the town's citizens hadn't had important food necessities. People ate the apples off trees before they were fully ripe and would have done the same with the pecans if they were able to get through the still-thick husks.

Mama had three hens who were laying. They tried to keep from cooking the birds, but if Daniel didn't arrive within a couple days with food, they'd have to resort to eating them.

In the past at this time of year, White Oak River, Bogue Sound, and out into the ocean, the water was covered with white-sailed fishing boats. Called the net-hauling season, it lasted until November. But this year, with no strong men in town, the heavy nets of fish couldn't be pulled in.

A gust of wind came up, and John quickly put his hand on his straw hat, holding the rod with the other.

Something out in the distant water caught Caroline's attention. She moved to the end of the piazza to get a better look.

A gunboat flying the Union flag entered where the ocean met the sound.

The hair on her neck lifted. "Oh, please God, no!"

Another large ship entered with some difficulty through the narrow and winding Bogue Inlet. At the beginning of the war, a fort on nearby Huggins Island guarded the inlet, but the guns and men on the island were taken to New Bern in March for its defense. The cannons were now in the hands of the Yankees, and Swansboro was left defenseless.

Another gunboat came into view.

"John!" Caroline called, but the strong winds carried her words away. She called louder.

He didn't turn. He did stand taller, looking out toward the ships.

Caroline ran into her room, snatched Ora off the floor, and dashed out to the stair landing. "Mama, Yankees are coming in ships." She hurried down the stairs.

Mama came into the passageway holding Hester's baby, David, her face ashen. "Where's John?"

"He's on the dock fishing, but he saw the ships." She ran out the back door.

John raced toward the house, holding his fishing rod in the air. "The Yankees are in the sound!" He reached her and stopped to catch his breath. He turned to look out to the water.

Seven Union warships had dropped anchor.

"What should we do?" She clutched Ora tightly, who cried out. Caroline gave her a couple bounces.

"We don't want them firing on us," John answered, still breathing heavily. "We need to somehow let them know there are no soldiers here, just old men, women, and children."

They turned to enter the house, but found Mama blocking the doorway. She stared out to sea with a vacant look in her eyes.

John took her hand. "I'm going to put on my clergy attire and run down to the town pier. I'll try to reason with them."

Mama nodded and stepped aside, still not looking wholly present.

Fear embraced Caroline. "What if they don't listen?" She called after John. "They could fire their guns from the ships and kill you." She ran and grasped his arm. "Don't put yourself in harm's way."

"They won't harm me if they realize I'm a preacher." He pulled her hand from his arm. "Don't worry." He looked her in the eyes, his calm and sure. He hugged her briefly and then hurried up the stairs.

Mama and Caroline embraced with the babies between them. Caroline couldn't find words to comfort Mama. Ora cried.

Hester burst through the front door carrying a bottle of milk she'd gone to buy from a neighbor with a cow. The fear in her eyes probably mirrored Caroline's. "There are warships surrounding Swansboro!"

"We know," Mama and Caroline answered in unison.

"John's going down to the pier to talk with them." Caroline tried to take a deep breath and couldn't.

John came downstairs dressed in his white high-collared shirt, black vest, black long-tailed coat, and black top hat. No one but a preacher or undertaker would dress in such a manner.

Caroline handed a still crying Ora to Hester. "I'm going to the pier."

"No." He walked past her. "There's nothing you can do."

She quickened her step to meet his. "The Yankees are more unlikely to shoot a woman than a preacher. And with both of us together, I doubt they'll shoot. I can't rightly let you go alone."

"I won't put your life in danger. Stay here. If anything should happen to me, Ora needs at least one parent."

"I'm coming with you."

He stopped and took her upper arms. "You're the most stubborn woman! We don't have time for this." He stared hard at her.

She didn't flinch or back down.

Whether John saw in her unstoppable determination or knew her words to be true, she wasn't sure and didn't care.

He nodded once, and they hurried out the door and down Main Street to the town's largest pier.

Stiff legs made it hard to walk fast. Her heart thudded like when the Yankees had come on horseback to her home in Pollocksville. She hoped John didn't notice her fear. He'd let her come, and she needed to act strong.

Some women and a few old men were on the pier. They wouldn't be alone. Relief flooded her. One of the homes along Front Street flew a white flag from its upper window.

The ships looked nothing like Papa's merchant ships. Some of them had double smokestacks, others one smokestack and one mast. The sides of the ships slanted in a diagonal, floating low to the water. Along these slanted walls were open windows with cannon guns pointed at Swansboro.

Two ships moved away from the other five and sailed closer to the mouth of the White Oak River.

The anchored boats rolled and pitched in the rough waters. They were close enough for Caroline to see hundreds of sailors in blue uniforms on their decks. With perhaps a hundred people left in Swansboro, they were greatly outnumbered.

The lead gunboat released a small launch with six men on board. They rowed up near the pier.

A man stood up in the boat. He wore a ridiculously flamboyant hat, double-breasted blue uniform, with large gold-fringed epaulets on each shoulder and a red waist sash. The rowboat rolled with the waves. He grabbed the shoulders of two of the seated men. "I'm Colonel Manchester of the Third New York Marine Artillery, under the command of Acting Brigadier General Stevenson. Surrender your town peacefully, and no one will be harmed."

John walked the short distance to the end of the pier.

Caroline's chin trembled. An arm went around her waist. Mary. She wrapped her arm around her sister's waist, and felt Mary trembling too.

"There are only women, children, and elderly men here," John called. "There are no Confederate soldiers. We're not a threat to you. We have no food and are hiding nothing."

Before the Yankee officer could answer, shouts went up from one of the gunboats headed toward the river. It had struck a sandbar and listed. Waves threatened to send it over.

The men in the rowboat conversed, but they were too far away for Caroline to hear. The officer sat, and the rowboat headed toward the disabled ship on the sandbar. When it reached the helpless gunboat, the officer called commands, but the words were lost to the wind. The ship would have been an easy target if Confederate soldiers had been near about.

Hundreds of men on the boat began undressing. Caroline felt the rising heat of a blush and looked away. She could hear shouts and splashes in the water. She couldn't stand the suspense and peeked back. The men were actually trying to drag the large ship off the sandbar.

John joined Caroline and addressed the townspeople. "I never thought I'd thank God for a sandbar. It bought us some time, but I fear if seven gunboats were sent here, they have a purpose."

A woman stepped forward. "We have nothing to fight with. We should surrender and let them come into town."

"And let them do what they did last time?" someone else responded. "My children and I are starving. We can't rightly let them take the meager amount of food we have."

More voices shouted opinions.

Caroline looked to John.

"We need to send someone to bring help," John called out. He turned to Mary. "Do you know where the Dragoons are?"

"I'm not sure. I haven't received a letter from Ned in a week, and even then, he didn't want to divulge their whereabouts for safety."

"Does anyone have a horse or know of someone who can ride and get help?" John asked the crowd.

No one answered. Either they didn't have answers, or they weren't fixing to volunteer themselves or one of their young boys.

"There doesn't seem to be anything we can do here on the pier," John told them. "Go home and hide your valuables and food."

"Who has either?" a woman complained.

"If you have a place to go, you may want to leave town. We're sure to be visited by the Yankees. Pray for the Lord's hand to protect us," John said.

The crowd dispersed, and Caroline and John walked back to Gibson House. Still trembling, she took his arm. "If only we hadn't let Daniel take our horse and wagon, we might could go to White Oak."

"You're right." His voice sounded strained. "We're in danger as long as we're in town. Perhaps we have a little more time to prepare ourselves for another raid. Does your mother still have her valuables buried?"

"Yes. The salt and pepper shakers are there too." What irony. Who'd care about salt and pepper shakers if they were killed? "Other than the chickens, there's nothing left for them to take except a little cornmeal. How can we hide the chickens? Should we eat them?"

"I don't know. It will be your mother's decision. Let's go talk to her."

Mama decided the chickens would be kept on the upper back piazza—still outside, but hopefully unseen and unheard.

Time moved slowly as they waited for an invasion. Everyone on edge, they acted unnatural. Caroline snapped at Hester when she told Ora to stop whining. Hester turned her back to Caroline and quietly cried. Mama retreated to her bedchamber.

A few brave women from church came to the house, asking for Reverend Mattocks. He met with them in the parlor. Caroline didn't know what they discussed, but they didn't stay long and left with their heads held a little higher.

After a few hours of unnerving anticipation, shouts went up from the direction of the river. Caroline went out onto the back piazza, shooing the chickens away with her skirts, and looked downstream.

The once stranded gunboat floated free of obstacles. Hundreds of soldiers still undressed, with their guns over their heads, waded through the shallow waters and came ashore. Men half-dressed shocked her. To have those same men carrying guns, horrified her. Her legs went limp. She gripped the piazza railing.

John came out and saw the scene. His expression hardened. "Gather the family in one of the back upstairs bedchambers and try and keep the children occupied and quiet. I'll stay by the front door and talk to them if they enter."

In Mama's bedchamber, Caroline waited in fear with the other women. Seeing those half-naked men made her afraid they'd try and have their way with the helpless women in town. Grateful to have John home to protect them, she tried to remain calm but also worried they'd take him away again.

Mama rested on the bed. Betsey stood next to her, fanning with an old *Harper's Magazine*.

Caroline placed her hand on Mama's skirts. "Can I get you anything?"

"No thank you, darlin'." She gave Caroline a weary look, dark circles under her eyes like smudged ash. "I'm grateful your husband is with us."

"Hopefully it will be different this time."

Ora toddled to Caroline and gripped her skirts in each little fist. "Mama."

Caroline picked her up, glad the child didn't understand the danger they were in or how vulnerable she felt. She nuzzled her neck.

Ora jabbered incoherently while fingering a button on Caroline's bodice. Caroline gave her a squeeze and vowed to protect her from the evil that had entered their lives. She moved to a chair and sat Ora on her lap. Even with the windows open, the room was stifling hot. Perspiration made her dress stick to her back. She brushed the moisture off her forehead.

Being trapped, she couldn't help but dwell on what had happened in Pollocksville—how she was wounded, almost compromised, and how all her beautiful wedding gifts and clothes had been ruined or stolen. And then again, when the Yankees turned life into hell after they invaded Mama's home in April, killed her animals, destroyed the kitchen garden, freed her slaves, and took John as prisoner. The memories fueled hate and anger. She clenched her jaw and squared her shoulders, helpless to keep any of it from happening again, but determined to fight harder this time.

Betsey stared at the floor as she fanned Mama in slow sweeps. Slaves were never allowed to sit in the presence of their masters. Caroline wished Mama would tell her to take a seat.

As if reading her mind, Mama said, "Betsey, please sit down. We could be in here a long time."

"Yessum." Betsey pulled a chair over next to the bed and sat, then continued her fanning. She looked uncomfortable sitting, like she'd rise again at any moment.

Hester swayed a sleeping David on her shoulder and gnawed at her lower lip.

Even though the windows were open, they faced the back of the home and little could be heard from town. Occasionally, Caroline picked up shouts and gunshots and what sounded like the boots of many soldiers running up and down the streets. As far as she could make out, the Yankees never came to their home. She prayed for Julia's and Mary's families.

When night fell, all became quiet. The women came out of the bedchamber, hungry and weary. Caroline found John sitting in a chair by the front door. As she approached, he stood.

"It's quiet," her voice wavered. "What do you think has happened?"

"I don't know. I'll go check on folks."

She nodded, hoping the soldiers had gone back to their ships for the night.

After eating a scant meal, she put Ora to bed and then went out to the piazza. Other than crickets chirping, the night was still, the hens asleep on their nesting boxes.

Small twinkling lights shined from the ships. She counted. There were still seven. If not so disquieting, she'd have found the sight as beautiful as the stars on a clear night. A breeze blew, and she faintly heard "The Battle Cry of Freedom" being sung by the Yankee soldiers. The tune was haunting, and the lyrics different than what her soldiers sang.

How could they proudly shout the battle cry of freedom when they trampled on women and children? What kind of battle were they trying to win?

The flickering lights on the dark water and beauty of the melody juxtaposed her feelings of anger and fear. "Let's pray they leave at first light." Even as she said the words, she didn't believe it would happen. John was right. Seven gunships didn't come to harass women and steal their meager fare. They had another mission.

CHAPTER FORTY-FIVE

Caroline waited over two hours for John to come home. When he finally arrived, they sat at the dining room table while Betsey brought in a cold fare of corn hoecake and honey—a meal only Negroes used to eat. Even worse, there was no longer fatback to give it flavor.

"They took sheep, chickens, and any food they found." John shared stories of Yankees stealing from homes, mostly along the waterfront. "They slaughtered all the animals before taking them to their ships. They said it was 'to appease their hunger.' I suppose the hunger of women and children means nothing to them. War turns men into uncivilized brutes." He rubbed his hand across his eyes. "McLean's store was broken into, and they stole tobacco and barrels of smoked fish and pork."

Caroline's stomach grumbled, and she fisted her hands. "I truly hate the Yankees."

"Oh, Carrie." He caressed her hand tenderly. "Hate is like spitting in the wind. It doesn't get on them but comes back to you. You're hurting yourself by carrying hate in your heart. They'll never realize your feelings, but it has the means to destroy *you*."

She raised her chin a fraction. "Well then, I'll try not to hate." But even she heard the lie in her voice. "But I do wish them all a life of misery and an afterlife in hell." She pulled her hand from his and ran up the stairs to her bedchamber. She didn't want another sermon.

She kicked a chair then plopped on the bed, hungry and weary. Why had she ever wanted to leave Hillsborough, where she never once saw Federal soldiers?

When John came into the bedchamber, she was already in bed with her back toward him, the candle extinguished. She listened while he undressed, put on nightclothes, and sunk into bed, the cornhusks crunching and crackling. Feather ticks were a thing of the past, but at least cornhusks were more comfortable than ropes.

He didn't reach out. "I know it's hard to see it this way, but God loves the Yankee soldiers as much as He does you and me."

Why wasn't John angry? She stared where moonbeams cast a soft blush along the wall, her chest still hurting with hate.

"This war will destroy you if you hate. I do understand your feelings, even if you think I don't." He sighed. "I didn't tell you this before because I didn't want you to know the horrible things I witnessed at Malvern Hill." He was quiet for a long moment.

She held her breath. Would he go on?

"No one should know the horrific crimes of war." His voice hushed in anguish. "I wish the memories could leave me." He rolled onto his back. "I wouldn't want you to have these same memories, so I'll tell you the facts and leave out the worst of the carnage."

Releasing her breath slowly, she kept still, afraid he'd lose his nerve and not share his experiences. She'd wondered if he'd ever speak of them. Her hate toward the Yankees was forgotten, replaced with deep love and concern for her husband.

"I watched men come into the hospital tent with bullet holes through every part of their bodies. Some were missing limbs or soon to have them amputated. Gaping wounds made faces unrecognizable. They called out to God in their suffering. Being a chaplain, I prayed with the wounded and dying every hour of every day."

My dearest John! How dreadful it must have been.

"I always had a prayer in my heart that my words brought peace and hope for a better life or hereafter. I'd never felt so much responsibility for being God's mouthpiece. It overwhelmed me to the point where I could hardly sleep, and if I did, I'd dream in vivid color of the same grotesque images I saw daily—mutilated bodies, gaping, crimson wounds, missing limbs." He swallowed several times.

He'd told her he'd leave out the worst of the carnage. How much worse had it been?

"Then one day, a wounded young man called me over to his cot, obviously at death's door. The pain on his face was so familiar by then that I didn't let it penetrate my soul. I knew that if I felt despair, I'd never be able to make it through the day or be of help to anyone."

She tried to imagine John holding back feelings of empathy. His experiences were obviously far harder on him than she'd ever imagined.

"I knelt by his cot and said, 'How can I help you, brother?' He clasped my hand with his bloody one. My first instinct was to jerk away, but somehow, I remained still as blood flowed down his arm and onto my hand.

"He said, 'I've performed the greatest of all sins. I have killed men.' Then his face contorted with anger and, as if spitting venom, he went on, 'I've murdered with hate in my heart, feeling every last one of them deserved to die. I obviously won't be permitted into Paradise. But I need to know, where will my soul go—surely not hell?'"

Something stirred inside Caroline deeper than her hate.

"The question of breaking the commandment of *thou shalt not kill* was asked of me several times daily. Many of the wounded soldiers wanted to understand what effect murder had on their eternal souls. Since they killed in the name of war, and under direction of their country's leaders, I told them they wouldn't go to hell. I hope I was right to say such things. I needed to comfort. Yet I hesitated to tell this soldier the same thing."

Where did John get his craving to help others? She'd never understood this aspect of her husband.

One of the chickens outside cackled faintly then settled.

"With my free hand I pulled my Bible from my pocket and read to him Matthew 6, verses 14 and 15—a scripture about forgiveness—and that he must forgive those who caused the hate to grow in his heart. If he could let go of the bitterness, the Lord would share in his burdens and replace them with joy. As I counseled him, I realized *I* held bitter and angry feelings in my own heart, that I too needed to forgive the men who tried to harm you in Pollocksville."

A warmth blossomed in Caroline, spreading into her chest, relaxing her shoulders and neck. How did he love her so completely?

"That night in my tent, I thought back on the details you shared about how Frank wounded and tried to take advantage of you. And how others stole our food and destroyed our home. I tried to imagine what it felt like to be them. Hopefully, they have loved ones. After all, they are someone's son, probably a brother or husband to others. They need to live with their own actions and perhaps someday have cause to mourn because of what they did to you and Ora. It's not for me to punish them."

She hadn't realized her experiences with the Yankees had affected John so thoroughly. He kept too many of his worries quiet, perhaps tangled into what he thought suitable for a man of God.

"Personal peace rarely comes overnight. I read my scriptures and pondered and prayed for many nights. I was eventually able to forgive them. I found once I softened my heart to my enemy, I allowed God to comfort me. I think to refuse to be comforted is to consciously spurn God." He softly exhaled.

And so did she.

"Eventually my bitter feelings have been given up and replaced with compassion. It's hard to recognize our blessings when we're bitter, but once I felt compassion, I wanted to share these feelings with you and express how blessed we are to have each other. I wrote you a letter. Perhaps you remember? I'm sorry now that I didn't give you the background behind the letter. My greatest joys have come to me through being your husband."

Caroline rolled over and was welcomed into her husband's arms. She rubbed his back. "Thank you for sharing your experience. I wish my heart could be as loving as yours."

John tightened his embrace. "Let's pray for understanding and safety."

And right there, he prayed to his Lord for that and more.

CHAPTER FORTY-SIX

August 15-16, 1862

Caroline and John's hopes and prayers were not answered.
The seven Federal ships still floated in the sound the following morning. Again, officers left their ship in a launch and rowed over. John, Caroline, and others—including Mary, Hester, and Julia—met them at the town pier.

This time, the men docked their boat and stepped onto the pier.

Colonel Manchester came forward. A tall man with a stern face, he had a goatee and long mustache, waxed and turned up at the ends. "I'm sending ashore a detachment under Quartermaster J. T. Sweet. All dwellings will be thoroughly searched for arms. If you allow the search, no one will get hurt, and we'll leave peacefully."

"I'm glad we seceded," a woman yelled. "I'd never want to be in a union with the likes of you."

Colonel Manchester didn't acknowledge her. His officers kept glancing across the crowd, hands on guns, and the colonel kept his eyes on John.

"I'm the local preacher, John Mattocks," John addressed the colonel. "In the country I grew up in, we were allowed by law to bear arms. If you take our property, you're stealing."

"We're at war here, Reverend. I'm sure you understand the logistics of war. We plan to be the victors and will take every weapon we find in your town, leaving its citizens unharmed if they let us make our search peacefully."

"May I go with your quartermaster into each home?" John asked.

"You certainly may not." The colonel looked condescendingly down his nose. "Wait quietly in your own home, and be a good example to the rest of the citizens."

John's demeanor was one of frustration, but he faced the crowd and said, "Let's do as he says and keep peace."

Caroline clenched her fists, but what could John do against six men with weapons and hundreds more waiting on the gunboats?

Following John's advice, the citizens went to their homes and so did they.

Four soldiers entered the Gibson House. While one guarded them in the parlor, the other three moved through the house. Unrestrained in their methods, they emptied drawers, wardrobes, trunks, and overturned furniture, all the while saying nothing. By unforeseen luck, they didn't search the piazzas and see the chickens. When they found no weapons, they left.

Caroline and the others went to work cleaning the mess the Federals left. How many times would she pick up after their destruction?

After dark, John again went to visit with the town's citizens. He came home with news that no one had been hurt. Richard Meadows, a young Confederate soldier on furlough because of an injury, had been captured and taken prisoner on one of the gunboats.

When Caroline arose Sunday, five gunboats remained in the sound. It was rumored two had left before sunrise and sailed west along the shore. John taught a sermon to the few who were brave enough, and perhaps at peace enough, to leave their homes. Caroline attended, but had a hard time concentrating on loving as God loves.

No one stayed to visit after the service, and before nightfall, all seven boats floated in the sound.

When John came home from his nightly rounds, Caroline was already in bed. Mama's supply of lamp oil had run out, leaving only a few beeswax candles. It was decided they'd retire at dusk each night until more oil or candles could be obtained. She hated lying in the dark, knowing the soldiers were near about while John wasn't at home.

Sometime later the door squeaked open. "Carrie, are you awake?" John whispered.

"Yes. I've been waiting for your return."

He sat on the bed, the moon lighting his silhouette. "I've been talking with men who snuck into town after dark. The gunboats that left the fleet this morning, sailed along the sound and up Hawkins and Queens Creeks. They'd destroyed the salt works at Jonathan Hawkins's, Newton Saunders's, and Charles Barnum's."

She rolled onto her back and stared angrily at the ceiling, well aware of how crucial salt was for the preservation of meat and fish, packing cheese and eggs, even preserving hides. So important, salt workers were exempt from military service.

"Not only the salt works, but every outbuilding on the properties. Soldiers armed with sledgehammers and axes broke up the brick furnaces, cast iron boilers, drying pans, and vats. If they couldn't break them, they used explosives. They set fire to barrels and buildings where the salt was stored. They even burned all the firewood used to boil the sea water."

Originally worried about what they'd eat next week, now she distressed over how they'd eat in the winter without preserved meats and vegetables.

"There was some violence at Hawkins's place," he continued, his voice distraught. "The soldiers freed forty-six slaves. His daughter threatened the Yanks with a gun, but they unarmed her safely."

Caroline's fingernails bit into her palms. "Where are our soldiers? Why aren't *they* patrolling the shores and keeping us safe? They must have known the salt works a target."

"I'd like those answers myself."

"And why has someone not come forward to ride out and find help?"

"I don't think there's a horse in town. If they weren't given to our own troops, then the Yankees already took them. Even the men who snuck into town tonight were on foot."

Caroline considered her next words carefully. "I can't rightly believe I'm saying this . . . but perhaps you should try and get help? Colonel Manchester said they only wanted our weapons, but they obviously also want our food, furloughed soldiers, and slaves. They've destroyed property and now the salterns. How do we know what they'll do next and when they'll leave?"

He stroked her arm. "You know how many times I've been gone when you needed me? I can't leave you. Let's hope Daniel will return soon. He'll bring our horse and wagon and, hopefully, food."

"I've been thinking about that too. He'll bring food and our horse, then the Yankees will confiscate them. We know he'll be coming into town from the west. We need to warn him."

"I wonder if there's some way to get word to him to bring it in the cover of darkness?"

"You could do that. If you go to find us help, leave word with homes along the route. Tell them to be watching out for Daniel to warn him of the situation."

John sighed. "I'm not sure I want to leave you for even that long."

"John, listen." She sat up and grasped his hand. "You're the logical candidate to go for help. No one will abduct a preacher. Head northwest and leave word along the way for Daniel. Go to Jacksonville and see if you can determine from those in charge where the Dragoons might be. Might could there be other soldiers who can come help us?"

John bowed his head and closed his eyes.

Was he praying? He often went to God before making decisions.

"If God is with you," she whispered, "some citizen along the way may even be able to lend you a horse."

He opened his dark brown eyes and gazed at her for a long moment. He bit his lower lip. "I feel in my heart you're right, and God will be with me." He held her. "But if anything were to happen to you or Ora while I'm away, I'll never forgive myself. Be brave and keep yourselves safe." He kissed her cheek.

"I will. Don't fear for us. If we have to escape before your return, I'll leave a note of our whereabouts in the pocket of my cape in the wardrobe."

CHAPTER FORTY-SEVEN

August 17, 1862

Caroline hugged John goodbye before he left with morning's light. The sun rose on the seven Federal gunboats anchored in Bogue Sound. A few soldiers patrolled the streets but didn't enter any homes or businesses, she guessed to remind the townspeople of their presence. Was this how it felt to live in Yankee occupied New Bern?

Somehow, they still had chickens. They made a mess on the piazza floor, but Caroline was grateful for their eggs that morning. After breakfast, she sat for hours on the settee in the parlor, watching out the window while Hester tended to the children. They had started taking turns with the babies while the other "stood guard" as sentinel.

Across the street, Julia came out her front door. Opening her parasol, she descended her porch steps. She no longer wore hoops, and her dress hems trailed in the dirt. She had no slaves to sew them shorter, yet still her dress was much better than anything Caroline had to wear.

Julia headed toward Gibson House, passing three armed soldiers, who said something to her. Chin held high, she replied, but Caroline couldn't hear what was said. The soldiers raised their brows in shocked expressions while Julia turned with a sweet, serene look. She couldn't have been more gracious in her manner.

Being a southern lady, she'd never utter a harsh word, but she'd obviously lacerated with the sweetest smile and nicest-sounding words. She continued her way to the house, mounted the steps, and came in.

Caroline remembered a day when no one entered until a servant answered the door.

Julia called, "Mama? Sisters, are you home?"

Caroline came from the parlor, and both Hester and Mama descended the stairs.

"Quiet, if you please," Hester whispered. "The babies are napping."

"Well then, let's all talk in the parlor." Julia led the way.

The rest of them followed and sat. The Yankees hadn't yet taken their furniture and carpets. It may have been because the Navy wasn't in need of saddle blankets, like the men who came to Caroline's home in Pollocksville.

Wishing it were like the old days when slaves brought in tea and cakes, she yearned for the way things used to be.

Julia sat by Caroline and pulled off her gloves, laying them in her lap. "I've sent word to Mary to come join us. Since our own men aren't here to help, we need to make a plan on how to survive this Yankee invasion." She looked at each of them with a satisfied look on her face.

Mama and Hester raised an eyebrow at the same time.

Caroline almost laughed.

"Is John here, Carrie?" Julia asked.

"No. I asked him to try and find our troops and bring them here. He's on foot. I don't rightly know how long it will take him."

Julia's eyes grew wide. "I declare!"

"He's heading northwest and will stop along the way to leave word of events in Swansboro and to watch for Daniel. I believe our only chance for food is if Daniel comes in at night."

Julia smiled with a gleam in her eye. "You're a wise girl, Carrie. Southern women are highly intelligent."

Mary let herself into the house. "It's only me."

"We're in the parlor, sweetheart," Mama addressed her.

"If enough of us go against our enemies," Julia explained, "we may be able to keep them out of Swansboro."

Hester laughed in disbelief. "Hush up! We're women. What can we do? We don't have weapons. Did you forget they have guns, Julia?"

Caroline felt uncomfortable about going against soldiers, even if they had a group twenty-women strong. "Hester's right. I had to fight off a Yankee once, and I never care to relive the experience."

Mama's mouth dropped open.

Caroline realized her faux pas. She'd deliberately not told her mother details of the experience because she didn't want her to think John hadn't adequately taken care of her.

"Caroline," Mama gasped. "What in heaven's name happened?"

"I'll tell you about it later."

Hester said, "This is foolishness. I'd walk to White Oak Plantation before I'd fight a Yankee. I've seen women leaving here on foot. It can be done."

Julia shook her head, pointing at her as if she were a naughty child. "Women can be as brave as men. We don't have guns, but I've been searching my house for anything that could cause harm."

Mama put her hand to her heart. "Julia, the soldiers aren't hurting us. Why not just do as we've been doing?"

"Julia's right, Mama," Mary said. "Being female might actually help our cause. They don't take women prisoners, and they won't be expecting us to fight back."

Caroline's mind swam with the idea. Her sisters were strong-willed, but she never imagined they'd consider causing someone physical harm. She couldn't fight a Yankee—unless he assaulted her like Frank had. She'd have lost that fight if not for Nate. "I may consider your plan if I see the soldiers might cause me or my family violence. Otherwise, I can't rightly imagine hurting someone." She looked at each face.

Julia clutched Caroline's hand. "If we have a plan and are united in strength, I believe we can make them leave us alone. They need to know we're not fixing to take their bullying and thieving anymore. They're stealing food from my children's mouths. I simply won't stand for it!"

"She's right," said Mary. "I'm closest to the waterfront and can watch their movements. They've been sending about thirty men into town at a time. There are more women here than thirty. We'll have them outnumbered, and I can let y'all know when we need to strike."

Julia pulled a lace hankie from her sleeve and dabbed her eye for effect. "I've lost my beautiful country plantation home, most of my fine gowns, and all my slaves. Daniel's business holdings are irretrievable." She actually sucked in her breath, like she truly didn't want to cry.

Caroline looked closely at her moist eyes.

"After this war, I can build a new home and have new dresses made, but I'll be hanged if I'll let them burn down my town house. I'm simply not going to let them take everything." Tears ran down her cheeks. "Especially y'all." She sobbed. "I can never replace my family. I love you dearly." She wiped at her tears.

With a sense of revelation, Caroline realized Julia's speech was genuine. Caroline had already given away her slaves and old way of life, but Julia only just was learning to survive without slaves to cook her dinner, dress her, and take care of all her needs. Caroline didn't have as far to fall because she was already near the bottom, whereas Julia had been at the top all her life.

Julia was often misguided by her pride but had always been good to her family. If she had any control over it, she'd never let any one of them go without. Daniel was even now out trying to bring them food.

Caroline put her arm around Julia's shoulders. "You've always been more than generous with us. Thank you kindly for caring about our well-being."

"We love you, darlin'," Mama added.

Mary still had a fierce look in her eyes and didn't appear anywhere near tears. "We're not asking to pick a fight. We just want to be prepared if the Yankees come into our homes again. I want the enemy to know we aren't weak. I'm tired of being fearful."

Julia regained her determination from Mary's words. She smoothed her hair and put on a sad smile, but now shrewdness lit her eyes. "I've a fireplace poker that didn't melt in the plantation fire and hasn't been stolen yet." She said "yet" like soldiers would walk in at any minute and take it from her. "I can keep its end in the fire at all times. Also, we can fill our kettles with water and keep them on the stove. As you know, boiled water can be truly painful on the skin."

Mary nodded to Julia and looked to the others. "They found the rifle I had hidden under the pig trough, but I do have tongs that Ned used for hog butchering. They're sharp as knives."

Mama straightened. "The Yankees took all our kitchen knives. Can y'all think of anything in my house that can be used as a weapon?"

"Do you still have shovels in the barn?" Mary asked.

"I've never entered the barn. I'll ask Betsey to check." She shook her head, as if trying to clear it of something. "In all my days, I never thought I'd hear my daughters planning what weapons they'd use to hurt someone. I'm not sure I want y'all to go through with this plan."

Hester looked between Julia and Mary. "Genteel ladies don't fight with hot pokers, shovels, and tongs. Are every one of you daft?"

"The men aren't here to fight for us." Mary scowled at Hester. "I realize we weren't raised to do such things, but someone has to take charge of the situation before it gets worse. We'll fight if we or the children are in danger. Let's pray the men will get here so this discussion will all be for naught." She turned to Julia. "I'll go make a visit to cousins Cassey and Charlotte. They may have weapons we're unaware of."

"Good idea." Julia nodded. "I'll visit other women we can trust and spread the word."

A noise in the hallway startled them. Caroline chided herself for not being more alert to her surroundings.

Betsey stood in the doorway, a look of determination on her face. "It'd give life some meanin' iffen y'all lemme help."

Caroline gauged the other's reactions. They were all smiling.

After Julia and Mary left, Caroline continued her watch at the window and tried to picture John safely making progress on his trek. The afternoon on the streets had been quiet, with only an occasional group of Yankees passing. The house itself seemed to be holding its breath for what was to come next.

As the sun began its descent, a few soldiers staggered down Main as if drunk. Another came into view. He stopped in front of the house and vomited into the flowerbed.

Caroline pulled back in repulsion.

More soldiers came by toting an unconscious Yankee. They laid him on the ground and came up the steps.

She hurried to the door as they entered. "What do you want here? We have nothing."

The soldier slurred, "Weee aint lookin' for nothinnn'—jus' a little helllp." The man staggered, reeking of alcohol, his pale face sweating profusely.

His partner, doubled over with his arms wrapped around his abdomen, groaned.

Caroline feared he'd be sick on the floor. Visions of cleaning up the calf's blood on that same floor came to memory.

"Think we beennn poisonnned." The man bending over moaned.

Good!

Mama came into the passageway. "Why do you think you've been poisoned?"

"My stomach hurts something awwwfulll! Some of my buddies are pukin'. All the men who drank that Hollaaaand womaaan's wine . . . are feelin' siiick."

"Well, I don't have any remedies here." Mama stepped forward. "All I can suggest is to minimize your activity. Go back to your ships and give yourselves a couple days of complete bed rest. You need to allow the body to heal itself." Wise and maybe a little sly, Mama wore a sincere look.

The men departed, and the remainder of the evening Caroline and her family were left in peace.

Around midnight, she hurried across the street to Julia's, stepping quietly up the stairs and tapping lightly at the door, hoping only Julia heard. After many minutes of no response, she thought to give up and go home.

A moment later, eight-year-old Billy called out in a strangled whisper, "Who's there?"

"It's Aunt Carrie."

On the other side of the door, furniture scraped across the wooden floor, then Billy opened the door a crack and peered out. Once satisfied it was indeed his aunt, he opened the door wide. "Whatcha doin' out so late, Aunt Carrie?"

Caroline stepped in and quickly closed the door. "I need to speak with your Ma."

Pulling the poker out from behind his back, Billy gave Caroline a sheepish smile. "She sent me to check on the door. Spooked me some, but she told me to be brave and bring the poker. I'm sure glad you weren't one of them rotten soldiers."

"You're very brave." Caroline patted Billy's arm. "Not only are you named after your granddaddy, but you act like him too."

Billy puffed with pride.

She ruffled his hair. "I'm sorry to have given you a fright. Run on to bed now. I'll show myself out later."

Caroline followed Billy up the stairs. He entered his bedchamber, taking the poker with him, and she tapped on Julia's bedchamber door. "Julia."

"Is that you, Carrie?" her sister asked.

"Yes, can I come in?"

"Of course."

A candle burned on the bedside table. Julia sat in bed, nursing her baby son, Walter. What did she think of the experience when all her other infants had been fed by wet-nurse slaves?

Caroline stepped closer. "Did you get any sick Yankees here tonight?"

"Yes, the drunkards! I scooted them off my porch with a broom. Who would've thought it'd be so easy to get rid of them? If we only had enough barrels of wine to float out to the ships and get them all drunk, perhaps we could win the war."

Caroline wasn't sure if her sister was serious or jested and she chose not to laugh. "Two came to Mama's house. They said they'd been poisoned. Do you think it's true?"

"I know it's true. I went asking around after the soldiers had gone out to their boats. Missouri Holland put rat poison in her barrels of wine, knowing they'd eventually steal it from her. Seems we aren't the only ones thinking to cause the soldiers harm. I told her of our plan."

CHAPTER FORTY-EIGHT

August 18, 1862

As Caroline tatted, the repetition of the knots and loops helped her relax. With her little finger extended slightly to support the thread, she passed the shuttle across her palm and around the back of her little finger, and then continued with her double stitch.

That morning, when she'd stepped onto the front porch and looked toward the waterfront, the streets had been emptied of citizens, but not of blue-uniformed soldiers who milled about as if they needed to torment helpless women. Five days into the invasion, more white flags flew from windows, the people of the town worn down and hungry.

Besides their local problems, the south was in a drought. The effects of which were severely felt everywhere. When Daniel had left, he was sure he'd be able to find food. Caroline had her doubts. He'd been gone over a week.

The past winter and spring had been unusually wet and created wheat rust, a fungus that had destroyed much of the wheat crop. Then drought had brought failed corn crops. Elderly locals had proclaimed 1862 the driest summer in their memory. And in occupied Southeastern North Carolina, the Yankees consumed much of what could be grown. They now inhabited most cities east of the White Oak River other than the Cape Fear defense district.

The drought created food shortages as well as hardships for Confederate soldiers. As if God were punishing the people of the South, northern crops, especially wheat, boomed.

Caroline made a noise of disgust in her throat. *Why must we suffer so?*

She pulled scissors from her apron pocket, cutting the thread, leaving enough to whipstitch it into the wrong side of the tatted baby collar.

As the sharp blades came together in a snip, she examined the scissors. They were a weapon. She pictured herself burying the pointed tips into the chest of a blue-uniformed soldier. She shuddered. Could she do it? She'd have to be closer to the soldier than she ever wanted to be. Julia's poker sounded like a better idea. She slipped the scissors back into her apron pocket.

Later that night, Julia brought the devastating news that Onslow County's sheriff of twelve years, W. D. Humphrey, committed suicide after writing out his will. A friend of John's, they'd served in the same Masonic lodge. It was rumored Yankee officers had occupied Mister Humphrey's lovely three-story colonial house and freed his eighty slaves.

Caroline found herself envying his escape from hunger and fear. But then she remembered he had a wife and seven children, and her heart broke for them, putting his actions into a whole new light. He was a coward.

The next morning, after Ora woke her with fussing, Caroline couldn't get back to sleep even though Ora did. Caroline dressed and went onto the piazza in the dark. The humid air pushed against her skin. Her skirts swished against the chickens' nesting boxes. They clucked softly and then settled back asleep.

The sun rose to show the seven gunboats.

She turned her back and looked upstream to the White Oak River, sparkling gold with new light.

Where was John? It was the third day he'd been gone. Two days would've given him plenty of time to get to Jacksonville and back with help. Perhaps he'd gone farther?

In the quiet of the morning, she found herself missing Papa. As she watched waves break on the shore and grasses bowing to the gentle sea breeze, she saw her home as an unseen connection to him. "Papa, if you can hear me, send help."

She turned to a sea of blue silk.

The Union boats marred its beauty. Men moved about on all the decks. Within twenty minutes, two of the biggest gunboats pulled anchor and left, headed out to sea.

She grasped the rail, reluctant to hope for the departure of all the ships.

Two more ships soon wended their way amid the marshes to Huggins Island. What was their interest? All that remained on the deserted island were the empty barracks and open-faced earthworks.

Before long, a force of about seventy men—more than usual for excursions into town—in an armed steamboat headed toward the pier of Swansboro.

She went downstairs.

Mama, Hester, and Caroline watched from the parlor window as about twenty Yankee soldiers marched up Main Street and out of town. The rest spread through the town's streets. Some stood at corners and waited with their rifle barrels resting against their shoulders, while others entered homes, some without knocking.

A nearby explosion rocked the house.

Caroline must have risen inches off the floor. Horror poured through her body and beat in her chest. Her mother and sister stared wide-eyed at her and then each other.

Both babies upstairs cried out.

"Oh, dear lord," Mama exclaimed. "What could that have been?"

Before anyone could respond, a bang sounded at the door.

Caroline jumped, fear racing through her. She glanced around the room for anything she could use as a weapon but saw nothing other than an empty glass lamp on a side table. If she used it to hit someone, it could cut her as badly. Louder and longer banging brought her from her thoughts.

"Open up," a man's angry voice yelled.

Caroline took a deep breath. "I'll answer. Stay here." She left Hester and Mama in each other's embrace.

She opened the door to a smell of gunpowder.

Two angry soldiers stood on the porch. One much taller than the other wore his cap pushed back and sneered with a look of superiority.

"Yes?" Her voice came out in a whimper.

"We're here to take from the rich and give to the poor." Both men laughed. The tall one propelled the door open and pushed Caroline away so they could enter. The short soldier had a limp, and the left side of his body tilted as he moved slowly down the passageway.

The tall soldier stood so close she could smell his stale breath. His sideburns wrapped his powerful jaw, his nose large and pocked, eyes small and hard. "Who lives here?"

"It's my mother's home. My sister and our two babies are staying here." She hesitated. "And a servant." She didn't want to make the same mistake as last time and not mention a slave, but she feared they'd take Betsey away.

"No men here," the man with the limp called to his companion.

The babies above had quieted.

"Let's fetch the food and get out." The tall one grabbed Caroline's arm. "Take me to the kitchen."

She forced her feet to move down the passageway and into the dining room. The room was lit with the morning sun, but nothing sparkled as it used to. The silver candelabras had been stolen months ago, along with the silver utensils and the china. She led the soldier down the catwalk into the cookhouse.

When she opened the door, Betsey turned in surprise. She stood before a big black stove, cooking eggs. When the Yankee stepped in, her eyes grew large.

The soldier pushed Caroline and she stumbled against a chair.

"Where'd you get those eggs?"

The spoon in Betsey's hand shook. "From the Mizzus."

He curled his lip at Caroline. "And where did the *Mizzus*," he mocked, "get eggs?" His face was the face of a man who knew hunger.

She stiffened. "From the neighbor."

"Are you lying?" He pulled his rifle off his shoulder. "I'll ask you again. If you don't tell me the truth, I'll start by shooting your toes off and work up from there." He pointed the gun at Caroline's foot, evil seeping out of him into the kitchen.

Her fear kept her from moving.

Another explosion rocked the town.

The soldier swayed.

Startled, she grabbed the chairback to steady herself. She had a fleeting image of the cookhouse sliding down the hill into the river, but the building stilled.

The soldier righted himself and again pointed the gun at her foot. "Won't be much left of that lame excuse for an island fort when my buddies are done over there. I'm thinkin' they might keep some of the dynamite for the town." Grinning, he squinted at Caroline. "Where did the eggs come from?"

The chickens were not worth dying over. Or were they? Would they all die if he took the rest of their food? He'd find the chickens eventually. It wasn't as if their hiding place was concealed. "They're on the upstairs piazza."

"Ha! You little vixen." Without moving the gun away, he scanned the cookhouse. "Get me that sack of cornmeal."

Betsey lifted the small cloth sack off her worktable and handed it to him, then scurried backward until she hit the wall.

The soldier glanced at the women briefly, seemed to decide they were no threat, and put his gun to his shoulder. "Don't move." He then walked around the room looking into cupboards and barrels, occasionally glancing at them. Finding nothing, he again aimed his gun at Caroline. "Both of you walk into the house in front of me."

In the house, Mama and Hester faced the wall in the passageway, the man with a limp pointing a gun at them.

Caroline shuddered at how small and vulnerable the women appeared.

"Good idea, Pete." The tall soldier laughed—a sound Caroline had learned to hate. "You two get up against the wall like the others."

She moved to the wall next to Mama, Betsey beside her. Sweat trickled down her back. Would this be the way she died?

"These ladies are hiding chickens upstairs. You keep your gun trained on 'em, and I'll go capture some birds to fry."

A rock dropped into Caroline's stomach. The babies were upstairs. Tears stung her eyes. She began to pray.

The babies will be all right. A comforting voice filled her soul, and somehow, she just knew the babies would be fine.

Thank you, Lord. She didn't understand how it worked, but she recognized the peace as a true gift from God as she continued praying for safety.

Stomping and a scuffle on the piazza above them ended when the clucking and squawking was silenced.

Ora wailed.

Caroline's eyes popped open. Wallpaper designs of hanging peaches on leafy branches blurred before her eyes. Her bosom burned again with the portent that all would be well. She knew it to be so. *Thank you again, Lord.*

The sound of the soldier's boots thumped down the stairs, but the crying remained upstairs.

She exhaled slowly.

"We'll be taking our leave," the soldier said to the one guarding them. "I've got a hankering for some fried chicken." His ugly laugh rang hollow.

"Three? It's our lucky day," the man with the limp shouted. "You women keep your noses to the wall and count to one hundred."

The men left, clomping down the porch steps.

Ora continued wailing.

Caroline had none of counting to a hundred. She quickly ran up the stairs to her baby.

Later, Betsey brought two shovels and a pitchfork into the main passageway, leaning them against the wall near the front door.

Actually using them seemed so far-fetched, Caroline rolled her eyes.

The marauding expedition continued throughout the day. More boatloads of soldiers arrived.

The noises from the streets kept Caroline at the parlor window. Why the soldiers decided to create added chaos on this day, she wasn't sure.

Soldiers slithered like snakes in and out of houses and businesses. Women and children abandoned their homes like gophers escaping their holes. The heat wave hadn't let up, and all the windows were open, making the noise of the town that much more intimidating.

Caroline stood and stretched, trying to relieve some of the tension. Her stomach growled. She decided she'd better check on Mama and help Hester with the children. As she entered the passageway, she found Mama and Hester in a huddle, whispering to each other.

Caroline moved closer, and the women stopped their conversation and turned. "What are you two discussing?"

Hester reddened, but before she could answer, the sound of children's cries came from the street. "Grandmama," one of them cried out.

Mama spun away from Caroline and Hester, snatched the pitchfork, and ran outside.

Caroline gazed at Hester. "Land sakes, what . . .?" But the truth of it registered in her mind before she could even voice the question. It was Billy crying for his grandmother. Mama must've recognized the child's voice as her eldest grandson's.

A nerve-shattering male shriek pierced the air.

Hester and Caroline glanced at each other for only a moment before they grabbed the shovels and sped toward Julia's house. Caroline's skirts almost tripped her as she took in the scene.

Two Yankees had Billy off the ground between them. One pulled at his legs, the other his arms. The one at his arms wasn't letting go but scooting sideways away from Mama, who wielded the pitchfork toward his leg, where she'd obviously already struck. Pinpoints of blood swelled on his pant. "Get away, woman. We're just havin' a little fun."

"Put that child down," Mama yelled.

Caroline was shocked to hear her mother's loud voice. Never had she raised her voice to anyone.

Julia rushed out her door, carrying her poker, the fiery red tip obviously having recently left the coals.

More soldiers gathered around. They had smiles on their faces, as if they'd come to the circus. "Looks like the women here know how to frolic," one of them called out. Others laughed.

Caroline felt a tap on her shoulder.

She whirled to find a blond Yankee smiling down at her. "Planning on digging your own grave with that thing?" His eyes traveled to the shovel in her hands.

She grasped the shovel tighter, quickly brought it up and swung it toward his head.

Surprise registered in his eyes. He jumped back but not fast enough to avoid the sharp corner. A streak of blood blossomed onto his face. He touched it as if he couldn't believe he was wounded.

Caroline, as shocked as he, held tight to the shovel. One of her hands stung with what probably was a splinter. She slowly backed up, ready to swing again if the soldier moved forward. From her peripheral vision she could see more soldiers had surrounded the women, taunting them.

She straightened her back. "I'll swing again if you won't leave."

The soldier wiped his cheek, smearing the blood across his face. "I have a gun. I could shoot you right now and be done with this nonsense, but I've no desire to make war on women." He reached out his arm. "Give me the shovel."

Caterwauling from other women running down the street gave Caroline pause. As a group, the women rushed the soldiers, swinging their weapons.

Betsey ran toward them with a clothesline pole in her gnarled hands, pointed straight at the crowd in blue, screeching like a crazed woman.

The blond soldier took in the scene unfolding and, for a second lost his concentration.

Caroline blinked, swallowed hard, and felt the weight of the scissors in her apron pocket. If she went at him with the scissors, he could easily shoot her. Instead, she stepped toward him as she swung the shovel with all her strength. With a thud, the shovel made contact on his shoulder.

He went down onto the dry dirt road. Dust flew up around him.

A rebel yell like Caroline had never heard before came from the direction of north Main Street.

A wall of gray uniformed men rode in on thundering horseback with guns pointed to the sky. Her heart pounded wildly.

Someone yelled, "Whip the Yankees!"

Warning shots fired all around, and Caroline realized the Confederates couldn't shoot into the crowd with so many women mixed amongst the Yankees.

Some Confederates trotted in amongst the people with weapons drawn.

The Yankee soldiers moved so quickly toward the pier, Caroline hardly realized they were the same men who only moments ago laughed and taunted. The spot where the blond soldier had fallen was vacant.

Horses galloped past as shots were fired.

Dust stung her eyes and clogged her throat. She coughed, waved her hand to clear her vision, and searched for her family. The smell of gunpowder and dust settled over her.

More shots rang out.

She ran toward the area she last saw her family and found, along with Billy, they'd moved onto Julia's porch. As she went to mount the steps, someone pulled her around. Fear grabbed at the pit of her stomach, and she went weak. The shovel fell to the ground with a *thunk*.

John gazed at her in wonder.

In her confusion and recognition of her husband, she trembled and laugh at the same time.

The Gatlin Dragoons had finally arrived.

John's eyes registered surprise and then concern. "What happened here?"

She bent over laughing until tears came into her eyes.

John held her arm while she tried to gain control of herself.

CHAPTER FORTY-NINE

September 30, 1863 - White Oak Plantation

The new year brought a horrific battle in Gettysburg but also a new life growing inside of Caroline. John had convinced Mama to move out to the White Oak country home, where they all waited out the war and Caroline's confinement. She gave birth to another girl September eighth and named her Lorena.

Eliza, Papa Koonce, and Kit had come for an unexpected call. Mama had only an unsweetened medicinal tea of rosehips to offer her guests, but they drank it eagerly while Betsey was in the kitchen trying to put together shortbread with just a couple handfuls of cornmeal.

Caroline tried to look cheerful enough to visit with them in the parlor. She listened to Eliza, while gleaning what she could hear from the men's conversation on the other side of the room. They spoke mostly of war news.

"She looks sickly, Caroline." A noise of surprise escaped Eliza as she pulled the blanket a little further off Lorena's fragile body.

"Mama thinks it's because my diet is so poor, but there's little we can do about that." Caroline pulled the infant close, wanting to take the blame and protect her daughter from ridicule.

"The tribulations of war affect more than the soldiers, it seems." Eliza wrinkled her nose, as if she smelled something rotten. "Lorena is quite an exotic name."

"We call her Rena." But Caroline was tempted to always call her Lorena in Eliza's presence.

"Ora and now Lorena." Eliza gazed at Caroline critically. "What ever happened to simple names like Jane and Mary?"

Even in naming her daughters, Caroline had done wrong. She smiled tightly and turned her attention to the men.

"The North Carolina 26th had the greatest loss of lives at Gettysburg," Papa Koonce said.

A sick feeling gripped her. The 26th was the Confederate regiment that had come to her home in Pollocksville. She couldn't recall a single face and was glad for it now that she knew most were probably dead.

The 26th's leader, Zebulon Vance, was the man who ate while standing at Caroline's piano and watched for Yankees after the battle of New Bern. He wasn't with his regiment at Gettysburg because he was now North Carolina's governor.

John shook his head. "The Union called Gettysburg a victory, but I don't understand how either side could claim victory with over 51,000 men dead."

"It surpassed Malvern Hill's fatalities." Kit gazed toward nothing. He had recovered from malaria, but his eyes never regained their brightness. He had no plans to return to war.

"I've read the Confederacy has a problem with men leaving to care for their starving families," John said. "There are supposedly hundreds of deserters hiding out in the mountains."

"One has to have sympathy for them. It seems as if the Confederacy feels there's an unlimited supply of bodies to draw on. The soldiers keep fighting and falling." Kit avoided direct eye contact with anyone in the room as he offered his catastrophic conclusion.

Caroline wished the men would change the subject. Couldn't they see the horrors Kit played out behind those haunted eyes?

John hadn't had interest in going back to serve as chaplain after bringing Kit home. He'd stayed with Caroline for over a year now. Hester's husband, George, still served in the 27th and had been in battles at Harper's Ferry, Antietam, and Fredericksburg.

No Yankees had disrupted their quiet lives at White Oak. While she was pregnant and felt the movement of the baby within, she knew joy for the fact that life would go on and there was something to look forward to. But as if the South's suffering was carried into her womb, Rena was born unwell, and reality invaded their life again. They were fighting battles they knew they couldn't win.

"With all the bad news around us, I think it's time I shared some good with you boys." Papa Koonce glanced over at Caroline, giving her a smile that stretched his large mustache wide, and then looked to both his stepsons. "I'm sorry Ned can't be here. I'll just have to tell him in a letter."

Ned had resigned from the cavalry in January and took Mary and their son to Duplin County where he felt they'd be safe. In August, he'd re-enlisted with the North Carolina 67th Infantry Regiment.

"By the grace of God, we still have a home, even with the Federal Army having achieved permanence in New Bern." Papa Koonce's dark brows knit together. "Over the months, our fieldhands took advantage of the proximity of the Yankees and gained their freedom behind enemy lines. Foraging armies have ravaged our crops and stolen our farm animals. With all that, and the drought last year, we've given up on farming the land." Papa Koonce glanced at Eliza, and she offered her hand toward him as if to say, *go on.*

"I make a substantial enough living as a doctor." Papa Koonce looked to John then Kit. "The land we'll no longer cultivate was your ancestral Mattocks land left to Eliza as her dowager right, and we'd like the money from the sale of it to go to you two and Ned." He gave his full attention to John. "We especially hope that it will help you establish a home of your own."

Caroline let out a small gasp, the news so unexpected. *A home of our own?*

"I found a buyer who paid in coin, not with Confederate money, which isn't worth picking off the ground." Papa Koonce smiled widely. "I have $900 apiece for you boys."

John was fixing to say something when Kit said, "I don't need it." He glanced at Papa Koonce and then to his mother as if he'd just awoken. He pulled back his shoulders. "I have a home and land and have freed my slaves. They chose to stay with me. Joe and Junior help me cultivate my land and I gave them their own. My medical practice is picking up. My needs are taken care of. I don't have a wife or children to support. Please give my share to John and Ned."

Caroline focused immediately on John to gauge his reaction.

He looked as stunned as she felt.

Tears stung her eyes. Could they really hope for a better life? She never wanted to live away from her family again.

ভেত্তেত্ত

In October, John visited Swansboro and bought three buildings— the church, the Academy, and a house—all next door to one another on Elm Street.

With daily bad news about the war efforts, Caroline was apprehensive toward feeling joy over her new home, yet she couldn't help but feel some contentment in finally having a home she and John could call their own.

John preferred they stay at White Oak as long as the war continued. As much as she wanted to decorate and live in her new home, when the enemy captured and finally held Swansboro in March, she was grateful for his decision.

She was also glad to have Mama and her knowledge of medicine because Rena cared little for thriving.

CHAPTER FIFTY

April 26, 1865 - Swansboro

Coming into Swansboro on the wagon seat, it appeared to Caroline as if the town had gone into a long, deep sleep. The air smelled of the familiar moist tang of the sea, but the sounds were different. There were no ferry bells or calls from the docks or people milling about the streets. No fishermen hauled their nets ashore for wash and repair.

The Yankees had occupied Swansboro for a year until news was finally received of the war's end. Julia had sent Caroline a letter about how the Yankees had set fire to a warehouse. Julia and her children, along with other women and children, put it out and prevented other buildings from burning. McLean's store still had scorch marks.

"There's where I hope to spend the rest of my life with you." John drove the wagon past the church and pointed to their new home—a white two-story Georgian facing the waterfront with piazzas on each level.

His ardent smile excited her as much as the thought of owning their own house. "Other than needing a little paint, it's lovely."

"I'll remedy that as soon as we can find some. There's plenty more inside that needs fixing." He pulled the horses to a stop.

Benny brought another wagon behind John's and helped Hester and her new daughter, Minnie, from the wagon. Hester had decided to live with John and Caroline, hoping George would eventually come back to set up a home of their own. He'd been taken captive at Appomattox and sent to the Old Capital Prison in Washington, DC, and then recently transferred to Johnson's Island Prison in Ohio.

"This town is a sight for sore eyes." Hester shifted the baby onto her other hip. "Carrie, let's go see what the house looks like."

The first floor consisted of a center hall, an exceptionally large parlor and sunroom, and a kitchen, and a dining room in the back. The second story contained four large bedchambers. It was empty of furnishings, some of the windows were cracked, and the whole house needed a good cleaning, but Caroline couldn't stop smiling as she toured each room with Hester.

John came into the parlor. "The horses are stabled. Are you ready to tell Benny and I where to put things?"

"Yes." Caroline was already moving toward the door.

After unpacking, John found her in the kitchen, organizing the meager supplies they'd brought. "I'm going to go check on the Academy. I'll be home for supper."

If he could find enough students, John wanted to resume operations at the school. He'd convinced Caroline to teach piano and sewing to the female students. He also talked about finding a way to teach the Negroes to read. But if he did, she wondered if the town folk would keep their children from attending.

After he'd left, Hester turned from where she washed a window. "I'm not sure what work George will find once he comes home."

If he comes home. Caroline tried to shake that thought away.

"Do you think John might need a teacher at the Academy?"

"It's yet to be seen how many will return from the war. John's not sure if boys who have taken on the toils of war will want to go back to school. Did you know they're saying North Carolina lost more troops than any other state?" Past feeling at this point, she stated it as fact and nothing more.

"The war cost the south everything but its greatness. We'll rally, you'll see."

Caroline wanted to be as optimistic as Hester, but how much sadness could a nation endure? Who had not lost a friend or loved one? Even Hester's son David had died of illness during the war. She'd suffered the grief without George. Other than coming home for two furloughs, George had been gone four years.

Rena splashed nearby in a pail of dirty water, and Hester moved right quick to pick her up. Rena's boundless curiosity and subsequent illnesses kept Caroline tuckered out. At Mama's, she'd find her sneaking into cupboards and toppling John's books. Once she even wandered into the woods. When ill, which was often, Rena endured it by looking at picture books, tracing her fingers along drawings, or singing simple songs.

Caroline said to Hester, "I'm going to like having you live with me. Just keep reminding me that things will get better. After all, they couldn't possibly get worse."

CHAPTER FIFTY-ONE

July 25, 1865

When Rena was almost two, Caroline again found herself with child. Considering Rena's delicate state, Caroline worried over the prospects of the new baby's health. What kind of world would this child be born into? Food still ran low. They ate any meat they could find—birds, raccoons, rabbits. Caroline would give anything to smell smoking pork and taste bacon.

Thinner than usual, the girth of her belly still made her clothes no longer fit. Daniel had been able to order bed ticking for an exorbitant $6 a yard, which cost even less than thick homespun the locals were selling. Her family no longer owned a loom. Even if they had, she didn't know how to use it. Remembering Spicey behind the loom during their childhood, Caroline briefly wondered how she was doing. Their early lives together seemed as if a dream.

Daniel had given Caroline five yards of the ticking. The fabric would have to do for a dress. At least it wasn't black. Most women in town were dressed in widow's weeds with tattered lace collars where they had fastened a framed photo pin of their lost love.

More than 200 people lived in Swansboro before the war, less than half that number lived there now. Some men came home with limbs missing, others as thin as their skeletons. They all appeared hungry and couldn't find enough to eat even now that they were home. The war had worn them down one death and disease at a time. How many stories had the soldiers held back from their loved ones? Never unburdening their souls of the horrors they'd witnessed.

Occasionally, John shared a brief story about someone who suffered spiritually, but nothing more. Nothing about how *he* suffered. He kept his anguish to himself and had bouts of sickness more often.

Ned returned from the war painfully thin with sunken eyes and a scraggly beard. He'd received no wounds, but his constitution was so impaired that he wasn't able to perform manual labor.

Mama came into town to help Mary. One day, Betsey asked if she could have a few hours at play with the young ones. Hester took the children to her at Gibson House and came back to help Caroline make her dress. They laid out a Godey pattern Julia had loaned Caroline and began cutting along its borders.

Caroline removed the sleeve template. "Do you think our burdens are God's punishment to the South for enslaving a race of people?"

"I think our trials have much to do with many decisions of evil men." Hester snipped along the fabric.

As they continued cutting the fabric and pinning the seams together, they spoke of who had recently returned from war and who never would. And if the new president, Andrew Johnson, being a southerner himself, had sympathies for the South and would help them with recovery efforts.

Caroline glanced up and was startled to find a waif of a filthy man standing in the doorway. "What are you doing in my home?"

The stranger wore no hat, his face scabbed, blistered, and peeling. His beard was filthy, his hair long and matted, his feet wrapped in paper and rags, and his britches and shirt tattered. Dirt clung to him like he'd rolled in mud and slop. He swayed.

Caroline tensed, fearing he'd fall.

With vacant and fevered eyes, as if in slow motion, he placed his hand on the doorframe to remain standing, and then turned his gaze to Hester.

Hester sprang from her seat. "George?" Just as he began to bend at the knees, she rushed to him and held him on his feet.

They'd been told he'd sustained wounds in his arm at Wilderness, Virginia, but Caroline guessed that was minimal in comparison to what he'd gone through in prison and since. He looked like an old man at twenty-nine.

She found the same anguished look on his face as she'd seen on so many other men in town. Their expressions mirrored perpetual exhaustion and defeat.

CHAPTER FIFTY-TWO

October 10, 1865

Sitting on the porch, Caroline tried to read to Rena while Ora shrieked with laughter as her friend Jonah threw golden leaves into the air and let them shower onto their heads.

"Read." Rena pointed to the page. "Funny flowers." Laying her head on Caroline's arm, Rena wrapped her little hand around Caroline's index finger. The child loved Hans Christian Andersen fairytales, and this was the third time that week Caroline read "Little Ida's Flowers."

"'But flowers cannot dance?" cried little Ida. "Yes indeed, they can," replied the student. "When it grows dark, and everybody is asleep, they jump about quite merrily. They have a ball almost every night.'"

Rena giggled and pushed herself off the bench onto her delicate legs. She wiggled her body, then twirled in a clumsy circle. "Dancing flowers!" Her laughter was as crisp as the autumn air.

When well, she was always full of questions and playfulness, but with Caroline in the seventh month of pregnancy, she didn't have energy to keep up. Rena had seen little sickness that summer, and just when Caroline had been hopeful that her health was finally improving, fall brought on sniffles, coughs, and sore throats.

"Shall we have some dinner?" Caroline asked.

"Peanut brittle." Rena smiled like she'd suggested a sumptuous feast, swiping wispy brown curls away from her eyes.

"No candy." Caroline laughed. "Ora come in now," she called.

Ora waved to Jonah and skipped to the porch, then hopped up each step with a thud, continuing her skipping into and through the house.

Rena tried to mimic Ora's skipping but couldn't quite get the rhythm, dragging one foot behind.

Ora came back to show Rena, who lit up at the attention her sister gave.

Caroline smiled to herself, content with finally having her own home and two daughters whom she loved dearly. She followed them into the house.

Later, as she undressed Rena for bed, Caroline noticed a few red bumps on the girl's tummy. "What are these?" She touched one.

"Don't know." Rena stuck out her bottom lip.

Caroline felt her warm forehead. "Do you feel unwell?"

"Tired." Rena rubbed her upper arm.

Caroline frowned. "Is your arm tired?"

Rena nodded. "And legs." She rubbed both thighs.

Caroline turned her around and saw more red spots on her back. "John," she called, trying to keep the alarm from her voice.

When he arrived, they looked Rena over head to toe. All the spots were contained on her mid-section. John immediately left to fetch the town doctor.

Upon the doctor's examination, he wasn't sure of the cause of Rena's ailments or how serious they might be. But by morning, her eyes were glassy with fever. She moaned and complained of head and body aches.

The doctor returned, and when he saw the rash had spread over her body, he asked Caroline to step out of the room.

He placed a hand on her arm. "I'm afraid she's suffering from typhus."

As if a rope squeezed Caroline's chest, she gulped for air.

"I'd suggest the room be darkened because of her sensitivity to light. Although not contagious, you may want to move your other daughter to another bedchamber, so she doesn't see her sister suffer."

Suffer. The word nearly a physical blow, it hit Caroline in her heart. *No, Lord, no.* Too weak to stand, the doctor helped her to a chair.

By evening, Rena's fever was so high she was listless, her lips dry and blistering.

As Mama had taught, Caroline draped wet tobacco leaves on Rena's body. Kneeling at her bedside in the middle of the night, Caroline took Rena's small, chapped hand. "My sweet angel." Since birth, Caroline suspected Rena wasn't to be long on the earth, yet somehow that knowledge never really made it to Caroline's heart. Not until now. *Please God, don't take my sweet Rena.*

By the third day, an air of stillness had settled into their home. Caroline administered dogwood and red oak bark tea, but as was true with Sarah and Papa, nothing helped. Rena had stopped talking, drinking, and eventually moving.

Late that night, Caroline knelt with John beside Rena, barely feeling the cold, hard floor as her baby girl took her last breath. Gasping for her own, Caroline doubled over. A crucial part of what made her thrive had left and would never return. She'd never be whole again.

Rena's small body lay so stiff, it was only an impression of who she used to be. An empty shell. Too still. Too pale. Too silent.

Caroline took up Rena's limp little hand, wanting her daughter to grasp her finger as she always had.

John cried into his hands. "God . . ." He moaned in a muffled voice. "Take care of our baby until we see her again." He wrapped her in a blanket and held her tight against his heaving chest. "My delicate angel you will always be." Sobbing, he reached for Caroline's hand.

She grasped his, her soul hollow. Would her unborn babe feel the burden of her agonizing grief and be born with sadness? She wrapped her arms around John and Rena and stayed that way for what seemed like hours as he recited what he believed about the afterlife.

The next morning, she forced her aching body out of bed and dressed in a black mourning gown, joining the ranks of most of the women in town. She found John in Ora's room, holding her close and speaking in low tones, telling her where Rena's soul went. Caroline knew well that he could comfort. She joined them in an embrace and wept again.

Hester brought a burying quilt and made a meal none of them had the stomach to eat.

After preparing Rena's body for viewing, Caroline snipped some of Rena's hair to be woven into a wreath. John penned the date of her death in the open family Bible at her side. It was one day short of Sarah's death, six years earlier.

If there was one thing Caroline could be sure of, it was that people could vanish as though they'd never been.

CHAPTER FIFTY-THREE

October 28, 1865

Caroline awoke to three strikes of the parlor clock, her weary body crying out for more sleep. She lay in the dark, listening for the voice of her dead child. It had been two weeks since Rena had left them, yet sometimes she still felt so near. Caroline rubbed her palm against the aching heaviness of her chest.

John had his faith to pull him through. Caroline was unsure how Ora managed her feelings, or if she believed her father's explanation of Rena holding hands with God. Because why would a loving God take a child from her mother?

Pulling up her legs, Caroline pushed with her feet, rolling laboriously to her side, away from the warmth of her husband's body. She listened to his heavy breathing and recalled their days of contentment as newlyweds. Much of her happiness related to John's good heart. She was letting him down by not recovering quickly. She hoped he'd endure her leaning on him a little longer.

The moon lit Ora's small form. Although she had her own room, she often came into their bedchamber during the night and curled up on the pallet left for her on the floor. Her breathing was shallow and hard to discern, but eventually her little chest rose. All was well with Caroline's only daughter.

The ache in her chest eased a little. Ora couldn't voice why she needed to sleep near them, but Caroline sensed Ora was lonely in the room she once shared with her sister.

The clock's rhythmic ticking and John's deep breathing were the only noises.

Why could he find sleep when she could not? She couldn't remember the last time she'd arisen refreshed and ready for the day. Her anxieties consumed her at night, leaving her defeated, battered, and torn to bits by morning.

Caroline coughed. She'd developed a nagging hack after Rena's death that still lingered. The baby stretched and moved within her. *It must be a boy. It simply must!* If it was a girl, she worried she'd see only Rena in the new baby's face. But if it were a boy, she was sure his presence would cheer the family. Even though John had never voiced it, every man wanted a son, didn't he?

An hour later, she still lay awake, feeling her active unborn child. John would be up by five, which made her decide to arise. She wanted to cook him a big breakfast. "Southern comfort food," Betsey called it. In reality, it was Caroline who needed comfort, but John would find joy in her trying to bring back their old life.

She slid her legs off the bed, moving slowly because of her girth. The cold wood floor shocked her bare feet and made her shiver. She stretched her leg to reach her shoes with a toe, sliding them closer, one at a time. Bending to pick up a shoe or putting on her stockings had become impossible now that she was in her eighth month, so she wiggled each bare, swollen foot into her shoes as well as possible, leaving them unhooked until later when Ora could do the task. She pushed herself upright, belly first, and took her dressing gown off the bedpost, pulling it around her large abdomen. Her unhooked shoes flopped as she walked.

Before breakfast was complete, John entered the kitchen. "Good morning, dove. How nice to wake to the smell of your cooking." He took her in a warm embrace.

She couldn't squelch her guilt in the face of his tenderness. "I'm sorry for my lack of strength in caring for you. You've probably thought I'd rather join Rena, but I do want to be here for you and Ora." She wanted to hold him closer, but her belly was noticeably in the way.

He kissed her neck. "Take all the time you need. How are you feeling?"

"My feet and ankles are swollen most of the day." She broke the embrace and returned to the johnnycakes and kipper on the griddle.

"Do you want me to finish the breakfast?"

She shook her head.

He took a seat at the table. "I received word I'm needed in Trenton." The Academy hadn't picked up enough students, and the black folk couldn't pay for his services, so he'd resumed his circuit duties the month before. "There are two marriages and six baptisms that need to be performed. I wrote Reverend Wilson, asking if he could take my responsibilities, considering your condition. But I received a letter from his wife yesterday explaining he's in Wilmington until the end of November." He shifted in his chair. "I don't feel right about leaving you, but I don't see another answer. If I leave tomorrow, I should be back a couple weeks before the baby arrives."

Caroline was disappointed but had long since resolved herself to the idea of her husband giving his time to God's duties. At least now there was no danger of Yankee invasion. "I understand."

"I saw Mother in town. She said you're welcome to stay with her. In fact, she insisted upon it. Her servants will care for your needs. I believe you'd prefer to be with your own mother, but with her at White Oak and just old Betsey to help, I feel you'll be better off with mine. What are your thoughts?"

Tingles of alarm surfaced along her arms. She shook it off as her fatigue. John was right, the idea of having servants wait on her sounded too good to be true. How many long years had it been? "I'd be happy to go to your mother's. When would we leave?" She pumped water into a cup and slowly added it to the already bubbling porridge.

He stood and poured himself a cup of coffee, then returned to his seat. "I'd like to take you today if you're up to it. I'll ask to borrow Ned's carriage. The springs are new, and you'd be more comfortable than in the wagon."

Touched at his concern for her comforts, she placed a plate of food in front of him and kissed the top of his head. Staying with his mother gave her one more week to pull herself together to be the wife and mother she should be. "That sounds fine. Ora will enjoy the attentions of her young aunts and uncles. I'll pack immediately."

John brought her to his lap. "Don't be in such a hurry and join me for breakfast. Ora won't be up for a bit, and it might be the last time we're alone for a while."

"I'll crush you!" Caroline lightly reprimanded.

John chuckled and brought his arms around her, pressing his face into her neck. "Your weight seems little more than when I first married you. Although the babe may seem large and burdensome, you're still quite slight." He kissed her ear. "You could use a big breakfast."

"I haven't had much of an appetite lately, but for the sake of the baby, I suppose I could eat."

CHAPTER FIFTY-FOUR

November 9, 1865 - Koonce Plantation Home, Carteret County

Caroline placed a cushion on the portico rocking chair and gently maneuvered her swollen body down.

Ora waved from the yard where she played cricket with her eleven-year-old uncle, Freddie.

A raw dampness in the cold air, Caroline coughed to relieve pressure in her chest. Instead of coming to Koonce Plantation, she probably should've gone to Mama's, where healthy teas may have healed her. She should ask Eliza's servants if they knew any remedies for the cough.

By Dr. Koonce's estimation, she had at least three weeks of pregnancy left. When she arrived at the plantation, he'd examined her and recommended she get off her feet as much as possible. He seemed more concerned with her swollen ankles than he did her cough. He'd since left for a medical conference in Raleigh.

She took Papa Koonce's advice and stayed in bed late each day. It was pleasant to have access to Eliza's staff of house servants. Of course, they were now paid for their services. Caroline knew better than to ask how much.

Hard as she tried, she couldn't warm to her mother-in-law's frigid demeanor. Eliza was all business and never found time to visit other than at meals, and even then, the discussions were minimal.

Ora didn't care much for her grandmother either, but she did love John's young half-siblings. They doted on her.

Ora and Freddie bounded up the steps past Caroline.

"We're going to play in the nursery, Mama," her daughter called.

"All right, darlin'." Caroline pulled herself up to follow. Warm liquid ran down her inner thighs. "Oh, my! What . . .?" She moved her skirts.

A small puddle lay on the white painted planks, steam escaping its surface.

She put both hands on her belly. Nothing felt different. She stepped away and more warm liquid dribbled down her legs.

"Eliza!" Caroline held her skirts and went inside. At the bottom of the stairs she called up, "Eliza?"

With feather duster in hand, a young servant came from the morning room. "Mistress Koonce out back, Ma'am."

"Will you run and fetch her? I'll be in my bedchamber."

The servant nodded and walked off toward the back of the house.

Grasping the rail, Caroline slowly made her way upstairs. By the time she sat on the bed, her abdomen had hardened. She was in labor.

Eliza entered. "Are you in need of assistance?"

"My waters have broken. Can a servant go for my mother?"

"Oh, dear. What horrible timing. If only Philip were here and not in Raleigh." She walked toward the window and then turned and retraced her steps. "Your mother is almost twenty miles from here. Even if I sent a servant now, he wouldn't arrive there until after dark, and then they'd travel here tomorrow. I fear that won't work at all." She turned and walked back across the room. "Kit's only a few miles away. We might could have him here within an hour."

Caroline never wanted a man to see her in childbirth, especially not young Kit. "I wouldn't feel comfortable with Kit seeing me in undress." Her face warmed. Worried her mother-in-law took her comment as foolish or an insult to her son's doctoring, she added, "But I'm sure he's a fine doctor."

Eliza stopped her pacing and gazed at Caroline. "He is. If you won't take his services, all I can offer you is Chany, an old midwife who birthed many of the Negroes on the plantation."

While relieved that Eliza didn't push Kit's doctoring on her, Caroline wasn't particularly happy with the alternative. Chany was one of those former slaves who were outright ornery and outspoken after the war. Caroline was surprised Eliza had even kept her on. A pain grabbed at her abdomen. "I believe Chany will do."

CHAPTER FIFTY-FIVE

After the baby was born, Caroline couldn't relax—her body rigid from the altercation she'd had with Eliza about the possibility that the child had black blood in him. Caroline admitted to herself that it appeared he might.

What about the story Mama had told her of Granddaddy Simmons fathering children with his slaves? Could Caroline have Negro ancestors? Dropping her head against the headboard, she didn't dare breathe a word of her thoughts. But what if Eliza read it on her face? Caroline turned away.

Chany, who'd delivered and cleaned the baby, went back to the bureau to rinse out the towel as Eliza stepped to the bed.

Stabbing Caroline with a cutting stare, Eliza said, "I would know my son's child. It's not his. Whose child is this?"

Tears slipped down Caroline's face, and she repeated what she'd said the first time Eliza had asked. "This child is mine and John's!"

Why couldn't she go away and leave Caroline alone?

"I insist you explain why this child has the traits of a Negro," Eliza said.

"I have Negroes in my family," Caroline blurted out.

Chany's back stiffened.

Eliza gasped. "Does John know?"

"Yes," Caroline whispered. She'd told her secret to defend her virtue, and now she regretted it. She covered her face with her hands.

"We must think of what to do with the child before John returns."

Caroline sat up, shocked by her suggestion. "What do you imply? I told you he knows. He'll understand how this happened. This is John's child. He'd never agree to give him away."

"And that is the precise reason we must take care of it before he returns."

"No," Caroline wailed.

"Pull yourself together and think. You can't rightly raise a black son. He'd be ridiculed, and your family shunned. You may say he's John's son, but who'd believe you? Do you want to have to explain the other darkies in your family and embarrass your mother, sisters, and the rest of your kin? You'd be ruining lives."

Caroline slumped. She'd lost the strength to argue with her overwrought mother-in-law. Obviously, Caroline would keep her baby. She'd work something out. What Eliza suggested was impossible. How could she give away her son? John's son! He'd be so happy to have a son. Caroline envisioned John playing with his boy, holding him close and kissing him—kissing a boy whose skin was dark and nose wide. No! It wouldn't happen that way. White people didn't raise black children. Perhaps the child would look whiter as he grew?

"Massa Kit's personal man done have a chile dat die a couple days back," Chany said. "'Haps with molassey-tit we git da babe to suckle and Spicey's milk come in."

"Spicey?" Caroline rose back up. "Chany, that's my childhood maid."

Chany looked surprised and then her eyes took on understanding. "Glory be."

Eliza enthusiastically picked up where Chany ended. "She's right, Caroline." Eliza's whole body became animated. "Spicey and Junior are the perfect answer. It's only been a couple days since the death of their child. The neighbors are distant, and perhaps they haven't heard yet, or if they have, they'll figure they heard wrong once they see Spicey with a baby."

Caroline wouldn't let them convince her to give away her child.

"We'll tell John and the others that the baby died," Eliza stated, as if the deed had already been done.

CHAPTER FIFTY-SIX

November 10, 1865

Caroline slept lightly that night. When she dozed, she dreamed of former black slaves surrounding her, reaching for the baby boy in her arms. She yelled at them to keep their distance, but they acted as if she'd said nothing and kept grasping for her child.

Suddenly they were gone, and she stood chest deep in the White Oak River, holding her son above her head. She recognized the riverbank in the distance as being where the Mattocks cemetery stood. She was at the curve of the river. She turned to look at the opposite bank, to Eliza's land, with her plantation house in the distance.

Caroline's arms trembled under the kicking, squirming weight of her child, all her energy focused toward keeping him unharmed and safely out of the water. The cold river rushed around her, yet she had a strong foothold. Downstream, her mother swam and then stood. Her face was old and hair gray.

"Mama," Caroline called.

"We are all part of the river." Mama smiled sadly.

Farther downstream, Granddaddy Simmons floated on his back.

Caroline spat at him, but it fell into the river and became part of the swirling water.

Someone was farther past Granddaddy Simmons that she didn't recognize, yet somehow knew her to be related.

Caroline shared the river with her family. She looked down into its swift red current. It wasn't water but blood. Her body shuddered in great quaking convulsions. She dropped the baby, and he disappeared beneath the surface.

"Help!" she screamed, searching frantically. Her hands found nothing. She dove into the bloody liquid but couldn't swim through the thickness. Suffocating, she came up for air, blood streaming from her hair into her eyes. "Help!" she called again and again, but no one remained in the river to hear her pleas. The baby was lost.

The current pulled her down, and she went under, drowning in a river of blood.

Caroline awoke with a start to a dark and quiet room. Covered in sweat, her lungs pulled heavy. She coughed to relieve the pressure and tried to roll over, but she hurt everywhere.

Sitting up, she peered into the cradle.

The baby slept on his tummy, swaddled tightly in a blanket.

Relieved that losing him had only been a dream, she ran her hand along his back. He was only a few hours old, and already she loved him.

Her joy over having a son was dampened by memories of Eliza and Chany saying he was black. Caroline suspected them right but would have to prove them wrong. Even if the child had black features, surely there was enough white to help him pass.

She knew John better than Eliza. Caroline witnessed his fondness for the Negro, and it would make no difference to him if his son carried their looks. Yet she had to admit, it made her uncomfortable. Through the years, John had somewhat changed her beliefs, but that didn't change the facts—the blacks were illiterate, lived hard lives of labor, and were a lower class than the whites.

The door to the bedchamber opened. Eliza entered, fully clothed for the day in a gray woolen dress buttoned to her chin, her hair pulled tightly back in its usual fashion. She carried a low-lit lamp, came forward and shined the light in Caroline's face. "We need to talk." Her voice was void of emotion.

Caroline's jaw clenched, but she said nothing. She brought her legs up to the bed, feeling the residual pains of childbirth. She leaned against the headboard, coughed, and waited.

Eliza said, "I'm your elder, wiser in the ways of life."

Caroline tried to comment, "You don't—"

Eliza put her palm up. "Hear me out." She dropped her hand. "I've seen many slaves born, and I recognize your child as black. With what you've told me of your family consisting of some blacks, we cannot wait to see how black your son will look. They *always* darken as they age. I've seen enough of his features to be convinced he won't pass. I'll not have my family brought down to the level of servant and ruined by gossip."

Caroline again tried to argue.

"Let me finish," Eliza said sternly. She walked around the cradle without looking in it and placed the lamp on the bedside table. She then pulled up a chair and sat erect, hands clasped in her lap. "I see no other conclusion than to give the child to Spicey."

Caroline's heart constricted as if Eliza held it in her fist.

"That doesn't portend you'd never see the child, although I do think it best for all concerned for you to cut ties. You may think I don't know my son as well as you, but I assure you, I do. He'd never agree to such an arrangement, and that's why we won't tell him. He must believe the baby died." Her callous eyes didn't blink. "If you love the child and John, you'd see the wisdom in this plan. You couldn't raise a black child and expect to be respected by white *or* black folk. You'd ruin the reputations of your family and mine—none of us allowed into landed society again."

Eliza knew every one of Caroline's vulnerabilities.

"Your black child can destroy my son's life and his capability to be successful. Even if you moved north or west, it'd be the same. No white people love the darkies enough to befriend them. John would surely lose his job. You and I both know he loves helping others and serving his God. What kind of man would he become if he couldn't teach the youth or do the things which make him feel worthy to wear clergy garb? He represents everything right and good."

How could've such a man come from Eliza?

"None of this addresses the safety of your family," Eliza continued. "There are those who hang men for no other reason than that they are black. Now tell me what you think but keep your voice down. Your earlier outburst was unforgivable."

She wanted to lash out at Eliza and tell her what an evil woman she was. However, Caroline was ashamed of what she had to say. "I think you're right in many things." Her voice oscillated.

Eliza's mouth dropped.

"But that does not change my desires to love and keep my child. How do I give away a son? He is your grandson—son of your beloved John. Do you have no feelings for either of them?"

Eliza remained straight as a ramrod. She was inflexible and appeared as if she'd sucked a lemon. "Your son has no familial traits that attach him to me. He is a black child, born of *your* ancestry. I will not claim him. But if it will help you by giving him to Spicey, I can promise to make sure he's cared for all his life."

"John will want him educated."

"John won't know the boy's his son and will not care about his education."

Ironic that Eliza denied her grandchild an education when she'd once told Caroline she needed to insure her children were educated. And Eliza just proved she didn't know her son so well after all. John would want him educated, no matter his color.

"Kit must know of Spicey's child dying. Surely the child has already been buried, and Kit would've approved the burial on his land," Caroline said.

"I believe you're right. Although I can hardly agree to it, I can see no way around telling Kit of the situation. I won't disclose its John's son. No, that would not work at all. Those two boys care for each other too deeply. He'd tell John. I'll explain to Kit it's the bastard child of one of my servants. That way, he won't question if he eventually realizes the child is part white. Or if others ask questions, he'll know the parentage is to be a secret. In fact, it would be best to disclose as little as possible, because if there's a story to tell, you can be sure there will be someone to tell it." Eliza stood and turned her back, then walked across the room to the window.

The baby fussed, and Caroline lifted him to nurse. By the soft glow of the glass lamp, she gazed at her son. How could he have come from her and John? He looked like neither of them, yet she believed she could see small traces of Ora's little face. He was a dark thread in the fabric of the family—an outgrowth of crooked and rotting branches of her family tree. He seemed all innocence, yet could his existence be some kind of curse? By keeping him, Eliza would label him a bastard.

As he suckled, Caroline cried. Tears dropped onto his face, and she brushed them away. She hated to admit it, but what Eliza said made sense. Her son would have no chance for a happy life if he grew up in Caroline's household. However, Eliza was wrong about one thing—Caroline *could* withstand being scorned if it was for her child. It was her son being shunned she wouldn't be able to tolerate. If he lived amongst the Negro, he'd have a better chance toward living a life of acceptance. It would be best for him to not know his parentage.

If she had to give away her child, there would be no one better than Spicey to care for him. Her heart was kind and good. Although Caroline hadn't seen Spicey in years, Caroline loved the woman still. She'd have to make excuses to visit so she could watch her son's growth and make sure he was well cared for. She'd beg Spicey to let him grow up thinking himself a legitimate member of her and Junior's family.

She lovingly ran her finger down the baby's cheek, feeling in her soul it'd be the last time she'd nurse him. If a heart could truly break, hers was shattering.

She loved John too much to let him give up his career. By giving away the child, she'd be protecting John from any sorrows and disappointments he might have from raising a black son.

Being a small newborn, the child nursed for only a short time before sleeping.

Caroline placed him in his cradle. "Eliza, although it will tear my heart out . . ." The words stuck in her throat. They were words that could carry her to hell. "The child will be better off raised by Spicey." Tears streamed down Caroline's face. In that moment, she hated herself.

ଓଓଓଓ

The first rays of morning peeked through the window to a brooding quiet. The walls smelled of deceit and guilt. In the corner lay a pile of blood-darkened linens—the scene of the crime. Linens not yet carried away because servants still slept. Eliza hadn't wanted anyone to be witness to the child's features and the fact that he had lived. Chany took him soon after Eliza left. Caroline had been mistaken, it hadn't been early morning at all, but the middle of the night when Eliza came to convince her to give away her son.

Perhaps Caroline could convince herself she never cared for the child?

She remembered the vivid dream she'd had of the White Oak River taking her baby. She grew up by the head of that river, where her ancestors had settled and where their history started. Just like the White Oak River and the tributaries that compromised it, there must have been a black ancestor whose blood flowed in her veins.

The dream showed there was no leaving the river, even in death. Whom she and her son were descended from would not change. She pictured the great White Oak River flowing into the sound and then the ocean, adding to the planet's waters—flowing like history into the world.

She coughed, and her chest hurt as she became aware of people moving about the house. Glad for the excuse of childbearing, she wouldn't be expected to leave her bed.

There was a light tap at the door. It opened, and a servant came into the room. "'Scusum, but I come for de laundry."

The girl picked up the bloody bedclothes and towels. The empty cradle was pushed up against the wall. The maid seemed to be deliberately keeping her eyes from its emptiness. Eliza must have told the servants the baby had died.

The lie strangled Caroline. How could she ever again function like a productive human being? The world had changed in the single beat of her baby's heart.

CHAPTER FIFTY-SEVEN

November 11-13, 1865

Were there circumstances decreed in Heaven, which against all odds came to pass on earth? Was a mother meant to have a son who, although expelled from her body, was not of her kind—a foreigner and intruder? Would God play a part in such an injustice? Why must she atone for her ancestor's sins? Questions spun through Caroline's mind until she thought she'd scream.

She pushed the covers off her hot body and slowly set her feet on the cold floor. Her head spun, and her abdomen cramped. She gulped deep breaths and coughed, which squeezed her chest. Steadying herself, she clung to the bedpost and pulled herself to stand. Warm blood gathered on the cloth between her legs. It was too soon for her to be up, but she'd go mad if she had to stay in bed with nothing to distract her thoughts of the child.

How could she lie to John as Eliza suggested? If he found out, he'd hate her, and she might as well be dead. For years she'd suffered hardship to keep John at her side—given up her parties and gowns, social outings, and her genteel ways. She'd given away her slaves and learned to care for him herself—keeping from him her real selfish desires. Was that love or some kind of deluded insecurity of her own? And now this. She knew without a doubt John would accept his son, but Eliza was right, he'd do it at the expense of his happiness. His career. His wife.

She raised her arms to give herself balance and walked across the dark room to a chair by the window. She fell onto it as if she were a bag of flour plopping into a wagon. Pain shot through her abdomen, and she grabbed her still loose belly. All this agony and discomfort for a child she'd never know.

Slivers of clouds slid across the waning moon's face. The earth was keeping time, marching forward, ignoring her sufferings. Rena was gone, and now her son—perhaps her only son—was lost to her as well. Caroline wanted to die and join her daughter. If she died, Ora would still have her father. Mary, whose blood and Ned's were the same as Ora's, desperately wanted another child. Perhaps they could raise Ora as their own? After a few years, she wouldn't even remember she had a mother named Caroline.

She pushed the window open. Frigid wind slapped her fevered face. She leaned over the sill, drawing icy air into her lungs. She smiled bitterly at the burn, trying to relieve pain with pain. Coughs racked her body.

She could pitch herself out the window. What kind of mother could she be to Ora, anyway? A mother who gave away her child—a fiend and a pitiful soul—one who deserved no one's love.

If she fell, people would believe she was feverish after birth. A woman in delirium could do anything unholy. It would save her from having to lie to John. Save her from the suffering that kept her chest constricted and jaw tight. Save her from the pain of losing another child. The pain of seeing John's face when he was told his son was dead. The pain of living with the lie day after day.

A sob pushed its way into her throat. She swallowed hard to keep it down. *Stop it, Caroline. You're the lowest of humans. You don't deserve to feel. You don't deserve the privilege of suffering.* She willingly let herself drift into a heavy darkness, free from agony.

"Missuz Mattocks," someone called, pulling Caroline away from the window. "Missuz Mattocks."

Caroline slipped free and hit the floor. Pain shot through her head.

Someone screamed.

"Open the window," Caroline pled. "It's so hot . . ."

Heat. Fire too near. The inside of her eyes burned.

Someone was talking. A soothing voice.

John? No, he was away. Always away. Never there when she needed him. Yankees in her home, grabbing her. "No," she screamed. The image faded as darkness consumed her.

ଓଝଓଝଓଝ

Someone squeezed her hand. "Carrie, can you hear me? Open your eyes, dove. I need you. Don't leave."

John's soothing voice calmed like a peaceful day at the beach. She could feel the warmth of the sand and hear the gentle waves against the shore.

Pain rushed to the front of her head, dark and unforgiving, carrying the memory of a son. A son whose black hair was too curly. Nose too wide. Blue spot. She moaned. Darkness swallowed her again.

ଓଝଓଝଓଝ

Her breasts were hard. Painful. Heat clung to her body. "Please, open the window," she begged, her voice not sounding like her own.

"Carrie! Carrie! Can you hear me?" John touched her shoulder. "Please open your eyes."

She could feel his breath at her neck. Too hot.

"Carrie . . ." he cried into her ear.

He was crying? Why was he crying? Our Rena died. Yes, that was it. Something heavy crushed her chest. Why would not John remove it?

It was dark again, but this time Caroline could see shapes. Lavender and lemon balm filled her nose. Sweat covered her body as if she'd been bathing in her clothes. Her head hurt, as did her breasts. She wiped the wetness from her forehead and then touched the strips of fabric wrapped tightly, again and again, around her chest.

Somebody stirred. A silhouette slumped in the chair next to her bed, breathing deeply as if in slumber.

"Who's there?" she whispered. Through her confusion, comfort came in knowing she wasn't alone.

The form stirred and groaned.

"John?" She touched his shoulder.

He fell to his knees at the side of her bed. "I'm here." His smile was sad, his eyes puffy and rimmed in red. He kissed her forehead and her dry lips. "Have you come back to me at last?" His tears fell onto her neck. He wiped them away. "Please stay with me." He cupped her cheek in his wet hand. "Can you drink?"

Terribly thirsty, she nodded.

He sat on the side of the bed and reached to the bedside table for a glass of water. "Can I help you sit up?"

She nodded again.

He slipped his hand under her and pushed her forward. "Here, I'll hold it for you. Sip it slowly if you can."

The water was cool, soothing her raw throat.

John gently laid her back and placed the glass where he'd found it. "I'm sorry we lost our son." His voice was a halcyon of his innocence.

But the words cut her, slashing across her flesh, crisscrossing where her heart used to lie, carving down to her empty womb.

"We'll have more children. God hasn't abandoned us," he said with what sounded like hope in his tone.

She tried to let his words flow into her like the water had, soothing the agony her heart felt. But they didn't and she looked away.

"We'll try again as soon as you're ready." This time he sounded tired and unsure. Not like John at all. "I'll resign my post." He cried again. "Can you ever forgive me for not being here?" He didn't try to wipe away the tears this time. His eyes pled with hers, as if he needed her forgiveness. *Her* forgiveness!

Another lie to endure.

She closed her eyes, hot tears falling onto her temples and into her hair. "You being here would not have changed the outcome," she lied. "You're my rock and have always been." She opened her eyes and marveled at the love John held in his.

If he knew what she'd done, he'd turn away and leave her alone in her sorrow, as she deserved. He had it wrong—he was the pure white dove, she the snake. Their union was a sham.

ଔଔଔ

"Mama, when did you arrive?" Caroline peered through heavy eyelids at her mother dressed in black mourning attire as she opened the curtains, letting sunlight stream through the window, stinging Caroline's eyes.

"I've been here for three days, darlin'." Mama stepped forward, casting a shadow across Caroline so she could open her eyes more fully. She brushed Caroline's hair off her forehead. "I feared I'd lose you." Mama's eyes were weary, but she smiled all the same. "The Koonces sent a carriage for me when they found you with fever." She sat on the edge of the bed, grasping Caroline's hand. "I'm heartbroken about the babe. I wish they would've waited for me before they buried him." Mama's eyes misted with tears.

Caroline hadn't realized there'd been a burial—a mock burial. The elaborate scheme had started without her. As far as she could remember, Eliza hadn't been to see her since *that night*. Perhaps she was deliberately avoiding Caroline, wishing she'd die.

"I'm having sage tea made for you." Mama squeezed her hand. "It should help dry your milk."

"Did you bind me, Mama?"

"Yes, child. There are cabbage leaves under the wrappings, which I need to change. I've been by your side for days. Your blood flow has been normal, even when you were delirious. I believe we are past the worst of pneumonia. Now all we need to do is help you get your strength back."

Caroline didn't deserve Mama's tenderness.

She smiled at Caroline sadly, misreading her thoughts. "I know your sorrow. It's one too many women bear. Find a place for it in your heart, and don't let it fester. You'll have more children, I am sure."

Mama could be held in the category of John's goodness, and in high esteem with God. Caroline was evil and belonged in Purgatory.

She didn't deserve either of these people. "When did John come?"

"He came the second morning of your illness. Kit searched without rest until he found him. John loves you, Carrie. He cried over the death of your son, but it was you he couldn't bear to lose. I don't think I've ever seen a man so consumed by the need for a woman."

CHAPTER FIFTY-EIGHT

December 1, 1865 - Swansboro

The next week, when Caroline was strong enough, John took her home.

Life should've returned to its routines and normalcy, but the corrosion of self-hatred produced deeper despair. She tried to find peace in sleep, but it was fleeting. She woke at the least sound, her heart so full of loss she had no room left in it to care for those still living.

By the second week, she began taking laudanum. A bed warmer became her companion instead of John.

"What do you need?" John often asked.

How could she explain that she longed to be free of life? Thoughts of Rena were compressed to an aching tenderness. It was allowing black arms to carry away her baby boy that had killed her soul.

During the day, Caroline performed small chores as regret chewed a hole in her heart. Whole hours at a time passed where she couldn't recall what she'd been doing. She often found herself in bed in the middle of the afternoon, Ora playing on the floor near about. The child complained little, but Caroline sometimes found her daughter staring at her in confusion.

John, true to his word, declined all clerical duties. He spent a few hours a day at the Academy, having enough students to keep him teaching Latin in the mornings.

It was on one of these mornings when Ora excitedly called, "Mama! Mama! Come quick. There are feathers in the sky."

Caroline set the broom against the wall and followed her daughter's voice to the parlor, where she stood on the hassock with her hands against the windowpane.

Fingerprints to wash off.

Ora turned, her face open with wonder and joy. "Mama, look!"

Caroline stepped behind the hassock. Outside, fat white snowflakes floated from the sky. Heavy snow was so uncommon in Swansboro that she'd only seen it on rare occasions during her childhood.

"What is it, Mama?" Ora's voice reverently breathed.

"That's called snow."

John suddenly rushed in with a burst of frigid air and a crisp smell of chimney smoke.

"Papa, you have *snow* on you." Ora giggled.

John's eyes were as bright as the child's. He closed the door and rubbed his hands together. Taking off his hat, he examined the snow on its brim and blew it onto Ora.

Her squeal of delight almost touched Caroline's heart. But she might as well have not been in the room with John and Ora wrapped in each other's glee.

"Get your coat and gloves, and let's go play." John helped Ora put on winter clothes as she hopped from one foot to the other. They were out the door within minutes, running down the street toward Gibson House, probably to the hill that sloped to the riverbank.

Caroline pulled over a chair to watch the snow blanket the houses. Eventually, the fire embers smoldered low. The room became chilly. Outside, everything was covered in white—no contrast other than wisps of gray smoke coming from chimneys. Nothingness was in front of her. Emptiness in the silence. Her house a coffin, suffocating under snow.

Hours passed, and eventually John's dark form emerged from the snow drifts. He carried Ora asleep on his shoulder. "I've tuckered her out." He quietly laughed then kneeled, setting Ora on her wobbly legs and pulling off her gloves, hat, and coat. He lifted her again. "I'll put her down for a nap."

When he returned, he placed logs on the fire and stirred embers with a poker. He brought a chair next to Caroline. "It's cold here by the window. Would you like to move closer to the fire?"

She shook her head.

He left and returned with her shawl, which he draped around her shoulders, and then sat. "How can I help you?" His voice was urgent but kind.

How could she tell him how she felt without exposing the truth? Never had she told him their son died, but she might as well have. Letting him believe Eliza's story was a lie in itself. "I need some time." She looked to her hands in her lap, pale and dry.

John leaned back in his chair and folded his arms across his chest. He sat quietly for so long Caroline wondered if he'd fallen asleep. She cocked her head slightly. He was awake. In fact, he stared intently at her with his mouth closed tight and jaw set firm. She was ready for him to ask what she needed, as he had so many times before.

"We may weep in the night but find joy in the morning." He might as well have said it in his sermon voice.

"And exactly what's that supposed to imply?" She clenched her jaw. "Is it because of your faith that you feel no pain?"

It was as though she'd slapped him in the face. His head jerked back, and his eyes opened wide. "Why would you think I feel no pain?" His face reddened. "Do I have to mope around the house to show grief?"

A stone dropped in her stomach. Her mouth opened, but nothing came out. He'd insulted her, and she deserved it.

"I can't bring our son back," he said. "He's dead."

The last word hung in the air as if it were a living thing. Did he hear that it rang untrue? She would never be able to tell him his son lived. His misery was her fault.

"Just like Rena, Sarah, and your father. He's gone from this earth never to return." John's eyes filled with tears. "I feel pain so deeply sometimes I can't breathe, but my belief that I'll see my children again someday will, in time, lessen my heartache." He swallowed. "Does it annoy you that I believe in Heaven?"

Caroline yearned for Heaven, but she wouldn't make it there. Utterly ashamed of herself, she looked toward the window. "No, it doesn't annoy me. I'm sorry if I hurt you."

"Look at me." He squeezed her cold, clasped hands.

The heat of his palm moved her somehow. How long had it been since he'd touched her? She wanted to let him comfort her, but it felt wrong when she was causing his pain.

"Carrie, please!" His voice tender, he stroked her hand with his thumb. "I've lost two children I cannot bear to lose you too."

Caroline's head dropped. She moved one hand on top of his but couldn't bring herself to tell him what was in her heart. How could they ever be close again with such a hideous lie between them? She'd cast her dark shadow over the good things in their marriage, and now they were dead. She'd brought sin and evil to what had been clean and pure. She couldn't hope for a future with John. Not anymore.

The logs popped, then the room fell as silent as the snow falling outside.

CHAPTER FIFTY-NINE

December 18, 1865

The crystal-clear sky looked as if it would shatter like ice if Caroline punched her finger through it.

Inside the parlor, Mama and John talked quietly about her.

They didn't know she sat on the porch listening. Who would've expected her to be out on such a bitterly cold day?

Every critical word they'd said was true. She was surprised John's voice showed concern, considering he now slept in the parlor and they rarely spoke to one another. Guilt pinched her. She swallowed to loosen her parched throat.

"I would've expected her to pull out of it by now," he said to Mama. "The death seems to have hit her harder than Rena's, and she didn't even know the baby boy like she did Rena."

"It might be more than the loss of her son," Mama answered. "I've seen it before, women getting melancholy after birth. I'll prepare her some—"

A wagon rumbled by, cutting off Mama's words and John's reply.

"How's she sleeping?" Mama asked.

"Sometimes when I awaken, she's not in bed. She roams the house in the dark."

Caroline was grateful John didn't tell Mama where he slept.

Nights were definitely the worst. She tortured herself worrying about their son. Was he thriving? Getting enough to eat? Was he clothed well enough during this cold December? Why hadn't she considered these things before making the decision to give him away?

Mama sighed. "Has it been helpful for her sisters and me to be caring for Ora during the day, or do you think Caroline would rise to being a mother again if we stopped?"

Caroline bit her cheek. She'd given away her right to be a mother when she gave away her son.

"I really can't say," John said. "I try to get her to talk, but she won't share her suffering."

"How are you holding up?" Mama asked.

"To be honest, seeing Carrie in mental anguish has been harder to endure than losing Rena and my son. Death I can understand and deal with through my faith and a belief that they are with God in a better place. Carrie won't let me comfort her in her mourning."

Caroline thought of the house they'd shared in Pollocksville—growing a garden, learning to cook, taking care of John and Ora. Could she ever again be that person? Was that her true self or the self she wanted to portray that she believed John loved?

"Might could she need a change of scenery," Mama suggested.

"Kit has invited us for Christmas. Perhaps we'll go there if she's willing."

Going to Kit's would bring her closer to her son. Could she spy on Spicey and her family to see how he was doing? Could she walk right up to Spicey's cabin and share an open interest in the child? Caroline wasn't sure what Spicey knew. Eliza could've said it was her servant's child.

John and Mama moved farther into the house where Caroline could no longer hear them.

Heavy, endless minutes dragged by. Her mouth went dry with the anguish of missing her son. Silence grew into a void as big as the ocean Papa used to sail upon. She filled the void with unfathomable guilt.

She didn't deserve Mama and John's concern, not when she'd made them suffer. She was being punished for her choice to give away her black child. Or was it an ancestor who chose for her? Perhaps the choice had never been hers. She was part black herself.

A deep ache spread through the empty space where her heart used to be.

CHAPTER SIXTY

December 25, 1865 - Kit Mattocks Plantation Home, Carteret County

The bleak-gray sky was an omen of rain. The wind had a bitter chill. Caroline tied her black bonnet under her chin, pulled the veil over her face, and turned up the collar of her heavy mourning cape. Dressed all in black, she should be leading a funeral procession, not taking a walk to the river.

She needed to get away from the Christmas festivities. Each of Ora's squeals of delight stabbed Caroline in the ribs. As the Christmas scene unfolded, her deceit hung above her head, governing her reactions. She didn't think she could love anymore.

Her son should be with them. With her.

Throughout the day, she felt John watching her. She had to pretend his eyes weren't making her squirm. Being estranged from him was her penance.

What finally pushed her outdoors was Kit's unexpected gift of a painting he'd done the day she'd found him at the river's edge. He'd captured the water's sparkle. Other than the river's blues, he'd used various shades of green for the grasses, trees, and distant hills. Kit had named it *Renewal*, explaining that green was the color of rebirth. He felt the river could restore life.

When John and Kit had gotten into a discussion of the cleansing powers of the waters of baptism, she'd left without explanation, the massive weight of her crime crushing her chest.

She walked without noticing her surroundings. The wind picked up and flapped her cape. At the river's bank, several white ibises used their long, curved orange beaks to probe for food in the mud. Her intrusion startled them into flight, and all quieted.

Perhaps that's why she heard the twig snap. She turned and scanned the landscape. The forest dark and dense, no one appeared.

She picked her way along the river's shore and then moved up to a drier, firmer path. She almost stepped on a snake and jumped back with a scream strangled in her throat. It took her a second to realize it wasn't a snake at all but shed skin. *If only it were that easy to shed my past.* She'd leave her mistakes behind and go on with a new life.

She'd once heard that if a snake couldn't shed its skin, it died. She understood that now.

After a few hours, she turned back toward the house and found what she sought. In a clearing, three cabins stood within a hundred yards of each other, each with a winter garden, smoke coming from the chimneys. She didn't know which was Junior and Spicey's.

Concealed in the trees, she walked around the clearing. Spotting one cabin with a clothesline of worn children's dresses and a few cloth nappies, she decided to try there first.

At the first knock, Junior answered the door.

Warmth flowed from within. She'd forgotten how large Junior was. Maybe this was a bad plan? She cleared her throat and pulled the veil from her face. "Merry Christmas. Is Spicey at home?"

"Sho'nuf. Merry Christmas to ya too." He sounded friendly, despite his looks. His eyes held her in acceptance. He didn't know. He must not know.

Spicey pushed around him. "Miss Carrie! Oh, what a pleasure seein' you at my door. What brings you here? You be lost?" She hadn't changed the way she pulled her long curls into a messy knot, tying it with a length of indigo cloth. Somehow, she still looked twelve.

Caroline envied her youth and young spirit. She missed her. "I heard you had a son. I brought him a Christmas present."

Spicey looked as if she'd swallowed the snakeskin Caroline had seen. Coughing, Spicey glanced at Junior, questions written all over her face.

"We'ze humble folk, but please do come in." Junior moved away from the door and pulled a shocked Spicey with him.

Caroline pulled from her pocket a silver rattle, once given to Rena by Julia, and handed it to Spicey.

Her eyes grew large at such a precious gift. "Law! This too gen'rous. Why you brung him such a thing?"

It perhaps was a foolish idea to give something so valuable yet useless. Caroline had no money to buy the baby a gift, and it was all she could find that she hoped John wouldn't notice missing. *Things* didn't mean much to him. But Spicey's innocence was clear. She didn't know the baby she now raised was Caroline's.

"I . . . I wanted you to have it . . . to show my gratitude for the service you gave me most of my life." It was a lie. Caroline hadn't considered Spicey's service, but as soon as Caroline said it, she realized she should've given Spicey that gift and many more. Not only for past assistance and comfort, but for what she did for Caroline's son now.

"Mam, what is it?" A girl of about four stepped up.

"This a rattle. Show the babe."

The girl took the toy and shook it before walking off.

Another child toddled to Spicey's side and grasped her skirts while sucking her thumb. She stared at Caroline.

The older girl knelt next to a thickly folded blanket on the floor. Caroline peered around Spicey.

Spicey moved aside. "Come see the lil' one."

Upper lip sweating, Caroline suddenly felt faint. She drew in a long breath and steadied herself. She stepped to her son and knelt next to the older girl, who was tinkling the rattle in front of the baby's face.

Caroline had been counting the weeks. The baby was now almost seven weeks old, and he looked healthy. Chany had been right. He had the obvious look of a Negro. And although not as black as Spicey or Junior, he'd darkened considerably since his birth. He watched the silver rattle with his deep brown eyes.

She wanted to take him in her arms and run away with him.

"He been my easiest babe." Spicey's distant voice interrupted Caroline's thoughts. "Other than eatin', he fine to sleep and watch the girls at play. They act like lil mammys to him." Spicey touched Caroline's arm. "Did 'cha wanna hold him?"

The pounding in Caroline's chest said, *No, leave now while you can*, but her heart longed to hold her son. "May I?"

"Sho'nuf."

Junior placed a chair near Caroline and beckoned toward his daughters. "Come now, girlies, lets go play wid dat hog bladda ball Mister Kit gives ya."

They left and Caroline sat.

Spicey placed the baby in Caroline's aching arms.

His face showed no features that said he belonged to her or John. He was a stranger.

"Ain't he the cutest?" Spicey tenderly observed the baby with love in her eyes.

Caroline shouldn't have come. But on reflection, perhaps it was good for her to see him content here with Spicey. What might have been, but never would be, wasn't worth considering. The best way for Caroline to survive was to forget she ever had a son.

Spicey gazed at her oddly.

"I'm sorry, did you say something?"

"I ax't how Ora and Massa Mattocks be."

"Oh, forgive me." Caroline tried to smile but failed. "We've all been low since my son . . . my son . . . left."

Spicey crinkled her brow. "Oh, I's sorry to hear it."

Caroline needed Spicey to know. She wanted the connection. It was why she really came. Maybe as the years passed, Spicey could report news to Caroline. If ever the baby needed anything, Spicey would know to come. "Do you know whose child this is?"

Spicey rubbed the back of her neck nervously and blinked rapidly. "'Tis mine." She glanced away and seemed to not know where to settle her eyes.

"Spicey, look at me."

Spicey brought her gaze to Caroline and bit her lip. "Are you here to take my babe?"

"I needed to see the child and to know he was well cared for. I also wanted to make some kind of arrangement with you."

"I don't unner'stan." A tear trickled down Spicey's cheek. She quickly swiped it away but more followed.

Caroline wasn't going to let Spicey's anxiety affect her. She wanted to be strong and clearly state her intentions. "The child is mine." As much as she tried to sound unemotional, her voice broke. She looked down. As if her chest suddenly expanded, something collapsed within her. A gasping sob came from deep inside.

Spicey pulled the baby from Caroline's arms. "Mistress Koonce say the babe be mine to keep." She hugged the child tight to her bosom, and he whimpered and squirmed. "This chile a black chile. How you say it be your'n?"

Caroline stood and took a moment to compose herself. She walked to a small window.

Junior and the girls were sitting on the cold ground, bouncing the ball between each other so the littlest one could participate.

She turned to Spicey, who was now jouncing the child, trying to calm his fussing. "What I say today is only between you and me, although if you must, you can tell Junior. I need his understanding too. John thinks the baby is dead. Do you understand?"

"No." With fear so evident on Spicey's face, Caroline worried Spicey would bolt out of the house.

"I can't rightly tell you why the child looks black, but I think I must have Negro blood in me."

Spicey gasped and stopped rocking the baby.

"I gave birth to him November ninth at the Koonce plantation home."

Spicey nodded at the date.

"The midwife, Chany, told me he had the signs of a Negro. John's mother believed it." Caroline shuddered at Eliza's accusations of infidelity. "She convinced me to give the baby to you."

Spicey's streaming tears fell onto the quieted baby.

"As much as I want to, I can't raise my child." Caroline's voice caught on her words, but she wasn't going to let herself cry again.

Spicey's shoulders dropped, and she breathed a sigh of relief.

"He looks blacker than when I last saw him. But Spicey . . ." Caroline again had to gulp a deep breath to keep her emotions at bay. "I've hardly been able to maintain my sanity with his loss." Her words tumbled over each other. "I need some kind of connection to him. A word from you occasionally, perhaps? Nothing in writing. Might could we meet secretly? I want you to tell me if he's ever in need of anything."

The two women stared at each other, and Caroline's heart expanded in hope. She wished Spicey would say something or at least acknowledge she understood. It was hard for Caroline to keep from demanding obedience of Spicey, as it had been in the past.

Spicey laid the baby on the folded blanket and wiped her apron across her face. She came to Caroline. "That babe the best gift I's ever get. I don't wan'cha hurting none, no how. I know'd what it's like losing a lil one." She grasped Caroline's hands in both hers. "The Good Lord blessed me in this gift to replace my own. I feel it meant to be. But I help you ever way I know's how." Spicey took Caroline in her arms.

The memory of the last time they hugged came back to Caroline. It was over four years earlier when she'd brought Spicey here, and the last day she'd served as Caroline's slave. Shame burned her face. Why could she not accept her deep feelings for Spicey?

Spicey pulled Caroline to her in a tighter embrace. The woman's warmth and goodness gave Caroline some relief from the sin she'd been carrying. She was filled with a love for Spicey as great as that for her own family and she missed having her in her life.

"It gonna be fine, you hear." Spicey rubbed her back.

A great wall of stone broke in Caroline's chest and a sob burst from her mouth.

Spicey rocked her gently.

Caroline's body shuddered in shame and guilt and grief.

Spicey hummed her hair-brushing tune and let Caroline cry until there were no more tears to shed.

Caroline pulled away. "I could never leave my baby with anyone but you, Spicey. You always took such good care of me."

Spicey's wide smile showed how truly grateful she was to hear the compliment. "I will love this babe all the more knowing he's of you and Massa Mattocks' blood. Don't you fret none for his upbringing."

Caroline was glad she'd come. She'd seen with her own eyes that the baby was healthy, and she knew Spicey would love and care for the child the way she'd cared for Caroline most of her life.

It started raining when Caroline left. Mud from the road stuck to her boots and hems, splattering her cape. Kit and John had spoken of the cleansing powers of water. Her cleansing was mixed with brown dirt that left stains.

As she walked toward the house, the rain came down harder, soaking her bonnet and cape. Moisture reached her skin. If water did have restorative properties, she'd not be polluted with the darkness of the lie she withheld from John. Perhaps her stain was her mixed blood, and no water could wash that from her. What color was her soul— black or white?

CHAPTER SIXTY-ONE

January 2, 1866 - Swansboro

Caroline rolled onto her back and stretched her hand. It'd gone numb from being curled into a fist as she slept. Her deceit had crept into her dreams.

The bed space beside her felt cold against her palm. The distant winter sun seeped through cracks on either side of the window shade. Late morning. Again, she'd neglected her obligations to make breakfast and prepare Ora for the day.

Her secret held her captive, destroying her relationships with her husband and daughter. She'd hoped with time the sorrow of her betrayal would fade, but the longer she kept it inside, the more it invaded her life. Seeing her baby had made it worse.

Covering her eyes, she let her breath out slowly. She couldn't continue this way—she and John going about their days in silence, filled with confusion. Sometimes she screamed at him with no sound leaving her mouth.

She'd finally concluded she wasn't protecting him by not letting him know they had a Negro son. It was a fact that was rightfully his to decide how to deal with. She had to tell him, even if it meant she'd lose him. She took a deep breath. It was time.

As she got out of bed, the frigid fingers of winter chilled the air and slowed her movements, but she didn't stop for slippers or a robe. *I need to tell him.* She went downstairs, following the noises coming from the kitchen.

John stood at the basin washing dishes. Ora was nowhere in sight.

Caroline remembered Mama had promised a day of games at her house, aware of Caroline's neglect of Ora.

John appeared tired as he lifted a bowl from the soapy water and stacked it into another.

"The baby," she cleared her throat and waited for him to turn around.

He glanced over his shoulder and pulled his hands from the water then dried them on a towel.

She prepared herself for him to hate her and gripped the closest chair. "Our son is not dead." The sharpness of her words sliced through the cold air with a beat of silence.

Caroline barely breathed as John turned.

His dark-circled eyes clouded. "What are you talking about?" He frowned. "Why have you come down in your nightdress? You must be cold."

"Did you not hear me?" Her voice went up an octave.

John put the towel down and came to her, lightly touching her upper arm. "You are distraught. Come sit, and I'll pour you a cup of tea." He moved toward the stove.

She didn't sit. "I've come to tell the truth, and I must say it."

He gazed at her with weary sadness.

"Your son did not die." She clenched her fists and hit one against the chairback.

The sadness in John's eyes deepened, and he shook his head. "I know you want to believe that—"

"You must listen to me. I gave birth to a healthy son, whom Chany declared had all the markings of a Negro."

A flash of shock crossed his face.

She continued as if her life depended on her getting every word out. "Your mother was there. She can tell you. She was the one who convinced me to give him away."

"Away?" John mouthed. His tortured look of comprehension almost made Caroline stop her explanation.

She looked away. "Chany showed me the marks—a blue spot and dark nail beds and groin. She said only black babies had such features. Your mother claimed the baby could not be yours."

John's eyes were flat with pain. "My mother claimed the baby could not be mine?" He echoed her words, but they sounded horribly wrong.

She wanted to take his pain away and opened her arms.

But he didn't move.

Of course, he didn't. She'd opened her arms to torment. She dropped them to her sides, the thickness of John's silence ringing in her ears.

John's face hardened, his nostrils flaring. "You had relations with a black man?"

"No! I'd never do that." Tears burned her eyes the way his belief in her betrayal burned her heart. "The baby is yours. I told your mother—"

"You gave birth to a black baby, and you and Mother covered it up by lying to me?" Anger colored his voice. "Where is the baby?"

"He's with Junior and Spicey. I saw him last week at Kit's. He looks blacker than when he was born. Chany was right."

John looked as if she'd punched him in the stomach. His dark eyes held her in place. "What have you done? Was it because I rode the circuit? Were you so lonely that you found satisfaction in another man's bed?" Anger rolled off him like storm waves against a cliff.

"No! John, what are you saying?" She swayed.

"Or did it start with that Yankee, Nate? Have I been duped by your false love all along?" The raw misery in his eyes chilled her.

"Of course not. Listen to me." The air left her lungs. The question of her loyalty to the only man she'd ever loved slapped her out of her grief and confusion. "I gave away *our* baby because of his obvious blackness—because some time in the past, a black baby was kept in my family because his or her blackness was *not* obvious."

His shoulders dropped a fraction.

"I've never shared my bed with anyone but you." Hot tears coursed down her face. "But you are right to blame me for the child being a Negro. It was my tainted blood that made him so."

He clamped his lips and still didn't move toward her.

She'd lost him because of her deceit. "At first I argued with your mother. She was worried about your family's reputation and your ministry. She came up with the idea to give the baby away and tell you he'd died. She was never convinced the child was yours." Caroline looked at the floor.

Silence rung through the kitchen.

"There is a stain on my family for what my ancestors chose," she continued. "I had to make a decision about a child who looked like he didn't belong to us. If the truth came out, he'd always be a reminder of who I am and what is in my blood—and my family's blood. We'd all suffer, not to mention our baby. Our child won't have a place in society unless others think him black." She moved toward John.

He stepped back.

She stopped and knelt before him.

He let his arms fall to his sides, but he didn't touch her.

She clutched her chest. "I've thought of nothing else these last two months, trying to decide if I should have done something differently. I believe he will be happier with Junior and Spicey as his parents." She bowed her head. "What kind of life could he have with us? He'll be happier with his own kind. Your mother has promised to make sure his needs are met."

John groaned. "Swear to me you've not had relations with another man."

"I swear!"

"Then this child is mine, and he is not dead?" A shocked understanding registered in his voice.

"Yes."

"Could you have not trusted me enough to help you with the decision of what kind of future our child should have?"

"I should have. I'm so sorry!"

He stared her down. The room grew smaller as her "sorry" lingered in the air. Because he didn't acknowledge it, the word became magnified.

"You had no right to take my son from me." There was a sting in his words, and his eyes showed just how betrayed he felt.

Caroline's mouth went dry. The misery he wore was worse than the day they'd lost Rena. Worse than when he'd found out his son had died. Worse than when he'd thought Caroline close to death.

What would he do with that pain? It seemed too much for one person to bear. She reached out to him again.

And he pulled back.

The agony of his withdrawal pierced her heart. The John she first married would never have done such a thing.

"In one thing you are correct." His voice was rich with contempt. "Spicey will make a better mother than you."

His words hit like a hammer, doubling her over. She stared at him in shock.

He looked back as if he didn't know her.

There were no words to defend herself because he was right.

He stomped out of the kitchen.

The crack of the front door slamming after him galvanized all her nerves. She crumpled to the floor. Pain consumed every inch of her in two deaths—she'd lost her son and her husband.

CHAPTER SIXTY-TWO

January 4, 1866

Caroline tried to close her heart, but she couldn't stop seeing the hurt in John's eyes. It tore at her already tender wounds. And there was no turning back.

Two days after John left, she found herself trying to go about life's duties as if he were gone on his circuit as people suspected. Only she knew she'd lost him forever.

She rubbed a cloth across the top of her piano, brushing through the thick layer of dust until the deep, rich wood showed its grain once again. The piano had sat quiet for months. She couldn't bring herself to allow the emotions music invoked.

She sat on the piano stool, lightly touching the keys, and recalled the time her serious preacher came to call, asking permission to court her. It was the day Papa gave the piano as a gift. Sweet Papa!

Smiling, she hit a few notes of the song she'd played that day. The piano had seen so much history and helped her express so many emotions. Slaves used to dust its keys, but no more. Both Confederate and Yankee soldiers had used it as a table while anxiously watching for their foes arrival. It had traveled in the back of a wagon to homes filled with both love and sadness. Lonelier than she'd ever been, she played a few more notes and then stood to finish her dusting.

She tried to imagine how John felt. The two women he loved the most, who he'd trusted with his soul, who should've loved him back with the same trust, showed him they did not. He had to be devastated. She ached to comfort him, but she was the last person he'd want to see, even if she knew where to find him.

Despite the torment of his rejection, Caroline somehow still experienced a little relief in telling him the truth. She no longer had to live with the deceit. The guilt no longer crushed her. Her misery now was for the loss of her husband. The telling of the lie had torn him from her.

Even though she'd gone through the motions of pushing everyone away, she didn't want to be alone. But she was. *Really alone.* With no one to turn to.

As she dusted the kerosene lamp, a small white spider crawled out from the glass globe. She peered into the shade. An intricate web spanned the area from the glass chimney to the concave curve of the shade's bowl. The spider returned to its web and settled in the center.

Ensnared in a web not unlike the spider's, she couldn't release herself from the tangle of bad choices. Would she fight to leave or let herself be eaten by deceit and the sadness of loss? Had telling John the truth released her from the sticky strings, or had she hurt the person she loved the most so deeply that she would no longer be able to free herself?

She squished the spider between her finger and thumb, then dusted the web away with her cloth. She *would* endure *and* survive. She'd allowed all this to happen. She could make it better. The choices she'd made were wrong, and she needed to do what she could to correct them. John had given her the tools to survive. He'd taught her there was always someone to turn to. She put her dust cloth down on the side table and left the room, climbing the stairs to her bedchamber.

There was an irony in that her ancestors' choices gave her pain, and she'd passed that pain onto others. Her mother-in-law had led her down a road of deceit because Caroline allowed herself to be led. If she'd been strong in the first place, as John was in his views of slavery and equality, she'd never have agreed to give away her son. She acted in a moment of fatigue and weakness and long-taught falsehoods. She could've found another way. She could've worked it out with John. Maybe they both would've come to the conclusion together to give the baby to Spicey and Junior. Or perhaps they could have kept their son and traveled west and found a home of acceptance. They would've had to leave their families, but at least they'd be together. All together. Husband, wife, daughter, and son.

She entered her bedchamber and closed the door behind her.

What was she to do with her pain? Where was she to put it? The fact that she had black blood in her and passed it to her son could not be changed. She needed to let go of any alternative lives she thought she could lead and accept who she was. Shame wasn't rooted in what she *was*, it was rooted in what she *did*. It was her choices that made her good or bad.

Like the great White Oak River, she'd chosen the easy way and let the currents take her where they would. But now she needed to swim against those currents and determine her own path. It'd take strength and work, but hadn't she been learning how to do that all along?

She stood for a moment at her bedside and forced her knees to bend to the God she hoped in her heart was waiting for her. "God, are you there?" She laid her forehead on her clasped hands. "I need Your help." She tried to feel a presence.

A wagon rumbled down the road.

"God? I want to free myself from sin." An ache pushed at her heart. "I need to know You can hear me. I know I've sinned. I'm not a strong person, but I want to be. Please show me how to repair my wrongs."

A sense of not being alone came over her.

She inhaled deeply and brushed the tears from her eyes, then again clasped her hands. "I've been judgmental and not loved others as I should. I've lied to the person I love the most." She sobbed at the words, remembering the agony she caused John when she'd told him his son still lived.

Minutes passed as she tried to gain control of her emotions. The hall clock chimed.

"I'm not worthy of Your love nor John's. Tell me what I need to do to bring him back." She paused again, waiting for an answer. Instead of an audible heavenly voice, a great pain consumed her chest. "Please show me the way. I know I've been unfair to John . . . and so many others."

There was so much guilt. Betsey's tear streaked face after Papa's funeral reminded her of just a small part of what she had to feel guilty for.

"*I think* I can make amends. I can try to accept Betsey as my aunt. I know I need to accept my own heritage. Help me embrace the black blood that is mine." She dug deeper into her soul. "Please forgive me for not accepting Betsey, or my son, and most especially for hurting John. Forgive my pride, lies, and betrayal." The anguish of imprisonment by her sins made her desperate to unshackle herself. "Please God, please help me. I know I'm unworthy but show me the way."

A small shaft of unearthly warmth spread through her body. As if a small ray of light suddenly broke through dark clouds. She desired more. She wanted the sun.

"Oh, God! You are here." The words deepened the realization. Fingers of light surrounded her heart and filled her mind. "How could I have denied Your existence?" Uncontrollable sobs wracked her body for many minutes. "I'm sorry I gave away my baby and deceived John. Why did I do it?"

She knew the answer—she cared too deeply about what others thought of her. The roots of her sins stemmed from pride. She needed to change. "Please God, help me change my desires. The sins of my forefathers were delivered upon my head, but that did not give me the right to hide my son and lie to others. What must I do?" Again, she listened for an answer.

Amazingly, the all-consuming warmth of love flowed through her body, stronger than if she'd actually heard the Lord say, "I love you." With the love came the light of hope. The guilt and sadness that had draped across her shoulders like a heavy shawl was lifted. Peace replaced its heaviness. Something dormant but familiar came to life.

Still on her knees, she straightened her back and lifted her head. Afraid to open her eyes and lose the feeling, she whispered, "I feel You." And then said louder, "I feel You, Lord." At the realization of His nearness and pure love for her, humility overwhelmed her. A God over as many children as there were sands of the sea had turned His sights to her. She was as sure of His listening ear as she was of her own existence.

"My Heavenly Father," she breathed reverently, "thank you for my life." She meant the words, even though it had been a life burdened in much affliction. "Thank you for my lovely children." Visions of Ora's sweet face came as true gratitude poured through Caroline for a healthy child. Rena had not been healthy, but Caroline still was grateful to have shared her short life. "Please Lord, keep Rena by Your side until I can join her. I know now she's in a better place. And thank you, Lord, for my righteous husband while I had him. I did not deserve such a good man."

Loathing to ask the question, but needing to know the answer as badly as she needed the breath she breathed, she asked, "Should I leave my son with Spicey and Junior?"

Yes, the affirmative answer immediately came to her. As to that, somehow, she had done right. The Spirit whispered to her heart that it was not for her good but for the child's. At last she found peace with the decision. She could accept the pain if her son did not have to feel it. He was safe and happy where he was. That was enough.

"Can you soften John's heart and show him the baby is where he should be?" Caroline did not receive an answer, but her mind and heart begged God that it be so.

"Please forgive me for allowing my pride to let me offend others. I should not have listened to Eliza. I should not have deceived John. My sins are great. Can You forgive me?"

This new love from God she'd felt only moments before filled her more fully. His light shown in her soul, healing every dark misdeed. She could not deny the truth of it. It excited her heart, mind, and body.

Her sins were forgiven, and the relief made her slump back to her bed. She quietly cried and thanked her Lord for such an exquisite gift.

Feeling God's love made her want to change. She must make a sacrifice to the Lord for His great love and forgiveness. What could her sacrifice be? She knew as soon as she asked. Her pride. She would no longer look at others as beneath her. "Please, Lord, help me be strong so I may follow through with these convictions. I want to set things right." His love made her want to change and correct all the misery she'd caused others.

A miracle had been given her. Her offenses were forgiven, and she'd witnessed the presence of a loving God, who was not one she should fear. He was a personal God. He took time to speak to her soul and allow her to feel a love stronger than anything she'd ever felt before. She was not overlooked, even in her shortcomings.

Flooded with well-being and comfort, Caroline finished her prayer by pouring out feelings of gratitude and promised to make amends with those she'd pulled into her acts of selfishness.

CHAPTER SIXTY-THREE

January 5, 1866 - Gibson Home

Caroline found Betsey in Mama's warm cookhouse, smelling of fried chicken livers and biscuits. Cold, biting wind whistled through the cracks in the door, wailing a ghostly cry.

"Mornin'." Betsey's genuine smile brightened her face.

With a lump in her throat, Caroline walked to the worktable. Thoughts circling, she wasn't sure where to begin.

Her gaze settled on Betsey's hands. She knew them nearly as well as her own. Before she'd married, they'd served her almost every meal, mended her clothes, made her bed, and bathed her in the cookhouse when Mammy Abby cared for one of Caroline's siblings.

Now, those hands wore wrinkles and brown spots. Dry and cracked from years of using lye soap, they had thick purple veins running across the back and around knobby knuckles grown big with arthritis. The index and pinky fingers curved either inward or jutted unnaturally out, like wayward tree branches. It looked painful, but Caroline had never heard Betsey complain.

It was time to let them rest. Caroline gently laid her hands on Betsey's. Youthful and pale contrasted with aged and weathered, like cream on toast. A perfect duo. The warmth of Betsey's skin calmed her anxiety.

Betsey returned Caroline's gaze.

How had she not noticed the deep wrinkles cutting into Betsey's forehead, trenching prominent cheek bones—lines that told stories of daily hardships and worries.

In Betsey's features, Caroline found Papa's familiar face, mostly in the woman's eyes. They were a comforting brown, like pliable silk, yet clear and not a gelatinous yellow like so many others her age.

Silence hung in the air, then Betsey smiled, her hollow cheeks filling with folds of loose skin. "Miss Carrie?" Her voice flowed warm. "Can I hep ya?"

Caroline collected her words while her heart sped up. "I think I'm hoping for something that cannot be mine."

"'Scus'm?" Betsey's face crinkled with deeper folds. She stood motionless.

"You're my Aunt Betsey, are you not?" Caroline gently squeezed Betsey's hands.

Shock shot into her eyes, and she flinched. "Yessum, I 'spose," she choked out.

"I didn't want to believe you when you told me you were my father's sister. If I had accepted you, perhaps your life could have been easier."

Betsey nodded once, a flash of something like pain moved across her features. Then she shook her head and stood a little taller. "There be no point in travelin' down that road. The past is not meant to be relived. Iffen we learns from it, then it have served a purpose."

Caroline had forgotten how positive Betsey always was. Perhaps it was her armor for survival. "I came here to ask you to forgive me for treating you poorly."

"Ain't nuttin' to forgive." Betsey cocked her head. "You never hurt me none, chile."

"Oh, but I did. I failed to make sure you were cared for after Papa died. I could have convinced Mama to set you free. I'm sure there are many sins on my head when it comes to your well-being."

"Yo Ma have cared for me jus fine."

"Wouldn't you have rather fled north before the War and been a free woman, not having to cook and clean for us all?"

"I can't rightly set my sights on sumpin' that never was. When ya can't find the bright side, ya polish the dull one."

Such a charming woman. "You're a better person than me." Caroline stepped around the worktable and took Betsey in her arms, hoping it wasn't too late to develop a relationship.

CHAPTER SIXTY-FOUR

January 12, 1866 - Swansboro

At the threshold of Caroline's door, Benny stood tall at fourteen, holding a two-pronged oyster rake. Her brother's cheeks glowed pink, and his eyes shone with excitement. "The tide's especially low. People are gathering at the oyster reef, just upriver a piece. If you wanna come, I'll teach Ora how to harvest."

"Oyster ridges can be sharp to handle for a girl not yet five." Caroline frowned.

"I've brought my old leather mitts for her to use."

Ora pulled on Caroline's skirts. "Please, Mama, please!"

"The day is fair, Carrie." Benny grinned. "Some people are even bringing a picnic." His hair, in need of a trim, fell over his forehead and almost touched his eyelashes.

"A picnic!" Ora continued to pull on Caroline's skirts, her face lit with hope.

"Very well. Let's put on an old dress so it won't drag in the mud."

Ora jumped and squealed.

Caroline gave her a look of disapproval. "You're a proper little lady, and I expect you to act as such, even while harvesting oysters."

"Yes, Mama," Ora called over her shoulder as she bounded up the steps to her bedchamber, not in a genteel fashion whatsoever.

The tide was indeed low. After a small picnic of nuts, cheese, bread, and cider, Benny and Ora walked to the reef where thousands of grayish-white oysters jutted out of the mud.

About a dozen people clawed up clumps, breaking off barnacles and young oysters with the sides of their hand rakes, tossing the large ones into wire baskets and the small ones back into the water for a future reaping. Past the harvesters, a netted, green glass crab-pot buoy bobbed on the water's surface.

Caroline sat on the riverbank on an old quilt. The day fair and devoid of wind, she'd chosen a light jacket. Stretching her legs, she leaned back on her hands, closing her eyes to let the late morning sun warm her face, and breathed in the musky smell of the river. She'd come back to life after being lost in the inert clouds of depression.

Since her redemption, her heaviness had been replaced with peace. She smiled at the new richness of happiness.

The dulled chatter of the harvesters and distant waves lapping the shore were calming backdrops to her thoughts. She regretted that she'd had to get to her lowest before she turned to God. Before she understood He'd always been there for her. His forgiveness complete, she was finally able to forgive herself.

She didn't know what awaited her around the next bend. She needed to think about the future and where she'd go if John never returned and she lost her home. Her life was bound to continue with hardships that threatened to break her, but as long as she held to the belief that through God's grace all would be possible, she could endure without John—although the thought greatly saddened her.

John probably thought her a failure. All the times he held concern for others and knelt in prayer for them, she now hoped he'd do for her. She then amended the thought and hoped he'd do it for himself.

The overwhelming feeling of God's love had stayed with her through the weeks. She could feel Him as she performed her tasks at home, even if she was only cooking a meal or playing with Ora. His peace draped her like a fishnet, catching all her good desires and blessings and making her feel accepted.

For years, she'd watched John have a relationship with God she didn't understand. God had always been just out of her reach, like mists off the morning river. Now she understood His acceptance and love. Yet during the past weeks, she'd still had times of weakness and self-doubt where she felt undeserving of His love. But she'd stayed strong.

She was free from bondage, but because of her past transgressions of pride, she'd always be robbed of having her husband's love and devotion and her family living together. But she would no longer let herself fall into despair. A small flame of hope lit her heart, and she believed it would grow bigger and brighter. Just as the brown grass around her would soon be green with new growth, she had something to look forward to.

She opened her eyes and looked at the grass and then the river's flow, knowing that what was passing would never pass again. She couldn't go back and start a new beginning, but she could start today and navigate a new route to progress to a better ending.

Benny's whistle caught her attention. With a grin, he raised a blue crab in the air. She waved her approval, and Benny bent to show Ora, hopefully teaching her about the pincers.

Upriver, a small boat passing Jones Island came into view with a lone paddler. The familiar black clergy hat made Caroline's heart leap. "It can't be," she said under her breath.

The boat came closer.

"Papa, Papa!" Ora jumped up and down on the marshy river bottom, waving her rake over her head.

Benny stood tall and waved too.

Caroline's heart slammed against her rib cage. She wanted to jump up and down as Ora was doing, but she didn't even know if she should lift her hand.

John smiled broadly and waved to his admirers by the reef. When he looked toward the riverbank, she knew the moment he saw her. His body stiffened, his hand and smile instantly dropped. He resumed his paddling and maneuvered the skiff around the crab trap and oyster reef, then brought the boat to the shallowest spot of water, pulling it onshore, about thirty yards from her.

Her body trembled with both anticipation and dread.

He headed toward her without looking up, watching his steps as he picked his way through the sedimentary and rocky river bottom, avoiding clumps of dead river grasses.

Ora and Benny bent once again to their task.

John stepped to the quilt's edge. "Hello, Caroline," he said dispassionately.

Caroline gazed at his muddy boots, hesitant to look at his face. She couldn't remember the last time he called her Caroline instead of "Carrie" or "my dove." She held her breath and peered up.

Grief had left its mark on him, and there was a vulnerability in his eyes she'd never seen before.

"Why are you traveling by boat?" she asked.

"Sammy has colic. I left him with my brother. Kit loaned me his skiff." Sitting, he kept his profile to her and his muddy boots clear of the quilt. "I talked to Mother."

Caroline's stomach seized. "The child is yours, John."

With his index finger, he traced a leaf pattern on the quilt. "I know."

His admission surprised her. She snapped her head up and caught a fleeting look of relief on his face before he masked it.

"It took a great amount of coaxing," he said, shoulders slumped. "But she finally admitted it was she who convinced you to give away the child."

"I'm so sorry." While she hadn't been the one to lie to him about the baby's death, she had continued his mother's deceit.

He nodded and sighed. "I'm sorry too. The moment I stepped out the door in anger, I was ashamed of myself. But I couldn't come back." He ran a hand through his hair. "After leaving Mother, I worked my circuit and put myself in the service of the Lord to forget all that happened. Of course, it was impossible." He leaned back, turning his face away. "It hurt that you didn't trust me enough to tell me the truth—to share the pain and help find a solution. You made the decision without me, which in my mind means you really don't love me."

"But—"

"No, don't interrupt." He rubbed his face as if he were weary. "When I continued down that road of thinking, self-pity gnawed at my soul. Your reckless decisions became about the way you hurt me, and I'd go in circles in my mind about how it shouldn't be about me at all. I was being selfish. And selfishness is the source of all sin." He hit his fist on the ground.

"John . . ." She reached out.

He didn't turn or acknowledge she'd spoken.

She let her arm drop.

"I've always believed the Lord only gave us burdens we could carry. I can't carry this." His head dipped. "So where is my faith?" His voice broke.

She moved across the blanket as close to him as she dared and put her hand on his shoulder.

He flinched but didn't pull away.

Hope as small as a white cotton seed blossomed in Caroline. "When Sarah died, you told me we sometimes have to lean on someone else's faith to get us through hard times."

"Yes, but—"

"Please lean on me right now."

"*You?*" The surprise in his voice moved through her like ice.

But she deserved it. And swallowed back the hurt. "You need to find peace, John. While you were gone, I learned true peace only comes from a loving God."

"Caroline . . ." He turned and stared at her, brows drawn.

"Papa!" Ora ran toward them with Benny close behind, toting the basket. "Look at our o-sters." She collapsed onto John's lap.

Brushing away tears, he buried his face in her hair.

"Did you see the size of that crab, Carrie?" Benny pointed to the basket. A large, blue crab sat near the top, partially covered by oysters and a few clams.

"She's a good size." Caroline tried to put excitement in her voice but failed.

John looked to Benny with red-rimmed eyes. "I wouldn't dream of asking for the crab, but can we enjoy in the bounty and have enough of those oysters for stew?"

"Of course." Benny laughed. "Ora was a good little learner and gathered half of those herself."

Ora gave Benny a look of adoration.

John lifted her from his lap and stood without looking at Caroline. "I'll go take care of the boat and meet you at home. Do we still have that slab of bacon we can add to the stew?"

She knew he'd only said he'd come home for supper, but she hoped he'd come home to stay. If not, she'd make the most of the short time she'd have with him. Her body tingled with the prospect. "Yes, and some milk and an onion. I'll get working on it immediately."

ଔଔଔ

Throughout supper, John said nothing to Caroline and little to Ora. Caroline guessed he desired the meal to end so he could be away from her.

After eating most of her stew, Ora yawned, and Caroline took her hand and walked her to bed.

When Caroline came back, she found John staring into his empty bowl. "Would you like to retire also?" she hesitantly asked.

"I'm tired, but I think we need to talk." He took his bowl to the basin.

In the parlor, she took a seat on the settee, and he sat across from her on a chair. The expression on his face was so severe, she wondered if she'd changed him forever.

"You look different somehow," he said, although that's what she was thinking of him.

"How do you mean?"

"I'm not sure . . . more confident, perhaps? Certainly happier." He frowned. "Which puzzles me."

"Well, I suppose I am happier. Until last week, I thought I needed to pay for my transgressions by being unhappy. I was wrong."

He tilted his head, questioning her with his eyes. "You told me at the river you'd found peace. How Carrie?"

She drew in a breath. He'd called her Carrie. "I discovered God loves me despite my foolish shortcomings and sins. And it will come as no surprise to you, but I've learned bigotry was a great limitation to my spiritual development. I'm coming to terms with who my ancestors were."

He shook his head, a light coming into his eyes. "Tell me more."

"I prayed to God and felt His love. He forgave my sins. It was a miraculous experience, John. I don't even know where to begin. It was as if my body filled with light and truth and warmth. I'll never forget it."

He smiled.

Seeing a smile on his face, no matter how small, made her heart skip.

He moved to the settee and took her hands in his. "It's what I've been praying for. If I'd realized the grief and worry you carried these last months, perhaps I could've helped you."

"It was something I needed to experience by myself. I don't know how to explain the surge of exquisite peace I sensed after being forgiven. I no longer felt broken. I was whole again."

"Broken is how I feel." Tears gathered in his eyes. "What are we going to do about our son?"

"I asked God if he should stay with Spicey and Junior, and He told me it was the right thing."

John's expression dropped and tears fell. "How?" He shook his head.

"I need you to receive the same answer. Will you pray about it?"

"I will." He squeezed her hands. "I've missed you, Carrie." He wiped his face. "I laid awake every night wanting you by my side. What we've been through is more than any husband and wife should have to endure, and I can only pray it will somehow make our marriage stronger. Only God can perform that miracle."

Tears spilled from her eyes. "I want that too. I love you, John. Can you forgive me for deceiving you about the baby?"

He gently ran his thumbs under her eyes to wipe away the wetness, his tenderness filling her. "I forgive you."

His words were the sweetest she'd ever heard.

He leaned forward and kissed her softly, his kiss so familiar, yet somehow new and full of promise.

Something broke free in her, and she let his kiss continue, adding her own love to his. She needed to show him her feelings hadn't changed but had only grown deeper and fuller. She pulled him closer. She was his, this was where he belonged, and she never wanted him to leave again.

CHAPTER SIXTY-FIVE

January 13, 1866

Songbirds chirped their greeting to the new day as morning rays filtered into John and Caroline's room. The warmth of his breath brushed her neck, and she snuggled back against his body. As he brought his arm around her, she drew strength from his embrace, hoping he'd look at her in this new light of absolution and not see her as the person she used to be. She was not her mistakes.

He kissed the back of her head. "As I prayed last night, I knew if I was to receive God's forgiveness for treating you poorly, I needed to apologize and make amends."

"But you didn't—"

"I did." He kissed her tenderly. "In my anger, I said you weren't a good mother. You've always been a good mother. And a wonderful wife. Thank you for loving me. I hope you can forgive me."

She was a good wife? It was something she'd wanted to believe for years. "I don't blame you for what you said."

"I'm still sorry I hurt you." He held her tighter. "I'm also sorry my work has taken me away so often."

His admission, more than she'd expected, made her feel giddy, and she smiled. "We're being given a second chance."

"Yes." He pulled away and started to unbraid her hair. "I was away from you too long, but I wanted to hang onto my anger. I had to know if you damaged me irreparably. And eventually, I knew you hadn't. I've been a hypocrite. How many times have I taught that one who refuses to forgive burns the bridge that he himself needs to cross?" He released the last twist and ran his fingers through her hair. "As sad as it makes me, I know now it's for the best that our son be raised with those he resembles. Our society will treat him more fairly that way, and perhaps God has something in store for him that we can't yet realize."

Although she believed his words to be truth, giving up her son was so final. She swallowed hard. "I need to see him one more time, and I think we should go together. It might be good for Spicey and Junior to know we both give our consent."

"You're right, and I can only pray I'll be strong enough to set eyes on our son and not carry him home with me." Tears blurred his words. "I think it will be the hardest thing I'll ever have to do."

She rolled over.

He'd propped himself on his elbow and wore an expression of torment.

She ran her hand over the morning stubble on his cheek. "I'm sorry I've brought this upon you. I no longer hold shame for my black blood, but it is what's caused our son to be brought up in someone else's home." She frowned. "One thing I'm still unsure of—although I've forgiven my ancestors, am I being punished for their transgressions? Is such a thing possible?"

John became thoughtful, as if he were sorting it out for the first time himself. "We're not born with sin upon us. God is not that cruel. Although we can be born with the consequences of our ancestors' transgressions, we do not have their sins on our conscience. Their skin color *is not* the sin. In your instance, the sin most likely was adultery or rape by an ancestor. You did not make that choice, and you will not be held accountable.

She closed her eyes in relief.

He kissed her forehead. "What we are responsible for is how we handle what we're given and how we'll let those experiences influence our lives. The Bible says that the sins of the parents are visited upon the children to the third and fourth generations. These sins are relative to acts *they* have performed. Your ancestor likely committed adultery. If he taught his children that it was all right to commit adultery, then his sins are visited upon the next generation. If they teach their children, who then teach their children, this false idea has reached the 4th generation. The curse is that they are teaching their children to sin. Who can break the curse or continued sin? You— the person who did not commit adultery. *You . . .*" He looked tenderly into her eyes. ". . . *you* have broken the chain of transgression."

She smiled. He'd released her from resentment and blame. He seemed to be saying he held her in high esteem, even. She'd broken away from generations of slave owners and their ideas of supremacy. She only wished she could break the chain of empowered men preying on women.

John laid his hand on her waist. "Now our children and our children's children will benefit from the principle of good things being passed down. We won't be punished for the choices of our forefathers unless we follow them in committing their falsehoods."

His explanation made perfect sense, and his words soothed her worries. She wished she had such clear understanding of God's ways. It was truly a gift of John's, fast becoming a blessing. He seemed to have forgiven her so easily. It hadn't even been a full day since she'd asked.

"What are you thinking?" Both his dimples appeared.

Caroline ran her index finger along one. "I'm thinking how lucky I am to be your wife. You're quite remarkable, you know."

He pulled her closer and kissed her in such a way that showed her their future together.

CHAPTER SIXTY-SIX

January 15, 1866 - White Oak River

Caroline leaned over the edge of the boat, dipped her hand in the cold water, and brought it out, wiping the wetness across her forehead, the coolness refreshing.

The river's low levels made the current easier for John to row upstream. Unseasonably warm for mid-January, icy cold December had dissolved into the past.

She smiled at John while he hummed a hymn under his breath. "It's interesting is it not, that only in your heart can you know you're forgiven? There's no scientific approach for that answer."

John pulled the oars toward him. "God has spoken to you through the Holy Spirit."

She nodded, remembering the burning in her heart and the enlightening warmth of truth flowing through her body. Leaning back onto her hands, she watched the water's gentle currents, sunshine sparkling along liquid ripples. *Renewal.*

John continued his hymn, softly singing the words in his rich tenor voice.

Come, thou fount of every blessing
tune my heart to sing thy grace;
streams of mercy, never ceasing,
call for songs of loudest praise.
Teach me some melodious sonnet,
sung by flaming tongues above.
Praise the mount! I'm fixed upon it,
mount of thy redeeming love.

Redeeming love—perfectly stated. Caroline sang the next two verses with him.

The wide river narrowed somewhat as they left the tidal estuary and traveled upstream toward their son. The salt marshes and wetlands left behind, they entered an area of thick forests. She deeply inhaled the smell of Carolina pine. As they traveled, the river waters eventually darkened from decaying vegetation at its shores. Occasionally, silvery fish swam close to the boat.

They rowed past the inlet of Hadnot's Creek, the river narrowing dramatically, carving a large curve into the landscape. The waters darkened further, reminding her of the dream she'd had the night of her son's birth.

She'd been standing in the river, holding the baby over her head. He'd slipped through her fingers and she lost him to the river's currents that had turned to blood. Had it been foresight disclosing that although she'd given away her son, he was still of her blood and somehow not lost forever? She could only hope.

"I love this part of the river," John said contentedly, the oars making the only other sound.

They passed under the shade of the trees for which the river got its name. She loved the area, also. They were near about the old Mattocks land. The river gave fertility and life to everything in view. She was as deeply rooted here as the great white oak trees around her.

They would soon be at Kit's plantation.

With a look of uncertainty, he pulled hard with the right oar, lifting the left out of the water, turning the boat into Cales Creek's inlet. "Are you still sure we should see the boy?"

She understood his reservations. It wasn't an easy thing she asked—to give permission for others to raise his son. What if she never had another son? Should she take the risk of getting pregnant again? More of her children could be born black. "I believe we need to do this for ourselves as much as Spicey and Junior. If you don't want to come, I'll understand."

"No, you're right. It needs to be done." He resumed rowing with both oars, quiet for a moment. "I just realized we're getting a *very small* taste of what God suffered when He gave his Son."

Caroline pondered his comment. "I'm ashamed to admit it, but I'm not sure I understand the death at Calvary. If I remember correctly, Christ took upon Himself the pain I felt at giving away our son and the subsequent remorse?"

"Yes, your pain and that of every other human being. I don't think anyone can understand His suffering in Gethsemane."

"It makes me feel ashamed that I added to His agony."

"As do I."

"It's truly a miracle. The price I had to pay was to give away my pride and hurt and anger." For her, no hardness of heart remained. Her agony had been turned to glory, the exquisite sweetness of being redeemed.

"Nothing can separate us from the love of Christ, except ourselves. He's the only one to take the pain away—fully away. The rejection of the atonement is what creates pain and an unchanging heart."

When Caroline was thirsty, Jesus offered the water of life. She drank and now prayed she would be satisfied eternally.

CHAPTER SIXTY-SEVEN

Kit's Plantation, Carteret County

Spicey answered at the first knock. Her face lit with a warm greeting of pleasure, until she saw John behind Caroline. "You come for the chile?" she whispered in alarm. Her face crumpled as if she were mortally wounded.

"No," John quickly said.

Spicey wrung her hands and then seemed to pull herself together. "Where my manners. Please do come in." She hesitantly stepped back and gestured them into her two-room cabin.

The cabin smelled of hog fat and sweet potatoes, and a fire warmed the room. Her two young girls—wearing clean but tattered dresses— sat on old blankets, which probably served as beds at night. With their fingers, they ate fried sweet potatoes off mismatched tin plates. They both stared wide-eyed at the visitors.

Caroline took the basket brimming with bottled garden vegetables, smoked ham, and fresh bread that John carried and set it on the table, then she brought Spicey into her arms.

Spicey returned the warmth of the hug, then backed up. "'Scuse the place . . ." she sputtered nervously. She pulled the only chair away from the small table and made a motion of dusting the chair off with her apron, but Caroline could see no dirt or dust on it. "See fit to take a seat." She looked from Caroline to John, as if she wasn't sure who she was offering it to.

John motioned Caroline to sit.

She didn't want to, but she also didn't want to insult Spicey. So Caroline sat.

John cleared his throat. "We're sorry to have come unannounced."

Spicey tipped her head to acknowledge John's apology.

"Caroline told me about the baby," he said.

Spicey's eyes darted to a curtain hung in the far corner. She turned to her girls. "Ya two run along an go see Granpappy Jack."

The girls placed their empty plates on the table and ran out of the cabin.

John motioned toward the curtain. "We've come to discuss the matter of his future."

Spicey's eyes moistened.

"Spicey." Caroline stood and took Spicey's small, chapped hand in hers. "As we said, we aren't here to take the baby. We're here to bring some resolution to the matter."

Spicey peered into Caroline's eyes as if to ensure she spoke the truth and relaxed a fraction.

John stepped toward the curtain, then turned back toward the women. "We're asking a lot for you to raise our son. Do you feel coerced in any way?"

Spicey's hand trembled in Caroline's. "Not rightly shore whatcha mean. If you ax'in if I's obligin' to care for the lil one, I think you should know he's part of my heart now. The Good Lord knew what my needs be. Ain't no suffering on our part to have Lil' John here."

John's shoulders dropped. He barely spoke above a whisper, "Little John?"

The agony on John's face splintered Caroline's soul, and she went to him, but he shook his head as if to tell her not to speak.

"No disrespect," Spicey said. "Junior an I decided on the name, not only for his daddy"—she visibly swallowed and tipped her head to acknowledge John as that father—"but cuz we want Junior to feel like he's the daddy too. Junior's real name be John, affer his own pappy." She started to fidget with her apron. "We can change the name if it gonna cause trouble. The babe never know."

John smiled sadly. "I understand your reasoning. Leave his name as it is."

Caroline had asked too much of John. If God hadn't placed in her heart that she was to leave the child with Junior and Spicey, then she was sure she couldn't press on by putting him through the heartache of not raising his son. "Do we need to leave?"

He shook his head. "I want to see the baby."

Spicey nodded once, went to the corner, and pulled back the curtain.

John sucked in his breath.

In a crudely made cradle, crafted of driftwood, lay their sleeping son. The child looked healthy and perfect. His little mouth moved as if he dreamed of suckling. He'd changed since Caroline's visit three weeks before. He'd filled out with pudgy cheeks, and his hair had become thicker, with tightly wound curls. He also looked more like John. She could see it now in the set of the eyes. She hoped the baby had John's dimples.

Spicey lifted the sleeping child from his blankets and handed him to John. The baby made a small noisy complaint, then snuggled into John's chest.

Face wet with tears, John glanced at Caroline.

Her heart shattered into pieces. She sent a quiet plea to God. *Comfort my husband.* She leaned her head on John's shoulder.

He wrapped his arm around her and tenderly kissed Little John's forehead.

The baby stirred, and the barest hint of a smile played on his face.

Caroline tried to gauge John's mood. Feelings of concern for him and loss of her child pulled at her soul.

Tears ran down Spicey's cheeks, but she regarded both John and Caroline with tenderness.

John sniffled. "You've done well, Spicey. He looks healthy. Please know when he or your family are in need of anything, we will do all in our power to supply it."

Spicey stepped to John's side and touched his arm, then looked to the child with a love only a mother could feel.

Little John opened his sleepy eyes. His brown-eyed stare gave an impression of contentedness.

John kissed the child again.

By leaving Little John here, they were doing what the Lord told them was right. John hadn't turned away from Caroline when she'd lacked faith, and he wasn't turning away from their God-inspired choice to leave their son to be raised by others.

Like a magnificent tapestry being woven before her eyes—stitched together with love and sacrifice—Little John's life intertwined with the events of history. The threads of past ancestors pulled tightly around him. Caroline prayed the fabric held strong and helped him feel secure.

CHAPTER SIXTY-EIGHT

Caroline and John found Kit pacing his foyer floor, still in his riding attire.

His shoulders sagged when he saw them. "There you are. Jack told me you'd come." He reached out with shaking hands. "I'm glad you're here. I've something important to tell you."

The brothers embraced. Glad for their relationship, she smiled. John could probably use Kit's consolation and hoped John would someday tell Kit about the baby.

Kit motioned to his parlor, which wasn't a parlor at all, but more of a man's study. If a woman ever came into his life, would he change his ways? "Come make yourselves comfortable, I have a story to tell you."

John lifted an eyebrow in question.

They settled in chairs facing Kit behind his desk.

"I need to tell you some things in a roundabout way, if you'll be patient with me." Kit creased his brow. "There's a purpose to my tale."

John motioned for Kit to commence.

"Since the war ended, have you seen the *Christian Recorder* newspaper with the hundreds of Information Wanted advertisements of former slaves looking for their families? Mothers searching for children. Husbands for wives. I get simultaneous feelings of hope and misery when I read them."

"I've seen them. I can only pray for their reunions," John said.

"One morning, about a week ago, I read of a daughter looking for a father sold from Sugar Maple Plantation, and a memory was rekindled. Do you remember when Mother used to take us there for family visits?" Kit asked.

"Yes, I do."

Kit nodded. "On one of those trips, I sat high in a tree to get a better view of the landscape. I guess I was an artist at heart even then." He chuckled. "Presently, two old male slaves came along and settled in the shade at the base of the tree. I sat as quietly as I could, and I don't think they ever knew I was there. They started in on recollections of the old days. They were fine storytellers and within minutes I became enthralled with tales of Africa and ship voyages. They also spoke of loved ones who had been sold away or died. They recounted names and gave descriptive stories of slaves' antics or their sorrows and beatings. I received an education up in that tree. I realized for the first time that perhaps slaves were people who had feelings just like me."

If only Caroline could've had that early education. How different her life might've been.

"Why that stuck with me is because I wondered if I heard one of the stories correctly." Kit frowned. "The rest of what I have to share is harder. We've always been honest with each other." He looked closely at John. "I want you to know I needed to find out the truth, and I think you need to know too."

Caroline wasn't sure she followed Kit's line of thought.

"If it's the truth," John said, "you should not fear telling us. Go on."

Kit studied John. "Last November, in the middle of the night, a black woman brought a baby boy to my home, telling me he was to live with Spicey and that my mother would be along to explain matters. The baby was light in color but appeared to be part Negro."

Caroline felt sick.

John grasped the arms of his chair, his knuckles white. "Go on."

"When Mother came later, she told me the child was a bastard son of one of her servant's and that she wanted nothing to do with it but would compensate me for any expenses he may incur. She said she heard Spicey could nurse-feed the baby. She was adamant Junior and Spicey raise the child. She said she never wanted to see him on her property nor ever to bring up his existence again. For being a servant's child, Mother seemed overly involved and emotional. It puzzled me, and I'm ashamed to admit, I wondered if he might be Papa Koonce's son."

Caroline sat positively still.

John nor Kit glanced her way.

"I didn't think much of it again, until you two were here for Christmas. Your son's death still shrouded both of you with despondency. It was to be expected, and I was sorry for your loss. I was most concerned about Caroline." He looked at her then.

Her hands cold, she tucked them under her skirts.

"As a doctor, I see melancholia that drives people to harm themselves. I recognized your state as serious. One day, when you headed toward the river, I followed you to make sure you were safe— for your own sake. I hope I didn't overstep my responsibility?"

Caroline shook her head no, staring at her lap.

"To my surprise, after you went to the river, you stopped at Spicey and Junior's. I had to ask myself why. I knew she was once your personal maid, and I thought it was reason enough for your visit. I tried to convince myself that was true, but the real truth wasn't hard to figure out." Kit hesitated. When he continued, his voice was kinder. "Caroline had a son the same night a baby boy was brought to my home. I think it too much of a coincidence to believe there were two babies born in that home that night. The child at Spicey's is yours, isn't he?"

"Yes, he is," John spoke without a flinch, claiming his child.

A hand flew to Caroline's chest.

Kit's eyes filled with love toward John. His kind gaze shifted to Caroline.

She released the breath she held. She didn't feel shame but worried what it meant to have someone else know their secret. She wanted John to explain the situation to Kit.

"It wasn't until last week when I read the advertisements that the story those old men told came back to me," Kit said. "The story was of the prettiest, light-colored slave on a nearby plantation. She was from Jamaica, and her name was Jamila. She was the favorite of the master of Howse Plantation. Jamila birthed him several babies. Some passed as white and lived in the plantation home, raised as the master's own. The old men at the tree spoke of the day the master decided he was tired of Jamila wanting to be involved with her white babies' upbringings. A beating ensued, and he sold Jamila to a passing tradesman."

Caroline shuddered.

"I just returned from the area of Howse Plantation, near Sugar Maple. It has since been destroyed. I went there to see what I could discover about Jamila because there was more to the story, and I needed to have it confirmed. I found only three freed slaves left. They didn't want to talk, fearing retaliation. I was eventually able to persuade them—money for their memories.

"When I described the old men under that tree long ago, they knew who I meant. Although long dead, they were famous for their storytelling, and their tales had been passed to the youngest generation. They had no means to prove the facts, but they could recount the story of our Mother's grandmother, Jamila, as if I was hearing it from the old men. My memories were correct." Kit peered more intently at John. "Your son looks like a Negro, John, because our great-grandmother was a mulatto slave."

John's jaw fell open. He jumped from his chair, startling Caroline. "I knew it! I somehow knew in my soul." Words tumbled from him as unstoppable as a rock rolling downhill. He laughed and turned to Caroline, pulling her up. "Don't you see? It's my blood that gave our son his features."

"Or both our blood," Caroline said, still stunned.

"Or both our blood," John echoed.

Their son was born of both his parents. His separation from them was not just her fault. The heavy yoke of responsibility lifted from her shoulders.

Kit stared incredulously. "I must say, I'm taken aback at how you are responding to the news. And I didn't realize Caroline had black blood."

"We don't know that she does, we only assumed. We may never know for sure, but it doesn't matter." John went behind the desk and pulled his brother from his chair, embracing him. He motioned for Caroline, bringing them both to him. "I feel whole somehow." He laughed as if he were drunk with happiness. "Seems there's a forest of family trees."

John's deep brown eyes found Caroline's.

Did he get those eyes she loved so much from a Negro ancestor? There was an openness on his face that ministered to her soul.

"The truth shall set you free," John said. "It was all about the truth. I just needed to be told what the truth was."

In the past, Caroline would've been devastated by the news of John's ancestry. But the past was far from her. It was as if a frosted window had been wiped clean and she could finally see clearly.

CHAPTER SIXTY-NINE

January 16, 1866 - Koonce Plantation Home

Caroline and John stepped into Eliza's house.

"To what do I owe this unexpected visit?" Eliza clasped her hands.

It was the first time Caroline had seen her mother-in-law since the night of the baby's birth. She appeared older. Certainly, more tired.

Caroline no longer held bitterness. Instead, she regarded Eliza as a woman who'd held deceit inside her for so long that its invasive fingers had robbed her soul of some of its light. She was what Caroline would've become if she'd not confessed her own lies.

In the parlor, Eliza shut the wide double doors.

John took a seat by Caroline, and Eliza sat across from them.

"We're here to discuss our son," he began the conversation.

Narrowing her eyes, Eliza stuck out her chin. "I told you everything when you were here last week."

"Not everything, it seems," John said firmly. "We've just come from Kit's. He told us of an ancestor you'd never mentioned to me before—Jamila of Howse Plantation. Your grandmother."

Eliza looked as if she'd stopped breathing. She gazed at John, but Caroline doubted she truly saw him. "You've been listening to lies that have circulated for years. If you continue with the lies, it can ruin us. Is that what you want?"

"I know the truth now, and I think you should admit it too," John answered succinctly.

"I will admit nothing. Do you have evidence to back up this *story*?" She said the last word as if it were a lie in itself.

"Only tales from those who lived on Sugar Maple." John didn't drop his stare.

Caroline ground her teeth but tried to remain calm.

Eliza straightened, looking ready for a fight. "Don't you realize your privileged upbringing and education is what made you who you are today? Would you prefer to live in a shanty and break your back in the field?"

John balled his fists. "Why didn't you tell me the truth when my son was born?"

Eliza's chin went higher, and she looked away. "Everything I've done is for my children. I've given you a life of advantage, and you are ungrateful." Contempt filled her voice.

"You've given me a fine life," he acknowledged through clenched teeth. "You've also been living a lie, which led to breaking up my family and almost destroying my marriage." He took Caroline's hand, squeezing too tightly. Veins rose at his temple.

Eliza's expression hardened. "Perhaps I did get carried away, but it was only to save you from heartache, not create it. Your son is the truth of our lineage. I wasn't going to have you raise a *Negro boy* for all to see."

Eliza had deceived Caroline in more ways than she'd realized, making *her* feel guilt over not wanting to give away her son, when in reality it was Eliza's own fear that drove her choices. Caroline grasped her skirts into her fists.

"That was for me to decide." John's voice rose in anger. "Not you!" He stood. "Do you realize what you've put us through? How could you—"

"No one is going to take away all I've done for my children because of my filthy ancestry," Eliza hoarsely whispered, her nostrils flaring.

With those words, Caroline's anger drained. There was a time she would've done the same for her children. Caroline and Eliza's eyes met. Fear settled into Eliza's. Caroline tugged her husband's hand, pulling him back down to the settee.

John had once told her it was a necessity for their society to believe ignorant things about the blacks' intelligence and worth in order to function. He said it was founded on fear. Fear kept Eliza from seeing the color of reality.

John took a deep breath. "We're living in a different time. No one will take anything from you."

"Society has not changed so much since the war. People will look down on me. I'll no longer be considered white and be able to move among the upper class." What Eliza believed she bore was in the tightening of her mouth and flexing of her jaw. She was a victim of her own social rules.

John rubbed the back of his neck. "One's pride will bring him low, but he who is lowly in spirit will obtain honor."

"Don't quote the Bible to me." Disbelief played on Eliza's face. "You would have me think my pride makes me a sinner?"

Caroline knew too well the weight Eliza carried.

"Your pride *is* sinful," John said. "We don't suffer from our sins for punishment or payment. The suffering is to change us."

"I don't need to change, and I won't sit here and be preached to. I'm your mother and demand your respect." Eliza's tone matched her severe expression.

"We can discuss this at a later time." John's voice became tight with anger once more. "There's too much enmity between us, and I don't want to lose my temper again." He moved to stand.

Caroline grasped his arm to keep him seated.

Eliza squinted. "What's between us is the thickness of church doors. You think you're better than me." Although it was meant to sound harsh, her voice broke at the end of her accusation.

Caroline touched John's leg to stop his response. "It wasn't long ago that I viewed life in the same way as you," she said to Eliza. "I lived in fear of losing my place in society. But the opposite of fear is not courage, but faith, which creates courage. And with faith comes peace. I no longer care what people think of me, only what God thinks of me. My heart is at peace, and I have finally found true happiness. You can do the same."

Eliza gave a wry smile as if she believed none of it. "The power of my son's persuasion has won you over. You can both preach to me all you want, but I will not claim my mixed heritage and embrace the Negro in me. Only shame is found in that."

Caroline shook her head. "Shame isn't rooted in what you are. Shame comes from what you do and how you act. We are all the same human race."

"No, it's what we believe about ourselves that determines how others see us." Eliza's face reddened.

"I remember you quoting that often as I grew up," John added calmly. "I now see its meaning more clearly. I refuse to let our different opinions of this situation break our family apart. How do you suggest we settle the matter?"

"I can't rightly see us ever settling the matter, and I won't acknowledge your son as my grandchild."

Leaning back, John returned his mother's stare, clearly choosing his words carefully. "Carrie and I have decided it best to let our son be raised by those he appears to look like, only because we feel it will be the safest and best road for him in life, and most especially because the Spirit directed us to such a decision. We will be in communication with Junior's family and make sure the child's needs are met, including a good education."

Eliza nodded once. "Then that will be no concern of mine."

John stood and reached to Caroline. "Don't hang onto what happened in the past, Mother. To have the right to make choices means you're free. To make wrong choices takes away your freedom."

In the buggy on the way back to Kit's, Caroline leaned on John's shoulder as he held the reins. She wanted to comfort him, for there was pain in his expression since his mother's adamant declaration of her exclusion of Little John in the family. Eliza's lies about who she was, a person of both European and African ancestry, was more than a rejection of John's son—it was a rejection of John. "I'm sorry your mother was so cruel to you."

"Why must she only see the color of skin?" Exhaustion slowed his speech.

"If she accepts her heritage, she'll have to admit and rectify all the things she's done wrong. A lifetime of mistakes and mistreatment of others." Caroline shook her head. How does Eliza even accept herself? Had Caroline fully accepted her own forebear? In her heart, she knew she had. She wished she could meet her African ancestor. She hoped the woman was as loving and kind as the African women Caroline had grown up with and that she hadn't been cruelly mistreated. The thought that she likely had made Caroline bemoan the sickness of the past and all the evils slavery had caused. She turned her head and wiped at tears.

John sighed. "I will mourn for Mother, but I will not join her in a hard heart."

It didn't surprise Caroline that he was already trying to work out forgiveness for Eliza. And if he couldn't, Caroline knew it would completely overwhelm him.

ଔଔଔ

That evening, Caroline and John dined at Kit's, drinking wine and eating sparingly of clam chowder and delicious warm and moist bread. Not as abundant a meal as in the years before the war, but the winter vegetables now planted in the fields gave them a hope of better things to come.

Kit finished his soup and laid down his spoon. "Dare I question how it went with Mother today?"

John wiped his mouth with his napkin. "At first, she denied the existence of black ancestors, but eventually she came around. She would not, however, agree to embrace her heritage. I assume she'll deny it again to anyone who broaches the subject." That same pained expression John had earlier in the day pulled at his countenance.

Understanding and sadness simultaneously flooded Kit's face. "And what is her stand with your son?"

"She will not acknowledge him as her grandchild." John cleared his throat.

Kit thinned his lips and shook his head. "Well, you can count on me to keep a watch over him, and I can report to you often. Junior and I have always been close. I've already deeded him some of my land, and he's started to work it. I can picture Little John being with us as we care for the plantation. I can teach him to ride a horse and act as a gentleman."

A memory came to Caroline of Spicey's skill with weaving and making clothes. "Spicey is an excellent seamstress. I'll spread the word and perhaps she can do that or find other employment she enjoys."

"Excellent idea," John said. "I'm glad Junior and Spicey will have the opportunity to sustain themselves, and that Junior can make his own decisions about his family. We need to make sure Little John receives an education too."

"He'll be schooled along with Spicey's other children." Kit agreed. "I wouldn't be surprised if Spicey will want to learn too. She'll need to understand sums and be able to keep records if she's to start a business."

Caroline's heart lifted. Kit was a blessing she hadn't expected. Although she'd always yearn for her son, she'd find his absence less painful knowing her brother-in-law watched over him. "Thank you, Kit. I hope we can somehow reward you for your service."

"No need. I have no children, and who knows when or if I will? I look forward to spending time with my nephew."

"Thank you, brother." A small smile crept onto John's face, giving Caroline some relief. "Knowing he is happy and cared for means a lot. I think we should start with helping Junior build a larger cabin."

Kit nodded. "I've already told Junior that he need only ask for the use of farm equipment. But we can discuss what more he needs. It's the least I can do for his lifetime of service to me."

Caroline glanced from John to Kit. They were imperfect, yet still men of God. They didn't see themselves as saviors, but to her they were. She clasped John's hand.

The next morning, Kit lent John and Caroline his buggy. As Sammy pulled them toward home, John wrapped an arm around Caroline. "Giving away our son is not going to destroy us. We're going to endure together."

She nestled into his embrace, safe and hopeful. She'd made horrible choices, yet John—with God's help—still loved her. She never could've imagined the Lord working in her life this way, but she was so grateful He had.

The End

For a limited time, receive a free novella prequel
White Oak Plantation: Slavery's Deeper Roots
to learn of the courtship of John and Caroline, and Spicey and Junior.
www.orasmith.com

AUTHOR'S HISTORICAL NOTES

I suspect readers will be surprised at how many of the events in this novel are based on true events. It took me twelve years to research the Gibson and Mattocks families. When I prepared to write the story, I worried over misrepresenting my family, and those worries almost kept me from finishing. In the end, I decided it was a story about what *I think* could've happened in my family given the historical documents I found.

Following are the events and details I do know as fact in somewhat of a chronological order from chapter one to chapter sixty-nine:

Susan "Caroline" Gibson was born into an affluent family. Her father William J. Gibson ran a shipping trade where he took barrels of turpentine distilled on his land from longleaf pine, along with barrel staves, planks, and other lumber to the West Indies. There he traded these products of the pine for sugar, molasses, honey, and fruits. The ships then sailed the Gulf Stream currents to the North American cities of Boston, New York, and Philadelphia where the commodities were sold. The 1860 United States Federal Slave Schedule records him enslaving thirty-five human beings. Their names were not recorded.

William Gibson owned a home and estate called White Oak Plantation in the present country area of White Oak near Gibson Branch Creek. His eight-hundred acres spread through both Onslow and Jones Counties. I don't know what happened to the plantation home, but it did survive the Civil War. Caroline lived there until 1890 with her mother. My grandmother had visited there in her youth and my guess is it was demolished in the 1930s. I wish I had asked my grandmother to describe it to me. In 2000, I visited the cemetery off Gibson Branch Road where I believe many Gibsons are buried. Only the headstone of Susan Simmons Gibson, Caroline's mother, remains partially above ground with dozens of unmarked graves surrounding her, the depressions in the earth approximately seven feet by three feet in shape. There are photographs of the town home in Swansboro, called Gibson House, and it looked as I described in this story. It stood at 302 Main Street on the northeast corner of Main and Elm Streets and was demolished in the 1970s. A bank was eventually built at that location, then another. But before the second bank was built, I was able to visit the cleared land and look down the green sloping hill to the White Oak River. Although there are now buildings on the hill and Highway 24 cuts across its slope, I could imagine it without those obstructions and with one of William's ships alongside the Gibson pier.

Caroline's sister Julia Ann Gibson married Daniel Ambrose Harget almost seven years before the opening of this story and already had three of their six children. Daniel Harget (later spelled Hargett) owned a home in Swansboro, "the brick store," a mill, and a plantation in the country. According to the 1860 United States Federal Census, he was one of the richest men in Onslow County with real estate valued at $17,000, and personal property valued at $33,100. He enslaved thirty people, which sadly would have been considered part of his "personal property value." Across from the bank on Main Street, is what is presently called the Ringware House (circa 1778 and on the National Register of Historical Places), possibly the oldest house in Swansboro and the place where Daniel and Julia Harget once lived. There are stories of the Ringware House being haunted, and piano music can sometimes be heard. Daniel's and Julia's descendants have no records of the size of the country plantation house or its exact placement because it was burned by the Yankee's during the Civil War. Some of Daniel's estate off Belgrade Road in Onslow County is owned by his descendants, and it's assumed the plantation home stood somewhere on that property. Julia Gibson Harget was truly a beauty, but her personality traits are conjecture in this story.

At the age of three, John Frederick Mattocks lost his father, John Frazar Mattocks. John Frederick had a stepbrother, Edward "Ned" Mattocks, and two full brothers, Joseph (died as a child in 1844) and Christopher "Kit" Mattocks. His mother, Eliza Foy Mattocks, was widowed for a year and a half before marrying Dr. Philip Koonce, with whom she had six more children. I found John's 1856 Passport Application, but whether he actually went to Israel or not, I don't know. I have a list of many of the highly academic books he owned, and among them are works related to the history of the Jews, so I assumed he had an interest. He attended Trinity, which became Duke University, and taught Latin and Greek at Swansboro Male and Female Academy, appearing to have had a rapport with the youth. He served as both a local minister and circuit rider as early as 1858. I possess his pocket Bible and large family Bible, in which he wrote on a front page, "This book is never to leave my family, Swansboro, NC

1860," with his signature penned. We have honored his wish. Through research, I found several court documents regarding John's debts. It appears he struggled financially most of his adult life, although his mother and siblings did not.

John and Caroline were married in the Gibson House in Swansboro by the Reverend James H. Brent of New Bern on 19 January 1860 and first lived on Elm Street in the rented or "borrowed" home of Abe Watson while he was in Florida. As a young child, John had inherited slaves from his father, but I found no proof of him owning or selling them before his marriage. After his marriage, in the 1860 United States Slave Schedule, he is recorded as having a male 40; male 21; male 21; female 24; female 16; and female 10. The genders and ages do not match any of the inherited slaves recorded in his father's court records. Since John was often in debt and had no land to farm, having enslaved people appears nonsensical and why I assumed the slaves came to him by his marriage to Caroline.

In a New Bern newspaper dated 29 May 1860, a story is recorded of John Wilkins "a supposed free negro" coming to John Mattocks's home late one night, asking him to sign a document stating Wilkins was not negro and could marry a white woman. John signed the paper, creating some unsettling feelings in others. I have no proof that John helped runaway slaves, only records showing he welcomed African American's into his church after the Civil War ended, when they were allowed by law to attend. In *The Christian Advocate* newspaper, John's one-sentence obituary is a scant bit of detail, and I believe a slap in the face from those white people who didn't like him. Other ministers were given half a page or more of tribute upon their deaths. In the same newspaper, on the same page as John's obituary, his aunt's obituary was long and filled with overblown prose. She was proslavery and did much to help the Confederacy.

Caroline's sister Mary Elizabeth Gibson married Edward "Ned" Ward Mattocks (John's half-brother) two and a half years before this story began. Ned Mattocks was four months old when his seventeen-year-old mother died, and he only knew Eliza Foy Mattocks as his mother. His father died when he was eight. In mercantile for most of his life, he had five acres where he raised swine and other livestock. He also had an interest in education. The 1860 United States Slave Schedule records that he enslaved eight people. I'm not sure exactly where he lived in Swansboro, but he bought and sold waterfront property there, and his son Willie built a house in the Colonial Revival style on Front Street, which may have been originally Ned's lot. He and Mary's first and possibly only child William "Willie" Edward Mattocks is not in this story, although he became a well-known citizen of Swansboro as an adult. Close to where the ferry from New Bern used to dock, the Front Street house, circa 1910s and on the National Register of Historic Places, still stands today and has for many years been used as a gift store. Its two-tiered porches and dormered windows look out over the East Channel Sound.

Aunty Ann Gibson Smith, the wealthy sister of William J. Gibson, lived decades longer than her parents, spouse, and siblings and had no mention of children in her will but named some of William's children. In the end, and not mentioned in this novel, Caroline also lived much longer than her parents, spouse, siblings, and all but one of her children, thus the mentions I slipped into the story about Caroline wondering what it would be like to be alone like her aunt. Caroline lived fifty-five years after John's death and never remarried. She was pregnant with their fourth daughter when he passed. She never had another son.

William Gibson did give all his daughters pianos on their wedding days or birthdays. The square grand piano once belonging to Caroline Gibson Mattocks is still in my family. My great-grandmother used to say her husband (Caroline's grandson) would part with her before he'd part with the piano. William bought the five pianos on a trip to Boston possibly in 1851. The date is stamped on my family's piano, which also includes the maker's name and location—Hallet and Davis, Boston. The piano has ornately carved barrel legs and looks as I described. I am not a pianist but have tickled its ivories. Someone in every generation has played the piano while family and friends gathered around it to sing. To my and my grandmother's enjoyment, my son played us the *Star Wars* theme, the tones a brighter timbre than a modern piano, and about one octave short of a regulation keyboard. I have also seen Julia's piano and a third piano believed to have belonged to Mary. They are similar in that they are each square grands but not exactly the same in style or maker. While I can't confirm it, I've been told the one belonging to Hester was hidden in a swamp to keep the strings from the Yankees during the Civil War invasion of Swansboro. It was said the Union troops wanted the strings to make cannons shoot a greater distance. This doesn't make a lot of sense to me, but perhaps there was some other reason?

Finding facts about specific slaves is almost impossible. Sometimes their first (rarely last) names were mentioned in wills, estate records, and censuses as a means to verify them as "property." In all its ugliness, accept in rare occurrences, they were not treated important enough to record births, marriages, or deaths in church records, government documents, or in family Bibles. The name of Spicey is fictitious, but Caroline would certainly have had a personal lady's maid. Betsey, Cozy, Big George, Jess, Moses, Keziah, Mahaly, Esther, and Jamila are also fictitious, as are the enslaved of Kit Mattocks. Although in the 1880 United States Federal Census, well after the War, a black servant is recorded in the household of Kit Mattocks with the name of "Alsey," age 66. Twenty years before, Kit enslaved six people according to the 1860 United States Slave Schedule: a male 50, female 45 (Alsey?), male 25, female 21, male 21, and male 18, thus I created Junior's family. Kit was a physician, as was his stepfather Philip Koonce. The freed slave Chany did exist, but I invented her character traits. Chany was inherited by Eliza along with slaves named Robert, Cathy Richards, and "man" in the will of Eliza's first husband, John Frazar Mattocks.

Caroline's sister Sarah died at age ten just a few months before this story starts, and I felt her death would play into Caroline's mental makeup. To read of this event and Caroline's courtship with John, see my novella *White Oak Plantation: Slavery's Deeper Roots*.

I have no record of John almost drowning when he was young and don't know what enticed him to serve the Lord, although I would love knowing that piece of information. My hope is, as others read this book, that some may also be descendants of the Gibson and Mattocks families and may be able to add their stories to mine. If you can, please contact me through my website www.orasmith.com. The details of the drowning experience in this book come from my life and something that has played into my own personal spiritual strength.

Hester Rebecca Gibson married George Washington Ward on 1 May 1860, when she was seventeen years old. Her descendants claim she was given her piano as a wedding gift. I am not sure of George's occupation before the Civil War, but afterward he was a schoolteacher and journalist. It was said "the underprivileged always had a supporter in him," and he was devoted to the Christian way of life.

On 4 July 1860, John did indeed speak at a Swansboro celebration with those attending as described. Although I don't have a copy of his speech, a newspaper article reports "After music, reading of the Mecklenburg Declaration by Mr. E.W. Mattocks [Ned] and National by Mr. C.S. Hewit, the Orator for the occasion, Rev Jno. F. Mattocks then arose and spoke at some length acquitting himself credibility as to the satisfaction of all present. He at one time spoke to the youth of the land, which was very touching and eloquent and should not be forgotten by them."

William J. Gibson, "Papa," died on 2 August 1860 without a will. Ned Mattocks was named as administrator in William's estate records. Although I couldn't find many records regarding his estate after death, it appears much of his land was not retained by the family, but his wife Susan was left the "dower house" in the country and a small piece of land around it. She also owned the Gibson House in Swansboro. I have found no records of William belonging to any church or his life events performed by a minister, which is true of most of his Gibson ancestors. I have surmised he was not Christian, but I could be wrong. The white handkerchiefs with black-lace edges mentioned at his funeral are in my possession, inherited through Caroline. This style was commonly used at funerals back then. I find it interesting that Caroline would have kept them as mementos.

It is not known if William had a mulatto half-sister Betsey, but it is true that Obedira Isler Simmons, Susan Simmons Gibson's father, mentioned three "Negroes" in his family Bible: Manda, daughter of Levina, born March 12, 1842; Pleasant, daughter of Levina, born August 3, 1844; George, son of Jude, born March 15, 1845.

Caroline gave birth to her first daughter, Ora Divine Mattocks, 27 April 1861, just fifteen days after the Civil War started. I am named after her. The name is Hebrew in origin and means "light." Ora Mattocks was very tenderhearted and kind in nature, so I tried to portray her as such. Just four when her sister Rena died, Ora was six before she had another sibling to grow up with.

War is never as black and white as some try to make it. When the Civil War erupted, the North fought to hold the Union together and, for the most part, didn't have strong views about freeing enslaved peoples. And although the South was built on an economic foundation of slavery, they didn't see the war as completely about slavery either.

There are whole books written on these views and subjects, and I won't try and explain either side. I don't believe the answers were easy for those who lived at the time either. But as I wrote this story, I did try and see it from the viewpoint of a Southerner, even if I didn't agree with some of their opinions. When Abraham Lincoln was elected president, not a single southern state had given him the popular vote. The Republican candidate was not on the North Carolina ballot. John C. Breckinridge took the presidential vote in North Carolina, and his supporters backed the Union, which gives evidence of Union sentiment in North Carolina and maybe plays into why North Carolina was the last to secede. The feeling of the South not being *represented* in the Union goes as far back as 1850 or earlier and is partially why the South eventually seceded. North Carolina's decision to secede was determined by a committee of delegates, some of the wealthiest men in the state who enslaved people, *not* by a vote of its citizens.

I wrote the story from what appeared to be the point of view of the majority of Southerners. Feeling their rights threatened, they had a real fear of losing their property and livelihood and wanted to preserve their way of life as they knew it. Kit Mattocks and George Ward enlisted in the 27th NC Infantry Regiment on 23 July 1861 at Camp Green. I do not know if Kit took a slave with him into war, but many enslavers did. He enlisted as a Private in Company I, but he was promoted to Full Hospital Steward in Company S in 1862. George served as a 2nd Lieutenant in Company I. The novel is true to the places and battles where they served.

Ned Mattocks enlisted 23 January 1862 with the Gatlin Dragoons, 41st Regiment NC Troops (3rd Cavalry) mustered to serve for Onslow's picket duty. They remained in the Cape Fear military district until 1863. Ned was 28 years old at enlistment and promoted to Full Sergeant on 8 June 1862. On 26 August 1863, he enlisted as 2nd Lieutenant in the 67th NC Infantry, Co H.

In this story, I mention John's cousin James Mattocks. John's father had four brothers and a sister. They appeared to be a close family with some of their business transactions tied together in the shipping of food goods. This shipping trade continues back many generations to the Mattocks/Maddox family of Maryland. James descends from Allen B. Mattocks, John's uncle, as does his cousin George Dennis Mattocks (not to be confused with Hester's husband, George Ward).

James enlisted in the Civil War on May 15, 1862 in the 41st Regiment, Company H, NC (3rd Cavalry), the same regiment as his cousin Ned. But James is best known for his inventive genius and mathematical skills after the war. John's cousin George Mattocks was in the 27th NC Infantry and had also enlisted at Camp Green on the day Kit and George Ward did. After the war, George Mattocks wrote a novel based on his experiences in the war. Although his novel was never published, it was enjoyed by his family.

When John was asked to ride a circuit in Jones County for the Methodist Church, he took Caroline to Pollocksville. It appears they did not take slaves with them. I own Caroline's book *Mackenzie's Five Thousand Receipts in All the Useful and Domestic Arts* (1829). It is "a complete practical library relative to agriculture, bees, bleaching, brewing, calico printing, carving at table... confectionary, cooking...disease...metallurgy...varnishing...wines" and so much more. Quite a remarkable book, I used it as a reference for Mama's beehives and medicinal practices.

New Bern was captured by the Union on 14 March 1862. The Confederate and then Union troops visiting Caroline at her home in Pollocksville are factual events. Her own stories told to her children and passed down in writing by her grandson John, whom she raised after the death of her daughter Ora, told of Zebulon Vance commanding the first of those to come through and stopping at Caroline's home for food. I tried to find proof of the claim and found a letter written by Vance to his wife about escaping New Bern. He wrote of stopping at homes where kind people gave the soldiers food.

I have a good imagination, but I'm not sure I would've thought to put Nate's story in this novel. Truth *is* stranger than fiction. Caroline told her grandson John, "As the Confederate troops retreated from New Bern after its capture, a battalion of the Confederate Army, commanded by Major Zebulon Vance, who later became Governor of North Carolina, camped in the yard...Being in retreat and afraid of ambush by Federal troops, these officers insisted on having their dinner served while standing. This meal they ate while using the piano as a table...The following evening the Federal troops arrived and also being afraid of ambush by fleeing Confederates, they also had their officer's meal served while standing, eating off the same piano...The next morning, before departing, the officers of the Federal forces who had been billeted in the home, had some of their troops enter the house, remove all the feather beds and while holding them at four corners on bayonets the officers ripped them with their swords, leaving nothing but the bed-ticks, as the feathers were blown with the wind. The officers then went into the house and picked holes in china vases, which they carried out on point of swords and had the troops shoot them to pieces by gun fire. In the face of this destruction, one of the Federal troops was found wounded under the front porch steps. He was taken in and nursed back to sufficient health so that he could be moved to New Bern and turned over to his command."

I don't know how the wedding gift silver salt and pepper shakers survived the Federal destruction and thievery of Caroline's household, but they did—perhaps overlooked because of their small size. They were given to me as a gift from my grandmother.

I couldn't determine which Union troops came to Caroline's house. Most likely, it was one of the companies from Pennsylvania. If that's accurate, they would have also been involved in the campaign to Roanoke and Hatteras the month before. While the name "Nate" is fictitious and not recorded in our family history, the story he tells of those events is based on historical information.

The brooch John gave Caroline, with the miniature picture of him, is pinned at Caroline's neck in a photograph taken of her when she was elderly. No one in the family knows what happened to it. I often wonder if she may have been buried with it.

The Union occupation of North Carolina began in August 1861 when Roanoke was taken. New Bern followed, then other ports captured, and then Fort Macon, about twenty-seven miles from Swansboro. The White Oak River became the division between the Union occupied areas and the defense district of the Confederacy. Union forces constantly raided Onslow County. Swansboro was first invaded 13 April 1862 by the 103rd New York Volunteers. They bound prominent men in ropes and irons, abused women, plundered homes and stores, and promised to return, telling the slaves to rise against their masters. At Gibson House, the Union soldiers killed a calf by cutting its throat and then dragged it across the main hall from the backyard to the front.

In the novel, I mentioned an attack on Fort Macon where William Harden Jones (3rd NC Cavalry, Co H) rode out to get help. I didn't

330 · Ora Smith

mention another story found in a pamphlet called "Swannsborough Seaport - A Profile" compiled by Thomas J. Reed, and in a couple other documents about Jones, "a midget" (said a local), during an invasion on Swansboro. "A detachment of Federal soldiers, whether of the 24th Massachusetts or of Cushing's detachment, captured William Harden Jones, a Confederate dispatch rider, in the upstairs bedroom of the John Mattocks house." He was pulled out from under the bed. Whether this was in the Gibson House or a house John may have been renting, I'm not sure. One story recalls Jones was visiting his parents who were staying in the Hawkins house, and another says Jones was visiting his wife. But all stories relate that he was captured in the house John Mattocks lived in.

Once owned by David Sanders, Palo Alto Plantation house (circa 1836) still stands. Sanders owned 9,500 acres where he grew mostly corn and cotton. The history of it being ransacked during the first invasion on Swansboro is true to description herein. It is now used as a wedding venue.

John took Caroline to Hillsborough where many Southeastern North Carolina refugees fled. I have little on their stay there, but it appears it may have been about this time that John was assigned as a chaplain in the Confederacy. I have no records on where or when he served, only family records stating that he had. The salary and wartime stipulations of a chaplain were true to what is stated in this novel. My heart still breaks to think of the thousands of young men John must have prayed with who were injured and dying. How did he succor them before battles, knowing they may likely not return? Such a tragic history!

Although the Harget plantation home was burned down by the Yankees, the land is still owned by Harget descendants. The original thousand acres was purchased by Daniel Harget in 1856, three years after he married Julia. Members of the family of William Davis Hargett (Julia and Daniel's son, known as Billy in this novel) recall two incidents of the Civil War. According to a letter in the Harget loose records folder (author unknown) in the Littleton room of Jacksonville Library, "William, then a boy first attending school, was riding a horse from the Harget home in the country to Swansboro, when Yankee soldiers took his horse and sent him home afoot. The Daniel A. Harget home, described as a fine structure on his large farm which was worked by slaves, was burned during the Civil War and the family moved into Swansboro. It is related that Mrs. Harget's piano stood under a tree at the site of the home for some time until it could be moved into Swansboro."

Kit was discharged as "disabled" on 1 August 1862. I do not know what his disability was, so I chose one of the most common types of illness for a soldier at that time—malaria. Being in the 27th NC, he would have served in the battles of New Bern (March 14, 1862), Seven Days (June 25-July 1, 1862), Malvern Cliff (June 30, 1862), and Malvern Hill (July 1, 1862).

The information written of the second invasion on Swansboro in August 1862, where over seven hundred Union troops from seven warships anchored off Swansboro, was gathered from newspapers, books, and personal accounts. Even the stealing of Susan Gibson's chickens on the piazza was reported in the *Wilmington Journal* newspaper on 4 September 1862. The salterns were destroyed, animals and food stolen, and Missouri Holland did poison her barrels of wine, knowing soldiers would steal them. I was thrilled to find an old newspaper for sale on eBay describing the only account of the Swansboro invasion I found reported by the North. *The New York Herald* newspaper 25 August 1862 states, "At half-past two o'clock we arrived off Bogue Inlet and discovered a white flag flying from a house in Swansboro, this town being in full sight from the sea...on the inland passage we learned that the Union had got aground, and that two-hundred of the Twenty-fourth Massachusetts men stripped off their clothes, jumped in the water, and actually dragged that vessel off the bar...the boys went on shore (some of them naked), holding their pieces high above water, and got some sheep and other things which were then eminently necessary to appease their hunger. On Saturday morning Colonel Manchester and two or three officers of the Marine Artillery landed on the dock of Swansboro. They were met by a dozen or more citizens."

The newspaper article goes on to tell of the town having nothing of consequence but cornmeal and how the Union searched every dwelling for arms, securing thirty pieces. "In the barrel of one was found a charge of thirty-six large buckshot, intended as the woman of the house said, for the Yankees. The women opposed the searching of their houses...The negroes, in many instances, gave us important information. All of these and others who aided us to such information, and who were desirous of leaving the place, were allowed to do so, by returning with the expedition to Beaufort." On the final day

"...another force was on shore at Swansboro, looking after the poor of that place. The boys of the Twenty-fourth got into a charitable mood and took from the rich and gave to the poor. How long these latter will hold what they got of course we do not know. In order that the rich ones might not take the chickens, etc., from the poor ones, all the live stock [sic] was killed before being given away...Several of the Marine Artillery who attempted to search a house for arms were set upon by nine women, one of the same threatening them with a red hot poker, another with a kettle of hot water, and the rest with shovels, tongs, etc. One woman had a clothes pole. Not desiring to make war on women, our men withdrew without searching the premises." Sadly, names were not given of those women who fought back, but I found it interesting that they were so fed up with the armed Yankees that they were brave enough to go after them with whatever they could use as a weapon. Fear, anger, and starvation can do that to people.

It appears the Confederacy was aware that Swansboro had been invaded but did not have the manpower to help the citizens. In a letter dated 19 August 1862 from Captain Edward W. Ward of the Gatlin Dragoons stationed in Jacksonville (Company B, North Carolina 3rd Cavalry) to Colonel Collett Leventhorpe, Ward writes, "I have men watching them closely, may go down until they can see them...They have taken one of mine a prisoner. If possible send me some artillery, if only two pieces, and if you remain in Wilmington send the express men to Golden Place to meet mine. My horses are badly used up."

John and Caroline's daughter Lorena "Rena" Bryan Mattocks was born 8 September 1863 and lived two years and one month. I do not know what she died of. In the Mattocks family Bible is a lock of brown hair wrapped in a small piece of paper. I've wondered if it belonged to Rena.

I'm not sure how John acquired enough money in 1863 to buy three buildings in Swansboro—a house, the church, and the youth academy. The money may have come from his mother's property inheritance from John's father as I suggested in the novel. The home he bought can still be found at 208 Elm Street and is referred to as the Hawkins House (on the National Register of Historic Places), being built by Bazel Hawkins around 1830. The other two buildings no longer stand.

Ned suffered greatly from his service in the Confederacy. On a pension application in 1903, he wrote, "I received no wound but came out with my constitution so impaired that I am not - nor have been able to perform very little manual labor." Photographs of him in middle age show him extremely thin.

Mary Moore Ward Smith, granddaughter of George and Hester Gibson Ward, wrote of George "His army duties took him all the way to Gettysburg, where he was injured, having been shot in the arm. He made his way as best he could through Virginia and then on foot most of the way back to Onslow County. During the long journey home, he was ill with fever from the wound and traveled with his feet wrapped in paper and rags, having long since worn out his precious shoes. Members of the family still living in Swansboro hardly knew him when he arrived." I could not find that the North Carolina 27th Infantry Regiment fought at Gettysburg in July 1863, but the regiment *was* at the surrender at Appomattox Court House, Virginia, on 9 April 1865. At that time, the troops would have received paroles enabling the prisoners of war to travel home without harassment by the Union. Tens of thousands made their way home by foot from Appomattox. This would have been the more logical history of George, but I can't be sure. George and Hester had five more children after the war.

Kit married in 1872 when he was thirty-one. His wife Christiana Sanderson had only one son, John Edward Mattocks, in 1873. I'm not sure if Kit owned a plantation but assume so since he had slaves. I don't know where it would have been located, and I don't believe his first home still exists. He served as a physician in Jones County during his adult life.

John and Caroline giving away a black child had only been a rumor until I found on a genealogy website where someone had placed within John and Caroline's family group record the son's name—John Edward Mattocks (yes, the same name as Kit's son)—and birth year of 1865. I searched for years to find who submitted that information. I finally found the gentleman's name and email address, but after numerous inquiries, he has never written back. Now the email address is no longer viable. Has the gentleman died? I can only hope with the printing of this novel that someone who has answers will contact me with more information about our lost John. Years after this discovery of Little John Mattocks, I had my DNA tested and found that not only did I have ancestors in Africa but that the lineage came through my mother, who descends from John and Caroline. As far as I can follow the circumstantial evidence, *both* John and Caroline may have had

African ancestors. Both of their families had enslaved people for generations, almost since America's English beginnings. That is many generations of slavery to step away from. Just how much the Civil War forced the separation I have no idea.

Through my research, I've never found for certain (I'm still searching) what family originally brought in the African ancestry. I chose the Howse line because I haven't been able to (yet!) find the parents of Lency Howse, my 5th great-grandmother on John Mattocks's family line. Also, as mentioned above, my 5th great-grandfather Obedira Isler Simmons, Caroline's mother's father, did record three "Negroes" in his family Bible. I wrote this novel before I wrote *The Pulse of His Soul: The Story of John Lothropp, a Forgotten Forefather* (published September 2020), where I came across the Howse family once again. A strange coincidence. I do believe the North Carolina family and that of Samuel Howse of England (in *The Pulse of His Soul*), who came to America in 1634 are related, but I have not found the exact connection. Samuel's grandson John Valentine Howse moved from Massachusetts to Maryland and died there in 1752. I suspect that to be the connection. But without documentation, I can't say for sure. Most of my North Carolina ancestors came from Maryland, including the Mattocks family who ran a shipping trade along the Eastern coastal port cities.

In areas where I had to use artistic vision to tell parts of the story, I pray they came as close to the truth as possible. I believe I'll see my deceased family members one day. I will ask their forgiveness of any mistakes I may have made. I created Eliza Foy Mattocks Koonce as the villain of my story because such scripts are crafted for novels, but I don't know her true character nor if she knew her ancestry. If I have misrepresented her, I hope she will forgive me. In her day, when bigotry abounded and the color of your skin could mean life or death, most any "white" person hid their African ancestry. Thankfully, today we cherish it.

Perhaps I modeled John as too perfect, but I fashioned him after what I knew of the men in my mother's family. They were true Southern gentlemen who cared tenderly for their women. I have handwritten letters from some of them to their wives or about their wives, and their love is astounding to me. They had no hesitation in saying "I love you," which some think was uncommon for the time. John was the only preacher that I'm aware of in my mother's North Carolina family, and I suspect he had a true love of God. His faith would've had to have been strong to take on the hardships of a horseback circuit rider, spending days and nights traveling in the elements through the swamps, hills, and forested areas of Jones and Onslow Counties. Much of the area is now considered the wilds of the Croatan National Forest where John could have seen and experienced thousand-year-old cypress trees, bogs, saltwater estuaries, deer, black bears, turkeys, insect-eating plants, peregrine falcons, poisonous reptiles, alligators, hundreds of varieties of fish, moonshiners working their stills, and slaves hiding out. If John were not near the hospitality of others, he'd have to hunt and fish his meals, sometimes spending the night outside, other times counting on the kindnesses of someone, perhaps a stranger. He'd spend his time preaching, spreading the gospel, baptizing, marrying couples, giving comfort at an ill person's bedside or as they crossed death's door, and listening to confessions. Nearly half of Methodist circuit riders died before the age of 30. After contracting malaria when traveling his circuit through swampy areas, John died 15 October 1868 when he was 30 years and 2 months old.

I abhor the deep racial division that sometimes rocks our nation. For the descendants of the enslaved and the enslavers I hope in some small way this novel helps toward understanding and perhaps reconciliation. There is a desperate need to learn our history, move past it, and resolve our differences through kindness and understanding. Exploring our DNA may help us all understand that we comprise many ethnicities, all equal and good. All the human race.

JULIA ANN GIBSON HARGET

DANIEL AMBROSE HARGET

MARY GIBSON MATTOCKS

EDWARD "NED" WARD MATTOCKS

HESTER REBECCA GIBSON

GEORGE WASHINGTON WARD

BENJAMIN SANDERS GIBSON   **ORA DIVINE MATTOCKS (AGE 12?)**

SUSAN SIMMONS GIBSON "MAMA"

(A PHOTOGRAPH OF WILLIAM J. GIBSON "PAPA" COULD NOT BE FOUND)

For more photos and history about Swansboro and its people, visit the Swansboro Historical Association, Inc. website: http://swansborohistoricsite.org/historic-walking-tour/ or the artist Mary Warshaw's blog at www.swansborohistory.blogspot.com

FAMILY GROUP RECORD

MATTOCKS AND GIBSON FAMILIES
of Onslow County, North Carolina

John Frazar Mattocks married in 1832 *Cassandra A.D. Ward* | *William J. Gibson* married in 1832 *Susan Simeon Simmons*

Edward "Ned" Ward Mattocks 1833

John Frazar Mattocks married in 1835 *Eliza Ann Foy (Koonce)*

Joseph Mattocks 1836 (died young)

John Frederick Mattocks 1838

Christopher "Kit" James Mattocks 1840

Julia Ann Gibson 1833

William Simeon Gibson 1836 (died young)

Mary Elizabeth Gibson 1838

Susan "Caroline" Gibson 1840

Hester Rebecca Gibson 1843

Sarah Frances Gibson 1849 (died young)

Benjamin Sanders Gibson 1851

Julia Ann Gibson married in 1853 *Daniel Ambrose Harget*

Mary Elizabeth Gibson married in 1857 *Edward "Ned" Ward Mattocks*

Susan "Caroline" Gibson married in 1860 *John Frederick Mattocks*

Hester Rebecca Gibson married in 1860 *George Washington Ward*

Read where the story begins in the novella prequel to
White Oak River

White Oak Plantation: Slavery's Deeper Roots
An enslaved young woman craves a family.
Her mistress desires status in society.
Can an unlikely bond change their lives forever?

Most slaves long for freedom. Eighteen-year-old Spicey longs for a sister. As an orphaned house slave, she's desperate to belong to a family—even her mistress Caroline's family. But Caroline is more concerned with courting John, the local preacher, than noticing Spicey's devotion or caring for her needs. Caroline doesn't even think to look past Spicey's skin color to see their relationship for what it is. But when the decision to protect a runaway slave causes them both to risk everything, will the chains of slavery keep them bound to a world of lies and prejudices or be the catalyst that sets them free?

ACKNOWLEDGEMENTS

This novel was almost twenty years in the making. For the first twelve years, I went to North Carolina once a year for a week to slowly research my ancestors while also raising five children in Arizona. I had my eye set on the goal to someday write a novel about five Southern belle sisters who were gifted pianos by their father, but when I discovered the story of John and Caroline giving away a son, I knew that's where the real story lay. Consequently, I had a lot of helpful advice along the way, and I want those wonderful people to know of my appreciation in helping me cross the finish line.

My deepest thanks to Vickie Mattocks, a partner in research and a friend. It was fun to share ideas and find records with someone who loved genealogy too. Who else would want to sit side by side in an archive and be thrilled at finding a loose estate paper, half torn and hard to read?

Frances Henderson, thank you for taking in a fellow researcher but stranger and being my first friend and hostess in Swansboro. Thank you for editing and teaching me the lesson on Split Infinitives. You are a patient lady! I will treasure my memories of cemetery hunting with you and you showing me the broken and leaning headstone of Reverend John F. Mattocks so I could fix it before it was lost to history.

Mel Guss, much thanks for helping me discover the Gibson cemetery in the woods on a cold November day in 2000, consisting of rows and rows of seven-foot by three-foot indentations in the ground, with the one remaining visible headstone of Susan Simmons Gibson ("Mama"). I will always remember your kind helplessness when you stood by and watched me cry over her grave. (Mel's wife is a descendant of Julia and Daniel Harget. She and Mel live on the land where the plantation used to stand.)

Thank you, Mary Fulford Moore, for giving me a place to stay and being a great friend when I came to North Carolina to do research. You love discovering family as much as I. Maybe someday I will write the story of our earliest ancestors who disembarked at an unsettled Chesapeake Bay? Thank you for reading the first version of this story.

I appreciate the kindness of Roger Kammerer who let me and fellow researchers go through boxes and boxes of genealogical documents in his shed. You graciously gave me permission to use in this novel a sketch of Reverend John Mattocks, drawn when a teenager from a photograph. I was never able to find the original photograph, and I'm hoping someone who reads this novel may know where it is located.

Thank you for the advice from my writing groups: The PP Ladies—Cindy Higginson, Sandra Scott, Evelyn Nelson, Anne Law, Lecia Crider, Jan McBride, Luann Roberts, and Kathy Olson. American Night Writers Association chapters of Salt River Scribes, Daytimers, The Write Stuff, and Time Spinners. And the small writing groups that branched off writing classes—Patti Hulet, Juliet Peterson, Margaret Turley, Donna Dustin, Anna Arnett, and Louise Laughlin. Your encouragement and suggestions made all the difference.

Thank you Pamela Goodfellow for being my first creative writing teacher. You believed I could do it, and that's what I needed to hear.

Dean Hughes, thank you for taking time to read a rough first draft of this story and giving a newbie direction. Your desire to help others write well is admirable, and I am grateful to be a recipient of your kindness.

Thank you to the many who helped with research and writing craft: Alex McGilvery, Steve Shaffer, Dennis Jones, Wayne Venters, and Ethlyn Sanders Hurst. Special thanks to Julia Harget Stephen's granddaughter Lottie Venters Kesler, who lived to be one hundred years old and gave me a tour of her Antebellum home. It was there that I saw Julia's square grand piano given to her by William Gibson, and also the biggest silver tea set I've ever seen that I wrote into the quilting bee chapter.

Thank you to my original 2014/2015 beta readers, who read a formidably long version of this story when it was called *Choices*. You all gave me helpful advice—Janette Penfield Rasmussen, Patti Hulet, Cindy Higginson, Sandra Scott, Mary Hydrick, Jill Hydrick, Amy Lake, Kamela A. Watson, William Reed, Catherine LaPorte, Carter Hydrick (who suggested the title be *White Oak River*), Christi Hydrick, Rick Hydrick, and Jordan Smith. You made me realize the novel wasn't ready and that I needed to go back to school for a Master of Arts in Creative Writing.

And thank you to my most recent beta readers—Christle Rawlins-Jackson, Paula Peebles-Bonds, Ann Grimes, Sandra Sorenson-Kindt, Angelique Conger, Susan Nelson, Cindy Higginson, Luann Roberts, Gwen Rogers, Zakiya McKelpin, and Fleming Lemon. Beta readers are a crucial step in understanding reader preferences. Thank you for your time and comments.

My editor, Lori Freeland, edited two manuscript versions of this novel and never complained. She is talented and wise, and I very much appreciate her expertise.

I will forever be thanking Rene Allen and Jo Ellen Guthrie for the many hours we read our scenes together. You two have heard every book I've written and gave thoughtful and constructive advice. The friendships we developed were the best payoff.

And thank you especially to my Heavenly Father and the inspiration that comes through Him.

ALSO BY ORA SMITH

Children's Picture Book
A Christmas Story of Light

Heritage Fiction
The Pulse of His Soul: The Story of John Lothropp, a Forgotten Forefather

The Cry of Her Heart
A companion novella to
The Pulse of His Soul: The Story of John Lothropp, a Forgotten Forefather

White Oak Plantation: Slavery's Deeper Roots
a prequel novella to
White Oak River: A Story of Slavery's Secrets

Unacknowledged
(to be released fall 2021)

Ora Smith, a genealogist who writes Heritage Fiction, creates fascinating stories about her ancestors based on true events. She loves nothing better than to be whisked off to past eras to meet those whose lives are worth sharing.

The Pulse of His Soul: The Story of John Lothropp, a Forgotten Forefather
Based on a true story of love and loss, family and faith.

At the height of Separatist suppression and enforced Anglican worship in England, Reverend John Lothropp meets and marries Hannah Howse. The witty, educated vicar's daughter immediately challenges his decision to put God before a wife. In a world spiraling into hypocrisy, tyranny, and betrayal, Hannah refuses to break from her Anglican roots. But when John comes face-to-face with his deep-seated convictions about religious freedom, he's forced to make a hard choice—renounce his orders with the Church of England to become an outlawed Separatist or conform and save his marriage, his family, and his life.

Considered one of the most important ministers to follow in the footsteps of the Plymouth Pilgrims, John Lothropp helped plant the seeds of religious freedom in America's soil and left a legacy of well-known individuals who influenced the nation's destiny.

The Cry of Her Heart
A companion novella to *The Pulse of His Soul*

Punished for her choice to leave the Church of England and meet illegally with the secret Separatist community, genteel Penninah Howse is thrown into Clink Prison with little chance of release. To survive prison under the evil of Bishop William Laud's tyranny, she must evade the advances of a malicious jailer, learn to live with a cruel cellmate, and battle the enemies of hunger, filth, vermin, and self-doubt. When Robert Linnell finally succeeds in buying visitation rights, her old and dear friend not only brings food, he brings hope. Is there a chance he'll find a way to secure her release? Or will this be her life forever?

Watch for another **Heritage Fiction** about Ora Smith's ancestors in
Unacknowledged
to be released fall 2021.

Unacknowledged

A mysterious letter written on a deathbed. A Texas prostitute who became the mistress of a famous and wealthy entrepreneur. A son born out of wedlock who may have grown up to be a notorious American celebrity. Those vowed to secrecy have died, but the world's curiosity is still very much alive. Don't miss *Unacknowledged*, Ora Smith's third historical fiction novel based on the fascinating lives of her ancestors.

Get free novellas, sign up for Ora's newsletter, and get to know Ora at
www.orasmith.com
amazon.com/author/orasmith
bookbub.com/authors/ora-smith
facebook.com/AuthorOraSmith
instagram.com/authororasmith
twitter.com/AuthorOraSmith

ABOUT ORA SMITH

Ora is an artist, genealogist, seamstress, lover of a good book, traveler, antiquer, upcycler, and history buff. She's one of those people who always has a project she's excited about. Although she's lived in Arizona since 1986, she spent her early life in Lake Tahoe, California, where her passion to write blossomed on a tranquil riverbank with a beautiful backdrop of the Sierra Nevada Mountains.

Made in the USA
Columbia, SC
19 April 2021